Anne Buist is the Chair of Women's Mental Health at the University of Melbourne and has over 25 years clinical and research experience in perinatal psychiatry working on cases of abuse, kidnapping, infanticide and murder.

She is married to novelist Graeme Simsion, with whom she co-authored the romantic comedy midlife rediscovery novel *Two Steps Forward*, and has two children.

This I Would Kill For is the latest instalment in the Natalie King series following *Medea's Curse* (2016) and *Dangerous To Know* (2017).

Visit Anne at
annebuist.com
or on Twitter
@anneebuist

*For Dominique and Daniel, now
on their own life journeys, and Graeme,
who shared parenting them with me—
hopefully we were 'good enough'*

And the king said, Divide the
living child in two, and give half to
the one, and half to the other.

1 KINGS 3:25

'He wants to take my kids off me.'

Jenna hadn't even sat down. The urgency of the statement, the hint of fear, were at odds with the cool, firm handshake. When she did sit down, she ignored the chair opposite Natalie's desk in favour of the armchair by the coffee table.

The request for a psychiatric evaluation had come from Jenna's lawyer. *Merely pre-emptive*. A legal report, and an attractive fee; Natalie did not expect she would have to appear in court. A welcome supplement to her pay cheque from the forensic psychiatry ward at Yarra Bend, particularly as she'd been ill and hadn't worked for much of the last few months.

'Why?' Natalie asked.

'He blames me,' said Jenna. 'For the breakup.'

She looked briefly unsettled; Natalie watched her regain control. There was a sense of strength, the lioness-protecting-her-young kind, but the lines around her mouth were deeper than they should have been at thirty-four; the puffy grey under her green eyes and the unkempt mousey hair suggested she wasn't getting enough sleep. Young kids.

Her style was inner-city greenie: bright coloured top, vaguely Peruvian looking, and baggy red corduroy jeans tucked into heavy boots undone at the top. She probably volunteered to help slow learners at the local primary school. Her marriage might once have looked magazine-perfect. Walks along the beach hand in hand, Sunday sleep-ins interrupted only by a boisterous rescue dog, helping the kids decorate cupcakes with Disney characters.

Except somewhere between packing the lunch box and Saturday morning sex she had ended up with two children, a mortgage she couldn't pay and an ex-husband who thought she was nuts.

Natalie waited—but Jenna had pursed her lips. She was not about to make things easy.

'He wants to punish you?' Natalie prompted.

'He feels entitled.'

'Entitled to what?' Was Jenna's ex-husband narcissistic? Antisocial? Did he think he could dictate the terms of a parenting order?

'He still fantasises about us getting back together.' Jenna stretched her legs out in front of her. 'Malik is used to getting what he wants—that's how his family are. He says jump and his mother asks how high.'

'Malik?' Natalie looked at Jenna's paperwork. Her surname was Anglo: Radford. The husband's name was Malik Essa.

'We hadn't exactly planned a family,' Jenna added.

The eldest child was eight.

'So this was all, what, back nine years ago, when you got together?'

'I meant my pregnancy with Chris. He's three and a half now. Chelsea isn't Malik's child. Her dad didn't want anything to do with us after I found I was pregnant. Never seen her, doesn't pay maintenance.'

'Where did you meet Malik?'

'Paris.' Jenna caught the flicker of response from Natalie and added, 'I got a scholarship. Three months. My parents looked after Chelsea. It was pretty amazing.'

'So, the separation—your idea?'

'You could say that.'

'Is there someone else?'

'No. But even after six months he can't get it into his head that I'm not coming back. He's...' Jenna paused, chose her words carefully. 'He's possessive. Thinks he owns me and the kids, Chelsea included. It all went wrong when I went back to work.' She reflected for a moment. 'Our life was fine while I played housewife and he knew where I was. The moment I was independent he didn't like it. Monitored my fricking...' Jenna pulled herself up. 'Checked my phone calls, even followed me to work.'

'Physically threatening?'

Jenna hesitated. 'No. Well...I think he threw paint over a guy at work's car but I can't prove it.'

'How about with the children? Any concerns?'

The hesitation again. 'No.'

'Nothing? Pushed you? Twisted your arm?'

Jenna shook her head.

'So,' said Natalie slowly. 'Tell me why you're worried he might get custody.'

Jenna moved in her chair. 'My lawyer said there are two types of judges. Women-friendly—the old-school types that think it's the woman's job to bring up the children. And the ones who think they're playing it fair.' Jenna grimaced. 'Turns out there's a third type.' She handed Natalie a news-paper clipping dated a few weeks earlier, headed *False Claims Leave Dads in the Cold*. Crusading journalist Mark La Brooy was taking up a right-wing senator's attack on the Family Court. Fathers were 'taking their own lives and those of others out of sheer frustration at the unfairness of the system'. Natalie's colleague and perennial pain-in-the-arse Associate Professor Jay Wadhwa had been quoted in support. As had a Family Court judge, from an earlier review of the Family Court: he felt dads were getting a rough deal.

Jenna pointed to the photo of the judge. 'That's the guy we got.'

This explained the need for a succinct, pertinent report from a strong advocate for women's rights. Jenna's lawyer, Ms Yang, was presumably aware of Natalie's reputation. But there was still a large missing piece. 'Why a psychiatrist?' Rather than a psychologist, maybe even one assessing the effect of the separation on the children rather than the mother.

Now Jenna gave the answer she'd been holding back.

'Malik... he knew me at a time when I... wasn't well, and I don't want him to think he can use it against me.' There was a nervous edge to Jenna's tone, but her look was all *don't fuck with me*.

It wouldn't be the first time an estranged partner had cited psychiatric illness as leverage to get custody — sometimes with justification. Natalie had minimal experience of the Family Court, but she imagined that, as with the other courts, a lot depended on how sympathetic and informed the judge was about mental illness. This one sounded pro-parent and perhaps had some catching up to do regarding the more recent move towards children's rights. Natalie wondered whether his other views were similarly archaic.

'Let's go through your psychiatric history then,' Natalie said. Familiar ground — doing the checklists, targeting the likely problem areas.

Psychosis, mood and anxiety disorders? Jenna admitted to a few mood symptoms, in response to current circumstances.

Eating disorders? Check: anorexia nervosa as a teenager.

'Dieting, exercising, throwing up. Just the usual.'

'Did you go to hospital?'

Overly long pause. 'No. And I'm over it. It was nearly twenty years ago.'

Noted. With a question mark.

Natalie leaned forward slightly. 'Is there anything you're not telling me? Better to tell me now than have my report thrown out of court because it doesn't address something Malik thinks he can prove.'

They'd both done drugs — dope and ice — in Paris. Not now.

Another question mark.

'Alcohol?'

12

'I used to drink a bit.' Not anymore, Jenna added, but Natalie put a question mark here too. Was this what she was concerned that Malik would bring up in court?

Natalie combed through Jenna's childhood, including her relationship with her mother and father. Parents not only provided a role model for parenting style—they also shaped personality and self-confidence.

Jenna's father, Stephen, was: 'strict, very involved, loving, emotionally distant and always there'.

Some contradictions—he can't have been 'always there' as he had a job and often had to travel for work—but Jenna was light on detail. He seemed to be the classic father who connected with his children—Jenna more so than her brother or twin sisters—by taking them to out-of-school activities like Little Athletics and ballet.

Talking about her mother, Mickie, Jenna took longer to come up with the five words Natalie routinely asked for. Eventually she said loving, anxious, tired—most of the time anyway—and overwhelmed. The fifth—drunk—explained the dominant theme of Jenna's early childhood: acting as carer for her younger siblings while her mother self-medicated her anxiety.

Jenna was matter-of-fact about it. 'We were fed and clothed. I grew up faster than I should have, but it toughened me up.' Rationalising a time she should have been cared for, rather than doing the caring.

There were no surprises in the rest of her history. Jenna was just anxious to keep her children, and there was no evidence of her being a risk to them, though she found the little boy—'his father's son'—a handful. Chelsea was the model daughter. Mostly well behaved; until recently, loved school. Maybe Malik was an angry ex, but Jenna gave her nothing to suggest he was dangerous.

Not quite as straightforward as the legal referral had suggested, but in the end not a difficult assessment. As long as she could get confirmation about the drugs and alcohol being confined to the past, there was nothing here that could be used to stop Jenna getting custody.

After getting some corroborative history, the report could be finalised and filed in the *Completed* drawer.

After Jenna left, Natalie cycled into the city, missing her Ducati with every turn of the pedals. Two weeks earlier, after she'd lost the motorbike in a fire, her first impulse had been to buy another. Immediately. She had allowed herself to be talked out of it. *Not good timing, Natalie*, Liam had suggested in their brief phone call.

Waiting to see Doctor Sandra Oldfield, Natalie avoided eye contact with the other three women. The two with enormous bellies moved in on the one with a baby capsule, making pre-verbal sounds while Natalie gritted her teeth.

She tried the mindfulness mantra to calm herself—getting these women out of her moment and leaving them to theirs— until her name was called.

'The ultrasound says nine to ten weeks,' Doctor Oldfield said, looking at her file. 'I gather you don't recall the date of your last period?'

'I wasn't regular after I stopped the pill.' Natalie had been ill. And who cared anyway?

Doctor Oldfield waved the referral letter and frowned. 'Your GP says you'd been taking lithium.'

'I'd pretty much stopped it. I thought it was causing the nausea.' Declan, her supervisor, had reluctantly agreed she could just take quetiapine. She was only on a low dose, which put her at risk of an episode of depression or mania but reduced the chance of problems with the baby's development.

Doctor Oldfield pulled off her reading glasses and sat back in her chair. Short brown hair, no jewellery apart from a wedding ring; maybe forty. Sensible clothes. Pictures of two young children behind her; a nanny was probably looking after them. Maybe two—alternating shifts.

'You have bipolar disorder.'

Natalie resisted the urge to bite back *Thanks for letting me know. Now I get why I've been taking medication and nearly topped myself before I was given shock treatment. And want to be high again more than anything else in the world.*

'You know there's a risk of defects?'

'Really?' Natalie didn't bother holding back the sarcasm this time. 'A risk of 0.05 per cent of Ebstein's heart anomaly. *If* I'd been taking a full dose of lithium, which I wasn't, and there are no known teratogenic links with quetiapine. I haven't been drinking, don't do drugs, am not overweight and don't smoke. Odds are in the bean's favour, I'd say.'

Doctor Oldfield frowned. Natalie assumed it was at her nickname for the foetus. That was pretty much what it looked like: a broad bean. With appendages.

'Bipolar disorder is hereditary. And you're likely to relapse postpartum. *And* you're single. Have you thought about the child?'

In the silence that followed—it felt like five minutes but was probably thirty seconds—Natalie wasn't sure she could reply. Then she said: 'I know it's hereditary. So is being a bitch. Though your kids will probably end up with your nanny's defects.' She stood up to leave.

She didn't pay on the way out; they could send the bill.

This usually only happened when she was high. Exactly the right response delivered in exactly the right tone. Cutting but calm.

It was only later she wondered if she'd overreacted.

Before finishing the court report, Natalie rang Jenna's parents. Her mother, Mickie answered.

'I think maybe… you should really talk to my husband. He's at the pharmacy. Working.'

'I was just wanting to get a little background. It won't take long.'

'I don't think…' Mickie trailed off.

'I'm sure you'll be able to help,' said Natalie. 'I'm just after some background on Jenna and her children.'

'Jenna's a good mother.' The automatic response. What followed, after Natalie didn't answer, was more revealing. 'She and Chelsea are about as close as a mother and daughter could be.'

Close—or too close? Eight-year-olds didn't need their mother to be their best friend.

'Does she have problems setting limits? Being the grown-up?'

Mickie hesitated. 'Not with Chelsea. Chris can be a handful.'

'Have you had any worries she might be drinking again?'

'No.'

The answer was too quick—more likely answering for herself.

'How's Malik with the children?'

'He's a good father. Looked after Jenna, too.' A sigh. 'You don't think he's likely to take the children to Egypt do you?'

Natalie had no idea and didn't imagine she'd find out unless it made the papers. Lawyers had better things to do with their (billable) time than keep people like her in the loop, unless they needed them for something.

Which was exactly what Natalie assumed when Beverley put Jenna's lawyer through to her only an hour after she'd emailed her report.

Natalie wondered what Li Yang wanted her to add to the report. Maybe Beverley had just forgotten to send through her CV.

'Doctor King? You're difficult to get hold of.' Li sounded like she was walking; Natalie could make out the click of heels on pavement. 'I need you in court.'

Natalie stifled her irritation. The assessment request had stated that it was unlikely that she would be needed to give evidence. There was a fee for court appearances but it barely covered her costs and, more often than not, she had to reschedule other patients. They must be really worried about this judge. She opened her diary, assuming the date would be a month or two out. 'When?'

'Monday afternoon.'

'Monday? Come on—no way the Family Court hasn't given you more notice than that.'

'It's not the Family Court. We're in the Children's Court.'

'The Children's Court?' It was one of the few institutions in the legal system that reacted quickly.

'Protective Services are involved. Jenna made a report to them and the police. Looks like our Egyptian friend has been abusing the eight-year-old girl. Sexually.'

So much for a straightforward case.

Friday night she was fronting her band at the Halfpenny. Natalie liked the idea of singing with the Styx until the baby dropped, but figured they might feel differently. She hadn't got around to telling them. She tried to picture what Vince's expression would be if she was still singing up until the bean made an appearance. Every inch the old-school publican—in his early sixties, tattooed arms, hair thinning, pasta-lover's waistline— Vince had an opinion on everything. Particularly what women should and shouldn't do. She put up with it because he was the band's biggest supporter. And, beneath it all, a decent guy.

Maybe she could start an all-female band and make a statement: *Preggers? Knocked Up?* Maybe not. There wouldn't be much future in it.

She wished Liam would turn up, but knew he wouldn't.

He didn't seem as convinced as her that the kid was his, and why should he be? It had only been the one time. Damian was the more obvious contender; except for the minor issue of him being infertile. Liam didn't know that.

'You need some certainty in your life,' Declan had said to her. 'If not for yourself, then for…' The bean.

Maybe after the DNA test had confirmed Liam was the father. If they were right for each other, it'd work out. If not—well, she'd sort her life out on her own.

'You're looking hot.' Shaun, the keyboard player, kissed Natalie on the cheek and patted her butt.

'You looking for trouble, boy?'

Shaun pushed back his straw hat and looked at her over blue-framed glasses that Natalie was certain were purely for show. 'Promises, promises.'

Cute, but so not her type. He'd grown a hipster beard and looked more Robinson Crusoe than bad boy.

Vince offered her a Corona, lime in situ. Natalie shook her head. 'Just been for a run. Can you fish out the Vitamin C wedge and put it in a glass of water?'

Vince raised an eyebrow. He handed the beer to Gil the bass player as he came past and added a fresh piece of lemon to a sparkling water for Natalie. 'Going soft on me?'

'Getting older,' Natalie said.

The weather was mild for September so the beer garden was open and there was a good turnout of students. By the time the Styx had warmed them up with some covers, the beer was flowing, the crowd raucous and Natalie and the band were enjoying themselves.

She'd just finished Pink's 'Fucking Perfect' when she caught sight of Damian McBride at the back, sitting by himself watching her. Last time she'd spoken to him it had been purely professional. A case they'd both been involved in. She wondered at the coincidence of the song—she had chosen to sing it for Damian once before. Then told herself to get a grip. She'd sung it lots of times.

When the band took a break, she weaved through the crowd to find him. His dark brown hair was a little longer, probably because he hadn't had time for the barber rather than a deliberate move to look less like a cop. Solid, square jaw, and the sort of good looks you take home to meet Mum. Beneath the veneer was a dogged determination and a surprising ability to read people.

He nodded. Noted her drink choice.

'You look good, Damian.'

'So do you.'

Natalie smiled, wiped the sweat off her brow. 'Feeling pretty good too. How's work?'

'Busy enough.' Damian hesitated, looked at his beer.

'I'm still having it—the baby—if that's what you're here to find out. It's too early for a test.'

Damian nodded again. 'You with O'Shea?' His tone left no doubt about his opinion of Liam.

'No.'

Damian cleared his throat. 'We were good together, you know.'

Natalie took a breath. They had been good for each other as recovery sex. But as partners? He would be a steadying influence and that might be what she needed, but it wasn't necessarily what she wanted.

And for him? He didn't know her well enough to decide if she was what he wanted. He was hardly likely to trust her now, anyway.

'If it turns out to be yours, you mean?'

'You know the odds I was given.'

'One in a million? Doctors can be wrong.'

'I'd be there.'

'What does "there" mean exactly?'

Damian shrugged. 'Half the care, I guess, at least out of work hours. I'd get paternity leave. Support you through the pregnancy. Help with the finances, whatever we decide is fair.'

Natalie glared at him. *Support*. Meaning he'd done his homework. Knew that, unmedicated, Natalie was likely to relapse and be *needy*. 'And we'd be what to each other?'

He was still looking at her. Natalie had managed to keep her voice neutral. If someone had designed a special purgatory with her in mind, she'd just found herself there. Vulnerable not to just one man, but two. Declan would have a year's worth of interpretations out of this. What deepseated insecurity and self-hatred had led her to this point?

Damian seemed to be considering his answer.

'Forget it Damian, it's not yours.'

Damian shrugged. 'Up to you and O'Shea what you do then, I guess.'

Nice and clear. The kind of guy he was. The suburban-house-and-car sort of guy that made a good cop and would look after his own mistake but not someone else's. 'Thanks Damian. I'll let you know when the daddy lineage is confirmed.'

'You're okay?'

Natalie felt that moment of vulnerability again; hated him for it. Hated him for caring. 'I can look after myself, okay? I don't need a nursemaid.'

Damian looked her up and down and smiled. 'No, don't suppose you do.' He stood up. 'Take care, Nat.' He kissed her on the cheek and walked away, taking her suburban family fantasy with him.

It was late when Natalie got back to her Collingwood ware-house apartment, along the lane with its bluestone gutters and graffiti-decorated roller doors. The globe in her garage needed replacing and she tripped over a cardboard carton just inside the door.

'Shit.'

She used her phone torch to navigate through the mess of boxes she had forgotten were there.

Bob, her cockatoo, screeched loudly from his perch on top of one. In the torchlight she could make out the handwritten English labels that had been pasted over the printed Chinese: Lego, yoyos, Bratz dolls...what the hell were Bratz dolls?

Blake's latest business venture. *Only need somewhere to store them for a week or two, Nat.* Four weeks ago. Natalie would have bet money that nothing was what the label said it was.

'Would this be a good time to be seeing you?'

The adrenaline shot through her. It might have been her PTSD—she'd been attacked twice. But who was she kidding?

This was Liam's voice, complete with the ramped-up accent.

The brogue that never failed to reduce her to a quivering mess. She wondered if he'd been at the bar. And bided his time, waiting to see if Damian had come home with her.

'Good a time as any,' she said.

Liam stepped into the doorway and turned on his own phone torch.

'What the…?'

His light had caught Barbie Dolls on the side of one of Blake's boxes.

'Don't panic,' she said. 'They're my brother's.'

'Let him go!' Bob announced, landing on her shoulder as he eyed Liam. The bird didn't like the prosecutor, and had saved his one non-Dylan misquote for him. She took the bird upstairs to his stand in the living space and fed him as Liam watched. When she had run out of things to distract herself, she took a deep breath and turned to him. She wanted to say a million things — *you don't have to have anything to do with me or this kid… I'm sorry, I just can't have a termination for a whole lot of fucked-up selfish reasons but I really, really don't want to fuck your life up as well* — but nothing came out.

'So, you're set on having this baby?' Liam had found a spot to sit among her paperwork. His voice was serious now, and the accent back to regular strength.

'Yes. But I can do it on my own.' With maybe her mother, a paid nanny, whatever was needed. How hard could it be? She was smart and she had more financial options than most of her patients. She sat across the table from him.

'And you think it's mine. Why?' His smile held little warmth.

Good to know where she stood. He didn't trust her — she had, after all, withheld information and bluffed that she'd tell his wife about their affair. Lauren had discovered his infidelity anyway and thrown Liam out, so that had been an empty threat in the end. But the fact remained that she had played dirty. She felt at the time that she had had a good reason — to protect her patient — and would do it again if she had to. But Liam had the moral high ground.

'You've got proven fertility: two kids. Damian…he and his ex-wife had tried to have a baby. He'd been tested. Results suggested I didn't need protection.'

'So, who else is in the running?' Liam's voice was steely. Natalie curbed her natural retort; he had the right to know.

'No one.'

'We had sex once, Natalie.'

'Last time I did biology classes that was all it took.'

'It's impossible that it could be McBride's?'

Liam sounded as enthusiastic about Damian's involvement as Damian had been about Liam's. Natalie supposed she should be happy that duelling had gone out of fashion. She was too familiar with the consequences that messes like this could generate. But these two men were well educated, rational, no history of violence. Hopefully that counted for something.

'No, just millions of healthy sperm versus the occasional one. Tilts the probability heavily in your direction.'

'I'll want a DNA test.'

Natalie shrugged. 'Sure. Then we'll all know one way or another.'

'And you want what from me?'

'Not a thing. Just whatever they need for the DNA match.' Natalie's patience was exhausted. 'Look, it's my decision. I get that it's unfair, but shit happens — and you weren't wearing a condom.'

Liam leaned forward, and appeared to choose his words carefully. As the Public Prosecutor, words were his tool of trade.

'If the DNA says the child is mine, I won't walk away.'

His fathering would probably entail a monthly cheque.

'If you need support now or later,' he continued, 'then I am happy to be there for that.'

She'd deck the next person that said they wanted to support her. 'I can organise my own support.'

Liam paused. 'If it's over between you and McBride,' he added, 'and you're interested in…' He shrugged. Words for casual sex with a pregnant woman appeared to be failing even him.

'I'll add you to the list of who to call if I'm horny.'

Liam stood up. 'I'll be leaving you to it then.'

She stood too, careful to keep her face impassive, refusing to acknowledge her pain to herself, let alone to him. Then he surprised her. There was a flash of vulnerability, a warm smile, and as he left he kissed her gently on the forehead. 'What I was trying to say…'

He stopped; shook his head. 'Stay in touch, okay?'

The Children's Court was tucked away just off William Street, where the other courts were located. When Natalie arrived, there was a line of people snaking up the hill: barristers and solicitors with briefcases, police officers, witnesses—experts and lay—all mixed up with the punters: women with prams and screaming children, tattooed men snatching a final smoke before going in.

'Renewal day for intervention orders,' explained the security officer as she dropped Natalie's backpack in the tray.

No sign of media; the court dealt with criminal cases against minors relatively infrequently and supressed names when they did. Also, unlike the Family Court, the Children's Court adjudicated over cases of families against the State, represented by Protective Services, and not primarily parents against each other. This case was going to be complicated— parents against each other *and* the State.

Li Yang, Jenna's lawyer, was waiting. Natalie could have picked her without the introduction: stick thin, short hair, knee-length charcoal skirt with matching jacket. Killer heels.

She was evaluating Natalie in return, and her impression was apparent: *You'll do, but you'd have been better without the blue streaks in your hair and the row of metal in your ear.*

'We'll be getting started again soon,' she said looking at her watch. 'Doubt the Protective Services lawyer will give you much trouble. Bit of a soft cock, and he's basically on our side anyway.' *Our* side meant Jenna's. If Natalie was on any side it would have been the children's—but she was impartial. At least trying to be.

Li Yang continued, 'Don't know Pam Warren, Malik's lawyer.' Not knowing her didn't stop Li offering her evaluation: 'Part-time Pam from the 'burbs. And we've scored Louise Perkins, who takes zero shit. Don't give her any absolutes. Say "I believe" and she'll believe you.'

Perkins? Maybe the magistrate was related to Tania, Liam's assistant prosecutor. Melbourne had its share of legal dynasties.

'Paediatrician gave his findings this morning,' Li added. 'No signs of abuse.'

Natalie was distracted by a black woman of about thirty, stunning in a bright yellow dress with hair clipped close to her skull. She was standing at the courtroom door glaring at a smartly suited man in his thirties who was on the phone. She looked vaguely familiar.

Li leaned in. 'Katlego Okeke. This could be interesting.'

Now Natalie recognised her—left-wing journalist. Wrote a column called *Not OK* for one of the dailies. What was she doing at the Children's Court?

'She's checking out Soft Cock,' said Li. 'The Protective Services lawyer. The guy on the phone.'

Li Yang disappeared before Natalie could ask for details about the abuse claims.

Natalie watched as the Protective Services lawyer caught sight of Okeke. He put his phone into his pocket. Early thirties, blue pinstriped suit, a little overweight. He mopped his brow and walked over to a middle-aged woman—a social worker Natalie had worked with before. Wanda? Wilma? No, Winona.

Winona spotted Natalie and introduced the lawyer—Harvey Alcock. Natalie barely suppressed a snort. 'We're here representing Chelsea and Chris,' she added.

'Do you think the child's been abused?' Alcock asked.

'I've only seen the mother. She didn't mention abuse. But...'

Winona crossed her arms. 'The guy's a sleaze.'

Alcock looked at Okeke who was moving into the courtroom. 'He won't get the kids.'

Winona leaned towards Natalie. 'He wants access to a child —a little *girl*—that isn't even his. What does that say to you?'

'I haven't met Malik,' said Natalie. Natalie knew better than to assume that the decision would be so straightforward— but a whiff of child abuse would have everyone playing it safe. In that sense, Mark La Brooy's line on hard-done-by dads was right.

The overhead speaker called them in.

The courtroom was small—and crowded. Natalie's eyes went to a man in an open-necked white shirt and loose trousers who had to be Malik. Olive skinned and black eyed, stubble on his chin, he looked like a movie star. He'd have been perfect in a white robe staring across windswept sand dunes…Natalie winced mentally as she caught herself. Could she blame her hormones for her mind going to mush?

Malik was sitting behind a generously proportioned woman in her fifties, in a skirt that was a fraction too tight, with bare legs and flat shoes. Pam Warren, his lawyer. Seated beside Malik was a well-dressed woman wearing a ton of jewellery with dark glossy hair under a loose head scarf. An older sister? If she was his mother, she was carrying her age well.

Natalie sat close to the door, next to Winona. Further down, Okeke was taking notes.

Jenna smiled tentatively at Natalie from the front row where she sat with a couple in their late fifties or early sixties— they had to be her parents. The father, Stephen Radford, was a big man who sat very upright. Hair a little long, thinning on top and greying at the temples; in comparison his wife seemed tiny, her long brown hair tied in a knot and her face strained.

'All rise,' called the bailiff, as the magistrate entered from behind the desk that sat above the rest of the room. *Don't sit in a chair higher than your patients: it makes a power statement.* In the court, it served exactly that purpose. Louise Perkins would not have been much taller than 150 centimetres. Silver through her brunette bob, probably mid-fifties. But she didn't need any help to look authoritative.

Natalie was called to the stand and sworn in. She stated her qualifications: medical degree and fellowship of the College of Psychiatrists. Twelve years of study. Plus nearly four years' experience as a consultant.

'You saw my client last week?' Li Yang began.

'That's right,' said Natalie, adding the date.

'And you don't believe she has a current psychiatric disorder.'

'That's correct.'

'What impressions did you have of her as a mother?'

'She clearly cares for her children. I think they are challenging at times, and she has difficulties putting up boundaries with Chris; but there are often behaviour problems after a breakup.'

'Or if they are being abused.'

'Objection, your Honour.' Part-time Pam, Malik's lawyer, was on her feet. 'There is no evidence of abuse and the witness hasn't seen the children.'

Li smiled. 'I won't pursue it.' She had made her point better than if Natalie had answered. Difficult behaviour was not uncommon when parents separated, but the specifics tended to be different if abuse was occurring. Natalie wasn't going to get a chance to explain that.

'If my client's daughter was being abused, what would be the risk to Christopher, her younger brother?'

'It would depend on who was doing the abuse,' said Natalie evenly. 'If it was someone who had access to both of them, there would be a risk of him also being abused, even though he's male—and in any case, there would be the problem of his exposure to what was happening to his sister and the culture that allowed it.'

Okeke started writing furiously. Was it the word 'culture'? Natalie had used the word in a general sense, to embrace whatever setting the abuse had taken place in—family, church, school camp.

'No further questions. Thank you, Doctor King.'

Part-time Pam knocked a folder as she stood up and spent a minute collecting the papers. Her clumsiness had done nothing to calm her client; Malik's edginess was palpable.

'Ahh… Did my client's wife say he hurt her in any way?' asked Pam.

'Physically, no.'

'Okay.' Pam sorted through her notes. Li rolled her eyes. Pam eventually found what she was looking for. 'Did she say anything that suggested Christopher or Chelsea was at risk from him?'

Natalie paused. 'No.'

Pam was fiddling with her notes again. Maybe they had fallen out of order when she dropped them. The delay gave everyone time to take in Natalie's answer.

'So somewhere in the few days between seeing you and making the report to police something must have happened, is that right?'

'I don't know.'

Pam squinted at the paper she was looking at, then rustled around for some reading glasses. 'If I told you that my client did not see the children in that time period—what would you say to that?'

'Sexual abuse is often not detected or reported immediately,' said Natalie. She was on firm ground now. 'Of all the types of abuse, it is the one that most often doesn't come to light until the victim is an adult. The victim may be threatened; they often know, or rather sense, the taboo surrounding the abuse. They blame themselves, collude to keep the secret. It's further complicated by the victim—and remember we are talking about children—being confused, often wanting to keep the love of the abuser. So it's possible that Jenna—Ms Radford—suspected something was going on but didn't tell me because she had no proof. There may not be physical signs—sexual abuse can take many forms.'

'That didn't stop her going to the police.'

Natalie flashed a look at Jenna, whose face was pale; when their eyes clicked she read *sorry* but also *help me*.

Mickie Radford was staring ahead and Stephen kept looking to his daughter as if he felt he had failed to protect her. Did parents ever stop worrying?

'There was no doubt in my mind that Jenna cared for her children,' Natalie said carefully. 'Coming to see me may well have been what prompted her to take the next step.'

Jenna mouthed a small *thank you*.

'Cares for them? Or feels she owns them, Doctor King?' said Pam.

'I believe... Jenna wants to do the best for her children.'

'And would she lie to do that, Doctor King?' Pam asked. 'Put what she believes to be her children's interests above the truth?'

'I can't answer that.'

'Have you read the article by your colleague Professor Wadhwa on false claims made by women in order to get custody and maintenance?'

The article that Mark La Brooy had quoted in his column.

Wadhwa had argued that the 'explosion of interest in childhood sexual abuse as a cause of trauma' following the Royal Commission into Institutional Responses to Child Sexual Abuse was giving every woman with a grievance a method to get what they wanted: an intervention order, more maintenance, payback for infidelity. 'Who,' he had enquired of Mark La Brooy, 'would dare, in this political environment, to believe the father?'

'I am familiar with *Associate* Professor Wadhwa's article,' said Natalie. 'It was an opinion piece without scientific basis.'

Katlego Okeke was scribbling. Pam opened her mouth, closed it and began again. 'But some women do make false claims?'

'In my experience, it's not common.'

'But Ms Radford has a psychiatric history.'

'All my patients have a psychiatric history.' Natalie saw the magistrate smile. 'Lying is only a criterion of antisocial personality disorder and factitious disorder, neither of which Ms Radford has.'

'But anyone can lie can't they?'

'Yes.' Jenna wasn't looking at her; Malik was.

'Could her history mean that she might be a risk to the children?'

'A psychiatric history doesn't make you a risk in itself; one in five people are affected by a mental illness and quite a lot of them are parents.'

'But what about the drinking, Doctor King? Isn't that what she does when she's stressed? Like now, without my client to help her?'

'I have no reason to believe Jenna has started drinking again.' This *was* something Jenna might lie about. Alcoholics were good at hiding what they were doing, and anyone who had had an eating disorder was a master. Conversely, Malik might say she was drinking even if she wasn't.

'But she used to, didn't she? Even when she had a young child.'

'Jenna... I believe Ms Radford maintains a job and isn't abusing alcohol.'

'That is not what my client is stating, Doctor King.'

'I have no evidence she is lying. But of course Mr Essa isn't living with her anymore so would have limited information.'

Pam looked annoyed that Natalie had managed to add the last point.

'You say she had an eating disorder,' said Pam.

'In her teens, I believe she would have qualified for a diagnosis of anorexia nervosa. But not now.'

'Are you certain?'

'Yes.' Jenna was slim and her choice of clothes tended to hide her weight—and today she was wearing a baggy black T-shirt. But there was no way it was dangerously low. Natalie caught Malik's incredulous expression. There was something decidedly unnerving about the look.

'But isn't it true that some people with eating disorders can struggle with food for years afterwards?'

'Yes.'

'Do you know how this struggle has influenced her mothering of Chelsea?'

'I haven't assessed Chelsea.'

'Would it surprise you to know that at times the household has had *no* food at all, not even cans in the cupboards? That Ms Radford has served up a single pea on each plate as the vegetable? Would that concern you Doctor King?'

'I would need to assess it, certainly.'

Malik looked at her triumphantly. Natalie mentally kicked herself for believing Jenna and her mother.

'What if she were parenting alone, as she is now? That would be a problem, a *dangerous* problem, for the child's safety, would it not?'

'Protective Services would assess that on a home visit.'

'While they're checking for the empty bottles.' Pam paused. Li Yang's hand pushed down on Jenna's shoulder.

'We've heard statements from family members and friends about how good a father Malik is. What's the risk to his son if he *isn't* allowed to see Chris?'

'Jenna is Chris's primary carer. She's the more crucial parent for him at this age.' Natalie paused. *Impartial*. 'But at three, he could have increased time with the other parent or family members, providing he's safe with them. I haven't assessed Mr Essa, but in general, a boy's relationship with his father is an important part of making him feel secure and helping him develop a sense of self. Possibly Mr Essa can help Chris make sense of why he and Jenna aren't together.' Like that would happen.

'Thank you.' Pam sat down.

Harvey Alcock took his time getting to his feet. 'Have you seen Ms Radford's statement about the abuse?'

'No.'

The magistrate threw a glare at all the lawyers, who

34

clearly should have provided the information to Natalie. Li Yang sent her junior across the floor with it.

Natalie took a moment to read Jenna's police statement.It was thin on specifics:

Not herself, withdrawn, not wanting to go to school which is most unlike her.

Asked me about getting pregnant, very distressed when I answered.

Natalie wondered about the exchange—a tense or emotionally charged response might have upset the child more than the reason for asking.

Wants to stay home with me all the time.

Doesn't want to go to Malik's house.

'What do you make of this?' said Alcock.

'I'm not a child psychiatrist.'

'But you have worked with children, haven't you?'

'Mostly aged three and under.'

'This is more than just reacting to her parents breaking up, isn't it?'

'Objection,' said Li. 'Mr Essa is not Chelsea's father.'

'I'm the only father she's ever known. I adopted her!'

Malik's outburst took the magistrate by surprise. It took her a moment to react. 'Mr Essa, please sit down. Ms Warren, please ensure your client remains in his seat.'

Pam whispered to Malik. He sat down, mouth set in a hard line.

'It could be just reaction to a breakup,' Natalie finally answered.

Alcock frowned. 'Surely not, Doctor King. What do you make of Ms Radford's statement regarding the child's mention of pregnancy?'

'Without assessing Chelsea, it's hard to say,' said Natalie slowly. 'It may have been brought up at school, she may have become upset because of her mother's anxiety. But it rings an alarm bell. Loud enough for it to be worth investigating.' And definitely worth checking out the teacher's observations.

'And would this abuse—' He caught Pam's expression '—were it happening, be disruptive for a three-year-old boy as well?'

'Yes.'

'And could he find it destabilising to see his father without his sister present?'

'He might.'

'It's true, isn't it Doctor King, that children are more at risk of sexual abuse from stepfathers—more so than from natural fathers?'

'Objection.' Pam. 'Doctor King is not a policewoman—or a criminologist.' Bad call, thought Natalie. The evidence was nowhere near as strong as people generally supposed.

Her answer would have helped Malik.

The magistrate frowned. 'I don't think this line of questioning is taking us anywhere. Do you have anything more, Mr Alcock?'

The Protective Services lawyer paused, walked to one end of the courtroom, then paced back to Natalie. Not for drama, but thinking time, Natalie thought.

'What about culture, Doctor King? How do you think Mr Essa's upbringing will impact on his parenting of a young girl? Alone?'

Katlego Okeke was sitting so far forward in her seat that she was almost in the next row. The magistrate had also noticed. Natalie felt like she was walking a tightrope over a volcano.

'I don't know anything about Mr Essa's upbringing.'

Natalie took little pleasure in the smile Malik sent her way. Jenna's father looked at her like she was the devil incarnate. Li Yang was letting Alcock go; probably happy for someone else to say the unsayable.

Louise Perkins was having none of it. 'Mr Alcock. At the present time we are not talking about anything other than the issue at hand, which is safety.'

'Certainly, your Honour.' Alcock's smile was forced.

'But the child's mother has expressed concerns to us

36

that Mr Essa belittles her, follows her and checks her phone records. Possessive. Patriarchal, you might say. Is this the sort of culture you'd want your daughter exposed to?'

'I can only reiterate that I haven't assessed Mr Essa.'

'But you have assessed Ms Radford, and the children will be safe with her?'

'Yes.' Careful. 'I believe so.'

'Chris is my son!' Malik was out of the chair again. Two security men appeared at the door.

'Sit down, Mr Essa. I won't tell you again,' said the magistrate.

Malik gave in to his lawyer arm-tugging and Alcock also sat down. 'I'm finished, your Honour.'

Louise Perkins turned to Natalie. 'The paediatric expert found no evidence of abuse, but I take your point that there may be abuse that doesn't exhibit physical signs. You're the only psychological expert I have in my court, Doctor King. So, until such time as the lawyers gathered here organise someone else, you'll have to do. I need to make a temporary custody and access decision today.'

The magistrate looked at her notes, but Natalie suspected she didn't need to. 'There's a lot of work to be done before I can make a ruling in the best long-term interests of the children,' said the magistrate. She looked at Malik. 'Mr Essa, I understand your distress if these allegations are without basis, but until we have more assessments completed—

including the police investigation—I must make a ruling that ensures the safety of both children. I am going to give custody of the children to Ms Radford—'

Jenna looked up; Natalie saw only relief.

'On the matter of access.' The magistrate frowned. 'I accept that Mr Essa has been father to both children. I'll grant weekend access—during the day only—to both children, supervised by Mr Essa's mother.'

Jenna's expression hardened and she turned to Li, talking frantically in low tones.

'Can we have a moment please?' said Li.

Louise Perkins nodded impatiently. Li turned to Alcock. Winona and Jenna joined the huddle.

'Ah, your Honour,' said Alcock finally, as he rose.

'Yes, Mr Alcock.' The magistrate didn't sound happy.

'Ms Radford wonders—and we agree—if the supervision could be undertaken by her parents. The children are familiar with their home and it's closer for her.'

'Are the children not familiar with Mr Essa's mother?'

Alcock cleared his throat. 'The reality is, Mrs Essa cannot be relied on to supervise adequately. Culturally…'

Malik was on his feet again. 'Chris knows my mother—' It was apparent he was referring to the woman beside him. 'Jenna's mother is a drunk.' Malik saw the two security staff start to move but remained standing despite Pam tugging at his arm. Jenna's father half-stood. His wife remained seated, looking down.

Okeke leaned forward again.

Jenna was now standing. 'She'll let Malik do anything, she'd lie for him, do whatever he asked!' Malik had moved out from his seat and the security staff stepped forward to restrain him.

'Enough of this in my courtroom! All sit down imme-diately.' The magistrate, all 150 centimetres, was worth several male heavies. Malik sat, but the two uniformed men remained beside him. 'Mr Alcock, has Protective Services spoken to Mrs Essa?'

Winona cleared her throat. 'Your Honour, Mrs Essa has not been interviewed but after assessing Mr Essa we do share concerns that… ah… cultural norms may differ and that Chelsea could be at risk.'

'What cultural norms would they be?'

Winona whispered to Harvey who replied, 'Mr Essa is considered the head of the household. We agree with Ms Yang that his mother might not be in the position to… ah… stand up to him.'

The magistrate frowned and addressed Malik's mother. 'Mrs Essa, you understand that supervision requires you to be with the children at all times?'

The woman with the arm of gold bangles nodded. 'Of course, if that is what is required. They are children. My family. I care for them as I did for my own.'

'Any other objections?'

Jenna looked like she had plenty, but the magistrate wasn't about to give her airtime.

Alcock conferred with Winona, who was shaking her head.

The magistrate turned to Natalie. 'How long will it take you to do an assessment? Both parents with the children.'

'A parenting assessment?' She had spare time slots. 'A month.'

'Then we reconvene a month from today. I trust there are no objections?' As Natalie locked eyes with the magistrate, the clear message was: *and make sure you have all the answers*. 'To be clear, Mr Essa will have weekend access, daytime only, supervised by his mother.'

Pam Warren and Alcock requested the right to obtain another psychiatric opinion if needed, and Li Yang nodded.

Brilliant.

Task one—decide if Jenna was one of Wadhwa's and Mark La Brooy's frivolous claim-makers, lying to keep things out of the Family Court, away from a judge she thought would be unfriendly. And if she was also lying about her eating disorder and her alcohol consumption. And if, regardless of that, she was still a better parenting option. And then try and convince the court of that.

Task two—decide if Malik was lying about the extent of Jenna's illness. And whether he was a low-life child abuser and, while she was at it, whether he was a paternalistic misogynist Islamic fundamentalist.

But really it was all about task three. How to ensure Chelsea and Chris were safe.

The first thing Natalie saw when she opened her iPad over breakfast was a *Guardian* column headed 'Racism in the Name of Child Safety' by Katlego Okeke. Shit.

> *Yesterday we saw the race card played in the Children's Court. Hardly news, you might say. Regrettable; but angry parents with much at stake will throw whatever is available to discredit each other—including racist stereotypes. Except it wasn't angry parents. It was a lawyer in the public employ, representing a government insti- tution: extraordinarily, the Department of Human Services...*

Okeke went on to skewer Harvey Alcock for labelling Muslims as child abusers and for maligning 'a grandmother, a quiet dignified woman who raised three children after her husband died', as well as for advocating in favour of 'a mother with a history of mental illness and alcoholism—but who had the compensating attribute of being white'.

After a robust critique of the way the various professionals in court had 'tossed the word "culture" about as a loose but invariably negative term to create a sense of danger', she concluded:

Magistrate Louise Perkins rightly dismissed Alcock's argument and allowed the grandmother to contribute to resolving the family crisis and creating a safe environment for the children. But when the voice of government is racist, how can we expect any improvement in attitudes to our refugees?

Which pretty much covered everything, thought Natalie.

Her toast was cold and she gave up on it and made herself another coffee. Protective Services would not be happy; they had enough image problems as it was. Natalie was grateful she had escaped a name-check. For a psychiatrist, all publicity was bad publicity. She'd been in the media before, and it had had Declan reaching for the blood-pressure tablets.

'Is this your case?' asked Beverley. She was outfitted in a yellow catsuit that made her look a little like a canary.

Natalie wished it had been something other than the Okeke article that had moved her secretary's interest away from the wedding-planning.

'Unfortunately, yes,' Natalie admitted.

'You aren't on Twitter, are you?'

'No.'

'Okeke has caused a bit of a storm. There are some awful trolls out there. And it's a sensitive topic.'

'What topic?'

'Get a Twitter account, then look up hashtag SaveOurKids.'

Natalie downloaded the Twitter app and found she needed a handle. After a moment she typed in @BobNotDylan and found it was already taken. Really? She added her birth year.

It didn't take her long to find the search function.

#SaveOurKids turned up hundreds of comments on Twitter in the preceding six hours. It was hard to tell who supported what but the Muslim theme was dominant. Okeke tweeted from @NotOKK and had posted a link to her article.

Right-wing journalist Mark La Brooy had replied.

Mark La Brooy @SayItStraight68: *Madness. Islam before women and now children. Kids need safe parents #SaveOurKids*
Others waded in:

Julie G @JoolieGG: *Maybe he's fine but unless we're sure why put kids at risk? #SaveOurKids*

Natalie skimmed through the rest—nothing that struck her as an intelligent contribution to the topic. Some people had too much time on their hands.

'I've been asked to do a parenting assessment on both Jenna and Malik,' Natalie told Declan. 'But the more I've thought about it, the more I want to run a mile.'

'Because of this?' Declan asked. He put down Okeke's article and turned to the pot of tea he had brewing. The lines on his face appeared like deep crevices in the light thrown from his desk lamp. She wondered if he saw anyone to help him shoulder the stress of suicidal patients…and fractious and rebellious supervisees.

'Having Katlego Okeke breathing down my neck won't make it any easier. But no, more that it's a poisoned chalice. Unless the kid tells someone Malik was abusing her, what does it matter what a parenting assessment shows? And how the hell do I do that anyway? I could do it with Chris—that's the three-year-old—but an eight-year-old? I'm not a child psychiatrist.'

Natalie had scoured the internet and her textbooks looking for tools—frameworks or questionnaires—to help with her assessment of Malik and Jenna. The forensic assessment tool she usually used was not suited for this purpose—it focused on the likelihood of a known sexual offender reoffending, whereas Malik was denying, possibly with absolute sincerity, that he was an offender at all.

Natalie's clinical skill was around diagnosing mental illness—mainly schizophrenia and serious depression, mostly in women—and assessing its impact on judgment and insight. It involved factors like the side effects of medication, or whether a mother's delusional system might incorporate the child.

Natalie didn't usually look at specific skills related to parenting. There were no guidelines that were helpful for cases like this, and certainly nothing that would withstand robust interrogation by the lawyers for either side.

So it was basically down to what the opposing parties said, and whether she believed them. But with their acrimonious relationship, anything they reported on the other would be unreliable. Forensic psychiatrists like her tended to think they were less gullible than general psychiatrists, but it didn't mean she could read minds.

'One assumes that the police will be investigating the abuse and a therapist interviewing Chelsea,' said Declan, pouring the tea. 'Hibiscus infusion. Have one?'

Natalie nodded, distracted.

'You know how to assess whether they have the capacity to put their child first,' Declan continued as he took his own bone-china cup and saucer and settled back in his chair. 'You haven't seen Malik yet; his developmental history will tell you a lot. And his attitude to the girl. If Malik can see Chelsea as a child with her own needs and desires, he's less likely to fit the abuser prototype. And Chris is young enough that you can at least assess their relationship.'

'I suppose I can hope Malik has an antisocial or narcissistic personality disorder. That'll make it straightforward.' But both Mickie and Jenna had said he was a good father to Chris—Natalie doubted it would be that clear-cut. 'Is there anything I should be particularly looking for in Jenna?' She took a sip of tea and winced. What the hell was she doing drinking hibiscus tea?

'You felt some degree of her need to control in your interview?'

'Yes.' Natalie nodded. 'Her need to control, and that Chris is challenging it.'

'There may be differences because of the genders of the

children, the different ages. As the older child, Chelsea will have had to adapt to her mother's parenting style, along with her mother's attitude to food and alcohol use—by eight she might even have become the parent in some ways.' Just like Jenna had with Mickie. 'That could explain her not telling her mother about the abuse. If she's seen Jenna fall apart under stress, she's already well versed in the dance of avoidance.'

'What if…' Natalie stopped herself.

Declan raised an eyebrow; waited.

'Wouldn't it just be easier for the court to say no to Malik? He's not the biological father.'

'Not Chelsea's. But he is Chris's,' said Declan. 'And the court will be aware of what a difference it can make to a child having a stable, protective, caring adult around, whether related or not.'

Could there be a scenario where Natalie could say Malik was a good father to Chris but not to Chelsea? Even if there wasn't any evidence of abuse, surely it would be better to just lean towards safety?

She could already see the Okeke column—or the La Brooy article. They'd have a point, too. Easy to see that approach as discriminating against all non-biological fathers, adoptive fathers, stepfathers…

But if she got it wrong and recommended Malik be granted custody, and he was an abuser?

The thought made her feel physically ill.

Jenna and her father were in the waiting room when Natalie arrived at work. She tapped Beverley on the shoulder; it was the only way to get her attention. Beverley—hot-pink pants-suit today—was listening to music in order to select what to choose for her big day. To be fair, she was typing reports at the same time, though Natalie wouldn't have been at all surprised if the lyrics of 'Walking on Sunshine' turned up in someone's psychiatric and drug history.

'Jenna doesn't have an appointment, does she?'

Beverley removed the headphones, also hot pink; a metallic sounding 'Ave Maria' leaked out.

'Jenna? No, but the poor pet was quite distraught when she rang in and I said you could probably find time.'

Poor pet? The impending wedding seemed to have turned Beverley to mush. She had the headphones back on before Natalie could respond.

Natalie looked at her watch—there was half an hour before the next patient. It would have to do.

Stephen Radford stood up as Natalie approached and extended his hand. He was a big man with soft features and an earnest look. His handshake was unexpectedly gentle. 'Just wanted to thank you,' he said. 'Court case was pretty tough on us all. Pleased to have you on our side.' He seemed to have overlooked her moment of being fair to Malik. Natalie remembered how he had kept checking on his daughter in court. Father and daughter seemed to be in similar positions, wanting to protect their children.

'I just want what's best for Chelsea and Chris,' said Natalie.

'Of course,' said Stephen, nodding and smiling at his daughter. 'We all do.' He looked awkward: because she was a psychiatrist or because he wasn't sure of his role, Natalie couldn't be certain. 'Let me know,' he said, 'if I can help at all.'

'I'm sure Jenna will ask for what she needs,' said Natalie. From what Natalie had seen of her, Jenna didn't need a psychiatrist to pass messages. She may have sounded distraught when she rang Beverley, but she wasn't now. If anything she appeared a little sheepish—and, though careful not to overplay it, grateful.

'Thank you so, so much for fitting me in,' she said before the door to the office had closed. This time she went for the upright chair by the desk—closer to the door, perhaps because she wasn't planning to settle in for long. Natalie took the chair opposite.

Jenna was in corduroy jeans, brown boots and jumper. Neat, no makeup, yet she gave the impression she looked after herself. Natalie couldn't quite pinpoint why; perhaps the way she held herself, a little like a ballerina. A certain poise, and she was working it hard.

'I want to explain,' she said.

'The abuse charges?'

'Yes.' Jenna took a breath. 'I know I told you... that there wasn't any reason for Chelsea not to see him other than he wasn't her father—'

'As far as the law is concerned, Malik is her father.'

Jenna stiffened and Natalie mentally kicked herself. There had been no need to remind her of this and put her offside. It was probably annoyance at Jenna for misleading her.

'I know. But he isn't... her father. I mean, I know he took us both on and at the time I was grateful. But he's only been there for half of her life. She'll forget him.' Her eyes held Natalie's, imploring. 'I know you can help… I was just scared.'

'There's two separate issues here.' Natalie took a moment to look hard at Jenna. Wondered if she was being played. 'Firstly, whether he's safe to be a father at all. And secondly, if he is, whether his relationship with Chelsea should or shouldn't be facilitated.' She thought of her own absent father, and knew how much she had suffered from not having him around when she was growing up. But better for a father to be absent than abusive.

'He isn't safe so the second issue doesn't matter.'

'But that would mean he wouldn't be safe to be Chris's father either.'

A wave of irritation crossed Jenna's face. 'He's fine with Chris. Chris might not do a thing I ask, but he knuckles under without a word if Malik tells him something. And… surely if Malik abuses girls it just means he's…well he isn't gay, I can assure you of that.'

'Being interested in children sexually is about attraction to children, sometimes but not always gender related. It's nothing to do with being gay,' said Natalie. She leaned forward slightly. 'I read your statement Jenna. It was… vague. Start at the beginning. How long have you suspected something might be going on?'

Jenna's shoulders slumped, the ballet-dancer pose gone. It was only a second before she straightened up, perhaps responding to some internalised monologue from her childhood. 'Soon after we separated. Nearly six months.'

Natalie nodded. Having lost his sexual partner, was Malik trying to replace Jenna with Chelsea? Natalie had had several patients who, as children, had been expected to take over their mother's role not just in the kitchen, but in the bedroom. In cases where there was no biological connection between father and daughter—and, according to some research, no early involvement in the child's care—an increased risk occurred of norms being distorted and relaxed to suit the man involved. It was driven by a mix of unfulfilled physical desire and a warped male-authoritarian view of their world.

'When Malik left, we were both too angry to negotiate having the kids,' said Jenna. 'But about a week later I rang Ama—Malik's mother. Chris was asking about his dad.' She paused. 'So was Chelsea.' Jenna shrugged. 'I said he could have them for the weekend and I dropped them off at Ama's.

Malik had moved in with his brother, Youssef, and the place was likely to be a pigsty. I thought Ama's would be better—she wanted to see them too. I heard later they slept at Malik and Youssef's, though.'

'And how were they after they returned?'

'Fine, I guess. Malik had fed them pizza and ice-cream and taken them to Luna Park so, you know, no complaints from them. I made sure he knew I was unimpressed about that, but I let him take them a few more weekends.'

Jenna had started fidgeting. This wasn't easy for her. *Or was she lying?* Natalie watched, looking for tells, well aware of studies that showed that professionals often missed them—or interpreted them incorrectly.

'It was just little things,' Jenna said in a rush. 'Chelsea started spending more and more time in her room. Then one morning, she didn't want to go to school. Said she had a stomach upset. I didn't think she was all that unwell, but I called in sick, let her have a day at home, and I was right, she wasn't ill. At first I thought something might be happening at school, like bullying or something. She denied it, school said they didn't think so. There was a problem with one girl, Matilda, but for her, not Chelsea.'

'Did she say she didn't want to go to Malik's? Or seem worse when she got home from seeing him?'

'No,' said Jenna. That seemed to contradict her statement to the police. 'Which was why it took me a while to work it out—the timing you see.'

'But the timing is also when you split up, Jenna. Maybe

she's been miserable about that. Afraid you might leave her as well.' Natalie kept her voice gentle. This wasn't about blaming Jenna in any way, but truth was, separations hit children hard—and children often thought they were responsible.

'I thought that at first, but…then there was the pregnancy thing. She asked how did you have a baby, and could children have babies.'

'It's normal for children to be curious.'

Jenna shook her head. 'No, it wasn't that.' She had that *I know because I'm her mother* look. 'I'm very close to Chelsea. I know her, and something is wrong. I mean, really wrong. Suddenly she's not talking to me, secretive, wanting to sleep with me. We used to do that, before Malik came to live with us, but that was a long time ago.'

'Has anyone else noticed any changes?'

'I'm the one who knows her, who sees her the most.'

'I understand that,' said Natalie, 'but the more corroboration the better. I'll need your permission to talk to her teachers, and her grandparents.'

'Yes, of course.' Jenna bit her lip, and Natalie saw tears welling in her eyes. 'I *know* he's abusing her. Please, please help me protect her.'

'You have to be well enough to have them in your care,' said Natalie. 'Tell me about your eating disorder and the lack of food at home.' Natalie made sure her expression said: *And no bullshit*.

'It's okay. Truly. Come and look in the cupboards; Protective Services already have.'

'You're saying Malik lied?'

Jenna hesitated, saw Natalie's face. 'It was a bit like the frump said. But only for a while, after I had Chris. I was depressed, looking back—I had to look after two children by myself until Malik got a visa. Breastfeeding, I lost weight and it seemed to trigger all that stuff from my teens. Took me a while to get on top of it again. But I *am* on top of it. *I'm* not the issue—Malik is.'

In a jerky movement, she picked up her handbag and rummaged. After a moment, she carefully laid down three large photos, one after another in front of Natalie. Natalie kept her eyes on Jenna, who looked directly back at her. 'I can't... I *won't* let him have my daughter.'

Natalie was in no doubt that Jenna thought her daughter was being abused. But Jenna's certainty didn't mean it was actually happening. If Malik was innocent and had to live with the suspicion, or indeed, label, of paedophile, it would have an effect on his employment prospects, affect where he lived and who he could be with. A stain on him for the rest of his life.

The assessment was going to have a lot riding on it. If Chelsea didn't come out and talk about the abuse, Natalie would need to come up with something definitive.

Jenna left the three photos of Chelsea behind on the table to remind her: one as a baby, eyes bright and alive laughing for the camera, another when she was about four in an embrace with Jenna, a poster for motherhood. And the final one—Chelsea, probably taken recently, sitting still and solemn, chin jutted out in tentative defiance. The sorrow and fear in the hazel eyes reminded Natalie of herself as a child.

How the hell had she ended up making an appointment with a male obstetrician? Let alone one located in a major teaching hospital where there were bound to be hordes of medical students hovering around. Was her mental acuity going to be on a downhill slide all the way to the delivery date?

Alex Lascelles, Natalie decided, was gay; camp anyway, and that might be his saving grace. Blond hair with foils and a button-down shirt that looked like it was meant to go with a velvet jacket and fob watch.

'You appear to be in excellent health,' he said after giving her written instructions about what to eat, where to deliver and what to take with you when you did. His secretary had already outlined the costs, which seemed an exorbitant price for one mistake—with a climax that was going to actually hurt. After paying for the bean to enter the world she might need to break into Blake's cartons of toys so it would have some entertainment.

Then there was the fact that the metal plates in her hips from the bike accident might cause problems, and the scars across her abdomen might not stretch: she'd need to see a plastic surgeon about that. This man was a bundle of laughs.

'Is there anything else you would care to know?' he said.

'I need a paternity test.'

Alex's expression didn't change; she could have been asking what her blood group was. 'There's now a non-invasive technique—a blood test. It's more expensive but safer.'

'I'll pay.'

'You need to be at least ten weeks… as you aren't sure of dates, best to wait a week.'

Only a week? Natalie felt a moment of panic; was she worried? Was not knowing easier?

'Here's the information brochure for the possible fathers,' said Alex. 'How many do you need?'

Riding home, she found herself out of breath on the slight incline past the university and made an illegal shortcut through Carlton Gardens. The *No bikes* signs made an exception for parents with children under the age of twelve;

hers was under the age of zero, and its mother needed to get home. *Mother*. Natalie pushed the idea down—it didn't sit comfortably next to any version of herself.

The warehouse that had always been her sanctuary seemed unusually quiet. The lane seemed dark and even the graffiti looked faded—more pathetic than edgy. Someone with a can and no talent had decorated the cul de sac beside her warehouse with red squiggles and she hadn't got around to calling the council about it. They'd only do it again anyhow.

She still hadn't replaced the globe in the garage. She bruised a shin on one of Blake's boxes, trudged upstairs, threw her bag across the room in frustration and nearly knocked Bob off the stand he had flown up to.

'Sorry.' She ruffled his feathers. 'Looks like it's you and me again tonight.'

Bob was more interested in his food container.

'It's not like I want a man living here,' Natalie told him. 'But it'd be nice to have one sometimes, you know?' She opened the fridge, closed it again. 'Actually, maybe more than just sometimes. Pregnancy doesn't seem to have decreased my libido.' She thought of how Liam had suggested keeping in touch. Thought about Damian's chicken casserole, and the way he did fish on the barbeque. Thought about going to the supermarket to get some real food—self-care as much as for the bean.

Instead, she opened a can of baked beans and sent a brief, to-the-point text to Liam. The speed of his response suggested his thoughts had been along the same lines as hers—and neither of them wasted any time when he did arrive.

Afterwards, snuggled together on the couch, they talked about the Children's Court case.

'What makes you think it's you who makes the decisions?' he said.

'The judge might make the final judgment, sure. But how can she do her job if I don't give her the right information?'

'What makes you so sure that any information you have is "right"? The law is about balance of risk and probability.'

'So are my recommendations.'

'But what if,' suggested Liam, tracing his finger down her neck, 'someone else tells the judge that, let's say, your patient is running a cocaine cartel and using the children as mules—facts you haven't been privy to?'

Liam had a point—but if she did her job well enough, wouldn't she pick that something was seriously wrong with Jenna—or Malik—even if she didn't know the details?

'You'll never know everything,' said Liam. 'Best information you have, with the best minds available. Or best mind in your case.'

She wondered if she was just too tired to argue, or that Liam really did make her feel better about the sort of work she—they both—did? There had to be something in his insights, in how they clicked, beyond the sex; when she woke up in the morning and saw he was still there she wasn't overcome with the urge to get him out.

Malik stood up and then sat down every time she passed him in the waiting room. Three times up, nervous smile and hopeful look, three times an embarrassed return to the chair. He was younger than Jenna, Natalie saw as she looked over the patient information sheet he had completed. Only thirty. And as good looking as she had noted in court—*about as trustworthy as a fox in a chicken coop* Beverley had said. Open-necked white shirt again, emphasising the honey tones of his skin, thin gold chain around his neck. Black hair over the shirt collar. A little-boy smile and deep black eyes. It was easy to see what had attracted Jenna—but Natalie needed to know what was beneath the veneer: not just psychiatric history but core values and beliefs, which he was likely to be pretty guarded about. Being a woman probably put her at a disadvantage.

And then the real issue—whether he was a child abuser. Was Jenna's certainty based on some visceral maternal reaction to a real situation—or redirected and misinterpreted concern and guilt about her own parenting and choices? Natalie had dealt with several child abusers and one child pornographer. Had there been any identifying feature? Perhaps a superficial charm, a readiness to manipulate and to see the world in a self-serving way. A way that allowed them to keep believing that the children needed their love and weren't being harmed by the abuse. A sense of weakness and a lack of integrity; an impression that the building blocks of the self were founded on sand. One man had thought he was doing the child a service. Natalie shuddered. Those men had made her skin crawl with their soft-spoken selfrighteousness.

But she didn't know if that was a detectable characteristic. She had already known what they'd done.

Malik followed her into her office, hesitating in the door-way. Natalie made the decision for him and sat at her desk. She wasn't doing therapy with this man, and needed to assert her authority from the beginning.

'Take a seat, Mr Essa. May I call you Malik?'

'Yes, please.' Malik smiled. Natalie gave him a curt nod and his expression became wary. He took out a business card and handed it to her. *Easy Tiger Imports*.

'Let me explain about this process,' said Natalie. 'Today I need to talk to you about your background, hear your story. You know, of course, that Jenna has already spoken to me. At the next appointment, I want to see you with Chris, and the one after with Chelsea. I'll be doing the same with Jenna. Protective Services and the police will follow up to interview Chelsea alone and I will not be a part of that.' Natalie waited for Malik to take it in. 'Any questions?'

Malik's expression was anguished. 'I would not know where to start.'

'Then let me begin,' said Natalie. She was about to ask for his response to the accusations and stopped herself. *Build rapport*. She had, she realised, already taken Jenna's side; yet she had never met this man and the court needed—demanded—impartiality. She thought of Liam's hypothetical drug cartel—after all, she wasn't God and couldn't know everything. Katlego Okeke's article and the biased and angry tweets in response came to mind. Was she any better, if she didn't allow Malik an opportunity to prove himself? She took a breath, smiled. 'How about at the beginning? Where you were born, about your early life?'

'But…' Malik stopped himself; there was an effort being

exerted. Malik wanted to appear reasonable. 'I was born in Cairo. I am the eldest. My brother is here with me and my mother. My sister is with her husband near Alexandria.'

His father, as Natalie already knew, had died when Malik was eleven. A lymphoma, said Malik. Malik's uncle had supported the family. It was Malik who had moved first to Australia and organised the others to follow.

'My uncle's business in Egypt, I started here. Importing,' Malik told her.

'Importing what?'

'All things. Someone wants something? We find it. We have the buyers: designer bags, children's toys, kitchen utensils. Anything. If you would like something for Christmas, let me know.' He smiled.

Great. A fake Gucci for her sister Maddison maybe? She thought of Blake's boxes.

No psychiatric history—either himself or his family. No run-ins with the law—though as a pre-teen he had been in a fight that had caused a lot of trouble at school, around the time his father died. Malik glossed over it, but it had been about his father.

No drugs anymore—and he'd only ever tried them 'once or twice', a downplay of Jenna's version; alcohol socially.

'Is it a religious issue for you?' asked Natalie.

Malik shrugged. 'Religion is not much of a thing for me. I was more observant in Egypt.'

'You drink at home?'

Malik hesitated. 'With my brother, some beers maybe, but his house is not really my home. Home is the house where Jenna is. With my children.'

'And when you were living there did you drink?'

'No, never. It would not have been good for Chris.' Forceful, a touch of self-righteousness.

'Chris?'

'When she was pregnant. You know your government made me go back to Egypt because my visa ran out? To leave her? If she had got drunk then and harmed him, it would have been on their heads. Now I worry again.'

Natalie let that go. 'Tell me about meeting Jenna, and your relationship.' Malik was still being cautious but it seemed that he was more likely to give away something of himself on a hot emotional topic—and there was no doubt Jenna was the button.

'We were together, in Paris. My uncle supplemented my scholarship so I could go to university there. Jenna was in the same student residence. Very sexy, fun. We were in love. She had this great smile. Has. It's been a long time.' His eyes sought Natalie's sympathy. 'Why has she changed? How can she say these things? These terrible things?'

'Let's stay back when you met. What attracted you to her?'

'As I said, her smile. She was fun. But also…' Malik frowned. 'There was some hurt perhaps.'

Jenna's knight in shining armour. 'You wanted to help her?'

Malik shrugged. 'Of course. And I was lonely.'

'How did you feel when she told you she was pregnant?'

'That it was meant to be.'

'But it wasn't easy for you. Coming to Australia. Taking on an extra child that wasn't yours.'

'Only the government made things hard. I was sent back to Egypt and missed out on *six* months of Chris growing up.' Malik looked torn between bursting into tears and ripping out the throat of any passing government official. 'When I arrived back, she stopped cooking. One night I find nothing in the cupboard, *nothing*. Chelsea was starving.'

'So what did you do?'

'We had an argument. Jenna was unreasonable.'

'Who fed Chelsea?' Natalie asked. Chris had been breastfed —all the nutrients going to him would have accelerated Jenna's weight loss.

Malik blanched. 'I…I left.' Which meant the child had remained hungry until the next day at least. 'But after this,' said Malik, leaning forward, earnest expression, 'I organise

57

the feeding of Chelsea and me.' He shrugged. 'I am not so good a cook, sometimes it was MacDonald's. But we ate.'

'How long did this go on for?'

'A few months. Then she got better. My mother was allowed to come. Things were fine, we were good, a family. Until Jenna went back to work. Why did she do this? There was no need. We were not rich, but there was enough.'

'She went back to work not long before you broke up, right?' Natalie asked.

'Yes.' Malik took a breath. 'I think perhaps this is where she met someone else.'

'You checked on her?'

'She is my wife.'

Natalie bristled. 'And did you find anything?'

'She makes lots of phone calls; some to men. When I asked her about this, she was upset, we fought, she hit me. I had to sit on her to stop her breaking all the glasses. Plates my mother gave us. In the end, I went to my mother's so Jenna can calm but then she says she does not want me back. She threatens *me* with an intervention order, when it is she that causes the problem.' Malik's speech had picked up speed, his tone heading towards a whine. So much for the knight in shining armour.

'When you argued did you ever hit her?'

The reaction was immediate. 'Never! Did she say this? It is not me that hits her, it is she that hits me!'

'When? Did she hurt you?'

'Once, she scratched me. When we fought, when she makes it so difficult for me I had no choice but to leave, or else I might…she makes me very angry.'

Different from Jenna's version. But…it fitted. Natalie couldn't see Jenna as being able to get him to leave by merely standing her ground; there was something not quite grown up about either of them.

'So Jenna became more assertive?' Natalie asked, careful to keep her tone level.

'Yes, yes,' said Malik. 'Aggressive. She thinks she can do what she likes, like she is still single.'

And he didn't like that—and Jenna not needing him anymore. Natalie sketched the cycle that they had become sucked into. Jenna trying to be more assertive. Malik becoming defensive and somewhat paranoid. Jenna withdrawing emotionally and ending up aggressive, pushing Malik away further towards paranoia and trying to take control—which resulted in Jenna pushing back and the cycle starting again.

People thought domestic violence towards men by women was less common than it actually was—partly because women did less physical damage, and partly because men were too embarrassed to report it. Either way, this type of violent cycle suggested both of them had insecurities that kept feeding it.

Jenna had broken free of the cycle... but had left Malik feeling inadequate. It was conceivable that in a situation like this a man might use the daughter as a substitute for his wife—one he could control.

'She married me, it is my name that they have.' Malik's voice trembled slightly. 'I adopted Chelsea, I am her only father.'

'And Jenna is their mother.'

'My son needs me, Chelsea too. Don't let her mess them up; let them at least have one parent who is stable.' His eyes had tears in them. 'Do you know what it is like? I found myself on edge when I was with Chris, my own son! Then I realise it is because already I dread handing him back. The house I live in now, it is...so...empty. Like there is something missing, and it is missing in my soul.'

Good performance. But even if he did miss his children, it didn't mean he wasn't abusing them.

Natalie took a deep breath. 'Malik, all I can tell the court is what I see. Tell me about these accusations.'

Malik shook his head. 'It is all made up. Perhaps her lawyer told her to say these terrible things? Is it for money? She must know I have little, that what I have I will use to support them. I have had the *police* come to my home. To my mother's home. She says this is worse than being in Egypt. I would be listened to there.'

'Jenna thinks… it is possible that abuse—or the separation— could result in the behaviours Chelsea is showing. Regardless, I don't believe Jenna is lying.'

Malik stood up and started pacing, running his hand through his hair. 'This makes no sense to me. Chelsea is just a child. They are making too much of it.' He stopped, his expression brightening. 'The other doctor said Chelsea was fine.'

Natalie shook her head. 'That just means that there is no sign of penetration.'

Malik flinched. He seemed genuine but Natalie watched him carefully as she went for broke. 'There are other types of sexual abuse. Having Chelsea touch your penis; or oral sex.'

He was visibly shaken. He flopped forward into the chair, head in hands. 'Chelsea is only a little girl, this cannot be possible. It is a mistake.'

It could be, Natalie reminded herself; Malik might not be able to handle strong women, but that didn't mean he was a paedophile. There was no physical evidence, and no statement from Chelsea herself. And sexual abuse might be perpetrated by someone other than the father or stepfather. She needed to cover this as well. Malik had a brother he was living with.

'Is there anyone else that Chelsea could have been left alone with?'

Malik's eyes narrowed. 'Perhaps Jenna has a boyfriend? She has been lying about me, so what else has she lied about? Please, you must help me.' He looked Natalie directly in the eyes. 'More important, even than this, you must help Chelsea.'

After he left, she slipped Malik's business card into her pocket, and found herself thinking more about him than she would have liked. Yet she found herself no closer to knowing the truth than she had been at the start of the interview.

When Natalie got home she had a shopping bag of salad ingredients: how hard was throwing some greens together and adding oil? She figured it would be a night or two before she saw Liam again, and until she had the DNA test results, they weren't going to be doing much talking about a relationship; anyway, he was juggling two kids part of the time in his apartment in South Yarra. Access was always ad hoc, usually related to urgent WHO meetings in Geneva, conferences or funding body meetings that overran. Associate Professor Lauren Oldham could organise the world's response to Ebola but not her own schedule. Or at least not in any way that might have been convenient for Liam.

She turned on the news, as much to fill the place with sound as anything, and was feeding Bob when she caught sight of Liam in the footage, standing behind a blonde reporter.

The child abuse Royal Commission. That had been the other bit of news from Liam. He'd taken leave of absence from his role as a public prosecutor to assist the Royal Commission.

'I'd hoped the hours would be better so I could be around for Megan and James,' he said. 'I should have known better. There's enough material here to keep a commission going for years. And I'm still working with the OPP to prosecute the cases in our jurisdiction.'

He hadn't said much else about the new role, but Natalie could see he was disturbed by what he was being forced to deal with. Hundreds of adults who had been in orphanages and church-run homes as children making graphic, explicit submissions of what they had been subjected to.

Natalie tuned into what Blondie was saying on the TV.

'Professor Wadhwa today gave evidence about the unreliability of memory…'

Great. Her nemesis—and former boss—was in a position to give both her and Liam a hard time.

When the doorbell rang she started. For the first time in weeks, she had a flashback to the stalker. She took a long, calming breath before checking out her guest through the spy-hole.

In the dim light Natalie could see a hooded figure walking restlessly before stopping to light a cigarette, then moving across the lane to look up at her windows. When he raised his face she could just make him out.

She opened the door. 'Blake?'

'You didn't answer your phone.'

'I had it turned off—means I don't want to be bothered.' Natalie stood in her doorway, arms crossed. 'You're here to get rid of the boxes?'

'That's what I needed to talk to you about, Nat.' Blake flicked his cigarette into the lane and followed her up the stairs. They looked nothing alike—he took after their mother. Willowy with long fingers; pretty, delicate features with dirty blond hair that he wore either in a ponytail or, like now, in a bun, and a trimmed goatee. And pretty, pale blue eyes that he had been using all his life, along with a hesitant smile, to get everything he wanted with as little effort as possible.

'I'm listening.' Natalie ate her salad—maybe a bit too much green; it would have benefited from a tomato—while Blake, who'd checked the bowl out and winced, poured himself some of the whiskey Liam had left.

'There's been a bit of a problem—'

'There's always a problem, Blake. But it's not my problem.

The stuff needs to go or I'll get a truck and take it to the tip.'

'You wouldn't!'

'I will. Blake, I have the Crown Prosecutor here some nights. If he thinks there is any chance of connecting him with whatever shit you are up to, we're both dead meat. I need it out. This weekend at the latest.'

Blake frowned. 'Nat, I just need another week, two at the most. The wholesalers have turkeyed on me. I need to find a new buyer.'

Natalie picked up her phone. 'I'm googling removal companies.'

'Good thinking! We can put it in storage. I can pay you back when I sell it.'

'I'm finishing my salad and watching a movie in bed. Be sure to slam the door when you leave.'

She couldn't recall the nightmare that woke her later. But unlike the others over the last months, it left her not with a fear of something or someone, but rather a feeling that she had done something wrong. A feeling that seemed out of place and time, and just out of reach. Was it the brief image of the hoodied Blake in the streetlight that had triggered her? Probably, but she refused to dwell on it. Refused to let her memories gain traction. She'd spent six months working on mindfulness and it had been more than three weeks since she had woken drenched in sweat, her heart racing and her mind frozen with fear.

At 5 a.m., unable to get back to sleep—assuring herself it was just her mind testing her randomly and that it wouldn't happen again—she got up and worked out in her makeshift downstairs gym, Lil Wayne blaring.

The photo of eight-year-old Chelsea kept flashing into her mind and she said to herself with each biceps curl what Declan would be bound to say: *Don't get over-involved. You can only do your best—give the court the facts and let them decide.*

Trouble was, no amount of Liam telling her that the law

was his domain could convince her that it knew what it was doing when it came to psychiatry, parenting and children.

But right now, she didn't have any answers either.

Jenna was late. Natalie made coffee and settled down to read the newspaper on her iPad. Two articles on the Royal Commission and in one of them there was an inset photo of Wadhwa. Apparently he didn't believe there was any compelling scientific evidence to support repressed memory as a genuine phenomenon. Natalie gritted her teeth; presumably he was waiting for someone to do a randomised control trial where half the children were submitted to abuse and the other half not, while researchers stood by with clipboards. The online comments were overwhelmingly critical of him.

She wondered if Twitter was still responding to Katlego Okeke's article; found that *#SaveOurKids* continued to trend. The tweets were coming from all directions—some responding to Okeke, some commenting on the Royal Commission and some that had nothing to do with either.

Okeke's supporters included some she may not have wanted:

Casey Hatton @caseyhatton85: *Muslim or Zoroastrian, doesn't matter. Any decision that recognises men's rights is a step forward*.

The detractors, some of whom seemed to have been prevented by the 140-character limit from developing their arguments in full:

My Bitchin Rules @MyBitchinRules: *Go back to Africa*.

And some who appeared to have inside knowledge:

Liza R @lizar82: @NotOKK *Why didn't you disclose he's not the biological father? #sjwbias #SaveOurKids*

Liza R's tweet had prompted a string of outraged replies, but no defence from Okeke.

Twitter didn't seem to have any mentions of Wadhwa. She checked out the lawyer, Harvey Alcock, and found that he tweeted under his own name, with a blue 'verified' tick. Nothing on the current case, but enough to confirm his politics:

Harvey Alcock @HAlcock75: *Religion of peace? You haven't read the Koran, have you?*

@HAlcock75: *If you're supporting same-sex marriage, you can't side with Islam. #cognitivedissonance*

Natalie didn't do social media—and this wasn't about to change her mind. But until her dealings with the Essa case were over, she needed to keep an eye on these feeds. She added a picture of her cockatoo to *@bobnotdylan82* and followed Alcock, Okeke and Mark La Brooy.

Jenna and Chris finally arrived for their joint assessment—twenty minutes late. Jenna looked flustered. 'Sorry. Chris has been impossible,' she said, watching the boy run up the corridor.

As they trailed after him, Jenna added, 'He's been behaving like a little shit. I can't get him to do anything. He just laughs at me.'

'What do you think's happening for him?' As opposed to eight-year-olds, Natalie did know a bit about babies, toddlers and attachment. Theoretically at least.

'He hates me.'

Not likely. 'Is there any other reason he might appear angry?'

'Because I wasn't doing what he wanted me to. *When* he wanted me to.'

'It must be hard for Chris to understand why he isn't with his dad.'

'He could be if Malik wasn't so…' Jenna shook her head. 'Can we just get this assessment over with?'

After retrieving Chris from the tea room, Natalie led the two of them upstairs and settled them into the room Gerry Milton used for his sand-therapy clients. It had a one-way screen, so she could watch Jenna and Chris together without her presence distracting them. Chris went inside without them, just as Jenna's phone went off in her pocket. She grabbed it, went to turn it off but stopped. 'It's Malik,' she said, looking at Natalie. 'He's been… Can I put it on speaker?'

Natalie hesitated. She stuck her head around the door and

saw that Chris had gone straight to the low central table with its neatly raked sand inset. Out of earshot. He looked suitably occupied and she thought he was old enough not to eat the sand, so she gently pulled the door shut, nodding.

'Malik? I'm about to see the doctor with Chris.'

'Chris? What have you done to him?' Malik sounded alarmed.

'I haven't *done* anything. Not that sort of doctor, Malik. Doctor King for our assessment.'

'I've told her you hit me. Are you drinking again? Have you told her about that?'

'Have you told her about checking my phone records? Ringing my boss because you found his number on my call list? Putting paint on the car? How about that, Malik?'

Natalie frowned, and gave Jenna the signal to wind it up. Having them continue an argument might give her insight into their relationship but was unlikely to leave Jenna in the right frame of mind for the assessment she needed to complete.

'I didn't lie, Malik,' said Jenna. 'I'm her mother, I know you've done something to her.'

'Fuck you!' Malik was almost screaming. 'My mother is right, perhaps I will go back to Egypt!'

Jenna hung up. But she had paled. 'They don't have passports. He couldn't get them, without my knowledge, could he?'

Natalie supposed anything was possible. But the authorities dealt with this all the time. 'Tell your lawyer you're worried. Let her take care of it.'

Jenna looked anxious, tapped her phone. 'There's a message here from my mother. Might be about Chelsea. Do you mind if I take it?'

Jesus, people and their phones. Natalie nodded and went to check on Chris.

The therapy room bore little resemblance to what Natalie had seen a few minutes earlier.

Figurines from the shelves that lined three of the walls

were strewn across the floor: soldiers, Disney characters; jungle, farm and sea animals. The meticulously arranged toys on the upper shelves marked the limits of the child's reach and provided an indication of what Natalie would have to reinstate.

What Chris had done with the sand was worse. When Natalie had let him in to play, the central pit in the low wooden table had been all Queensland tourist brochure; now it was more post-Tsunami aid request. There was as much sand over it as in it, to say nothing of the handfuls of sand this little *monster* had thrown around her colleague's formerly pristine office. Had the pit been deeper than the ten centimetres needed to fuel children's imaginative play, Natalie would have considered turning him upside down in it.

The little monster stomped on a figurine as he held onto a plastic tiger and growled, then looked at Natalie for her reaction. Part of her wanted to laugh: the child was so obviously playing for attention. But the other part of her wanted to hose the gel out of his black spiked hair, strip him of his Osh Kosh outfit and tell him to behave himself. Then head plant him. Or maybe head plant his parents?

Instead, she shook her head. Chris crossed his arms as if to say *Bring it on*—and Natalie started to see where Jenna was coming from.

Maybe Natalie really didn't know that much about three-year-olds after all. Smack his bottom? Besides being illegal, it would only show the unfortunate short-term effectiveness of brute force—and he'd probably get enough of that message elsewhere. Trouble was, she had no authority with this child, no relationship. Which left—what?

Natalie took a breath, dropped to the ground and started screaming, pummelling the floor with her hands and kicking her legs in the air. She grabbed one of the figurines and banged it into the floor. Threw another one. Out of the corner of her eye she could see Chris staring in bewilderment. He had backed off, mouth gaping and eyes wide; no longer in charge—just a bewildered three-year-old boy. No more than thirty seconds had passed. Natalie sat up, crossed her legs and brushed the sand off. 'See? I can do that too.' Her hair shed sand every time she moved. But at least she had the child's attention.

Chris looked relieved when Jenna came in minutes later. Natalie withdrew after quietly explaining the protocol to Jenna, leaving them to play. Natalie squashed herself into the observation room, between old files and boxes of paper and envelopes. She made herself as comfortable as possible on one of the boxes and sat to watch through the one-way screen. Jenna had been the stay-at-home mother with Chris, and therefore his primary attachment figure. It was from Jenna that Chris had acquired a template for future relationships—and that was what Natalie wanted insight into. Of course, not even the best mother could prevent adverse consequences if a young child was dealing with sexually predatory behaviour from the other parent.

The sound system was emitting a low buzz but she could still hear over the top of it. Chris started wandering around the room.

'Come and play, Chris,' said Jenna, picking up some of the figures. 'This is your favourite. Superman.'

Chris looked at his mother and started playing with the cord for the blinds. 'Superman's stupid. I like Thor.'

'Come play with me, Chris.' Jenna picked up some other figures and started to put them back on the shelf. Out of order; Gerry Milton had them all in clusters. His OCD would go into overdrive. 'Look Chris. Lions and tigers, remember, we saw them at the zoo?'

Chris wandered over but didn't appear interested. He pointed to some figures he couldn't reach and Jenna handed them to him. Jenna's phone must have vibrated—she pulled it out of her pocket and looked at it. Really? Chris didn't know Natalie was watching, but Jenna certainly did. Did she really think this was how to be a good parent? Or was she just too preoccupied with the abuse from Malik?

Chris quickly got bored. He looked up to his mother, who was tweeting or texting. He threw a figure at her, hitting her on the leg.

'Ouch!' Excessive: it couldn't have hurt much. Chris threw another one. Any reaction as far as a child was concerned was better than none at all. This one missed.

'Why don't you make a farm? There's some ducks and sheep there.' Jenna pointed. Natalie felt like yelling, *Help him—enjoy it with him!*

Chris picked up a figure and put it down, rolling over onto it. 'Don't want to play with a farm.' He moved across the floor like a commando.

Jenna leaned forward and put together some fences, added a couple of random animals. Checked her phone. Bit her fingernail. Chris tried to put up some fences next to hers but knocked everything over, more accident than deliberate. Frustrated, he threw another figure across the room.

'There's some Lego there, Chris.'

'I'm Thor,' Chris said in a booming voice.

'Okay, Thor then.' Jenna sat down and collected all the Lego in a pile. 'How about we make a zoo?'

'That's stupid.'

Jenna's expression conveyed childlike hurt. Chris smiled and strutted around the room, returning to kick her Lego blocks.

'Suit yourself, then.' Jenna sat back on the chair, missing the look of what Natalie took to be confusion on Chris's face. Followed by more kicking and throwing.

After fifteen minutes Natalie had seen enough. She used the intercom to ask Jenna to get Chris to help her tidy the room.

'Pack up time,' said Jenna. She stood up, as keen to leave as her son. 'Come on Chris.' Her voice carried no conviction. Chris was already at the door, trying to reach the handle. Luckily he couldn't. 'Chris, help Mummy pack up.' The tone said: *You'll do this if you love me.* Jenna started to pick up the toys that now decorated the room. Chris moved from the door to the desk, but with no intention of engaging in the task.

The room got packed up—more or less: but Jenna did it all. Except the sand. That was a job for the cleaners.

Ama hadn't seen the point in talking to Natalie when she called, but after Natalie explained she needed to hear both sides of the story, she said, 'Of course, there is much I can tell you about Jenna.'

Natalie was sure there was. 'I want to talk about Malik— you know him better than anyone.'

'Malik is a good father.'

'I was actually more interested in hearing about what he was like as a child.'

Natalie couldn't see Ama's expression at the other end of the phone, but the pause made it clear she couldn't see why that was relevant, and she answered the questions that followed with barely disguised impatience. There were no surprises. A good boy, always 'responsible'—which was more than Ama could say for Jenna.

'What was his relationship with his father like?'

There was a hesitation. 'His father died young.'

'But before he died?'

Ama sighed. 'His father was a security guard. There was a bank robbery. He was not the same after.'

So Malik's father had PTSD? Natalie thought of the veterans she had cared for and the impact the trauma had had on their ability to relate to their families. If the bank robbery was shocking enough it might have had similar psychological effects.

'In what way?' Natalie asked.

'Why does this matter now?'

'How we parent is affected by how we were parented ourselves.'

'I raised Malik and his brother and sister. Uri's brother too, was a good man; he helped.'

'But Uri was Malik's father.'

'Uri was a coward.'

Okay.

'What happened?'

'My friend's husband, the other guard, was killed. Uri gave the criminals his gun.'

'Was anyone else killed?'

'No, but he could no longer work because of the shaking, the nightmares.'

'It sounds terrible. For you all,' Natalie said.

'Mostly for Malik. He defended his father's honour but boys are cruel—the child whose father died beat him up, put him in the hospital.'

This was the episode Malik had downplayed. Ama clarified that it had happened after Uri had died, and was at pains to point out that he had got through it and done well at school, gone onto university. He'd had one long-term girlfriend. Ama hadn't liked her.

'She was always demanding he should be there and then, when he was, she just complained.'

'One more thing. I wondered if you could think of any way Chelsea might have... maybe heard a TV show where people were having sex? Exposed to sexual matters in any way at all.'

Ama snorted. 'She is a child. My son is a good father. He has done none of these things Jenna says.'

'Do you—did you look after Chelsea often?'

'Of course. When Malik and Jenna were together I would have both children. Mostly I see Chris because he is not at school. *She*'—sniff—'would often leave him with me. Because of work. Maybe you should ask her these questions.'

'And Youssef? Did he see much of the children?'

'Youssef does not live with me. He comes for dinner sometimes. He is a good man too.'

And if he wasn't, Natalie would be the last person Ama would tell — before the cops.

'Have you seen Chelsea since the separation?'

'At first. But now, not for some months.'

'How do you think she was taking it, the separation?'

'She is normal. She likes to see my son. Malik is good to her. It is Jenna; she has a problem in her head.'

Malik was looking around the waiting room warily, Chris on his knee. The only other occupant, a dishevelled man talking to himself, looked more 86 tram on a Friday night than doctor's office. One of Natalie's colleagues worked closely with the public mental health service, and bulk-billed some of the clientele who had chronic schizophrenia and substance abuse issues.

'I wanna go home.' Chris glared at Natalie.

'Maybe this time you can play trains with your dad?'

'I wanna go home. Daddy, I wanna ice-cream. I want it NOW!'

The shout jolted Malik. He frowned at his son. 'That is enough Christopher. I told you the ice-cream depends on you being good.'

Christopher mimicked the frown, looked like he was going to yell again then thought better of it. Malik smiled at Natalie. 'It's okay to say that, isn't it? I mean all parents bribe their kids, right?'

'You wouldn't be the first.'

Natalie led them up to the playroom Chris had been in with his mother. The sand had been cleaned up — and the table lid was firmly in place.

'Have a play together,' she told Malik. She avoided looking him in the eye. She just wanted to get this assessment — and Malik — out of her life.

Malik nodded, walking into the room with Chris and checking it out before he sat down on the floor next to the toy box. Natalie positioned herself in the observation room. By the time she got there, Malik and Chris had constructed half of the train track and were well on the way to completing it.

'Try that piece,' Malik suggested, pointing to a bridge that was part of the set.

Chris frowned, picked it up, tried to attach it and couldn't. Natalie thought he was about to chuck it but instead Malik intervened.

'Try it the other way, maybe.'

Chris looked at him, paused, tried again, copying his father's mimed actions. This time it clicked. There was a look of triumph on the child's face. Malik smiled in recognition of the boy's achievement. Chris looked at the animals and picked up a plastic tiger and put it in one of the railway trucks.

'A zoo car, perhaps?' asked Malik.

'The tiger is going away,' said Chris. A few minutes later he had a train running around the track, tiger onboard, shouting in delight.

The two looked like an advertisement for fatherhood. Natalie's stomach clenched. What she knew about fatherhood hadn't come from experience but from textbooks: reciprocity, joy, positive expectations… and she'd seen Malik put up appropriate boundaries. Maybe Malik was acting, but Chris was three. Even if he knew he was being watched, he wouldn't know which boxes he was meant to be ticking — and he seemed to be ticking them all. Malik was providing to Chris what his father had perhaps given to him before he died — a stable, caring role model who was helping him build his self-esteem. It went against every ounce of Natalie's intuition to believe that he could do this for one child and abuse another.

But Chelsea was a girl. And he hadn't been there when she was a baby. Was that enough to make the difference?

When it was time to clean up, Malik remained in the chair, encouraging like a cheerleader. Chris completed the entire task then grabbed his father's hand to drag him out—and on to their next adventure.

'I couldn't fault him.' Natalie was feeling frustrated.

Declan scratched the bridge of his nose where skin was peeling; he'd been bushwalking and must have forgotten the sunblock. 'Maybe that's because he's doing a good job.'

'With Chris, he is.'

Natalie thought back to the contrast in how the two parents had handled him. Took a sip of tea—English Breakfast today.

'Chris isn't the problem—with the right parenting, he can settle quickly. His behaviours are a response to his mother. Jenna seems frightened of Chris; she certainly isn't taking an adult role. He picks that up, and he's scared too, because when she's around there seems to be no adult in the room. And rather than be good—perhaps like his sister was—he does the boy thing and acts out of control.'

'Which Jenna interprets as anger.'

Natalie nodded. 'Her own father was—is—the patriarch, and she let Malik run things when they first got together. But she's grown a lot, I think. Malik couldn't cope with her need for independence, and she couldn't cope with either him or Chris trying to boss her around.' Natalie frowned. 'She did stand up to Malik though, and left him.' Albeit with some histrionics.

'She may fear that if she takes charge with Chris he won't love her.'

'That fits—she felt that when he said he hated her, he

really meant it. Which upset her. Her fear of not being loved didn't keep her with Malik, though. I wonder why not?' Natalie could see Declan was going to wait for her to make sense of it. He took a bite of the homemade ginger biscuits that were on offer—Natalie had already had two.

'Okay, possibly it did,' Natalie continued, 'but something shifted; and that something has to be that she needed above all to protect her child.'

Not all women in similar circumstances had been able to do what Jenna had; too often they turned a blind eye, consciously or subconsciously. Natalie had been involved in one case where the mother had stood by her husband even after he had fathered a child with their daughter. In the face of DNA proof, the mother had chosen to see her daughter as some kind of temptress. At fourteen.

Whatever shortcomings Jenna had in managing Chris, she made up for it with her willingness to protect her daughter.

'You don't think she's lying about the abuse?'

'Not deliberately. But that doesn't mean she's right. Sixty–forty as to whether there's a basis or not. Jenna's complicated; obsessional…but with some borderline and histrionic features too. I wondered if she might be a little jealous of Chelsea's relationship with Malik.'

Declan rotated his glasses around in one hand. 'It would fit with the sense of the hysteric in Jenna. What was her relationship with her father like?'

'Better than with her mother; he took her to things, a bit like Malik seems to have done with Chelsea. But I sense it wasn't close. Maybe he was the unemotional patriarch type, or maybe just because he was away a lot—probably to escape the alcoholic wife. He's still involved, trying to support her.'

'You're seeing both parents with Chelsea as well?'

'Yes, though I'm not sure what I'll get out of it. Eight-year-olds aren't exactly my strong suit.'

'You're not assessing Chelsea, rather her relationship with her parents. Just look for how comfortable she is with them.

Their willingness to let her talk. A sense of the dynamics. Whether Jenna is prompting or pushing her in one direction, Malik in the other.'

'I have nothing on Malik that suggests he's abusive. I've heard him get angry at Jenna, but that's hardly diagnostic. His father… died young. He suffered with PTSD. Ama— Malik's mother—saw the father as weak.'

'So Malik has a need to prove himself?

'Probably, though he says all the right things. It makes sense of why he liked Jenna needing him. But I have no evidence that he's so invested in the need for domination he could justify the abuse of a child. And he was very credible when he said he didn't.'

Declan looked at her over his glasses. 'Credible because it is the truth? Or because he's a psychopath?'

Natalie closed her eyes, tried to relive what it felt like to be with Malik.

Around one per cent of the population could be classified as psychopaths. Often intelligent, frequently charming. Usually good liars. They weren't all obviously cold-hearted— the more successful ones had learnt to read others' cues and feelings in order to use them more effectively. In the past, she had been alerted by a sixth sense, a feeling that something was a little off.

Could Malik have fooled her? She was sure she'd seen some genuine emotion. But then psychopaths did feel emotions—just not for other people.

'At times, he was kind of pathetic,' said Natalie. 'He whines when things don't go his way.'

Declan took a biscuit. 'You don't have to like him for him to be innocent.'

'There's a bit of "poor me" about him at times. I think Jenna becoming more assertive and confident undermines his sense of self—and fragile narcissism would fit with an abuser profile. The "all about me" and no regard for his children's needs and fears.' Maybe his dad *was* weak—like father like son.

'Does anything in his background meet criteria for narcissism or psychopathy?'

'Not really,' Natalie said, partly wishing it had. She liked pieces to fit together and this jigsaw was more like she had two different puzzles mixed up together. 'I pushed his mother as hard as I could. She's obviously going to try and make him look good but short of calling Egypt she's the only person I can check with. The only thing was a not-great relationship history—only one former girlfriend back in Egypt. I had the sense he may have got paranoid about her too. He certainly crossed the line as far as I'm concerned in checking Jenna's phone records and watching her at work.' She thought of Okeke. 'I wonder how much is cultural?'

'You're not assessing his culture—you're only assessing whether he is a good enough parent for this culture.' He walked over to his bookcase, and went straight to a volume on child psychiatry. 'Winnicott says it best, though Jude Cassidy has a nice way with words too.' He looked up. '*I'm here for you, and you're worth it.* Which is to say, does the parent you're assessing see their child's individual needs and provide them with unconditional love and support? This is independent of gender, race and age.'

Did either Malik or Jenna, really? Wasn't there too much of their own relationship, their own issues getting in the way? A thought of the bean flashed into her mind, and she shook her head. She couldn't let her shit get in the way.

'How about the intrusive checking, monitoring—evidence for insecurity and need to control? Not the sort of thing that you'd want in a father,' Natalie said.

'But how do you know he would do that with a daughter? And is it really enough to stop access?'

If that was the standard, half the parents she saw wouldn't get to see their children.

Declan patted her hand. 'You aren't Solomon, Natalie. Let the judge make the decision—just give her what you see and don't see, and an evaluation of the risks.'

Natalie had gone out on a limb before for her patients, at the risk of breaching ethical guidelines or even the law. She had a sinking feeling that this case might push her to do it again.

She thought of Jenna's plea: how could she possibly let Malik have Chelsea if there was any risk?

'And Natalie?' Declan looked pensive, usually not a good sign. She waited. 'Have you seen your mother yet?'

Natalie stifled a retort. She knew Declan had her welfare in mind, and was concerned she wasn't adequately supported. But her family—her business.

She took a breath. 'No, but I will.' Eventually.

Liam turned up late to the Saturday gig at the Halfpenny. Saturday was his son James's sports day: the kid was in his second year of high school and seemed to be aiming for the Olympic decathlon if the number of his after-school activities was any indication. On top of soccer and cricket, depending on the season.

Natalie quashed the resentment. Liam was a great dad, and if he wasn't asking after the bean, that was okay for the moment. She didn't want any man sticking around with her because of a baby. But she needed to fight for its right to have a dad. She couldn't help but want something better for her own child than she'd had.

Liam was smiling at her, and she winked and sashayed her butt as she sang. There was only a small crowd but it was an enthusiastic one. A guy up the front yelled, 'I'll have a bit of that, luv.' She laughed and called back: 'In your dreams,' in between verses. She was feeling good.

After the last set, she found Liam at the main bar.

'You still going to do that with a belly?'

'Any business of yours?'

Liam shrugged, turned back to his drink. She could tell from the way his eyes dropped at the corners that this wasn't his first whiskey of the evening. He smelled of booze and cigarettes.

'You been working?'

'Tania's been helping me put together one of the Royal Commission cases they've recommended prosecuting.'

The pert Tania Perkins, his co-counsel. He was sounding more stressed than she'd ever seen him before. Was it that he was essentially doing two jobs? Or Tania?

'Tania smoke, does she?'

'Tania?' He frowned. 'No. Jealous?'

'Should she be?' They both turned to look at who was speaking. Neither of them had seen Damian approach. His expression gave nothing away—apart from a possible desire to flatten Liam.

Shit. When she'd told Damian she wasn't in a relationship with Liam it had been true. Now, less so. Liam's mask was in place, the slightly amused expression he wore as he ripped people to shreds in court.

'Good to see you're still on water,' said Damian.

Natalie stiffened. 'I haven't had the test yet.' She was past ten weeks now.

'Amnio, right?' Damian was looking at Liam as he spoke.

'I think technology has improved lately,' said Liam. Natalie hadn't discussed it with Liam, but wasn't surprised he knew it was all down to a blood test. Damn men and their pissing contests.

'I'll send you the information,' said Natalie, grabbing her jacket. 'You'll need to give some blood.' Natalie waved goodbye to Vince, who had clearly overheard the exchange. He was watching them as if he was wondering how much it would cost to have a hit man knock off both Liam and Damian.

Liam caught up with her by the time she turned into her laneway.

'So, who's the smoker?' Natalie asked without looking at him.

'Lauren. She says I drove her back to it.'

'Ah.' He was seeing Lauren? Didn't they just hand the kids over like batons? Natalie vaguely recalled Liam had been trying to get his ex-wife to sit down and sort some of the details out. 'How did it go?'

'Great. If negotiating with Medusa is your idea of fun. Think you've got one thing sorted and she comes from a totally different, illogical angle.'

'You did marry her.'

Liam looked miserable. Shrugged. Work was getting him down, but the more Natalie was seeing him, the more she thought the problems on the home front were the root cause of his stress. Lauren might not ever have been the sort of wife that put his slippers out for him but, until Natalie, they'd found a way of making their lives work.

Natalie felt a fresh wave of guilt. As much as she wanted him she wondered, if she could go back in time, whether she would have done things differently. Would they be able to find a way to make it work together? For him, her, his kids—including the bean. They reached her warehouse and Liam poured himself a whiskey while she got herself another water.

'Any progress with the kid arrangements?'

'No.' Liam paused, couldn't bring his eyes to meet hers. 'She knows—suspects—I'm seeing you.'

'And?'

'To paraphrase: "Let her anywhere near the kids and I'll tie you up in court for the next ten years."'

'Can she do that?'

'Over money? Probably. Custody? Maybe. Her lawyer has already sent me a list of blatantly ridiculous requests. Doesn't seem to have heard of no-fault divorce.' Liam swallowed some more whiskey. 'She's going to turn the kids against me.'

'They're teenagers, or near enough. They aren't stupid. They can work it out for themselves.'

'Before they're thirty?'

Natalie didn't answer that—she still had father issues at thirty-four.

Liam changed the subject. 'I spent most of the day talking

to one of the witnesses for the commission.' He downed a slug. 'Or at least we hope he will be. He can help us put away a schoolteacher who's been abusing kids for years—but it's all down to him. The other victims are either dead by car accidents and suicide or too alcohol or drug affected to be any use. Or they're unwilling to testify. Without Michael's testimony the guy gets to keep hurting kids. But he's one of yours, I'm afraid.'

Natalie raised an eyebrow. 'I take it you mean he has a psychiatric illness. The witness or the teacher?'

'Witness. Been in and out of hospitals since he was a teen. You're going to tell me that was caused by the abuse, right?'

'More than likely.'

Liam ran his hand through his hair. 'I don't get it. He was in a home. Got beaten regularly. Not great—you know from my background how not great I really think that is—'

Natalie knew about Liam's da'. The Irish stereotype: get drunk; beat the wife and any kids that got in the way; repeat.

'It's just that...' Liam struggled for words; unusual for him. 'I got beaten and I got through it. Sure, it had an effect on me but not... Well, Michael can barely hold a conversation without bursting into tears.'

'For one thing, Michael isn't you,' said Natalie. 'We all come into the world with vulnerabilities, and if you're lucky, some resilience—kind of depends then what type of shit goes down. What family are there for you. Roll of the dice stuff. If you're unlucky, you encounter what you are least equipped to deal with at the most vulnerable time.

'Trauma as a kid can have a really toxic effect. You haven't formed yet, you haven't worked out who you are. Your stress levels spike easily and that actually makes chemical changes in the brain. Kind of a psychic scar with a physical basis. But it doesn't just make you anxious or depressed, the way it would if it happened as an adult—like with the war veterans. It actually shapes your personality—who you are, how you think, how you behave.'

Liam looked into his glass, probably hoping it would refill itself.

'The other thing in the mix,' Natalie added, 'is who does the abuse, how often, and the severity—it all plays a part. And whether your mother stood around and let it happen.' She thought of Chelsea. A father figure as the sexual abuser, someone who was trusted, and who was there in the home where the child needed to regroup and feel totally safe, was the worst of the options. Mother excepted.

Family abuse created toxic relationships and mistrust for the rest of the child's life. Jenna had at least got Malik out of the home, but the sense of home itself would have been ruptured.

'Sexual abuse,' added Natalie, 'adds an extra twist to the betrayal—and is even harder for a child to make sense of. It can distort all their future intimate relationships.'

'So why was your boyfriend there tonight?'

Christ almighty, had he been listening to anything she had said? Was this what he'd been stewing over? 'Your guess is as good as mine. Keeping his options open I suppose.'

We were good together, he'd said. Should she have waited until the test before letting Liam back in her life? Seemed only she was sure the baby was his—though Damian couldn't really have much hope the one in a million chance would come through. She'd burnt her bridges with him now.

Liam rolled his shoulders, stretched his neck. 'Think his preference would have been to deck me.'

Natalie suddenly just didn't want to deal with this; she had enough of her own problems without the men in her life behaving like adolescents.

'I need to borrow your car.'

Liam looked up. 'The Lotus?'

'If you have another car I don't know about then I'll take that. I need to go to Sunday lunch with my family tomorrow.' She took a deep breath. 'You can join me if you don't trust my driving.'

She watched Liam wrestle with the answer. 'Do you want me to come?'

'All I asked for was the car,' Natalie said. Wondering even before she had finished why she couldn't just say yes.

Natalie had managed to avoid the family Sunday lunch for most of the year while she was in hospital with depression and then living down the coast recuperating. She'd been back over a month now; as Declan had reminded her, she couldn't delay it any longer. At least in the Lotus the drive out to Warrandyte, on the outskirts of Melbourne's east, was kind of fun—although if there were speed cameras on the freeway, the car's owner was not going to thank her.

The long driveway wound through the thick vegetation that would quickly become a death-trap in the event of a bushfire. Natalie took the potholes at a pace that was possibly faster than Liam would have preferred, and drew up in front of the long ranch-style house. The surrounding veranda looked out across the pool to paddocks and a creek: ten hectares that had once been home to sheep and three of her half-sister Maddison's horses, but now held only one ageing thoroughbred, a few geese and an arthritic old English sheepdog called Hercules.

The car sent a spray of stones clattering against the garage door as she attempted a handbrake turn. Easier to look impressive on a bike. Hercules meandered out to check on her, gave one bark, slobbered over her boots and returned to where he'd been sleeping. She rolled her shoulders in preparation for two hours of purgatory. Maddison and her husband Miles, along with Blake, were already there.

'Bloody hell!' Her stepfather Craig was on the deck, beer in hand, gut lapping over his chinos. 'Psychiatry must pay better than I thought.'

'It's on loan.' Natalie strode past him, through the glass doors to the living area, wishing she could down a bourbon. She felt as if someone had turned up the dial on her thought processes; ideas had been jumping around her mind throughout the drive. She threw open the fridge door and grabbed a mineral water.

'Nice to see you, Natalie,' said Jan, her mother, meaning *Why didn't you ring and why haven't we seen you for so long?*

She was wearing a long colourful top over black leggings, golden hair in a bob that was getting close to needing a trim, long earrings and a large pendant around her neck. Elegant and unfussy. Natalie was in black leather and a T-shirt sporting a Megadeth album cover: *Killing is my business* with a skull and crossbones. Sometimes Jan and Craig probably wondered if Natalie had been swapped in the nursery.

'I'll set a place.' Maddison was in four-inch heels, with her glossy blonde hair in a French twist. Really?

'Check out Nat's latest wheels,' said Miles through the open door, leaning on the balustrade. 'What's LO73?'

'The registration.'

'I think he got that, Natalie.' Maddison to the defence. 'Presumably it stands for something?'

'Presumably.' Natalie sat down as Maddison half-threw a placemat at her. Natalie considered boomeranging it back. Didn't.

Shit, this was how she started to get when she was going manic. Had she brought any extra pills?

The men wandered over to check out the car. Maddison rolled her eyes as Jan turned to the oven to check the potatoes, her face colouring in the escape of hot air. Natalie looked out at the pool on the other side of the dining space and had a sudden urge to throw her clothes off and go swimming. Would Jan notice? There wasn't a bulge yet, but her mother had a sixth sense about these things. *Deep breath. Concentrate.*

'Are you okay, Natalie?' Jan asked quietly.

'Yes, Mum.' Natalie didn't meet her eyes, but saw the tell-tale sign that her mother was worrying—looping strands of hair behind her ear.

'We're thinking of having Christmas down the beach, what do you think? We could rent a house, a friend's in Portsea. Plenty of room. You could… bring a friend if you wanted.'

Damian for lunch, Liam for dinner maybe.

'I'm working through Christmas.'

'You can come down for the day, surely.'

'Go like the clappers does it?' Craig returned from checking out the Lotus and sat down beside her.

'With me at the wheel, what do you reckon?' These days, Craig was way easier to deal with than her mother. What you saw what was what you got.

'Natalie you really…' Jan bit her lip, shook her head. 'Are you getting another motorbike?'

'Not unless I can find one with a side car.'

Maddison frowned.

'What do you want one of those for?' Blake grabbed another beer.

'The baby.'

In the nearly thirty years Craig and Jan had been together, it was probably the only time there had been silence in the King household at a Sunday lunch. Natalie folded her arms. *There*, she told Declan in her mind. *I did it.*

Craig was the first to speak. 'So, ah, Natalie, are you trying to tell us you're pregnant?'

'Is… ah, the father…?' Jan had put down the plates with a clatter, and was trying to compose herself.

'I'm sorting it out.'

Her mother sat down. 'I'm not… if it's what you want then. I mean, we'll be there for you of course.'

'So,' said Natalie. 'I figured before I become a mother I should know who the grandfather is. You know, my dad? Biology and all that.'

Jan's expression changed immediately; a steeliness that Natalie knew well. But it was Craig who jumped in. 'Natalie, we've been through this before.'

'And we'll keep going through it until I find out. For Chrissake I'm thirty-four. I'm a psychiatrist. I think I can handle anything you throw at me. Chances are I've imagined a good deal worse than the reality. Child abuser? Syphilis? Rape? Bring it on.'

'Enough.' Jan's tone was more fire than steel. 'This isn't the time for this discussion.'

'But it's never going to be the time, is it?' Natalie glared at her mother, anger as raw as when she had been having the argument sixteen years earlier. Now, though, for the first time there was a nagging sense that she should have known better than to keep backing her mother into a corner. That she'd engineered this train wreck.

'What about the father of your child?' Maddison looked shell-shocked. Natalie wanted to giggle.

'Maddison, there's no need to aggravate the situation.' Jan had regained some of her composure.

'She'll expect you to look after it, Mum, I bet, while she swans around playing Doctor Important. God, my friends are still snickering over that television clip where she karatechopped the lawyer on the court steps.'

'It was more Tae Kwon Do than karate,' said Natalie, no longer able to hold back the giggles. 'And he's most likely the father.'

Maddison stared. 'Oh, just peachy. She doesn't even know whose it is. Well count me out. I'm not going to have anything to do with this.' She picked up her handbag, swung towards Jan. 'You want to condone her behaviour, be my guest. But don't put me down on the list of babysitters.' Then she burst into tears. 'I can't believe it, she's done it again.'

Craig, Jan and Miles all spoke at once. Blake looked at Natalie and shrugged.

'She hasn't done...'

'You don't need to…'

'Honey I know we were going to…'

'Yes,' said Maddison, sniffing and clutching Miles's arm. 'This was meant to be *our* announcement. Our baby is due in April!'

'Oh, how lovely,' said Natalie. 'So is mine.'

'There were probably better ways of breaking it to them, you know,' Blake yelled to her as the air streamed over the open top of the Lotus on the way back to town. He'd been happy to catch a lift with her rather than their sister; they'd left her talking babies with Jan and Craig.

'Better for who?' Natalie sighed, wondering why she did things so badly when it came to her family. Natalie hoped she'd made it up a little by letting Maddison have use of the cot that had belonged to their grandmother. And first option on names, however unlikely it was that they would both come up with the same one.

'So who *is* the lucky dad?' asked Blake. 'The Lotus owner?'

'None of your business.'

'Come on Nat. You know what it's like not knowing….' He followed the train of thought. 'You remember your dad, don't you?'

Did she? Sometimes she thought so, vague thoughts, more impressions than anything else. Music? Laughter? And then a different feeling. Something that made her stomach knot. Had he abused her? Was that why Jan had cut him out of their life?

'Hope your man is good at his job.'

'Why?'

Blake tapped the speedo. A hundred and fifty. Shit. She eased off the pedal. Had she taken her quetiapine last night? Did she need to be back on lithium? She had been feeling good, but maybe that was just because the morning sickness had finally stopped. At lunch though, she should have been able to keep it together better than she had.

'You need to get your stuff out. I mean it,' said Natalie.

'I can't find anyone to help. I just don't have the networks. I know there's people that'll pay… I just can't find them.'

Networks. Why did that sound familiar? Sounds like… works, perks, jerks… Malik! She grinned, fixing the steering wheel with her knee jammed up under it, as she rummaged around in her pockets. She fished out Malik's card. Imports. 'Here, try him. He might have a truck. Just don't mention my name. I'm serious about that.'

Tonight—extra quetiapine.

Natalie had made Jenna and Chelsea's appointment in what was usually her lunch hour; Malik was coming in straight after so that she could complete the assessments involving Chelsea in one sitting. Natalie had wondered if she needed to tell Jenna she was providing lunch. Eating disorders were, primarily, about control. Often in families of origin there were rituals or expectations about food and eating—if children picked it up as being a parental issue, it could become the basis for a power play. Refusing to eat was one of the most effective ways for a child to evoke a reaction.

Natalie had seen girls with anorexia nervosa sending their mothers—distraught, desperate women—shopping miles away because they had promised to eat a particular cake from a particular shop. One of her patients had gone into cardiac arrest at thirty-two kilograms. Amazingly she had survived and, in the end, recovered. Largely, Natalie thought, because after the near-death experience her parents acknowledged they were powerless and stopped trying to control her.

Chelsea was recognisable from the photo that Jenna had shown her, though not as obviously sad. She was seated in the chair next to her mother in the waiting room. Jenna was in her signature baggy red corduroy jeans, and a multi-coloured windbreaker with a label from an outdoor shop. Chelsea looked small. She had shrunk back into the seat, as if she hoped she could disappear into it. Long blonde hair fell into ringlets; she was in jeans and a long mauve T-shirt with a picture of some Disney heroine Natalie couldn't identify.

Natalie walked over to them. 'Hi, Jenna.' She lowered herself to the girl's height. 'You must be Chelsea. I'm Doctor King. Thanks for coming along.'

Chelsea's big blue eyes made her face seem all the smaller; she was like a miniature doll. Very, very pretty: the quintessence of the innocence that paedophiles were attracted to.

Chelsea looked up at her mother.

'Come on Chelsea, we're going together,' said Jenna.

Chelsea wriggled out of the chair, took hold of her mother's hand, and followed Natalie down to her office. The coffee table there was covered with plates of food: dip, cheese and biscuits, white bread with hundreds and thousands (eight-year-olds love them, Beverley had insisted), a selection of chocolate and plain biscuits, and some fruit. As well as a bottle of water and another of a red soft drink.

'Seeing as we have to meet over lunch in order to fit you and Malik in,' said Natalie, 'I organised some food. Chelsea has to last here a while.' She smiled at them both; Chelsea was looking at the food with interest, but Natalie thought she saw a tightening of Jenna's expression. She ushered Chelsea to a seat, placing herself between Natalie and her daughter. Chelsea looked to her mother, and sat back.

'So, Chelsea,' said Natalie, 'I was really pleased your mum could bring you to meet me. Do you know what sort of doctor I am?'

Chelsea looked at her mother, then Natalie and nodded. 'A doctor that looks after feelings.'

Natalie smiled. 'Yes, I guess I am. How do *you* feel about being here?'

Chelsea shrugged.

'Are you hungry? Because if it's okay with your mum, you can have whatever you like.'

'Go ahead, Chelsea.'

Chelsea seemed to be wrestling with what, if anything,

to choose. There was an edge to Jenna's tone which, in this relationship, meant something like: *Don't select the unhealthy foods or you'll get fat*. Chelsea stole a look at the plate of fairy bread. Natalie picked up a plate and helped herself to some biscuits and cheese. She turned to Jenna.

'How's Chris going?'

'Chris? As impossible as ever.' Jenna ventured a small smile. 'I think it's a male thing. He seems fine with my father and Malik.'

Chelsea had managed to get a piece of the fairy bread with sprinkles without her mother noticing, but promptly dropped it.

'Don't worry,' said Natalie quickly, seeing Chelsea's expression. She grabbed the waste paper basket and scooped it up. 'Try another—my secretary made them especially for you.'

Natalie suspected she missed a terse glance from mother to daughter. Whether it was that or the horror of having messed up the floor, Chelsea just took a plain biscuit and sat back on her chair.

'How do you get on with your little brother, Chelsea?'

'He's fine.' Chelsea took a bite of the biscuit. 'Well, when he isn't being totally annoying.'

'I had a little brother,' said Natalie. 'I remember he was really, really, annoying. He used to want my toys all the time.'

Chelsea nodded solemnly. 'So does Chris. And he's very noisy.'

'It must be quieter when he's at his dad's.' There was, she thought, the slightest flicker, a tightening at the corners of Chelsea's mouth. Because she knew Malik was a taboo topic…or because she was afraid of him?

'When did you last see your dad?' Natalie asked.

'Not for ages.' If Natalie had had to say, she would have said there was longing rather than fear in Chelsea's voice. Natalie looked at Jenna, whose stare held a challenge. Had she been defying the court order?

'We get to have girl time then, don't we Chelsea?' Jenna weighed in. Her smile was too bright and made her look edgy. If Chelsea had been a baby she would have found her mother's expression scary. But at eight she wasn't looking at her mother, and instead focused on Natalie.

'Chris gets to go but I stay with Mum.'

'Which is fun, isn't it?' said Jenna.

Chelsea, nodded, eyes on the floor.

'What do you enjoy doing with your mum, Chelsea?'

'Roller skating.'

'Both of you?'

'Mum used to ice skate too and we went to the ice rink once but we don't go often.'

'Roller skating along the beach is a bit warmer,' said Jenna. 'We sometimes go on a Sunday. Chelsea's really fast.'

Chelsea smiled. She ate the rest of the biscuit.

'What else do you like to do with your mum, Chelsea?'

'Reading, and she's really, really good at making things. I got top marks for my French lesson because Mummy helped me make this gigantic' — Chelsea jumped up onto tiptoes and stretched her hand high above her head — 'tower... thing.' She looked to her mother.

'Eiffel Tower,' Jenna said.

'And we watch Harry Potter.' Chelsea sat back down, but her voice was more animated, even if her smiles were tentative. 'But I've only been allowed to see up to *Harry Potter and the Prisoner of Azban*.'

'Azkaban,' her mother corrected.

Chelsea lowered her voice a fraction. 'It's a bit scary.'

Natalie let them talk about the *Harry Potter* stories — she must have been the only person in the world left who hadn't seen or read them — and watched Chelsea relax as the topic diverted from food, welcoming her mother's involvement in the conversation. Chelsea tended to look to her mother for approval or if she didn't know the answer to Natalie's questions. But she didn't appear depressed, or at least not severely so. Nothing that wouldn't fit with a parental separation and an awareness that food was a sensitive issue.

Natalie didn't expect much else. Protective Services had yet to interview Chelsea with a child therapist; there had been a mix-up with times, and Jenna's parents had taken her two hours late. Winona had said she would ring Natalie when they had the report. As far as she knew, Chelsea had still not said anything directly about abuse. Which might only mean that she was good at keeping secrets.

One thing was clear: Chelsea was smart and she was in tune with her mother. If she believed staying quiet was necessary for her mother's well-being, it would be hard to crack her defences.

As the clock ticked over to 1 p.m., the phone on the desk interrupted a conversation about ballet classes and her teacher, Mrs Ambrose.

'That'll be Beverley telling me Malik is here,' said Natalie.

It was hard to watch them both for a reaction so she focused on Chelsea. But Chelsea turned first to her mother— and then the mask went up.

'Perhaps if you could wait outside, Jenna?' said Natalie. 'Beverley will send him in.'

When Malik came through the door Natalie had her head down pretending to write notes. But she was watching Chelsea.

There were two possibilities as she saw it, each with variations.

The first was that Malik was an abuser who had coerced his adopted daughter into sexual activity and threatened or bribed her not to say anything. As a result, Chelsea might be directly fearful of him. Alternatively—or as well—she might feel some sense of connection, sharing a secret that she hadn't made sense of, but which gave her some power. The fear would still be there, but harder to find, and unlikely to come out until she was older.

The other possibility was that he wasn't an abuser and Jenna had misinterpreted her child's distress. Or deliberately lied to influence the custody decision. In which case Chelsea's reaction to Malik would be confused, given her mother's animosity. But even if Malik adhered to the 'children should be your friends' style of parenting—unlikely, judging by his behaviour with Chris—there wouldn't be any sense of Chelsea and him against the world.

Chelsea wasn't looking at the door and didn't look up when Malik came into the doorway, and, still standing there, said softly, 'Go Chelsea, Go Chelsea, Go Chelsea.'

It was a strange way to greet a daughter he hadn't seen in weeks. But Chelsea, eyes still down, sported a huge smile.

She risked a quick look up, then looked back down again. But the smile was still there.

'Come and have a seat, Malik,' said Natalie.

He moved to the chair next to Chelsea's, pausing for an instant before sitting down, arm outstretched as if to ruffle her hair. She still wasn't looking at him and he thought better of it. Probably worrying how Natalie would interpret it.

'Missed you Chelse,' Malik said as he sat down. 'When I watch the football your uncle Youssef is cheering for Man United.'

There was a pause, and Chelsea looked up, smile gone, and in a sing-song voice said, 'Chelsea, Chelsea, Chelsea.'

Now Natalie got it. They were soccer fans. And naturally they supported Chelsea Football Club. Or at least Malik did, on her behalf. For the next few minutes they talked sports results. It gave her a chance to watch Chelsea, who was clearly enjoying the interaction.

'I have to confess I've never watched a soccer match,' said Natalie.

'It's football.' Chelsea sighed with a melodramatic hand gesture; it made her look a little precocious. 'It's fun — we have a team at school but we're not very good. I'm better at singing.'

'You're a great little singer,' said Malik. 'How's school? Mrs Ambrose still giving you top marks?'

Natalie was quite certain Craig wouldn't have known any of her primary school teachers by name. She thought of the bean, wondered for a moment if it would have a father to kick a footy with or to know the name of its teachers. Maybe the bean would like motorbikes and bicycles — more her thing than ball sports or giant Eiffel Towers.

'I got three stars for reading and writing.'

'And maths?'

Chelsea frowned. 'Only two but that was because Ethan was making too much noise in class and I couldn't hear.'

Malik nodded gravely. 'Well, get Mummy to explain it, okay?'

'Grandpa helps me with maths.'

'Is that where you go after school?'

Chelsea nodded.

'She used to go to my mother's, but now there are always excuses,' said Malik to Natalie, anger barely concealed. To Chelsea he said, 'Teta misses you and sends her love.'

'When you were seeing your dad, Chelsea, were there other things that you liked to do with him besides football?'

'I like riding my bike. Daddy taught me to ride and we'd go to the park together. Sometimes Mummy came but on Sundays she likes to stay in bed and Chris would watch TV so we could go all around the park, just me and Daddy.'

Malik was upholding the tradition of fathers having all the fun.

'And he makes banana fritters.' Probably not high on Jenna's healthy foods list. Natalie noticed that Chelsea had finally helped herself to a slice of the fairy bread.

'Feel free to have something,' Natalie said to Malik, who still looked uncomfortable. It wouldn't be easy. The brief access, the unfamiliar environment, knowing he was under scrutiny. He looked like he was deciding whether he should say something, and he finally let it out. 'Chelsea, I had hoped you'd have come over to see Teta and me, last weekend, with Chris.'

Chelsea froze, the mask back in place. Because she was scared of going, or because her mother had stopped her?

Malik turned to Natalie. 'Jenna wouldn't let her come, even though the court said she had to. What should I do? Get the police to drag her out? Charge Jenna? I will, you know, it's not right what she's doing.'

He had become oblivious to Chelsea, who had shrunk back in the chair. Natalie gave him a warning look but he blundered on. 'She's doing it because she thinks she will have to pay me maintenance, that is what my lawyer thinks. In her fancy job where she hangs around with other men and—'

'Malik, enough.' Natalie didn't want to frighten Chelsea but her tone was firm enough to stop him mid-sentence.

Chelsea looked like she was going to cry.

'I wasn't thinking,' Malik mumbled, hand out and squeezing his daughter's arm. She didn't flinch, but she didn't look at him either. 'Can I give you a teddy bear hug?'

Chelsea shook her head. In a quiet voice she said, 'I want to go to my mum.'

Malik's expression fell. He looked like he'd been slapped. Natalie was grateful the girl didn't see it.

'Okay, Chelsea, that's fine. She'll be out in the waiting room.'

Chelsea hesitated and Natalie took her to the door. At the door, though, she stopped, turned around and ran full tilt into Malik's waiting arms.

'You have a problem.'

Natalie had cycled to Li Yang's office—it was the easiest way to navigate the city in peak hour when the trams were overflowing with commuters, and not far off the route home. Yang's room was small and the floor was almost completely covered in piles of papers and books.

'What problem?'

'Malik.'

'We already know he's a problem.'

'Maybe not the way you think he is. I can't give you anything.'

Li frowned. 'You've gotta be kidding me. How about the stats about de facto fathers abusing their kids?'

'I don't do stats,' said Natalie. 'I deal with people— individual cases. Stats mean zip.'

'Jenna is her biological mother.'

'And no one is saying Chelsea shouldn't be in her mother's care. It's about access. I haven't seen anything concrete I can put in a report that shows he has abused her.'

'All we need to show is that there is a risk it might have happened. Or might happen.' Li drummed her fingers on the desk. Her iPhone lit up. 'Hold on.' She picked it up and walked out of the office, calling for someone. She returned a few minutes later. 'He's a misogynist. Of course there's risk. Would you want him bringing up your child?'

Natalie felt her irritation rise. 'Jenna appears genuinely worried, but is there anything else going on? Like might she have to pay Malik maintenance if he had regular access or custody?'

Li waved her hand dismissively. 'She has a good wage, a solid worker. He's in "importing" whatever that means. And it's his family's business. They're good at hiding things.'

Natalie narrowed her eyes. 'So he *has* asked for maintenance?'

'It's immaterial. He's a risk to her daughter. Just because the media got bad publicity for chasing those poor kids around Lebanon doesn't mean they weren't in the right. That mother had been granted custody in an Australian court. The father had no right to refuse to give them back.'

'Is there any way Malik can leave the country with them?'

'Something you're not telling me?'

Natalie shook her head. 'I just imagine the Egyptian government will support him—he's a citizen—rather than Jenna.'

'Let him try running. I'll have him in jail faster than the ink can dry on the order.'

'Jenna?' Natalie called when she got home.

'Yes.'

'I'm just finishing my report and there's something I'm not clear about. I need some clarification.'

There was silence at the other end of the phone before Jenna said a cautious 'Yes?'

'If Malik gets access or shared custody do you, or might you, have to pay maintenance?'

Natalie could almost hear Jenna thinking. 'Maybe. Which stinks if you want to know. I couldn't manage if I had to pay him. I'd have to move in with my parents. He earns way more than what he told my lawyer—his family are covering for him.' She made no effort to hide her bitterness. 'I just want him out of my life, Doctor King. And out of Chelsea's.'

'Winona Ellis from Protective Services.' Beverley put the call through.

'Hope you've got something on the sleazebag.'

A picture of the last hug between Chelsea and Malik went through Natalie's mind. 'Why?'

'Because our child psychologist saw Chelsea this morning and couldn't come up with anything other than general symptoms of trauma.'

Which was good—if it meant that there wasn't abuse, but not good if she just couldn't find anything definitive. 'Maybe Jenna has overreacted.'

'I suppose you think we did, too. You have no...'

'You didn't have a choice. Where are the police at?'

'Nothing at this stage. Not pursuing it.'

'So Malik might get access,' said Natalie, more to herself than Winona.

'Not if we can help it. We've got a witness with impeccable quals to say he isn't fit.'

Natalie let out a sigh of relief. They must have organised their own parenting assessment. With an eight-year-old involved, that would mean a child psychiatrist. Excellent. She wasn't in this alone.

Later she wished the child psychiatrist had been with her at dinner. Liam texted to warn her that he was bringing Megan. She had to meet his kids some time, but she was surprised at how anxious she felt.

Even in school uniform, Megan looked more than three years older than Chelsea. She stormed past Natalie without saying hello, found a beanbag in the hallway—the Bridge of Sighs that crossed the lane—and plugged herself into her iPad with her back to both of them.

Liam shrugged.

'Give her time,' said Natalie.

103

They gave her too much time. When dinner was ready and they called her, she was no longer sitting there.

'How did she get past us?' Liam asked in bewilderment.

There was a hidden door at the end of the walkway. But there was no way she could have found the handle, was there?

Apparently, yes.

Lauren answered the phone and Natalie could hear her views on Liam's parenting skills without the need to be put on the speaker phone. But yes, Megan had turned up. *Traumatised*.

The description would also have fitted how Liam looked.

'At least I can stay the night now.' He forced a smile.

The sex did help. But both of them had too much on their minds. Natalie woke when it was still dark, and for a minute had the sense of being very small, the room around her full of shadows and, in the corner, something lingering from her dream that she couldn't make out.

A scream faded in her mind. Hers? She felt fear, and then a terrible deep wave of guilt. And was aware of a single eye, seemingly dislodged from its socket, looking at her.

She was frozen. No interpretation needed. Not PTSD re-emerging, or past abuse. Just good old fear of commitment. No wonder Jenna and Malik were pushing buttons. She had avoided being tied to men in her life—it was going to be harder to do when the bean was born. She rolled closer to Liam, breathed him in, and for once didn't fight the comfort that his presence gave her.

Natalie had the day off—a whole day of nothing to do except see Declan and make sure Blake collected his boxes. She had gone back to sleep after her nightmare but woke feeling exhausted, and hadn't been able to sleep again after Liam left. She had a sense that she was letting everyone down.

Just what she didn't need to dog her all day when she was planning to indulge in some nesting behaviour. Or at least clean up. The baby was going to have to fit somewhere and right now she'd have to wrestle a crib in between an electric guitar and two acoustics, three oversized speakers, piles of books and journals, CDs and DVDs and several items of furniture she'd taken when her grandmother went into the nursing home. Maybe one of the small tables could be turned into a change stand?

'You're a star,' Bob announced from his perch as he watched her move items around—mostly just making a mess somewhere else.

'That's me, Bob. Star screw-up. Hope you're going to enjoy being an uncle. Feel like babysitting?'

The morning passed slowly, and was only made bearable by the background music, which had her thinking about some new songs for the band. But she wasn't going to be with them much longer, was she?

In the clean-up, she found her old baby book. Her mother

must have left it there—Natalie couldn't remember ever taking it. She made herself a smoothie and flopped onto the sofa to leaf through it.

Natalie Eve Carmichael born 3.10 a.m. 1.09.82 6lbs 5oz looking like any baby, face screwed up. 'Never did like to cooperate,' her mother had told her.

A piece of hair, light brown then, rather than the red-brown (with blue streaks) it was now, was trapped under the clear plastic album page cover. Natalie tried to picture her mother's face if she put a coloured streak in the bean's hair. And Damian's expression. Liam would roll his eyes and say something like, *You'll turn her into a conservative voter with religious tendencies—only way she'll be able to rebel.* She? A boy might be easier. Less identification.

A footprint and hand print. She stared. They were so… *small*.

There were pictures of her later, too. Some with her mother, others with her nan, and then with Craig. Under the first of these was written *Craig King with daughter Natalie Eve King, 24.12.86.* 'You were each other's Christmas present,' her mother told her as a child. 'The adoption papers arrived the day before Christmas.'

Adopted when she was four. Just like Chelsea. Was that what these dreams were about? A childhood trauma she couldn't recall? Natalie thought uneasily of the Royal Commission, of all the patients she had seen scarred by abuse. Maybe she'd been damaged that way too, and it had increased her vulnerability to bipolar disorder. Or were her dreams because she identified with Jenna, fiercely independent and having to battle her own mental health demons to make it as a single mother?

The doorbell rang and Blake was standing outside, grinning; a large truck behind him with the engine running.

'Told you I'd organise it,' he said.

Natalie wasn't about to argue. She was sure it was only because Liam was so busy that he hadn't questioned her harder about the boxes, most of which Bob had decorated with white streaks.

She threw open the large wooden downstairs doors and heard them creak on rusty hinges. They were at cargo loading height—level with the truck doors. Liam wouldn't be able to get the Lotus in there even after the boxes were removed.

Blake and an olive-skinned man started throwing boxes into the truck. It was slow work and the muscle man was more adept at it than Blake, who was always good at finding activities other than the one at hand. He grabbed one of the beers Natalie brought down long before the task was over and stood close to Natalie, leaning in to her.

'Found a job yet?' said Natalie.

'Yep.'

'Really?'

'Working with these guys,' said Blake pointing to the truck with its black and yellow emblem. *Easy Tiger Imports.* Shit. That was Malik's company. She peered at Muscles who smiled back. Yep, he looked like Malik—his brother Youssef more than likely. The last thing she needed was a personal and ongoing connection with Malik, particularly while she was assessing him for court. She cursed herself for giving Blake the card. She'd been on the edge of mania and hadn't thought it through. Natalie looked around. No sign of Malik. She threw a beer to Muscles who had heaved the final box into the truck.

'Any more where that came from?' said a voice from the truck, and it was only then Natalie realised that there was a third man, at the wheel. Malik. He was now standing half out of the truck, one foot on the running board, a hand on the top of the cabin, another on the open door. He was taking in the view of Natalie in a pair of skimpy shorts—and making no attempt to hide his interest. And a smile that suggested she owed him.

Declan changed the record—the old-fashioned vinyl variety. It sounded like Mahler. When he sat down again he asked, 'And how are you?' He had the ability to focus completely on who he was speaking to and give the impression they were the only person in the world who mattered. Mostly Natalie found it comforting. Today she frowned. Why the concern? Because she was having a baby?

'Declan, if you mean about the pregnancy, I *have* told her. My mother.'

Declan leaned forward. 'You sound angry at her. Your mother had to make choices then, just as you do now.'

'And those choices had consequences. I need to know about the past before I can move forward. I feel like I'm... stuck. Sometimes... I think I can remember my father, you know?'

'Don't push it, Natalie. If and when the time is right, then you will remember what you're ready to manage.'

'But I want to know now!'

'This isn't just about you.'

Natalie knew that; had a moment of sympathy for Jenna's need to control. She hated the vulnerability.

Then she took a breath. 'Confession time.' Declan watched with a serious expression as she told him how Malik had ended up at her house.

'Boundaries, Natalie.'

'I know, it was stupid.' And a bit manic.

'You need to tell the court about your conflict of interest.' He didn't need to add *and error of judgment*.

'I will.'

'And what are you going to say to the court about him?'

'I'm still no closer to being able to say whether Chelsea's safe or not with Malik.'

'What would you do if you were the judge?'

'Err on the side of caution, no matter what racists—or anti-racists—were saying about me in the press,' said Natalie. 'I, of all people, should know what it's like to miss your biological father, but Chelsea's going to have that anyway. Her biological father hasn't even met her. It's sad to deprive her of a loving father figure, but better than the possibility of giving her over to one who abuses her.'

'But if Malik is innocent?'

'You think I'm wrong?'

'I think you should consider how you would determine if she was being abused—at least to a level of evidence you were happy with.'

'I wouldn't do it at all,' said Natalie. 'I'm not a child psychiatrist.'

Declan smiled. 'But it would be... good for you, Natalie. Good for the girl too.'

Natalie raised her eyebrow. 'How do you figure that?'

'Chelsea has been assessed by the system and is now at risk of falling through the cracks. If Jenna gets custody it will be over, no more need for interference. But you could persuade Jenna to bring Chelsea to see you, so you can help Jenna with her parenting and Chelsea with her demons.'

'You think it'll help my demons too. About my father.'

For a second she felt that sense of guilt again, the frozen view of the world from a child's eyes. And the single eye staring at her.

Declan put his glasses down. 'What do you think?'

'You're going all analyst on me. I think I don't need the aggravation. I'd have to do individual sessions. I really know nothing about eight-year-olds. Because I'm not a child psychiatrist, I'd need supervision, ideally on the other side of a one-way screen. It could take weeks, months even.'

'You're not due until April,' said Declan mildly.

'No way.'

'Can you take this call?' Beverley handed her the phone without waiting for an answer and turned back to her mobile. Today she looked like a bumblebee, black stripes breaking up the yellow. 'You there? No, I told you we need the big room. Jack has a huge family. Oh, and we need wheelchair access—'

Natalie glared, but the effort was wasted: Beverley was fully focused and forging ahead. Unfortunately, not with work. Her latest mission was badgering Natalie to sing at the wedding.

'Doctor King speaking.'

'This is Malik Essa, Doctor King.'

Great. Damn Beverley and her wedding; she could have at least put the call through to Natalie's office. She was aware that all the people in the waiting room were watching her. A woman in lurid purple and matching lipstick smiled encouragingly.

'Yes?'

'The court case is tomorrow.' She knew that. Malik paused. 'I... miss my son, Doctor King. Chris... he needs me.'

'I know.' Natalie reminded herself to stick to murderers in future. 'I'm not the judge. I don't make the decision.' She turned her back to the audience and kept her voice as low as she could.

'But the lawyer... she says your evidence is most important.'

'I…' Natalie bit her lip. Malik's voice was breaking up. Sure, she had to be impartial. But she was a psychiatrist, and right now she wanted to be healing, not trying to dodge shots being fired in someone else's dispute. 'Your kids love you, Malik,' she said.

There was a whispered thank you before he hung up the phone. And Natalie was left with the uncomfortable knowledge that she should have added: But I can't prove you didn't abuse Chelsea. And if she couldn't do that, the safest option was still for Chelsea—and maybe Chris—to remain in Jenna's care exclusively.

Natalie had planned to stop off at the supermarket but as she got on her bike Liam texted. *Sorry have to work late. Will crash at South Yarra.*

She got back to her warehouse and showered, lingered in front of the mirror as she dressed. She still looked okay; bit of a belly maybe. Well, that was only going to get bigger. She thought of her pregnant patients, bloated and tired, worn out by their estranged relationships, the pregnancy and their children. Was that what was going to happen to her?

She looked at Damian's text. *Had the blood test.* He was still holding out hope that the bean might be his. Reminding her he would be an involved father. Was he still thinking there was a possibility of them working out? Surely not.

The blood test. She hadn't got hers. She was busy…but not that busy.

Liam would be working with Tania. Cute, blonde like his wife. Natalie's age. Single. Tough. Liam had form. Maybe he wouldn't even think twice about someone on the side.

Question was, did she want to fight for Liam? She heard Declan: *This isn't just about you.* She felt like smashing her fist into her punching bag, but instead gritted her teeth and pulled on her leather skirt and tank top and over-the-knee boots. No underwear. She took the tram into town.

Liam's offices were on William Street, between the County and Family Court buildings. An after-hours buzzer brought a security man to the door: he recognised Natalie and waved her through. The metal studs on her boots and outfit sent the metal detector into a frenzy—they both shrugged, and she took the lift to the tenth floor. Most of the lights were off but Liam's door was open, paperwork strewn everywhere. No one in sight. But there was noise from Tania's office further down the corridor.

What would she do, Natalie wondered, if she caught them at it? Was that what she was hoping for? To give her the excuse, that it was all his fault, not hers? She didn't like Tania particularly, but she reminded herself that her issue was with Liam. Although if Tania was hurt in the crossfire Natalie wouldn't be heartbroken.

Involuntarily she remembered the first time Liam touched her. The electricity, the sense of invincibility. She gritted her teeth, strode forward and eased Tania's office door open.

Tania, long fringe over her face, was on the floor showing a good deal of leg and, from Natalie's angle, cleavage as well.

Natalie stood in the doorway and smiled at Liam. The only thing surrounding Tania's shapely body was a collection of files on three sides. Liam was at the desk, sleeves rolled up and top shirt button undone, tie discarded on the desktop where it was half-covered in paperwork. He looked tired.

His first look was surprise, then he stretched his shoulders and neck and grinned. The mischievous grin that usually heralded the removal of clothing. She leaned against the door frame, smile matching his.

'I think that might be enough for tonight.' Liam hadn't broken eye contact. He was aware of the game she was playing and was up for it. His look said *I'm yours*. It didn't say for how long.

'Well I guess I'll just be going then.' Tania sounded

peeved. She stood up, straightened her short skirt and picked a file off the desk, tossing her asymmetrical fringe as she did. 'I'll keep looking tomorrow and in the meantime I'll finish this tonight at home.' She remained standing. When no one moved she turned to Natalie. 'Liam's office is down the hall.'

Natalie looked at the other woman, whose face said all that the words hadn't.

Liam was only seconds behind her, closing his office door, pulling her to him.

'Don't trust me, hey?'

'Is that relevant?' Natalie pulled away from him, walked over to his desk and sat on it, turning back to face him. He watched her kick her boots off then walked slowly to her, kneeling before her, hands on the flesh of her thighs.

'You know I still think you're the hottest woman I have ever fucked don't you?'

'Ever fucked? How about the hottest including the ones you've ever wanted to fuck?'

Liam's lips went to the inner parts of her thighs as his hands worked around under her bare butt. 'You might need to remind me.'

'First here then,' said Natalie, leaning back to rest on her elbows, bending her knees. 'And then... maybe on Tania's desk. If you're up to it.'

Liam needed a glass of whiskey—two glasses of water for her—in between. But he was up to it.

Natalie arrived as the overhead speakers were asking for parties involved in the Essa case to proceed to courtroom three. As she sat down, she wished she'd had time to ask if the child psychiatrist, or psychologist, had already presented their findings. And what the findings were.

The courtroom was even more crowded than it had been the first time. Katlego Okeke was back—this time in a red turban and a red and green dress. Li Yang was seated, reading the newspaper. Jenna, in black, and her father were behind the lawyer, neither looking comfortable. In Harvey Alcock's place were what looked like two law clerks poised to take notes and a woman with neat files marked with orange stickers poking out the sides. Further along, Malik was sitting alone. Ama was directly behind him, but no sign of Pam Warren. Natalie leaned forward and tapped Winona on the shoulder.

'Where's...' she tipped her head towards Malik.

'Couldn't afford the lawyer,' Winona whispered. 'He's representing himself.'

'Really?' That explained the tearful phone call—he was desperate.

'You don't know the half.' Winona tried unsuccessfully to suppress a smile. 'After the debacle in the media, we've got a QC.'

Natalie stared. She'd never seen a QC in the Children's Court. Protective Services were in self-protection mode.

'You've probably heard of him,' added Winona. 'Richard Tatterson. Better known as the Dictator.'

Li Yang caught sight of Natalie and got up, leaning over. 'We haven't quite finished with the last witness; we had to take a break for some paperwork to be printed out—it'll be a little while before you're on. You can get coffee.'

Natalie shook her head. Aside from the quality of the court coffee, she wanted to hear what the child expert said.

The doors swung open and a man swanned in as if he owned the place; had to be the Dictator. Pinstripes and light blue tie. An elegant man in his fifties who looked good and knew it even as he squeezed in between the law clerks. Slumming it, Natalie imagined, compared to his usual court; here there would literally be no space for theatrical gestures.

Louise Perkins took her seat and asked for the witness to return to the stand. He was, it transpired, sitting behind Natalie.

Wadhwa. Natalie tapped Li's shoulders. 'He knows nothing about children,' she told the lawyer.

Li smiled. 'He's not here about Chelsea.'

Natalie sat back. So why in the hell *was* he here?

'Since he won that defamation case,' Winona whispered, 'he's become the celebrity psych for hire. Untouchable.' She managed to keep a straight face. 'After Malik's lawyer used his report at the last hearing, they can't protest about us using him now.'

'So, given his stand on women making false claims, why *are* you?' Natalie was struggling to keep her voice to a whisper.

'He never said *all* accusations were fabricated. The article establishes him as a sceptic, so it adds to his credibility if he says that he believes a particular claim.'

Natalie looked at Malik—he was being targeted directly, then. He looked as if he knew it.

'So, Professor Wadhwa,' the Dictator asked as he adjusted his tie. 'Your examination of the… Mr Essa? Would you be good enough to summarise your findings?'

'Mr Essa has features of an antisocial and paranoid personality disorder.' Wadhwa cleared his throat. 'This means that he is not able to feel empathy. It also accounts for the morbid jealousy I was discussing earlier.'

That explained the morning session. Li must have gone for the angle about Malik being dangerous to Jenna. Now where was the Dictator going? Natalie flashed a look at Malik; his head was down and he was writing furiously. Ama, sitting behind him, was whispering angrily but he appeared to be ignoring her.

'So, Professor Wadhwa.' The Dictator drew out the title. 'What sort of father does a *psychopath* make?' The terms *antisocial personality disorder*, *sociopath* and *psychopath* were generally used interchangeably—the Dictator had chosen the one that had the worst public perception. Natalie's skin started to prickle.

'Oh, not very good.' Wadhwa shook his head, his expression almost comically horrified. 'Violent, possessive, no respect for the law, no remorse, this is very bad for children. Bad role model, perhaps also in the genes. In studies, antisocial fathers have a higher likelihood of antisocial sons. There is also evidence on brain scans—' Wadhwa, making frequent references to notes, delivered what sounded like a literature review from a PhD thesis.

Natalie saw Malik's hand tighten on the pen. But it was Jenna's expression that arrested her. She was smiling. Smug even. She had to know what Wadhwa was saying was bullshit—this was not the man Jenna had described to her. Not as a father anyway.

Wadhwa had claimed that the majority of sexual abuse accusations made in the context of custody disputes were false. Natalie didn't believe that—but she was not naive enough to think that it didn't happen at all. She wondered if Jenna had planned this from the start. Maybe she had hoped to get by without using the abuse claim, but when Malik decided he wanted the kids—and some maintenance—she'd gone for broke. Or had things taken on a life of their own?

116

It wasn't as if Jenna could have predicted Okeke would get involved and that a QC would be brought in as a result—with Wadhwa in his wake.

'So Mr Essa is not someone who could put his child first?' the Dictator asked when Wadhwa finally stopped.

'That is completely correct.'

'And that would apply to sons and daughters, and quite separate from abuse claims?'

'This is so, yes.'

'Thank you, Professor Wadhwa.'

Malik was on his feet before the Dictator had sat down. The magistrate got in first. 'Mr Essa, may I remind you to keep your questions brief. And non-inflammatory.'

Malik nodded. There were bags under his eyes.

'Professor Wadhwa, you saw Mr Essa on one occasion, is that right?'

'Mr Essa? You? Yes, that is so.'

Malik was clearly trying his best to be professional but his emotions were etched on his face and in his voice. Natalie found herself sitting on the edge of her chair.

'How long was that appointment?'

'Two hours.'

'It was…' Malik stopped himself. 'Is it possible it was less?' The anger in his tone was barely concealed.

'This was the time slot in my diary.'

'But you took two phone calls and…'

'Okay Mr Essa,' said the magistrate. 'You've made your point.'

One to Malik. Not bad against a QC's witness.

'And how is it,' Malik continued, 'that in barely an hour and a quarter you can say so clearly that I… Mr Essa… has a personality disorder?' Malik picked up a sheet and started quoting from it—it sounded like the psychiatrist's diagnostic bible, DSM. The internet made everyone an expert. 'It is a lifetime disorder…not to be diagnosed on a… a…' He looked down. 'Cross-sectional interview.'

Wadhwa gave him a condescending look. 'I am an experienced forensic psychiatrist, an academic. I rely on years of clinical practice and research that I can hardly waste the court's time explaining.'

'But,' Malik pulled out another sheet of paper. 'An antisocial personality disorder requires at least three of seven criteria.'

'Indeed.' Wadhwa looked to the magistrate. 'He was most irritable with me…'

Who wasn't? thought Natalie.

'He also lies about the abuse and there is no sign of regret.'

Regret could be hardly expressed for something you were denying. Louise Perkins raised an eyebrow; she seemed to get this.

'Professor Wadhwa, is there more to it than that?' she asked.

'Of course.' Wadhwa looked at his report. 'As a child he was a problem at school. Involved in fights.'

Natalie frowned, remembering what Ama and Malik had said about his childhood.

Wadhwa turned to Malik. 'This is also necessary for the lifelong criteria.' Turning back to Louise he added, 'And the court has seen his violent behaviour first-hand.'

Malik hadn't done himself any favours at the last hearing; but interrupting a magistrate was hardly violence. He looked like he was defeated. He sat down and raised his head to ask one last question. 'Did you see Mr Essa at all, even once, with his son?'

'This is not necessary for a diagnosis of personality disorder.'

'But did you?'

'No. This was not necessary.'

At least Wadhwa wasn't claiming to be a child expert.

Wadhwa was excused, walking past Natalie without even glancing at her. The magistrate looked at her watch.

'I see the next witness is here but as we're unlikely to finish with her before lunch I propose an early break. Reconvene at one p.m.' The QC wasn't objecting, so the disruption to Natalie's day wasn't going to carry much weight; she'd just have to ring Beverley and get her to reschedule her afternoon patients. Katlego Okeke, from the look of how much writing she was doing, would be using the time to submit an entire manuscript to her publisher.

Natalie took her place on the stand and went through the formalities of swearing in and her statement of qualifications.

Li Yang asked the first question without standing up or looking at her.

'You talk about reflective functioning on page six.'

It took Natalie a moment to realise she was meant to answer. 'Reflective functioning is the capacity to see the world from, in this case, the child's point of view. That is, to see the child's needs and feelings as separate from your own.'

'So, empathy.'

'That's part of it.'

'And it's important?'

'Yes, very. It is the crux of good parenting. No parent can do it all the time, but if you can't do it at all then the child's world becomes frightening, confusing and cold: who can they turn to when their needs are very real but the adult can't perceive them and doesn't validate the emotion they are experiencing?'

'And you say Mrs Essa has this capacity?'

Natalie took a breath. 'Yes, but…'

'And Mrs Essa could learn to be more reflective?'

'I believe so.'

'What about Mr Essa's mother?' Li, still sitting, leaned forward across the table.

'I have spoken to her,' said Natalie, avoiding looking at Ama. And Okeke. 'From Jenna's point of view, her mother-in-law will always put Malik first. Mrs Essa's comments to me—in one telephone call—were consistent with that view.'

'Do you have any idea regarding Mrs Essa—senior's—care of Chris?'

'I haven't seen her with Chris. She is deferential to her son, though, and has strong opinions which are more... old school; at odds with Jenna... culturally.'

'Excuse me.' Louise Perkins leaned forward. 'Ms Yang can we move on please? The witness hasn't assessed the grandmother.'

Natalie saw Ama smile triumphantly.

'Though I trust, Doctor King,' continued the magistrate, 'that you aren't saying there is a problem with old-fashioned methods *per se*?'

'Ah... no, I'm not saying that.' Which didn't mean she *couldn't* say it. Smacking for starters.

'Doctor King,' Li said. 'My client is the primary carer, correct? The children's primary attachment figure?'

'Yes.' Natalie would have liked to add that, at eight, Chelsea had less need of this as a constant than she had at a younger age, and even Chris at three, would be unharmed if he spent time apart, like at preschool, but she wasn't given a chance. Li handed over to the Dictator.

'Doctor King.' His smile reminded her of a cat. A big, smug one. 'Can you please tell us about your assessment of Ms Radford in more depth.'

Natalie read from her report. 'She is an intelligent women who clearly cares for her children. She—'

'I meant her diagnosis. Or rather, absence of one.'

'Jenna has some depressive symptoms as a result of her circumstances. These do not qualify for a major psychiatric disorder. Her eating disorder is past, not current.'

'And does she have a personality disorder?'

'No, she has—'

'And I see in your report that you don't believe Mr Essa does either. '

121

'No, I don't believe—'

'But Doctor King. Surely you just heard Professor Wadhwa outline the criteria of antisocial personality disorder.'

Natalie turned to the magistrate. 'If I could be allowed to finish, I would like to explain that under stress both Jenna and Malik have accentuations of underlying less-functional personality traits emerging. It doesn't mean either has a personality disorder.'

The magistrate's mouth twitched; she didn't like having a QC in her courtroom and for a moment Natalie was a co-conspirator. 'Yes, I'd like to hear more about this.' Her look to the Dictator said 'button it'. He smiled, a tiger now: just a hint of teeth.

'Jenna has some struggles with sense of self. She has some dependent, histrionic and borderline traits as well as some obsessional ones; under pressure she may become more dramatic, or revert to trying to control her environment. Being unable to do so will increase stress. Even her eating disorder can be viewed as a maladaptive way of dealing with intrapsychic conflict.'

Jenna was looking at her. No smile. More a death stare.

The Dictator had regrouped. 'That's hardly very damning, is it Doctor King? The late Elizabeth Taylor was histrionic, was she not? She had plenty of children as I recall without being reported as dangerous. So, what about Mr Essa?'

Natalie was aware of a second stare now directed towards her. 'Malik has paranoid traits. Perhaps in part cultural…' She winced as Okeke narrowed her eyes. 'Perhaps in part a function of the relationship, how he reacts to what he perceives as being goaded. His need to know Jenna's every movement was a large part of why they broke up.'

'Come, Doctor King, it was more than just a need to know, wasn't it? It's a clearly dysfunctional characteristic in any culture… and don't these disordered aspects of his character become additive? Along with the antisocial ones?'

For a lawyer, Tatterson knew his psychiatry.

'Except he doesn't have any. At least I've seen no evidence of them in the maybe four hours I've spent assessing him and questioning his mother.'

The Dictator's expression would have given Jenna—and Elizabeth Taylor—competition. His hand was on his chest as he paused and pushed his shoulders back. 'So you are saying a professor of psychiatry is wrong? That her Honour imagined the aggression that happened here previously?'

'No. Well yes. That is, he has some traits—the aggression. When provoked, as I understand it. There is no history of physical violence against Jenna or the children. The only—'

'Excuse me Doctor King. What do you mean there has been no violence?'

Natalie stared at the lawyer. Jenna gave her an embarrassed half-shrug and looked away.

'At the last access visit,' the Dictator continued, 'we have eyewitness testimony of Mr Essa shoving Mr Radford, Jenna's elderly father.'

Mr Radford was hardly elderly. He was under sixty, and more strongly built than Malik. She wondered who'd shoved who. Mr Radford's glare in the direction of his son-in-law suggested a less than cordial relationship.

'I can't comment on the event—I wasn't there,' said Natalie. Why did she have the feeling she had just walked into a trap? 'But, as you described it, it was not against Jenna or the children.'

'Really?' The Dictator looked smug. 'Ms Yang has submitted to the court that he has also…' The Dictator picked up a report and read: '…*physically intimidated Ms Radford, twisted her arm behind her back and thrown Chris across the room.*'

Three times Jenna had denied this in the initial interview. Had the hesitations before answering been because she was lying then? Or was she lying now? Natalie found her eyes searching out Jenna again. *Twisted her arm behind her back*. Jenna had used Natalie's own words. Her head was down, avoiding Natalie's gaze. Natalie squared her shoulders.

'Jenna denied any such occurrence in my interview. And I did ask.'

The truth, the whole truth and nothing but the truth. That was what Natalie had sworn to uphold. 'The sexual abuse? That Jenna may have been unsure about; perhaps she only suspected it. But there was no reason to deny any past physical abuse to me. She had already left Malik.' The Dictator looked like he had found himself on the back foot and wasn't sure how he'd got there. 'And I've heard of only one fight as a child. Hardly abnormal.'

'Excuse me Doctor King,' The magistrate intervened. 'You're saying these claims have only come up recently, after your interviews?'

'I was unaware of them until just now.'

The magistrate wasn't finished. 'And are you telling me that he was not antisocial as a child?'

'He was a good student, your Honour—he got a scholarship to study in Paris. After that fight when he was twelve, it was Malik that was hospitalised. There is no evidence of lying, stealing or killing of animals that are common in people who become antisocial.' Natalie smiled her own tiger smile back at the Dictator and caught Malik's small punch in the air.

'Could he not be lying?' The Dictator was back on the attack.

'Yes, he could. But I did seek corroboration—his mother tells the same story. And, unlike Jenna's, his story has remained consistent.'

For a moment, the court was silent.

The Dictator made one last attempt. 'But you agree surely that monitoring of his children as he does his wife would not be good parenting?'

'There is no reason that he would be jealous of his children, Mr Tatterson. And I could only speculate about what his aptitude in parenting a teenage daughter would be—a lot of people aren't very good at that.'

Mr Tatterson gave her a tight smile and sat down.

Malik was already on his feet. 'So, Doctor King, you did see me with my son did you not?'

Natalie tried to address her answer to Louise Perkins. 'I have seen both parents with Chelsea and with Chris.'

'Can you explain your report? About Jenna not being able to manage my son?'

Natalie didn't look at Jenna or her father, continuing to focus on the magistrate.

'Jenna struggles to manage Chris and tends to take his behaviour, especially withdrawal, as rejection. She struggles with limits and wants Chris to like her. Children his age, particularly those going through a messy parental breakup, need firm boundaries. Chelsea tries to please her mother, who is not always aware that her own issues are getting in the way. None of these are issues that would prevent her from having custody. She needs education and support.'

'And ah... Mr Essa?'

'Chris is clearly bonded to his father. And appears to respect him. At the least, Malik—Mr Essa—is able to put limits around him.'

'Why is this important?' Malik sounded like he genuinely wanted to know the answer.

'Because children Chris's age are testing out just what they can do—if they aren't given boundaries then they face the anxiety of being uncontained, rather than learning how to deal with limitations, with not getting their own way. And they become at greater risk of anxiety and behavioural disorders.'

A light went on for Malik. 'So you mean Jenna's parenting could make him antisocial?'

'In a child that would be a conduct disorder. That may become antisocial personality disorder, particularly if the male role model is violent.' Natalie stared pointedly at Malik. 'But as I said, Jenna was only—'

'And how was Mr Essa with his daughter, Doctor King?'

'There are some clear positives between the two.'

'Do you think I abused her, Doctor King?'

Shit. What to say? The truthful answer was clear. But what if she was wrong? The safer option still was to ensure Jenna got custody. And it would be easy—one line—to back her up. Perjury, but surely she could live with that if it meant Chelsea would be safe…

The law, Liam, said, was his domain. She wasn't Solomon. Natalie took a deep breath.

'I haven't been able to establish if Chelsea has been abused or not.'

The magistrate frowned.

'But what do you think?' asked Malik.

Natalie felt her chest constrict. Would she ever forgive herself if she sent Chelsea back to an abuser?

'Objection, your Honour.' The Dictator looked as if he was wasting his time in kindergarten. 'Doctor King has explained—'

'Yes, I know, Mr Tatterson.' The magistrate looked frustrated. 'Doctor King. My problem is that the child was interviewed and there was nothing definitive there either. I will allow Mr Essa's question. At least you have seen Chelsea. What *do* you think, Doctor King?'

Natalie thought of her dreams, the father she fantasised about. Her gut feelings… No. It was about the evidence, not feelings—that was her job. Her impartial assessment. Then she remembered her conflict of interest and her promise to Declan to inform the court. Shit.

'I can only say it's possible. To be more certain, a number of individual sessions with Chelsea, over weeks or months, would probably be needed. Ideally, with a team watching behind a one-way screen, maybe combined with therapy to help decrease the stress of the separation.'

'Your Honour, this is all hypothetical and fanciful,' said the Dictator. 'Ms Radford is clearly able to offer the child a safe home without having to put the child through all this.'

'Sit down, Mr Tatterson.' The magistrate glared at them all. If everyone ran their courtroom like her, cases might be settled a good deal faster.

Malik had the floor again. 'Doctor King, is it possible my wife made this up?'

The magistrate intervened. 'I'm not allowing that question Mr Essa. Sit down.' She was looking frustrated. 'What about Ms Radford's police statement?'

This was the question Natalie really, really, didn't want to answer.

'Your Honour, I'm afraid I don't know. It...' — Natalie took a deep breath — 'would fit with Jenna's... tendency to exaggerate. And her need to control. But...'

Louise Perkins looked at her pointedly.

'I have to tell you... while I don't feel it has in any way biased me, I may have what might be viewed as a conflict of interest. It has come to my attention that my brother is currently working for Mr Essa.' Could she say anyone in their right mind would sack Blake and that she'd take Malik's side? Poor Malik. She'd just handed him a gift and was now taking it back. The QC pricked his ears up.

Louise Perkins took a deep breath, shaking her head in disbelief. 'Okay. This is how I see it. I have one psychiatrist who has support for Mr Essa but a conflict of interest. Mr Essa, in turn, is defending himself against the court's advice. I have another psychiatrist who may well be being paid enough taxpayers' money to attract the attention of the Audit Office giving me mumbo jumbo that supports Ms Radford. And no one has spent any significant time with the child in question through all of this. Can I remind all parties that this is not a criminal court, or even the Family Court? That we are after what is in the best interests of the child?'

She looked at the two lawyers, then at each parent.

'You,' the magistrate said, pointing at Natalie, 'seem to know what is needed and have already met the child. Can you see Chelsea until you can give me a better answer?' Her look

127

said both: *Don't fuck with me* and *Keep her safe*. She added, 'And see the grandmothers while you're at it.'

Natalie began to say she wasn't a child expert but stopped. Better her than Wadhwa. And it seemed she'd dodged the conflict-of-interest bullet.

The magistrate looked around. 'On the matter of grand-mothers, where is Mrs Radford?'

Jenna's mother? It was a good question. Maybe she had Chris. There was some hasty consultation.

'Mrs Radford has been unwell, your Honour,' Li Yang finally said.

'All right.' She addressed the next question to Jenna. 'Your mother-in-law has cared for Chris and Chelsea in the past?'

'Yes.' Jenna's reply was reluctant.

'Safely?'

'Not if she let her son abuse my daughter.'

The magistrate ploughed on. 'She loves them?'

'Not as much as she loves Malik.'

The magistrate narrowed her eyes. 'Very well. We will set a court date in three months' time. Chris is to have weekends with his father. Chelsea is to go on weekend days, supervised by Mrs Essa. Oh, and Ms Yang.'

'Yes, your Honour.'

'The court takes a very harsh view of parents who do not abide by its decisions. If Ms Radford continues to prevent access I will have her for contempt, is that clear? Meaning' — she looked hard at Jenna — 'I will lock her up.' She paused for effect. 'Court adjourned.'

Louise Perkins had left the room before her ruling had sunk in.

Natalie was still dealing with the thought of seeing Chelsea individually. She looked up to see Malik hugging his mother. Ama looked delighted, and to be sure there had been gains for their side. Natalie didn't imagine for a moment that any supervision Ama provided would be rigorous.

Jenna's expression was stony. Her father was still in his seat when she came over to Natalie.

'You lied, Jenna,' said Natalie.

Jenna leaned into Natalie. 'There are no rules when it comes to protecting your children,' she spat.

'Political Correctness Puts Children in Danger' screamed the Herald Sun above Mark La Brooy's by-line.

> *Have we lost even the most basic common sense in our efforts to appease the moaning minorities? Women, 'people of colour', the ever-widening LGBTTQQIAAPPH2O community (if you haven't been keeping up: lesbian, gay, bisexual, transgender, transsexual, queer, questioning, intersex, asexual, ally, pansexual, polyamorous, hijra, two spirit and— just in case there's some previously unimagined deviance we've overlooked—other. Or perhaps that's where we forgotten heterosexuals fit). And, of course, Muslims.*

Wasn't La Brooy's usual hobby horse fathers' rights? Natalie wondered exactly how he was going to turn that around so he didn't have to be on Malik's side. She read through a half-page diatribe about political correctness taken to another level of stupidity and a plucky single mother doing the right thing by throwing out the violent de facto, to the final paragraph:

> *Yesterday, at risk of contempt of court, a woman trying to protect her child was ordered to hand that*

child over to a violent, unrelated man who has been accused of abusing her.

How could this happen? What has brought us to a place where two women—psychiatrist and judge— bend over backwards to support a male aggressor? Guess. What group are we most afraid of offending? What group do feminists inexplicably put ahead of the sisterhood—and apparently even the welfare of children? Yes, our man is Muslim.

There are a lot of men out there justifiably angry at being denied access to children they love— but this isn't a triumph for them. It's a triumph of political correctness over common sense. Again.

Natalie shuddered. At least La Brooy hadn't mentioned her by name. Yet. What was it with these columnists? They took one angle out of context and distorted it to support their argument. He hadn't mentioned Wadhwa and the psychopath diagnosis; she could only assume his research had been at best lazy. Malik hadn't assaulted anyone. And he wasn't unrelated to Chelsea—he was her adoptive father. The truth was often murky, and murkier still in the context of mental illness and custody battles.

Beverley found her in the coffee room.

'I take it this is you that Mark La Brooy is talking about?' Beverley said pointing to the paper. 'Have you seen Twitter?'

Natalie felt a stab of anxiety. She couldn't afford to get into trouble with the College of Psychiatry or the Medical Board—she and the bean would be relying on her income if she didn't want to become dependent on Liam. She reminded herself that Beverley had seen the original Okeke article, and typed her reports. It didn't mean anyone else could identify her from the article. She felt her chest constrict when she found the tweets that had put Beverley into a spin.

Pearl Salter @PearlS: *Psychs easy to fool for one hour a week—out of 168. Mothers see the other 167. #SaveOurKids*

The insider was back:

Liza R@lizar82: *Good article but why don't you tell us Professor testified that 'father' is a psychopath? #PsychBitch way less qualified.*

And My Bitchin Rules @MyBitchinRules, was back too, replying to Liza R: *Stepfather, psycho, Muslim. 3 strikes but they give him the kids. Average white guy (me) has to fight for 3 years for weekends.*

Apart from Liza R—who could be anyone from the court clerk to Winona's best friend's cousin's workmate—the tweeters seemed to know little about the case in question—it had just set them off on airing their own grievances.

'Do you follow this sh...stuff?' Natalie went in search of Beverley who was busying herself sorting files.

'It keeps me in touch,' said Beverley, not looking at her. 'I like to know what's happening.'

This wasn't the sort of happening Natalie had any interest in. 'It's all bullshit.'

'You get a lot of that too,' Beverley conceded.

Natalie was grateful that the College and the Medical Board were even less likely than her to be following Twitter.

'Feel free to reply on my behalf,' said Natalie. She thought of all the people involved in the Essa case. With the possible exception of Wadhwa they were just trying to do their best in an imperfect world. Even if Jenna had fabricated a story, she had done so—at least in part—to protect her children.

'What exactly do you think I should say?' Beverley paused from her filing.

'That they should all get a life,' said Natalie. She turned off her phone. But the sense of outrage stayed with her all day.

Royal Commission work had taken Liam to the country for several days. 'I'm over curry and pub food.' He was on his hands-free as he drove back along the freeway. 'I'll pick you up; let's eat out.'

That meant his local French bistro, France-Soir, near his apartment on the other side of town, where they were served by lean Frenchmen, skilled multi-taskers with accents nearly as sexy as Liam's. They delivered the best French onion soup and fries she'd ever eaten.

'Aren't you meant to have a steak with the fries?' Liam asked.

'Nope. This bean must be vegetarian. I'm all kale and Brussels sprouts now.'

Liam looked at her. 'You doing okay?'

'Better than you; you look like you haven't slept in the last three days.' She took a breath. 'I had the blood test today. They're just waiting on you.'

She'd run out of excuses; when she admitted it was fear that was stopping her, she had gone straight to the pathology lab.

Liam poured himself another glass of red. He'd ordered a bottle and had already demolished half. 'Your boyfriend already done his?'

'*Damian*. He texted me to say he had.'

Liam nodded, took a slug. 'He seems to think there's more chance it's his than you do.'

'Wishful thinking. He said he had been told he and his

wife had a chance of one in a million without intervention.'

Liam looked at her. 'He's in love with you, you know.'

'Oh, come on.'

'He came to see me.'

Natalie stared. 'He...? And you didn't tell me?'

Liam shrugged. 'It was just before I went away.'

Natalie crossed her arms. Waited.

'He just wanted to make a point.'

'And that point was?'

'That children are better off with their parents.'

Jesus. 'Let's just wait until the result, okay? Then we can get on... Just get the test, Liam.'

Liam nodded. Neither of them needed any extra grief.

'How was the hearing?' Natalie asked.

'These stories...' He shook his head. 'I don't know how you do it.'

Liam thought he was tough. But hearing stories of abuse in graphic detail, one after another, took a different sort of toughness. And expertise. The legal profession was being thrown into this without the benefit of her training—and without having someone like Declan to debrief them. But Liam did have her. This was what they did well together— their work, their passions, bouncing everything off each other.

'Tell me about them.'

Liam shook his head. 'Aren't pregnant women meant to be wrapped in cottonwool?'

Natalie laughed. 'Do you think pregnancy is going to give me a personality change?'

'I'd rather drown the memory of them than talk about it.'

'Like your dad?'

Liam stilled. Put his glass down. 'I am *not* my father.'

'No. But you're too busy being tough to allow yourself to be human.'

Liam swilled the wine in his glass. 'Not sure that talking helps. I know it's what you do, but...' He shrugged. 'Michael has agreed to testify, which is great. But every time he talks about what was done to him... seems to make him more vulnerable. Like he just relives the pain.'

'That may be in part because it's been bottled up for years and years. And because it happened when he was a child, stole his innocence. You bottling it up...' Natalie shrugged. 'You'll explode. Booze kills you in all sorts of ways, not just the way it made your father die in your eyes.'

'This what it's like being on your couch?'

'Truth hurts. And it will hurt Michael too. Retraumatising him before it liberates him and helps him move on. Has he got supports?'

'His parents are dead. Has a sister, some friends through the survivor-support organisation.'

'Encourage him to use them.'

Liam nodded. 'Exercise is meant to help, isn't it?'

'Help what? Stress? Yes.'

Liam grinned. 'Good. I know what I need instead of talk.'

From the look, Natalie didn't think they'd be waiting around for dessert.

But it turned out there were more urgent matters to deal with. James, Liam's son, was sitting on his doorstep waiting for them when they got back. He looked like he'd had a growth spurt that his weight had yet to catch up with.

Liam hesitated but only for a fraction of a second. 'Hey mate, what's up?'

James looked miserable. When he saw them—or rather, Natalie—his expression turned to defiance. He looked at his dad. 'I want to move in with you.'

Natalie realised quickly that she wasn't wanted, and moved to listen from the next room.

James had kick-started his teenage years with O'Shea flair. Lauren had caught the boy drinking, hadn't been impressed with James's arguments about why he should be allowed to and read him the riot act. Liam, after talking to Lauren on the phone, hadn't been any happier than her. James and his friends had raided the liquor cabinet and one of them had thrown up everywhere.

Natalie's mind wandered as she waited for Liam to resolve the issue with James. She pulled out her phone and fired up Twitter. She did need to know. Not like Beverley, to 'stay in touch with the world'; she needed to know what these idiots were saying about her. About Malik.

#SaveOurKids was still going strong. Did Beverley tweet under her own name? Natalie did a search and couldn't find her. She did a search for *#PsychBitch* and any chance of sleep, already looking unlikely, vanished. Eighty-two tweets.

Kevin R Moor @kevinrmoor: *abusive parents need to be sterilised, stop wasting taxpayers money on this shit #PsychBitch.*

Jamie Z @easyzee: *#PsychBitch medication made me zombie.*

Kids Really Matter @KidsReallyMatter: *Most psychiatrists madder than their patients #PsychBitch.*

'PsychBitch' seemed to be any and every female mental health professional who'd made a decision that their patient disagreed with. Wasn't exactly uncommon in her field. Nothing about Natalie—yet it was unsettling.

It was after midnight before Liam came to bed.

'So, is he going to stay here for a while?'

'Probably better he lets her cool off for a few days. But I'm not around enough after school for him to live here, and given the drinking issue—Jesus, he's only thirteen—he needs some supervision. Not that Lauren is any better at that—she's going to get her mother to be there after school for next week.' He slipped in under the sheets. 'And she couldn't resist a *like father like son* comment.'

Ouch.

'At least...' He stopped himself.

'At least what?'

'Doesn't matter.'

'At least what, Liam?'

Liam sighed. 'At least James is unlikely to risk any further drama by telling Lauren you're here.'

Natalie watched the shadows on the ceiling. She was wide awake and doubted she'd sleep anyway. 'You need to keep the issue of Lauren and you separate from you and your children.'

'I don't need a lecture. Lauren's already given me one for the night.' Liam was tired, irritable.

Natalie knew she should leave it alone, but suddenly the whole avoidance of talking about their relationship, tiptoeing around Lauren—it just wasn't okay.

'So your plan is to hide me? Like you're still married to Lauren, just living apart?'

'Don't be stupid. It's just...I need to sort out the money, the access, everything first.'

'Actually, you're right,' Natalie said quietly. She got out of bed and started to get dressed.

'Natalie, for Christ's sake get back into bed.'

She ignored him.

'Natalie, it's late. We both need to sleep.'

'And I will, Liam. At my place.' Natalie turned to him, surprised at how calm she felt. 'I'd like to be able to help, even if it was just supporting you, but I can't. I really, really don't want to come between you and your kids. But I can barely help myself at the moment, and that's who I need to put first. Me and the bean.'

She wasn't really angry at him, just tired. 'You probably don't want my advice, but James came to you because he respects you. He needs a role model who is true to himself. Be calm and rational with Lauren, but don't give away part of yourself—because that's just as likely to lose the kids as it is to keep them.'

She kissed him, and stepped back quickly before he could stop her. 'I think we need to wait until things are sorted out before we see each other again. I mean really sorted out. Get your test—I'll ring you when I get the result.'

He was calling her back, and as she left the building he was on the balcony, towel around his waist saying he'd drive her, but she was already flagging down a taxi and heading back to the only life she felt comfortable with. The one where she relied on herself and no one else.

Natalie texted Declan late morning: *Need to talk. Will be there 6pm*. He hadn't replied but she knew his last patient was always five o'clock. Which meant he'd be done by 5.50, and sure enough, at 5.51 a thirty-something woman in an elegant suit walked out with her head lowered.

Declan's look of surprise told her he hadn't seen her text.

'I'll only be five minutes,' said Natalie, still winded from cycling up the Northcote hill, dodging the trams.

Declan nodded, looking a little put out. It wasn't 'her day'. He ran his hands through his hair.

'Would you like a tea? I'm rather in need of one,' he said.

Natalie used the time to suck in some deep breaths, wondering for the first time if she really would have to get a car. A family sedan with a baby capsule. As she paced the room, Declan's notepad caught her eye. She went closer, stared at it.

'Why do you have my mother's number on your pad?' she blurted out as soon as Declan came in, a cup of tea in each hand.

Declan put his cup down, sat, waved for her to take the one he had made for her, waited until she did.

'Your mother rang me. She left a message and asked me to call her back.'

Natalie stared at him. 'What the...? Jesus, Declan, I'm an adult. I don't need my mother checking up on me.' She thought of her last conversation with Jan, the messages on her phone she'd ignored.

'Why do you think she rang?' said Declan.

'I don't have to think. I know. Doesn't mean it's your business.' Natalie felt the familiar anger rising inside her, the anger between herself and her mother that she couldn't ever seem to rid herself of. Declan watched and waited. 'She's worried because I'm pregnant and she doesn't know if I'll cope, okay? She's upset I let loose again about my father and may think I'm manic. Overall? Probably hoping you'll talk me out of this pregnancy.'

'I suspect she knows you well enough to know no one has ever talked you out of anything that you wanted to do. Assuming you want to do it.'

Natalie ignored the implied question. 'Were you planning on ringing her back?' There were boundaries he'd be crossing if he did that without her permission.

Declan took a sip of tea. 'What would you like me to do?'

'Ignore her. No, better still, tell her about boundaries and confidentiality and to mind her own business. I'm old enough to look after myself and she's got no right going behind my back. And you've got no business talking to her.'

'I wouldn't speak to her about you without your knowledge and permission.' Declan's calm authority remained the one reliable thing in her life.

Natalie shrugged. It was her mother who'd asked the hospital to call Declan in to see her when she was in rehab—angry and depressed—at sixteen.

'Okay. Tell her I'm fine.' She gave a hint of a smile. '*Will* be fine.'

Declan nodded. 'Did you want to see me because of the altercation with her?'

'No.' Well, maybe it was one of the reasons. Along with Liam and her messed-up life, another dream that had left her feeling guilty, the tweets, Chelsea and... just too much on her mind. She couldn't wait another week to talk to Declan.

'Take a look at this.' Natalie pulled out Mark La Brooy's article. 'I'm about to be caught in La Brooy and Okeke's crossfire.'

'This,' said Declan after a few moments, 'is about agendas you have no control over.'

She explained about the tweets—after explaining what Twitter was. Declan looked a little out of his depth. 'Surely it will blow over? It doesn't sound like it is actually anything about you.'

'But it's… like it's bad enough having Jenna and Malik's life in the public arena in court. But this is… well it's like whole lives are being judged by people who bring their own agendas and no knowledge.' Natalie was pacing around the room. 'It's pulling everything down to some lowest common denominator. Worse than reality TV. How can you make an argument in 140 characters?'

'You can't, Natalie. Let it go. Focus on what's really important.'

He was right of course, but it didn't make her feel any better. It was the unfairness, the hiding behind Twitter handles that incensed her most. At least Okeke and La Brooy were up-front about who they were and what they stood for.

'I'm seeing Chelsea, individually—your idea as I recall.' Natalie sat down. 'Tomorrow. And I need you there. I want real hands-on supervision.'

Declan had his hands clasped in front of him. 'You don't think I might need a little more notice?'

'Oh. Yes, of course. So tell me what to do. And when to make the next appointment. I want you there on the other side of the screen. Two heads are better than one—and I can't afford to mess this up.'

'Have some tea.'

Right. Tea.

'I owned up about the conflict of interest but it did more harm than good—any points Malik had scored were taken away and now I'm on Jenna's blacklist.'

141

'Your magistrate sounds like a seasoned and balanced professional,' said Declan. 'Let her do her job. And you do yours.'

Jenna's smile was tight when Natalie came to collect Chelsea from the waiting room. Malik and his mother were picking Chelsea up afterwards—organised by Protective Services—which probably wasn't helping Jenna's demeanour.

'Hi Chelsea,' said Natalie, after briefly acknowledging Jenna. 'We're going up to my colleague's office because that's where all the fun stuff is, but I need to talk to your mum first. Do you mind waiting here? Beverley will get you anything you need.'

Beverley—remarkably demure in an ice-blue dress that resembled a bonbon—smiled from her desk. Jenna followed Natalie reluctantly, taking an upright seat.

'Jenna, whatever you have or haven't told me is in the past,' said Natalie, looking directly at her. 'I want to help Chelsea. Help her adjust to not living with her dad, find out if she is being abused.' *Or if you made it up.* 'I—we—need to do what's right for her.'

There was a long moment of silence and Natalie wasn't sure that Jenna was going to reply. In the end, she said in a tight voice, 'I'm her mother. *I* know what's right for her.'

Natalie could see the anger—but just maybe there was also some pain and anxiety.

'I get that,' said Natalie, 'but you're dealing with your own stuff. It's pretty hard to know what's best for someone else when you maybe aren't all that sure what's best for yourself.

Think of how difficult Chris is being, struggling with the adjustment.' Jenna stared in silence. Natalie tried again. 'I could see that Chelsea *really* wanted to please you. That means that she'll sometimes do things that she *thinks* you want.'

For a moment Jenna looked confused.

'Can you remember back to when you were eight or nine? Can you think of any time when you wanted your mother or father to do something and they wouldn't and you weren't able to tell them?'

Jenna's expression glazed over but Natalie pushed on. 'Like maybe a birthday and you wanted a doll and they gave you a book? A time when you knew you couldn't just tell them because it might upset them?'

Natalie was about to give up when Jenna, in a soft voice, said, 'Yes.'

Her expression was hard to read—vulnerable yet angry, guilty yet defiant. Then the moment was gone.

'I really wanted a birthday party at the fairy shop, but my mother said I was too old.' Jenna shook her head. 'I wasn't. We went to the Pancake Parlour but it wasn't the same; my mother thought it was and I let her think that.' She looked at Natalie. 'I ask Chelsea. I listen.'

'I know, Jenna, but things get in the way even when both of you try to do the right thing.'

'But…' Jenna stopped. 'I don't know why you can't hear me. I *know*, I mean deep down in my gut, Malik is abusing her. This isn't about me. It's about me trying to protect her, to be a good mother.'

'I do hear that Jenna,' said Natalie. 'And if he is, I promise I will do everything in my power to find out—but you need to work with me. I want the truth.'

'I've *told* you the truth,' said Jenna. 'He hasn't ever hit me or the kids, okay? Like I said. But the court… I don't trust them, okay?'

To not make her pay maintenance? Or to not see the world as she did?

'Let me work with Chelsea, Jenna. And if there's proof I'll get it.' Natalie took a breath. 'But you have to promise me, Jenna, that you will *not* coach your daughter into saying things.'

Natalie caught a brief look of guilt. She curbed her irritation. Maybe Jenna truly believed Malik was a threat and that the system wouldn't deliver a good outcome. Natalie couldn't really blame her for breaking the rules to achieve what she thought was right.

'Promise me, Jenna. I swear, I'll find out if you do—and it will harm your relationship with your daughter.'

'I'm not about to tell her to say Malik's stuck his dick up her,' said Jenna angrily.

'I didn't say you were, Jenna.' Anger was Jenna's defence against being in the wrong—but Natalie wanted to keep her on side. 'I know you love Chelsea, and I want to help that connection be as strong as it can be.'

'I will do anything for Chelsea,' said Jenna. '*Anything*.'

Chelsea hadn't moved from the position where they left her. Natalie invited her to come upstairs and at Jenna's nod, Chelsea followed, looking around cautiously. When Natalie opened the door to her colleague's office, Chelsea stood in the doorway, eyes widening.

'Is this a doctor's office?'

Natalie smiled. 'A special sort of doctor's office. Your usual doctor needs to look into your ears and eyes and check the outside—I'm much more interested in finding out how you feel. And playing'—Natalie's arm indicated the room — 'with interesting things can make that easier.'

The sand table had its lid fastened, but besides the figures on the shelves, there was a large doll's house and a small table with pens and paper. Chelsea's eyes flickered towards the doll's house.

'We can play with whatever you like,' said Natalie, wondering what she'd do if Chelsea went back to Jenna.

Chelsea didn't move.

Damn. What the hell did eight-year-olds like?

'Are you worried about your mum?'

'I guess. She's kind of unhappy.'

Natalie nodded. 'It's tough, isn't it, when grown-ups have fights and you get stuck in the middle. Bet you feel you need to fix it sometimes.'

Chelsea didn't look at her. 'Sometimes.'

'You know, it's okay to be unhappy; like it's normal. Not all the time, but after something bad happens. And then things get better, faster, if you talk about them. Your mum will be able to sort it out for herself, by talking with her grown-up friends.'

Chelsea sighed and looked at the doll's house. 'My nanna and grandpa have a house like that,' she said, pointing to the two-storey construction. Beneath a red tiled roof, the front section was removable. The front door was also red, the panelled windows had curtains and flower boxes.

'Do you mean the one they live in, or that they have one for you to play with?'

'Live in,' said Chelsea, coming closer so Natalie could close the door.

'Would you like to play with this one?'

Chelsea thought about it and shook her head. She stood awkwardly, shifting her weight, looking like she wanted to be anywhere but where she was. Natalie knew the feeling. She was cursing Declan in her mind for getting her into this and then not being there—though it was her fault for not giving him enough notice. He was organised to come to the next session, but right now if she didn't do something, the kid looked like she'd bolt and there would be no next session. Natalie wondered how long before the bean would feel like that too.

'Let's draw.'

Chelsea shrugged and sat down at the table.

Okay, Child Psychiatry 101.

'Can you draw yourself?'

'No, that's too hard. I'm not very good at drawing people.'

'I'm sure you're better than me,' said Natalie. She did a quick stick figure. 'This is as far as I got in art and my teacher told me not to come back.' A slight simplification. Natalie had been fifteen and drawn a picture of two people having sex to get under the art teacher's skin. She'd succeeded.

Chelsea looked serious. 'Mrs Ambrose said I did a really nice picture of our class, but my friend Amy's was way better.'

'Maybe you can do a picture of you and Amy?'

Chelsea considered this carefully, and spent time assessing the pens. In the end, she chose the coloured pencils with fine tips, rather than the crayons or paints, and carefully put them out before starting. She spent nearly ten minutes drawing, concentrating hard, before announcing she was done.

Natalie had no idea if the picture was typical—it seemed good for an eight-year-old, mostly in proportion, and details like the bow in Amy's hair and buckles on her shoes were not what she would have expected. Both girls had long hair and were wearing dresses. 'We're going to Amy's party,' Chelsea explained.

'Where is she having it?' Natalie was right in her assumption that girls' parties hadn't changed a lot since she was that age; they were *occasions*.

'Last year she had one where we dressed up as characters. I was Alice. Ethan went as the Mad Hatter. This time it's a sleepover.'

Natalie tried to picture a dozen eight-year-olds sleeping over in her warehouse, but her imagination wasn't up to it.

'It's in a week,' Chelsea said. 'I'm giving her a makeup set. Mummy said I might be able to get one for my birthday too.'

It was, apparently, critical what the present was: 'No one gives dolls, unless it's the Sylvanian family.' Whatever they were. What you wore also counted: 'I got a new dress but I don't always.' Then there was who you invited (or didn't): Matilda hadn't been invited because no one liked her. Did bitchiness really start this young?

In the picture Amy was smiling, but Chelsea was not.

'How are these two feeling?' Natalie asked.

'Amy is happy because it's her birthday.'

Natalie nodded. 'And Chelsea?'

Chelsea tilted her head and thought for a while. 'I think she's tired,' she finally announced.

'Why's that?' Natalie asked casually.

'Because she's been very busy with homework.'

No great reveal there.

'Can you draw a house, too?' asked Natalie.

Chelsea began then discarded her attempt and started again —after anxiously checking if it was okay to have another piece of paper. Natalie filed the reject for Declan to comment on.

Chelsea appeared to be struggling to decide what type of house to draw—her mother's, grandparents' or Malik's, perhaps? In the end, she drew a two-storey house like the doll's house, humming as she did. Natalie vaguely recognised the tune but couldn't place it.

'What's the song?'

Chelsea didn't look up. 'What song?'

'The one you're humming.'

Chelsea frowned. 'Oh, that. Just a kids' thing. A teddy-bear song.'

This didn't help Natalie identify it. Probably one her mother had sung to her.

'Do you have a teddy bear?'

'Nope.'

Chelsea looked bored. She stood up and wandered over to the shelves of figures and selected one.

'Who's that?' Natalie asked.

'Princess Jasmine,' said Chelsea, in a *how could you not know that?* tone.

Chelsea sighed. '*She* is beautiful. And she has Aladdin who has a genie and a magic carpet.'

'If you had a magic lamp like Aladdin,' asked Natalie,

remembering more from her child psychiatry things-to-do list, 'what would you wish for? Three wishes only, though.'

Chelsea thought hard, looking at the characters in her house. 'Could I wish for all the Sylvanian family?'

Natalie smiled. 'You can wish for anything you'd like.'

Chelsea nodded. 'They have a *really* great caravan.' She saw Natalie's look. 'The Sylvanians are a family of animals but they still live in houses and caravans. There aren't any there.' Her head indicated the shelf. 'I checked.'

'And wish two?'

'Am I allowed to wish for more wishes?'

Natalie laughed. 'No, but it was worth a try.'

Chelsea thought some more. 'I'd really, really like to go to Uxor. I guess it'd be okay if Chris came too.'

Uxor?

'And who else?'

'Mummy and Daddy.' She had said it before she had thought about it. Shrugged. 'It's only a wish, not real. Mummy doesn't want to go. She says I can't go to Egypt until I'm grown up.'

Not Uxor. Luxor. Natalie's skin prickled.

'Has Daddy said he'd like to take you?'

Chelsea nodded. 'I'd see the pyramids and get to ride a camel.'

And be a long way from her mother and out of reach of an Australian court.

'And the third wish?'

'Anything?'

Natalie nodded.

'Then,' said Chelsea, 'I'd wish for a big house in the country with my own room and a pony.'

'That's kind of a lot in one wish.'

'Well Mummy says I can't have a pony in the city so I have to have a house in the country to have the pony.'

'And your own room? Don't you have your own room at home?'

'Sure,' said Chelsea. 'And my own one at Nanna's too.'

149

'And at your dad's?'

'I slept in Uncle Youssef's bed there, ages ago.' Fortunately, Chelsea wasn't looking at Natalie.

'Did you?' Natalie hoped her tone was neutral.

'Daddy didn't have a spare one and Uncle Youssef was staying with a girlfriend.'

Natalie breathed a little easier.

'At Teta's I'm going to have my own room too, but I'm not allowed to stay there.' Chelsea looked to the door. 'Are we finished?'

Malik and Ama were waiting with Chris in tow when Natalie finished the session. Chelsea smiled cautiously at them both and took a seat next to Malik. Natalie left her there while she spoke to Ama.

Ama appeared no more pleased to talk to Natalie in person than she had been on the phone. Or rather, she was pleased to have an opportunity to bag her daughter-in-law, as long as she herself didn't come under scrutiny.

'What do you think is the cause of Chelsea's changed behaviour?'

Ama arranged her gold bangles along her arm, lounging back in the chair. 'Doctor King, this is obvious I think. Chelsea is a normal girl. She wishes to please her mother, but her mother says bad things about my son. What can a child do?'

'Tell me about her. What is she like?'

'She is a good girl. What is there to say? She helps me in the kitchen and we cook together. Not like her mother, who is' — Ama circled her finger next to her head, bangles jangling— 'a bit crazy with food.'

'And with Chris?'

Ama shrugged. 'It is normal for some arguments. Chris is much younger, annoys her.'

'What about with Youssef?' Natalie smiled. 'How does she get on with him?'

'Youssef is not around so much. He goes out. With friends.

But soon he goes to Egypt and maybe finds a girl to marry there.'

Did Ama know about the Australian girlfriend?

'What sort of issues did you have with Jenna's parenting? Apart from the food?'

'No issues,' said Ama whose tense demeanour and angry tone suggested the opposite.

'Did you disagree about things Chelsea or Chris were allowed to do, or not do?'

'No.'

Natalie squashed her frustration. She had the feeling it wasn't so much that Ama was lying; more that Natalie wasn't asking the right question. Eventually, Ama couldn't contain herself.

'It is not wrong that my son follows her,' said Ama. 'I do not trust her, not ever.'

'You think she was playing around?'

'I think the women here...' Ama stopped herself. 'She should have been home looking after my son and children, then this would not be a problem.'

After Ama left, Natalie rang Blake.

'You still working for Easy Tiger?'

'Yep.'

It must have been a record. 'Do you know when Youssef is off to Egypt?'

'Next month, I think. They asked me to do a couple of extra runs.'

It made her think of gun running. She really watched too much television. 'Can you do me a favour?'

'Yeah, sure.' Blake sounded hesitant.

'Keep your ears open for any hint that Youssef is taking anyone other than just himself.'

There was silence.

'And let me know, okay?'

'Sure.' Blake sounded like he had already dismissed the request.

'And Blake? Really, really, do *not* say I asked you this.'

Katlego Okeke had wasted no time in responding to La Brooy's column.

Mark La Brooy doesn't like being called a racist— he's threatened to sue more than once—yet could there be a starker example of racism than his column last week, commenting on a child custody decision he didn't like?

Natalie scanned it. A few references to the vilification of refugees… bromides about quality of parenting not being dependent on gender or ethnicity… the obligation of the judicial system to 'ignore stereotypes or even statistics' about race or religion… then back to Mark La Brooy's racism.

We know he's carrying a banner for 'men's rights'. The no-surprise surprise is that it turns out that he means 'white men's rights'. Because, for the first time, Mark La Brooy came out swinging for the woman to have sole custody—no access at all for the man.

Why? Mother—white, religion not stated. Father— Egyptian, assumed Muslim. If the father had been white, Mark La Brooy's column would never have been written.

'Has this hit Twitter yet?' Natalie asked Beverley.

'It will have been on Twitter before the ink was dry,' said Beverley.

'Why do I just know that @MyBitchinRules will miss every one of the good points here and just focus on being negative?'

'Okeke gets a lot of Twitter grief.'

'So does hashtag PsychBitch.' Natalie felt she was taking the grief for all of the female members of her profession. The others were probably smart enough not to be on Twitter.

'I'm keeping an eye on it for you.'

On Natalie's next day off—most of which was spent writing reports while ignoring the mess around her, including Bob—she organised to meet with Mrs Ambrose, Chelsea's teacher. The school was only a couple of kilometres away and the spring weather was encouraging, so she set out on foot. The public primary school was presumably one the bean might end up attending.

She tried not to scope the place, but it was hard not to wonder how the bean and her would fit in. Better hopefully than Jan and Craig had with Natalie—she hadn't done well in the private system where their rules-and-results mindset, which her parents thought she should adopt, was at odds with her need to speak her mind.

School had finished and there were only a few stragglers left in the concrete playground. One mother was leading her impossibly small child in an impossibly oversized shirt and shorts out the gate as she entered; the mother looked transfixed by a conversation that appeared to be about dinosaurs. Was this compulsory learning for future mothers or could she delegate that to the father? Had Liam ever talked to James about Tyrannosaurus Rex? It was easier to imagine Damian in that role.

Dismissing thoughts about the impending blood test results, Natalie headed for the main office where she was directed to classroom 3A. A woman in her late thirties whose features suggested an Indigenous heritage was pinning a picture on the wall. She introduced herself as Gaylene Ambrose and greeted Natalie with a broad smile. 'What do you think about this?' she asked, nodding to the picture.

Natalie took the opportunity to compare it to Chelsea's. The figures were not as advanced in details or form, but the subject was one she couldn't imagine herself thinking about at primary school. As far as she could tell it was the Refugee Olympic team being adopted by Australia. In this depiction, it looked like they had had to swim all the way.

'Does politics really start this young?' Natalie asked.

'We're not meant to encourage it,' said Gaylene, 'but they get it at home.' She shrugged and smiled mischievously. 'Only fair to let them air it here.'

The joys of an inner-city electorate with a Greens member, Natalie suspected. Her own electorate. Housing prices had escalated in the last thirty years and though there were refugees in the public housing, most of the households were middle-class professionals.

'I came to talk about Chelsea Essa,' said Natalie, taking a tiny seat that pushed her knees up against the desk. She pulled out a permission form signed by Jenna and Malik.

Gaylene gave it a perfunctory glance. 'Chelsea's doing her second year with me, so I know her well.' The teacher pointed to a front-row seat. 'That's hers. Amy Walker, her best friend, sits one side and Matilda Highton the other.' Seemed like the personal politics from Chelsea's pictures were played out on a daily basis.

'How does she get on with them?'

'Amy is her best friend but Matilda is the one that's desperate to be. Between you and me, she'd be far more loyal and deserving. Amy suffers from princess syndrome — Chelsea's a smart girl, but she's totally mesmerised.'

Smart, but beholden to the domineering bossy girl. Possibly an appealing sense of certainty for someone dealing with their parents' separation.

'What's Chelsea like in class?'

'Generally quiet, compliant, a joy to have here.'

Which might mean that she was actually depressed or anxious; some children, especially girls, tended to withdraw when they weren't managing psychologically. Faced with similar circumstances, Chris was bouncing off walls. He'd be causing havoc by the time he got to school if Jenna and Malik didn't manage to contain him with some tough love.

'Have you noticed any change in the last six months, since her parents separated?'

Gaylene thought a moment. 'Not really. There was a bit of a kerfuffle a month or so back, but I'm pretty sure Amy was behind that. And then more recently when Matilda didn't get invited to Amy's party.' Gaylene sighed. 'We suggest to parents that either the whole class gets invited or it's very small. The Walkers decided to ignore that suggestion. Or more likely Amy nagged them into it and they gave in for an easy life.'

'Chelsea though. Is she quieter, more withdrawn, less interested? More daydreaming, more sick days?'

'Perhaps a little.' Gaylene looked at Natalie curiously. 'What's this all about?'

'I'm just trying to determine for the court how much the breakup is affecting Chelsea,' said Natalie.

'Well she isn't alone. Matilda's parents broke up last year and there was an intervention order out against the father for DV. He turned up to try and get the children— there's an older boy as well—and we all but went into lockdown.' She narrowed her eyes. 'What is expected of teachers is *too much*.'

Natalie wasn't about to disagree, if for no other reason than the torture she had inflicted on her own teachers.

'You said *perhaps*?' Natalie prompted, shifting in the chair and nearly tipping it over.

Gaylene nodded, got up and went to Chelsea's desk and took a couple of books out.

'See here,' she said, flicking through some pages. 'Normally she'd have done twice as much just because she would finish early and get bored. Now she just keeps the same pace as everyone else.'

Natalie took the books. The outside had neat careful letters with Chelsea's name and year and her teacher's name. Inside the pages were meticulously filled out; the first half had borders around them in different designs and colours. The last ten or so did not. A definite change.

'What are her favourite things?'

'Reading and drawing; most of the children like drawing, but she's a very good little reader. Comes up with some extraordinary questions.'

'Like?'

'She read *The Lightning Thief*. It's kind of a modern Greek classic, quests and monsters.' Gaylene shook her head. 'Chelsea pestered me to explain about why Percy, the hero, felt he had to save the world. Seemed like she had seen his bad behaviour and getting into trouble and couldn't work out how or why he had changed. Can you believe it?' She laughed. 'The others that are up to reading it just love the adventure. But not Chelsea. She has an old head on those shoulders.'

The head might have got a bit older and sadder because of what was happening at home. No sex-related questions at least.

'And has she been off sick at all?'

Gaylene shook her head. 'Maybe one day. She had a twisted ankle and couldn't do sport for a while, but still came to school.'

'Does she like sport?'

'I don't think so, but a lot of the girls don't. They prefer to stay indoors. They generally like the cross-country because you get to go to the parks, but Chelsea had her sore ankle then and stayed back with me.'

'Who takes sport?'

'Ted Beahre.' Gaylene laughed when she saw Natalie's

look of disbelief, and spelled the name out for her. 'His name's Edward. Doomed to be nicknamed Ted wasn't he?'

'Does she have any other teachers?'

'Fiona, the Year Four teacher, takes them for Japanese; a student teacher occasionally.'

'Could I speak with Teddy? I mean Ted? Is he around?'

He was in the staff room. Natalie had a hard time supressing a grin—he looked like a teddy bear: short, slightly portly—workouts perhaps not as tough as they had once been—soft features and a smile that would have made him a contender to run *Play School*. The smile faded when Gaylene introduced Natalie.

'What's it about?' The tone wasn't aggressive, but there was a clear defensiveness.

'I'm treating her,' said Natalie. 'There's been some issues since her parents broke up.'

Was it her imagination or did Teddy Bear relax a little? 'Sure. I'm about to leave, though.'

Natalie offered to buy him a coffee at one of the cafés along his way home. He hesitated, then agreed. Natalie sensed that he was doing so only to avoid being seen as uncooperative.

'Tell me about Chelsea,' said Natalie as they walked.

'What do you want to know? She's one of the easy group.'

'Easy group?'

'Yeah. There's three groups—the easy ones do as they're told and you know you can rely on them. The troublemakers you can rely on to do something they shouldn't and you watch them really closely when there's an opportunity for havoc or danger, like when you're spread out on the crosscountry run.'

'And the third group?'

'They're the troubled kids. They can cause trouble, sure, but they're mostly struggling. Got some Aspies in that group, good kids but they look at a ball like they've only ever seen one on a computer screen. Others are...' He shrugged. 'You're the shrink. I don't know. ADHD, depressed? Both? I do my best to help them.'

'So Chelsea's never needed extra help or caused trouble?'

Ted flashed her a look. 'No.'

They arrived at a café with bright coloured outdoor tables and chairs, and both ordered coffee. Natalie had had her quota of tea for the day.

'Anything about her ever worry you?'

'Nope.'

Why then wouldn't he look at her when he said this? Natalie's skin started to prickle. There was a softness about the man; he would have been easy to write off as a kindly teacher who liked his job. Possibly, maybe even probably, gay. But she remembered the softness that had been weakness in some paedophiles she had interviewed. He was hiding something.

'Chelsea missed a few sports lessons and the cross-country. Was there any suggestion she was playing on a lesser injury to get out of running for any reason?'

'Like what?' Ted was now looking right at her, lips tight.

'Like some other kid or kids might trip her up or something.'

Ted shook his head slowly. 'The troublemakers group, all boys incidentally, pick on one girl, an overweight kid who's doing it tough. I stay with her when we go out—she's one of the slower ones anyway so it means I bring up the rear. Chelsea would be among the fastest girls. She probably could have outrun most of them.'

Natalie tried a different tack. 'Have you met her parents?'

'Yes.'

'Tell me your impressions.'

Ted added some sugar to the coffee that arrived. 'Her mother's a bit helicopter.'

The parent that got overinvolved—didn't surprise Natalie. But surely most parents were 'a bit'. 'In what way?'

'There on the sidelines, which is fine, but probably a bit too keen that Chelsea gets into everything.'

'And her dad?'

'More relaxed.'

'He comes to things too?'

'Yeah. As I recall, Chelsea tends to go to him first, like when she won last year. Eyes really lit up when he told her she had run like...' Ted thought. 'Ivanovic. EPL player, Chelsea I think.'

'Was Jenna part of that exchange?'

Ted shook his head. 'Think she's preoccupied with the little boy, Chelsea's brother.'

'Have you seen anything odd with Chelsea? Anything at all? Particularly, maybe, with the boys?' Sexual behaviour was not uncommon in children who were being sexually abused—and there had been the questions about pregnancy.

'Who sent you?'

Wow. Defensive or what?

'Like I said: I'm working with Chelsea.' Natalie paused. 'Who do you think I might have been sent by?'

Ted shook his head, anger barely concealed. 'Forget it. Nothing. All I want is to do my job.'

Natalie looked at him hard, wondered about taking a gamble, and if she did, which way to play it. 'Look,' she said finally, 'I'm a psychiatrist and no one has sent me with a special agenda. But I do want to help Chelsea, and every instinct I have says there is something you aren't telling me. Want to come clean now, or do you want me to find out later?'

'I don't have to talk to you. You aren't a parent.' He left before she could say anything more.

Natalie sat in the beer garden at Grumpy's on Smith Street, lucky enough to grab a table just as a couple were leaving. She wondered if she liked this better than France-Soir. More down to earth. But the food had been pretty brilliant at Liam's local, with a touch of French flair she could get used to.

'Looking good.' Damian's voice came from behind her, calm as ever. He kissed her cheek and the touch, however brief, was welcome, like a small reminder that she wasn't totally alone.

'Me or the bean?'

'You're still in one package aren't you?'

'I'm fine.' She sounded curt; knew he'd pick that. She took a breath. Damian had taken his tie off but looked like he was still in work clothes. The dark blue trousers and white shirt, though not uniform, still screamed cop. Maybe it was the short hair—he'd seen the barber. Or just that he looked so damn squeaky clean, schoolboy smile and all.

'Bad news?' he asked as he sat down, beer from the bar in hand.

'No, what makes you think that?'

Damian smiled; more like sad older brother than schoolboy. 'It isn't only shrinks that read body language, you know.'

Natalie shrugged. 'It's been a shitty week. I don't have the results yet, if that's what you're thinking.'

'Problems with O'Shea?'

Natalie took a sip of water. 'Among other things.'

'He hasn't gone back to his wife, has he?'

'No, no; nothing like that.' Had Damian sounded hopeful? 'Just... well, he has kid problems and he needs to sort them out before...'

'Before what, Natalie?'

'Nothing. It'll work itself out one way or another.' She took a breath. 'Any chance you can get me info about a schoolteacher?'

'So this is work?'

'No.' Natalie rubbed her head. Well, actually, yes. Otherwise she'd have told him when he texted that she didn't think seeing him was a good idea. Particularly if Liam was right, and Damian still had hopes they'd get together.

'Look,' she said. 'This guy was hiding something and I've got an eight-year-old I'm working with even though I *never* work with eight-year-olds and the judge has landed me in it and so has Declan and that's just my work life let alone anything else, like the tweets about me and the case and my brother is working for my patient because I was stupid enough to give him a card and I'm still angry at my mother and—'

'Whoa! Take a breath. I don't understand half of what you just said and that may be a good thing.' His look said *When did you last take your meds?*

Natalie closed her eyes and tried to tap into mindfulness, but couldn't even think of one line of the mantra. Breathe. Yes, that had to be part of it. Breathe. Concentrate. Could she? On what?

'Can you check out this teacher for me? Teddy Bear. I mean Edward Beahre. Find out if he is being investigated? I really need to know and—'

Damian looked startled. Because of the weird name or had he heard of him? 'I'm Homicide, Natalie. I can't ask those questions without a good reason and couldn't tell you even if I did get an answer.'

162

Her breathing seemed to echo in her head, like sounds bouncing off canyon walls, booming noises swirling around her. She got up and exited the garden, through the bar and onto the street. It took Damian until the next corner to catch her.

'Natalie, stop.' His arms were around her. Confining. Claustrophobic. But also containing. She hit him but there was no swing. He wouldn't have even felt it as he held her to him, until slowly she could breathe.

'Better?' Damian asked after what seemed like ten minutes had passed.

She nodded. 'Shit. Sorry. I just... oh what the fuck. I *am* fucked.'

Damian grabbed her arm. 'I'll walk you home and we'll order take-away. And maybe—' He was grappling with how to tell her she was acting nuts.

'Yeah, I'll take some extra meds.' Another quetiapine. Minimum risk to the bean and probably better than the buzz of adrenaline that was heading its way unless she got on top of things.

Damian phoned for a pizza and she risked the salami. The baby had most of its bits now. Then, at his suggestion, they went for ice-cream.

'They're prettier than the ones I had as a kid,' said Damian. He was looking at a concoction of bright green, chocolate with bits of Crunchie bars and a pink scoop with marshmallow. 'Not sure they taste any better.'

'Our tastebuds have altered. Ice-cream then, bourbon now.'

'Is it hard not drinking? Because of the pregnancy?' Damian sat down on the bench beneath three large gumtrees.

'No.' Natalie looked at him. He wasn't just protecting a baby he seemed to think might be his. He had his guard down and was interested. In her. 'Actually... the only difficult thing is... the uncertainty.' She took a breath. 'I'll have the results soon.'

Damian nodded. 'You know—I always figured I'd love being a dad. When I found out it wasn't likely to happen, it really rocked me.' He smiled. 'I guess you're going to think I doubted my manhood or something?'

'Did you?'

'No. It just meant there was going to be something missing. I haven't really resolved it yet.'

'Missing, as in, no son to ride the waves with?'

Damian looked a little sheepish. 'Hadn't occurred to me.' He thought for a moment. 'I guess if I had a girl I'd picture her dancing. Maybe a boy too, if he didn't go the footy or surfing route.'

Natalie's eyes widened. 'Dancing?'

'I was state under-eighteen Latin-American runner-up.' He grinned. '*Robbed* of the trophy.'

Natalie started laughing. Thought of herself at sixteen watching *Flashdance* and deciding, with her leg in a cast and her pelvis smashed up from the bike accident, that she'd never dance like that but that maybe she could sing like Irene Cara. She saw Damian's expression and took his hand. Time to head home.

'I like the idea of you dancing. It's just that—I would never have guessed it. And I'm usually really good at guessing things like that.'

Damian squeezed her hand. It felt better than it should have. He was probably imagining himself taking his daughter to a deb ball. Jesus. Any daughter she had would be sneaking out the upstairs window to get to a heavy metal concert, not letting her dad teach her the cha-cha.

'So you're waiting until this result?'

'I guess. Hoping.' Damian offered her a lick of his key-lime-pie ice-cream.

'You told me you were infertile, right? One in a million?'

There was just a fraction of a pause. 'That's what the specialist told Caitlin and me.'

Caitlin who had gone on to have a baby with his mate. Natalie breathed a little easier.

By the time they arrived back at the warehouse the ice-creams were finished. Damian didn't look like he expected an invitation in, brushing her cheek with his lips before he turned to leave. There was a noise behind them in the cul de sac and they both tensed.

Her first thought was that it was Liam preparing for pistols at dawn. But it was Blake.

'My brother,' said Natalie. Damian smiled, extended his hand.

'Damian,' she added, 'is a cop.'

Blake's smile dimmed a little. After the door was closed he went to the windows, probably to check that Damian had really left.

Natalie put a hand on his shoulder. 'So, what's up?'

'Nothing.' He saw her expression. 'I'm missing a box. Must have left it here.'

'Toys, right? One box of Chinese knock-offs? I can see why you're worried.'

Blake ignored the sarcasm. 'I'll just get it now, okay? Youssef's in the truck.'

'What's in the box, Blake?'

'I told you. Toys.' Blake was already disappearing back downstairs to look for it. Natalie was right on his heels. Sure enough, there was a box, hidden under her gym gear. She crossed her arms and stood between it and her brother. 'I want to see what's in it.'

Blake assumed an injured look, but he opened the box.

Bratz dolls. Blake went to close the box flap. He was still smiling. But sweating. Natalie reached into the carton. Were these things stuffed with drugs? If so, she'd fucking well call Damian back. They seemed hollow…Natalie dug deeper. Hit something that wasn't a Bratz doll box. Pulled at it. Blake's smile was decidedly forced.

This box was labelled in Chinese. She opened it and stared. 'Shit, Blake—what the fuck… a gun?'

'It's a toy,' said Blake, 'like I said.'

Natalie picked up the gun. Looked at it closely. 'Might not be real, Blake, but they're still illegal. Right?'

Blake shrugged. 'They aren't doing anyone any harm. And I've got a buyer.'

Malik? Natalie shook her head. Didn't want to know.'Just get rid of them.'

Natalie's nightmares came back in full force, and even more vividly. She woke alone in the middle of the night to Bob announcing, 'Shots fired out!' She stared at the ceiling and tried to pinpoint what was worrying her. Not the replica guns, surely. Was it Ted Beahre? Or the thought that she'd got it wrong with Malik, or that La Brooy, Okeke and Twitter would annihilate her? Followed by the College and Medical Board?

On balance, the evidence still pointed to Chelsea being upset about the breakup and nothing more. And Jenna (if you were charitable) was exaggerating and jumping to conclusions. If you weren't, she was calculatedly lying.

The dream left Natalie with unease, guilt and fear. The hollowness in her stomach was like the time their dog had escaped and she had heard the squeal of tires, the thud. That moment when you still had a little hope, before the worst was revealed. The thoughts and feelings whirled in a nonsensical spiral... and the base of the tornado was an eye that was both accusing, and, it seemed to her, immensely saddened.

She took an extra quetiapine but still couldn't sleep. The phone by her bed drew her in. She searched #PsychBitch to see if there were any references to her, wondering briefly if she was paranoid. The hashtag had been getting an airing.

Man Under Fire @ManUnderFire: *Feminist + psychiatrist + child abuse paranoia = lethal cocktail for men #PsychBitch*

#PsychBitch could refer to anyone.

Liza R @lizar82, the insider: *@ManUnderFire PC psychiatrist + fear of being called Islamophobic + traitor to feminism = lethal cocktail for kids #PsychBitch*

That one was probably her.

Julie G @JoolieGG: *@ManUnderFire @lizar82 Its never*

that simple. People doing their best in difficult situations just like you guys.

Maybe she needed to follow some of these people too? She added them—and @MyBitchinRules—to her list: following seven, followers one—who seemed to be some sort of automated scammer—number of tweets, zero.

It was a long time before she slept again and if she dreamed any more, she retained no memory of it.

In a move that was out of character, Declan had rescheduled their weekly appointment for an earlier time—the morning of Chelsea's second session. Natalie assumed he had more instructions for her. They met over breakfast, which Natalie knew he usually reserved for a browse of the papers. He had a pot of hot coffee waiting and she could smell bacon and eggs cooking; she was glad she was over the morning sickness phase.

'You'd better have a look at this.'

Not about Chelsea's session after all. Shit. Had La Brooy or Okeke finally named her? It couldn't be Twitter—Declan didn't know the first thing about social media. Natalie took the paper from Declan's hand—not a newspaper at all. A letter from the College of Psychiatrists. Contacting Declan as her supervisor, so he could discuss it with her.

There has been a complaint... Natalie skimmed it, looking for the name. The Chair of the Ethics committee, Ken Rankin, a man with a perpetual frown, had signed it. Though it didn't say who had complained, it didn't have to. Wadhwa.

Natalie's hand and jaw clenched. 'This isn't fair. I told you about this. He's the one who didn't get a corroborative history, had the short interview, and didn't see Malik with Chris or Chelsea. Malik is good with the kids. After the last session—'

Declan put his hand up, shaking his head. 'Take a breath.'

Natalie forced herself to put the letter down rather than

throwing it across the room. How dare Wadhwa report her. She should have reported *him*.

Lack of expertise… contradicting each other gives a poor impression of the profession.

'Like it or not, Professor Wadhwa has his supporters. And a point: psychiatrists get bad enough press as it is.'

Declan let his words settle in. It took all Natalie's willpower not to let out exactly what she thought of the professor, his expertise and his qualifications. Maybe she'd drop a line to Okeke, pointing out Wadhwa's associate professorship was in administration—at a university without a medical school. 'It doesn't mean your clinical acumen is being questioned,' Declan continued. 'The College have me supervising you for a reason, Natalie. To ensure competency—stability—to practise.'

Natalie winced. Psychiatrists knew the cost of stigma— yet here she was feeling its full force inflicted on her. The label, her past indiscretions, would always dog her.

'I haven't done anything wrong.' Natalie knew she sounded like a sulky kid; but then Declan was acting like he was her father.

'I have already spoken to the College,' Declan continued. 'As you have indeed been doing the right thing, both by talking to me, and in your clinical approach, there will be no further action.'

'But it's a black mark, right?'

Declan shook his head, topping up her coffee. 'Think more of it as a reminder to proceed with caution. The cases you deal with are difficult—already this one has made the news and, as you noted, you could easily get caught up in the media blow-up.'

'You were the one who said I should see Chelsea.'

'Which I pointed out to Professor Rankin. What happened in your session?'

Natalie reluctantly pushed Wadhwa to the back of her mind and brought Declan up to date with her work with Chelsea.

'Bringing the doll's house up first in conversation was her subconscious speaking,' Declan said.

'What makes you think that?' Natalie had relayed the conversation with Chelsea verbatim. It hadn't struck her as odd—merely that it reminded her of her grandparents' house.

'Because of the picture. This picture.' Declan was holding the first attempt at a house that Chelsea had discarded.

It was a house like the doll's house, but with attics.

'So you think she is saying something about a real house?'

'More about her room,' Declan said. 'I'm mostly concerned about the windows.'

Natalie looked at the windows in the picture: two downstairs, two upstairs, two attic ones.

'What about them?'

'It has attic windows, which the subsequent drawing doesn't.'

'Maybe she just had a favourite story with a house like this. *Anne of Green Gables* or something.'

'Possibly. But there is this.' Declan pointed to curtains on the attic windows—but missing on the main ones.

'Secrets? Things to be hidden?' Upstairs where bedrooms usually were.

'Get her to play with the doll's house,' Declan finally said.

The session was at 2 p.m. Declan arrived at half past one and spent fifteen minutes charming Beverley, who promised to invite him to the wedding.

'He sees things,' said Beverley to Natalie, oblivious to the fact that it really wasn't the sort of comment psychiatrists welcomed.

Natalie dragged Declan up to the little room on the other side of the screen.

'Instructions?' she asked.

'Don't push too hard,' said Declan. 'Let her get comfortable.' He paused. 'And Natalie.'

'Yes?'

Declan looked into the sand therapy room for a moment,

170

lost in thought. 'Before you let her go,' he finally said, 'come and confer with me.'

Chelsea was with her mother in the waiting room. She gave Natalie a small smile and headed towards the stairs.

'How is she?' Natalie quickly asked Jenna, watching Chelsea's back as she headed to where the sand therapy room was.

Jenna pulled a bright-coloured beret over her ears. 'How do you expect?' The surly expression of a teenager who hadn't got her way. But there was anger as well, and a hint of something. A haunted expression that Natalie recognised but couldn't place. She hadn't seen it before in Jenna.

'Has something happened?'

'Yeah. Malik abused her, remember? And now she sees him every week. Thanks for that. Do you know how that makes me feel?' Jenna turned abruptly and left, nearly bowling over a patient coming to visit one of Natalie's colleagues. She didn't offer an apology.

Chelsea was already in the therapy room, browsing the shelves. Natalie flashed a look towards the screen as she closed the door. Declan would be focused on the patient rather than her. But it was hard not to feel self-conscious.

'I thought you might like to play with the doll's house,' Natalie said.

The sand therapist was still away, which was just as well. One blast about the misfiling of figures was better than a weekly telling-off.

Chelsea shrugged. Natalie sat down on the floor and eased off the side of the house to reveal the rooms. Chelsea knelt beside her. 'Can I put furniture in it?'

'Whatever you'd like. Have you seen the shelf with the tables and beds and chairs?'

Chelsea crawled across to the shelves and picked out the laundry set—a washing machine and dryer. 'This house doesn't have a place for these.'

'Maybe the garage?'

'The mum will get wet when she washes the clothes.' Chelsea added the laundry set to the garage nevertheless and then chose some figures—Princess Jasmine and Aladdin—and put them beside the house. 'But now it's a nice day and they're enjoying the sun while the cleaner's working.'

Chelsea took a few more minutes selecting furniture. 'Will I have to move?' Chelsea seemed to be talking to herself—or rather, Princess Jasmine was asking Aladdin.

'Have you seen your new room at Ama's—your grand-mother's?'

'Yes,' said Chelsea. She wasn't looking at Natalie and suddenly froze. Turning around, she looked like she was going to cry. 'You won't tell, will you?'

Natalie felt bile rising. Shit. She couldn't keep secrets, not if it was the one she was looking for. Natalie looked at the screen but wasn't sure what she expected to see there; Declan was the one with the view.

'Won't tell what, Chelsea?'

'I wasn't meant to go to Teta's last week. Mummy said I was going to come straight home after dinner at the Pancake Shop but we went for a chocolate drink at Teta's, but it was my fault. I really wanted to see the room because Teta said she had bought me a Disney doona with *all* my favourite characters *and* Daddy said he'd got me a lamp that had the Egyptian gods on them, not just the Percy Jackson ones.'

Chelsea's lip trembled; Natalie smiled and the girl seemed to take this as her secret being safe. 'Daddy said he'd tell me the real Greek misses.'

Misses. 'Myths?'

'Yes.' Chelsea turned back to the shelves and picked a selection for the lounge room. Soon the doll's house room was cluttered with furniture.

'So where does everyone sleep when they get tired?' Natalie asked.

Chelsea put herself—Princess Jasmine—on the pink bed.

She then turned her attention to the living room, next door, on the upper level. She put Tweetie Bird—her mother?—on the couch at one end, and Bart Simpson—Chris, presumably—on it. Then she found a chair and had Aladdin sit on it. She hovered over where to put it, eventually electing to keep it separate from Tweetie Bird on the other side of the same room.

Nothing complicated here. Chelsea felt alone, felt her mother was more tied up with Chris than her—and her father was isolated as well. Probably felt responsible in a way that would make sense only to her. Already she was learning to keep secrets—before long she'd be playing her parents against each other for what she could get out of them. Did she know instinctively that Jenna would be jealous of Malik giving her presents, while she might have to move back to her parents' to save money?

Chelsea added someone she called Anna from *Frozen*, and Lisa from *The Simpsons*, to the bedroom and they had a pyjama party.

'Was that what Amy had?'

'This one is at Matilda's,' said Chelsea. 'We had popcorn and pancakes and red lemonade and Matilda was sick.'

'Was it just girls?'

'Yes, except for Matilda's dad.'

Wasn't there an intervention order out on Matilda's father?

'Do you go to Matilda's a lot?'

'No. Amy doesn't like her.'

'But do you?'

Chelsea thought about it. 'She's okay.'

'And Matilda's dad?' Natalie watched Chelsea carefully. She appeared to not have heard.

Natalie repeated the question.

'He's okay. He doesn't live with them either.'

So just some similarities that were both comforting and unsettling?

Natalie checked her watch. Fifteen minutes to go. She

excused herself and ducked into the room where Declan was sitting.

'Instructions?' Natalie could see Declan had taken a page or more of notes.

'Get her to draw a tree.'

'A tree?'

'A tree that would go next to her house. And then get her to put a nest in it.'

Trees? Nests? Natalie tried to remember what this might show but if she had ever learnt it, she hadn't retained it. So much of what she did was learnt and cemented through repetition with real people and their responses. There just hadn't ever been enough children in her six-month child psychiatry term to try anything more than once; most of the rotation had involved sedating aggressive pre-psychotic and drug-addicted teenagers.

'Okay, Chelsea,' Natalie said when she returned, 'I wonder if I can get you to do some drawings for me?'

'Sure.' Chelsea seemed relaxed.

'Can you imagine a tree that you'd like to have in your garden, maybe next to your house?'

'A tree? Like a treehouse, or just a tree?'

'Let's start with the tree.'

Chelsea looked at the pile of paper and pulled out a green sheet, and a brown pen. Her tree was small, taking up only a quarter of the page.

'No leaves?'

Chelsea shook her head. 'It's winter.'

'So would you like a treehouse in it? Or maybe a nest?'

'It's not big enough for a tree house,' Chelsea said with authority. She selected a yellow pen and put a small tightly drawn nest among the top branches. 'You can't see the bird because it's only an egg and the mother is hiding it.'

'What,' Declan asked her minutes later when Chelsea had been returned to a sulky Jenna, 'do you make of that?'

'That she feels she needs protection. And wants her

mother to protect her?' Natalie stared at the drawing. 'It's bleak, too. No leaves. Nest exposed.' Natalie started to feel uneasy. 'She doesn't come across as depressed, yet... I guess she doesn't smile much.'

'I thought her distinctly serious.'

Chelsea had always been 'good', but had she been serious? Was this a change? Not significant enough alone, but... Natalie looked back to the drawing. There was something else odd about the tree, what was it?

'We'll come back to that,' said Declan. 'Let's go and look at the doll's house.'

Natalie followed Declan into the room where she and Chelsea had been minutes before. Princess Jasmine was still busy partying with Anna (Amy?) and Lisa Simpson (Matilda?).

'Thoughts?'

Natalie looked at it. 'She's separate from the family, in the bedroom she dreams of, her brother is occupying her mother. Aladdin is, I presume, Malik. He's also apart from Jenna and Chris.'

'Anything strike you about the positioning?'

Natalie looked back. She recalled Chelsea's moment of indecision about where to put Aladdin.

Then she saw it. Her stomach did a somersault.

The bedroom furniture was all around the bed—and separate from it, was a chair. Right up next to the door. Like a barrier.

On the other side of the door, in the living area, was Aladdin.

Declan put the drawing of the tree on the table. 'This shows a nest—the quintessential expression of a protective home—and she has made it a fortress, high in a tree. But the branches are weak and it can be seen by everyone, so she is still in danger. It is also rootless, lost, floating without a base. And this—'

Declan pointed to something Natalie now realised looked

at odds with the rest of the barren stick form: a knot high up the trunk before the thin branches stretched out.

'If we think of the trunk as her eight years, then the knot is in the most recent year. And the knot?' He looked at Natalie. 'The knot, in this child, in this tree and with that bedroom... is abuse. Probably sexual.'

'What do I do now?' Natalie and Declan were both in her office.

What she wanted to do was to ring Jenna and apologise— to say *Don't let Chelsea out of your sight, you were right.*

'I got it wrong. It has to be Malik,' Natalie said.

'You don't know that, Natalie.'

'I was so sure Jenna was misreading things, blaming Malik because it suited her childcare and financial circumstances.'

'Maybe she is.'

'Is this enough to take to court?' Natalie could just picture Louise Perkins' look of disbelief that a knot on a tree meant anything other than the child couldn't draw straight lines.

'Not yet.' Declan looked worried though. 'Chelsea is clearly developing a relationship with you. She tested you— told you about seeing her bedroom at Ama's, was worried you would give her away, but trusted you.'

'I should tell Protective Services.'

'Chelsea's grandmother was there, supervising her. They didn't breach the conditions—just didn't tell Jenna they were going to show her the new room.'

'So. What do I do?' Right now, hoping for a genie to appear and grant wishes seemed like a good option.

'The next session,' said Declan, 'she will tell you.'

And if she didn't? After Declan had left, Natalie found her thoughts racing in circles. Worry, not mania. But stress could

177

lead to mania. Or depression. She gritted her teeth, determined not to let Jenna and Chelsea's case send her spiralling down. The bean needed her—it might not have anyone else.

Beverley found her in the coffee room.

'You haven't started tweeting have you? Or got one of your friends to?' Beverley was looking disapproving, but rather like a favourite schoolteacher. Even Natalie had had one of those. In primary school, anyway.

'No.' But as soon as she said it she wondered. Her sleep was so disturbed and more often than she liked she was getting her phone out while she waited for an extra quetiapine to take effect. The meds did make her drowsy; maybe she had tweeted and couldn't remember.

'Did you ever reply to those #PsychBitch trolls?' Natalie asked.

Beverley gave her a studied look. 'And say what?'

'Oh, I don't know,' said Natalie. 'How about psychbitch will certify you and throw away the key? Or your wife is better off without you? Or remember the symptoms you take the pills for?'

'One of us got out of the wrong side of bed I see.' Beverley eased out of her stilettos and rubbed a bunion. 'I am not going to last for a whole wedding in these. Maybe just the bridal waltz. As it happened,' said Beverley without drawing breath, 'I did. Reply.'

'And?'

'I told them they were inflammatory, unfair and ridiculously childish and no wonder their wives left them. Oh, and I said if the side effects included impotence then the women of the world would sigh in relief.'

Natalie had to credit Beverley for her flair. 'And their response?'

The smile disappeared. 'A few hundred replies.'

'Let me guess, they weren't giving you the thumbs up.'

'There were some anti-male sentiments,' said Beverley, 'but from the remainder there were five suggesting I became a nun, three that I have body parts sewed up, eight that I have them removed and two death threats. One said he knew where I lived.'

'Oh my god.' Natalie wondered at how composed Beverley looked in the face of this onslaught. 'You need to go to the police.'

'No, you do. I did it under the handle of @nataliek.'

'You didn't!'

'That's correct.'

It took Natalie a moment to register what she meant.

'What do you take me for?' Beverley sounded mildly irritable. 'However, *had* I made any replies, which I did not, under any name, that is exactly what would have happened. People have lost jobs and relationships and killed themselves over social media campaigns.'

Natalie quickly checked her account. Still zero tweets from @bobnotdylan82.

'Someone, however, has been quite active.' Beverley fished out her phone, opened the app and did a search. When she handed it to Natalie it was apparent the search had been for a particular user: @KidsReallyMatter.

Kids Really Matter @KidsReallyMatter: *drk should look herself in the mirror. Madder than patients*

Natalie tried not to react. She was just being overly sensitive, seeing things that weren't there. Wasn't she? But Beverley had seen it too. drk meant Doctor King. Maybe. And if it did… who the hell were they and what did they know about her?

'It might be coincidence,' said Beverley. 'Though someone has leapt to… well… someone's defence.' She grimaced as she pulled up another profile and Natalie recognised this one: @JoolieGG. 'Unfortunately,' Beverley added.

Julie G @JoolieGG: *Who of us doesn't have some bad moments?*

Kids Really Matter @KidsReallyMatter: *@JoolieGG I don't have to see a shrink.*

Julie G @JoolieGG: *@KidsReallyMatter maybe you should.*

Kids Really Matter @KidsReallyMatter: *@JoolieGG And maybe u r one of her patients.*

Natalie was very careful to keep her mask up. 'Whatever. But rest assured, Julie G isn't me or anyone I put up to it.' And hopefully not a patient, at least as far as she knew.

'Good. Stay well clear.' Beverley put her phone away. 'It probably isn't... well... don't worry about it. Not like there aren't lots of Doctor Ks. I just worry because I've been watching it since the court case. Most other people won't have been.'

Which was probably true and Natalie tried to reassure herself of this. But there was the uncomfortable problem that if drk was referring to her... who knew about her history? Her last stalker had been an IT geek who had managed to access her psych records. But he could hardly be tweeting from jail, though she supposed he could be getting someone else to do it for him. Natalie was still seeing his sister—she was doing well, and had cut all contact with him.

And there were all the staff who had looked after her only eight months earlier when she'd been an inpatient, being treated for depression. Of course, none of them were allowed to say anything...but under the cover of online anonymity? What if they spelled out her name, in full? And the College found out, or her patients?

Natalie allowed herself a moment of self-pity and then thought *fuck it*. This was what her patients had to deal with all the time. Stigma. It stopped people getting help, stopped them getting insurance; in one case it had caused her patient to be dumped by her partner.

It didn't stop Liam she thought, even though she had worried it would. She had underestimated him.

But she didn't want to think about him. Instead she told herself: 'Suck it up.'

That night in bed, though, it flooded back. All the cognitive rational feedback in the world wasn't going to work while Natalie slept. Her nightmares woke her, and she sat up gasping, her sheets wet with sweat.

There was something new in this nightmare—the eye took form. Though she could remember nothing else, there was a vivid picture of a teddy bear with a missing eye lying on the floor. She could hear a distant echo of a nursery rhyme *round and round the garden* and a churning feeling, a certainty, that she had done something wrong and that life would never be the same again.

It wasn't a good idea. Declan would certainly have told her not to, if she'd asked.

Natalie didn't even know she had it in her head until she was at the edge of the Fitzroy Gardens, about to cycle through the avenues of aging elms bursting with spring growth. Instead she looked over to the city and thought she could make out the cream brick tower where she knew Wadhwa had his rooms.

She had turned left before she had thought it through. Perhaps she was hoping that Wadhwa would be out, or too busy, and she could say she had tried. She needed to do something. Something to help her understand if she had got Malik so wrong. It wouldn't hurt if she could get him off her back either—though she had to admit that with their history she was more likely to inflame the situation.

Wadhwa's office was on the eleventh floor of a twelve-storey building that was dwarfed by the other towers at the top end of Collins Street. An eighties building, it was probably slated for redevelopment, but the interior was neat and modern enough. There was no secretary at the desk, nor people in the waiting room. Natalie pushed the buzzer and opened the door, then stood wondering what to do next. After a minute, a door at the end of the corridor opened. Wadhwa looked out and frowned when he saw her.

'Professor Wadhwa? Do you have a moment?'

'Do you have an appointment?'

Obviously, no. 'I only need a few minutes.'

'Oh, very well then, come along. I am nearly finished here anyway.'

Wadhwa's office looked clinically austere, apart from a photo of a woman in a sari holding a baby, with a boy of about two beside her.

'So what is it you are wanting?'

'To talk about the Essa case.'

Wadhwa looked at her blankly.

'Malik Essa. You thought... you diagnosed him with an antisocial personality disorder.'

'Yes. This is correct.'

No point saying that he didn't have enough information. It wasn't what she wanted to talk about anyway. 'Did you...' Natalie stopped. 'We've both worked in the forensic system,' she finally said. 'We've both seen psychopaths. So tell me — what did I miss? I mean on mental state. Did he *feel* like a psychopath, that he was lying? What did you *sense*?'

Wadhwa frowned, linked his hands together and regarded her over the tips of his extended index fingers. 'In Yarra Bend, I see many people, people with mental illness who have done terrible things. Sometimes, mostly even, because they have a chemical imbalance, their mind does not work well, they hear their own thoughts as voices, reality for them, it is not so clear.'

Natalie stifled her irritation at the lecture. She knew psychosis from the inside — she knew how it worked, how it felt, how it looked and the trouble it could get you into. Her bipolar had only ever taken her to the edge, where lights and colours had taken on new meanings... but it had been close enough.

The inmates at Yarra Bend mostly had a severe form of schizophrenia, often untreated and sometimes undiagnosed before they ended up in custody. Not only did it jumble their thoughts and tangle their beliefs in a way only they understood, if left to run its course untreated the disease often led to cognitive decline as well.

At least Natalie's bipolar responded to treatment without affecting her ability to think and work when she was well; many of the world's creative heroes who had suffered bipolar had been largely untreated and continued working. At least until they killed themselves: Woolf, Hemingway, countless others. Her own bipolar hero was treated—and still working as a psychiatrist.

'But at Port Phillip'—Wadhwa was referring to the men's prison, where Natalie had only briefly worked when she was training—'there, I am asked to assess many men whose thoughts are perfectly clear. They try to fool people, but they do not fool me. These are the men that Mr Essa reminded me of.'

'I agree he doesn't have a psychosis,' said Natalie. 'But I thought he was genuine. He loves his kids, they seem to love him.' She thought of Chris building a railway with his father, their mutual delight. Of Chelsea's smile when Malik had sung 'Go Chelsea Go', and how she had run into his arms.

'Love?' Wadhwa let out a snort. 'Of course the abuser loves his victim—when she makes him feel good, powerful, omnipotent.' He leaned forward. 'Particularly if he gets away with it.'

'But I didn't get any sense...' Natalie stopped herself. From Wadhwa's expression it was clear he thought she was not only mistaken, but wilfully so. 'I want to understand. Chelsea is being abused. But I need to know... how I missed it, so it doesn't happen again. After all, don't ninety per cent of women make false claims?'

Wadhwa waved his hand, but gave no indication that he'd picked up the sarcastic reference to his assertion. 'This is a matter of record. Spurious claims that can easily be disproven.'

Yeah? How? In Natalie's experience, most people weren't great liars but in Family Court battles there was a lot of bitterness to wade through, beliefs about children that had too much to do with ownership—and often money at stake. She wondered how many cases he had actually seen.

'So why did you believe this one?' Natalie asked.

Natalie caught Wadhwa's involuntary glimpse at the photo on his desk.

'Is that your children with your wife?' Natalie asked.

'Yes, my daughter Jiya and son Jayesh.'

'It makes you more protective, doesn't it?'

'Always, Doctor King, children must be protected.' Wadhwa sat back, and looked at Natalie with a serious expression. 'Your Mr Essa. You wish to know what it was that had my nose twitching, is this right?'

For her it was hairs raised on the back of her neck, a tingling from head to foot in the presence of psychopaths—a feeling she hadn't experienced with Malik. She nodded.

'I have much experience Doctor King. You, too, will have in time.'

Providing he didn't get her disbarred.

'I think, though…' Wadhwa rubbed his temples, then pulled out a file from his drawer, flicked through it. 'What made me feel Mr Essa was a psychopath? I will tell you.' He put the file down. 'Your Mr Essa was impatient, believed I was stupid and that the process was nonsense. This is not so strange. But embedded in his narcissism was also a self-justification. He alternated between being my friend—the idea that I as a man would understand him—and being my rival. Bulls in the same pen. This, Doctor King, is a sign that he is unsure of himself as a man, and I have seen it before. With *this* man.'

Wadhwa pulled out a newspaper cutting from his top drawer. There was a photo of one of the teachers that the Royal Commission had determined should face charges—the one Liam was helping Tania prosecute.

Shit. Had it taken a man—or at least the man-to-man dynamics—to see what was hidden behind Malik's exterior? If so, she had let herself be conned.

Cycling home, she stopped in the Fitzroy Gardens by the fairy tree and model Tudor village, and found a bench near the café. At this time of day people were not lingering; she watched commuters listening to podcasts and talking on iPhones, immersed in their own worlds. She wondered if her own world would ever take a more certain shape.

Natalie thought about Jenna's ferocious need to protect Chelsea. Not so different from Wadhwa. And if they were right—it meant that her own determination to be fair and impartial, to leave the law to the lawyers as Liam had insisted, meant she had delivered Chelsea back to an abuser. She thought of how in the past she had taken the law into her own hands—or rather, kept back information—for one of her patients and their child. She wished she'd done the same this time.

It was a black mark against her as a psychiatrist. And this time, as a potential mother.

Poor bean.

Mickie and Stephen Radford, Jenna's parents, brought Chelsea in for her next appointment. After cancelling it twice. In the end Natalie had had Beverley threaten to tell Protective Services. Not that they would have done anything, but the Radfords wouldn't know that.

When they eventually fronted, Natalie took the opportunity to speak to them, leaving Chelsea in the waiting room. Beverley smiled sweetly and mouthed 'wedding songs' at Natalie. She seemed to think Natalie singing at the wedding was appropriate payment for childminding, which was not in Beverley's job description.

'We're worried about Jenna and the children,' said Jenna's father.

'Jenna can't miss any more time off work,' Mickie said. 'Particularly now she's paying all her own bills.' Mickie's expression suggested disapproval, but Natalie was unsure of what. Maybe it was just the inconvenience to her. There was something birdlike about the woman, her skin taut under foundation makeup, lines clustered around the corners of her mouth and eyes as she watched Natalie. Jenna's bone structure was recognisable there, but in Mickie the years had turned the brightness in the eyes to a dulled wariness.

'She's doing it tough financially?' Natalie remembered the whole issue about maintenance — whether Jenna might have to pay Malik if he had access — and how he managed to hide his income. And Chelsea, in her play, had mentioned having to move.

'This whole business has been very tough on all of us,' said Stephen. 'We're happy to help her out any way we can.'

Natalie paused. 'You're helping out with the children more?'

'Someone has to.'

Natalie turned to Mickie, who was letting her husband do the talking.

'I understand you haven't been well.'

'I have a number of health issues.'

Natalie smiled, confident Mickie would elaborate, and didn't have to wait long.

'I've had migraines since Jenna was a child. Can't do anything but lie down in the dark. I was on morphine back then.'

'Poor Michaela was very distraught, not being able to care for the children as well as she'd have liked,' Stephen said.

'And now?'

'Not as bad.' Mickie avoided eye contact. 'But I'm picking up Chelsea most days, and Chris had a cough and couldn't go to childcare, so I had him. My son was nothing like as active; Chris is exhausting. I had him overnight as well and he got his finger stuck in the bathplug hole and I had to get the fire brigade. Chris thought it was all wonderful because he got to wear their hat and sit in the fire truck, but I couldn't move the next day.'

'How do you find Chelsea?'

'Chelsea's fine. Always been easy, much easier than her mother was.'

'What was Jenna like as a child?'

Stephen took over again. 'Active, could do just about anything she set her mind to, and had a real mind of her own.'

'Like?'

'Like she wanted to go to Little Athletics, demanded to go. Then out of the blue decides she doesn't like it anymore and nothing can persuade her to go back, even though we were rostered on for the rest of the year to help out.'

'Steve had to keep going without her,' Mickie added. 'It was ridiculous, but she just wouldn't budge.'

'It's been tough—then and now. Michaela's beside herself with worry. She had to see a doctor, her nerves have got so bad.'

Natalie started to get an idea of what living in this household had been like—everything had to be about Mickie; the children's emotional needs were secondary.

'You had four children, I understand,' said Natalie to Mickie. 'Including twins. Must have been hard.'

'I just did what a mother needs to do,' said Mickie, 'then, and now.'

Anything: that's what Jenna had said she would do. Natalie had the sense Mickie's *anything* would have fallen short of Jenna's criteria. Different circumstances... and different personalities. Jenna had the capacity to see the world from her children's point of view, and often did. In Mickie's case, now at least, she had tunnel vision.

'Can I ask...I'm wondering how you got on with Malik?'

'He was Jenna's choice,' said Stephen. 'We just wanted her to be happy.'

Natalie looked hard at them both. 'Do you think he's abusing Chelsea?'

Stephen's expression was indecipherable—not the sort of thing his generation talked about. Mickie's lips tightened. 'That's what you said.'

'No. I said it appears she's being abused. It isn't the same thing.'

'I've no idea.' Because she didn't want to think about it. Mickie had closed down emotionally a long time ago. Or used the bottle to deal with whatever emotions she hadn't been able to ignore. 'Seems to me there's far too much attention... the media is totally preoccupied with it and I find it all quite distasteful.'

It was the stick-your-head-in-the-sand-and-hope-it-goes-away attitude of previous generations that had allowed priests and family members to abuse children for decades. Natalie contemplated letting her get away with it. But grandparents had an important role in children's lives, and if Jenna was working and Malik didn't have access, then the Radfords would be especially important.

'Jenna was a very imaginative child,' Stephen was saying. 'And Chelsea even more so. I rather think… Well, she isn't very reliable. She says what she thinks you want to hear.'

Natalie looked at the couple. 'Can you give me an example?'

Stephen nodded. 'Jenna has been…pushing her. Asking her all sorts of questions about Malik. Next thing I know, Chelsea was watching television and asking if the man was going to take the ladies' clothes off! But that was exactly what Jenna had asked her… seemed to me she just regurgitates it.'

Damn Jenna.

'It would be better not to quiz Chelsea,' said Natalie. 'I'll keep what you've said in mind—it's why I'm not asking her direct questions. But unfortunately, these things do happen. Yes, they are distasteful—but we can't pretend they don't happen, because the impact is huge. Even if it's stopped now, Chelsea will be affected throughout her life. Like her psyche has a scar that can be pulled off at any time by triggers that remind her of feeling alone. And being betrayed by those she trusted.'

It was hard to interpret Stephen's expression—it could have been an earnest attempt to make sense of what she was saying—or just an older man who believed he knew the world and was humouring her.

Mickie looked at her watch. 'Do you wish to see Chelsea? Because we have to take her on the hour.'

As they left Mickie turned around. 'Jenna's always been a survivor,' she said to Natalie. 'She could wrap her father around her little finger, and after that it was her boyfriends. She's good at getting what she wants.'

Mickie wasn't about to change her views easily—but at least Natalie had tried.

Chelsea joined Natalie but without enthusiasm. She looked pale.

This session, Declan had said, would be the one at which she would disclose her abuser—or at least give them enough to take to court. As long as Natalie didn't mess it up. Or unless Chelsea just told her things Jenna had told her to say—either directly or indirectly. Natalie forced a smile.

'How's your week been, Chelsea?'

The girl shrugged.

'What would you like to do today then?'

Chelsea didn't respond, and continued to ignore Natalie when she proffered some options.

'I kind of get the idea that you're feeling pretty sad,' said Natalie. She stopped. Actually, while Chelsea's expression was sad, that wasn't what she was conveying.

'Maybe not just sad,' Natalie continued. 'I wonder… are you a bit angry?'

Chelsea still didn't respond—but Natalie had the sense she was listening.

'Last week,' said Natalie, 'I was pretty worried about you. I know your parents worry too.'

There was a quick look up. Chelsea's mouth was in a firm, grim line.

'Everyone wants to make sure you're safe, Chelsea. Sometimes it's kind of hard to know what is best, even for grown-ups.'

'I'll never get to stay in the new bedroom at Teta's.' Chelsea's voice was soft. They were both sitting on the floor, and Natalie shifted position, earning an alarmed look from Chelsea.

'Maybe one day.' Natalie wished Declan was there to tell her what to do. *Go with your instinct* he would say. But was her instinct right for an eight-year-old? A feeling was welling up inside her she couldn't quite make sense of; a feeling that something wasn't fair… Anger. But not just what she had sensed in Chelsea—this seemed to be her own.

'Sometimes it's hard to make sense of feelings,' said

Natalie. 'And sometimes you are angry and upset with someone you love and that's even more confusing.'

'Daddy will have to go on holiday by himself.'

Natalie's skin tingled. Holiday? Meaning Egypt? 'Luxor?' Chelsea shrugged.

'I know he'll be upset,' Natalie said. Chelsea had tears in the corners of her eyes and Natalie wanted to give her a hug—but at the moment she was part of the problem. Another adult to have to dance around and satisfy. 'But your daddy's a grown-up, Chelsea, and grown-ups know how to deal with feeling bad. He'll have people he can talk to—it won't mean he won't be sad or that he doesn't miss you, and he'll still love you, but he'll manage those problems. And he won't blame you, okay?' Ideally. It didn't always work out like that.

Chelsea now looked more miserable than angry, which might have been an improvement. Natalie wasn't sure.

'These sessions,' said Natalie, 'are for talking and playing and managing feelings.'

'I don't feel like talking.'

Natalie's heart sank. What had happened after the last session? Did Chelsea blame her? She *had* to get something this session. The last week had been agony, thinking about knots in trees and whether more were being added—an entire scarred trunk—because of her inability to convince any court on soft data.

'Maybe only talk if you feel like it,' said Natalie. 'We can draw or play in the doll's house or even the sand pit?'

Chelsea frowned. 'Mummy said…'

After a moment when she didn't continue, Natalie prompted her. 'What did your mummy say?' She added: 'She may be right.'

'That I was coming so you could find out about Daddy.'

Just as Stephen had indicated. Natalie made a note to personally wring Jenna's neck. 'What do you think that meant, Chelsea?'

'Mummy thinks Daddy is mean to me. Like the war-ock in the book I had.'

War-ock? How many children's books was Natalie going to have to scour? Maybe she'd start the bean on bicycle maintenance manuals.

'I have bad dreams about witches and war-ocks.'

'Warlocks.'

Chelsea nodded.

'How about you try and draw that dream? Maybe if it's on paper it won't be in your head to be in a nightmare anymore.'

Natalie chose a large piece of white paper—and put the crayons out. Messier, less controllable. She wanted Chelsea to put feeling into the picture.

There was plenty of that. Along with the humming—was it a self-soothing technique?

'Is that "Round and Round the Garden Like a Teddy Bear"?' asked Natalie. The thought came from her nightmares not from the tune. Had she been listening properly, it was obviously not what Chelsea was humming.

Chelsea shook her head. Sang the first line of the chorus. She looked vacantly at the picture.

'"Teddy Bears' Picnic",' said Natalie. Her mother had sung it for her—or was it her Nan? Teddy bears everywhere.

Chelsea nodded, and kept drawing.

At the end of the session, when Chelsea had left with her grandparents, Natalie was left staring at a picture not of witches or bears or clowns, but of one monster. Mostly formless, but it was hard to go past the size of the monster's hands in comparison to the central body mass. And the clear phallic form in the lower half where legs should have been.

'Treat this as a new notification, Winona.' Natalie was on the phone to Protective Services as soon as they had left.

'What's happened?'

'I've just seen Chelsea. I can't tell whether it happened recently or where or by whom. But I have clear evidence she is being abused.'

Natalie outlined what Chelsea had drawn.

'Jesus Christ. Told you he was a slimebag. We'll get an emergency court session.'

'It'll be enough, won't it?'

'It's not a name or a video, but this isn't a criminal hearing. Might not convict Malik, but it'll be enough for the Children's Court to indicate risk. I wouldn't mention the tree, but both you and I know little girls don't draw monsters with penises unless they are being abused.'

'It might not be Malik,' Natalie warned. 'It's taken her this long to trust me... it could be in the past.'

'She also drew it now Malik had access back; reckon that's pretty persuasive myself.'

'You'll try to get Chelsea and Chris back to Jenna's sole care?'

'You got a better suggestion?' said Winona. 'Email a summary of what you just told me in the next ten minutes.'

It took fifteen minutes—five for the phone call to Jenna, who didn't say 'I told you so'. No need to.

In the *Herald Sun*, Mark La Brooy was getting personal.

> *Last month I shared my fear that political correctness might have led to the Children's Court delivering an eight-year-old girl back to her abuser. It gives me no satisfaction to be proven right.*

'Liar,' snorted Natalie, almost amused—until she read the next paragraph.

> *A professor of psychiatry—an expert whose assessments the Royal Commission has relied upon—was unequivocal in stating that the stepfather was a psychopath and a danger to the child. But the judge preferred the opinion of a non-specialist junior psychiatrist—Natalie King, who, incidentally, has a history of instability and poor judgment.*

The rest of it was his usual outpouring about the intellectual games of the regressive left, and Natalie barely registered it. She put down the paper feeling sick.

Mark La Brooy appeared to have a direct line to the Children's Court. Or maybe the department's high-priced lawyer. And who else?

Unstable? Natalie felt like demonstrating it. *Breathe,*

she told herself. If La Brooy had searched her name in the archives, he'd have found the story of her leg-sweeping Liam off his feet in front of the courthouse steps a year earlier. Nothing about her mental illness and treatment was in the public domain. Why didn't he just mention the steps episode, then? Was he fishing? Did he know something else?

Ken Rankin would be on the phone to Declan before his morning Weetbix. And then what? A disciplinary hearing, or did they just rescind her right to practise—guilty until proven innocent? Play it safe when the public were at risk? She needed to ring her professional indemnity insurers. Could she sue La Brooy? Demand a retraction…

Not really an option. What was particularly galling was that the right-wing arsehole was basically correct. She didn't want to be upset that he had put her name in print: she wanted to be upset for any harm she had caused Chelsea. But her livelihood was on the line. And that meant the ability to pay her mortgage… and support the bean. To say nothing of her sense of self.

Natalie threw her coffee mug at the wall and it shattered; the sound sent Bob into the air, seed kernels adding to the mess as they fluttered through the air and landed across the books and papers strewn across the floor. *Unstable*.

'You're a complete unknown!'

'Unfortunately not,' Natalie muttered.

It would take the College less than a minute to connect this article with Wadhwa's complaint about her. And if they were on Twitter? Add DrK and #PsychBitch into the mix. Brilliant.

Twitter was right onto it.

Liza R @lizar82: *If they'd believed the mother instead of #PsychBitch abuse would have stopped weeks ago #unforgiveable.*

Kids Really Matter @KidsReallyMatter: *#PsychBitch finally gets it right. Maybe she's back on her meds.*

Man Under Fire @ManUnderFire: *@KidsReallyMatter*

Meds or no meds, they don't get it right all the time. Mistakes about child abuse have disastrous consequences #PsychBitch.

Natalie stared at the last texts and her hand was trembling so much she thought she'd drop the phone. *Meds.* Was this a wild stab in the dark or did someone know she took mood stabilisers? Would anyone else see this? Her skin seemed to turn cold. If she couldn't work... if this meant the College said she wasn't fit... She wanted to weep at the unfairness of it. Doing the right thing, getting help was what was now likely to get her into trouble.

She wanted to talk to Liam about it, but she'd ignored his calls and would continue to do so until the DNA result next week.

Declan was the obvious alternative, and better placed to support her as a psychiatrist. But she wanted... She wanted not to be judged. For someone to just say life was shit and give her a hug. Her mother would do that—but quite aside from her being out of bicycle range, there was Natalie's own longstanding belligerence, which she just didn't seem to be able to get over. It was partly why she didn't want to talk to Declan either.

'You underestimate your mother, Natalie. She loves you,' he had said. 'You'll need her.'

Natalie hated needing anyone. Better to do something for someone else; keep busy, focused. At the moment it was Chelsea who was most on her mind. She rang Damian.

'How are you?'

'Brilliant,' Natalie lied. 'You know how I asked you to check out that teacher?'

There was an audible sigh down the line. 'Natalie, you know—'

'There was a teacher indicted to stand trial from the Royal Commission.'

'Yes,' said Damian cautiously.

'Could you get a list of the schools he worked at? See if he overlapped with Ted Beahre?'

'Natalie—'

'You would if it was your daughter.'

'Jesus, Natalie. There are a lot of teachers and schools.' There was a pause. 'Okay, I'll see what I can do—but only because it's public record anyway, okay?'

Not really. And no way he was going to look and see if he could find out who @KidsReallyMatter was, so no point asking. When she hung up Natalie still felt restless, so she went to get dinner at the pub.

Vince was able to do what all good publicans did—he gave her an ear, a lemon squash and a burger.

'How about I become a full-time singer and give psychiatry away?' She thought she was sounding slightly hysterical but she was pretty sure that as yet it was just stress, not pre-mania.

Vince's ruddy colour looked darker in the dim evening light that reflected off the glasses hanging above him. 'One of those jerks gonna look after you, are they?'

Natalie laughed, but heard an edge to the sound. Like she might lose control and start screaming or crying. 'I take it that's not a vote of confidence in my ability to provide with a career in rock 'n' roll.'

Vince shrugged. 'Seems to me being a doc pays pretty good. And it took you a long time to get there.'

But her angst wasn't really about being a psychiatrist anyway. Well, only in part.

'What sort of mum do you reckon I'll be, Vince?'

Vince grinned. 'Bet you gave your mum a tough time. And you both survived it, didn't you? You'll be fine. With or without the jerk.'

Natalie smiled; almost felt like she meant it. Vince was good therapy. 'Thanks Vince. You're probably right—my mum did lots of good things. I just need to get over—'

What? That she wouldn't ever find out who her father was? Or that he had abused her? Was she really so stuck on some fairy-tale ideal that she had got hooked on as a child?

'What were Adrianna and Benny like as teenagers?'

Natalie asked Vince. She knew Ben with his pink mohawk because he did security at the bar, and Vince had twisted her arm to sing at Adrianna's wedding five years earlier. Luckily, he didn't know Beverley to pass this information on.

'I don't do weddings, Vince,' she had said.

'Everyone does Italian weddings.'

As there were five hundred guests, he'd been more or less right. And despite herself, she and the band had enjoyed themselves. The wedding party had had tears rolling down their cheeks at her version of *He's a Rebel* with the three Castentella brothers playing the doo-wop role—the youngest, Nick, leading them. He didn't have a bad voice, and had been hilarious camping it up, Vince wiggling his butt and Tony, the quiet one, rolling his eyes. Nick had even managed to get Natalie on the dance floor, though even to this day she couldn't recall how he'd managed that. Dancing was not her thing, and she hadn't got close to keeping up with Nick's moves. Not that anyone seemed to mind. The groom and his attendants were all bikers and were glowing as if the song was written especially for them.

Natalie didn't think this would work at Beverley's wedding, but she couldn't think of any suitable dentist songs.

'You've seen Ben's hair,' said Vince. 'Carmel thought he was gay, cried every night till I convinced her he was two-timing her best friend's daughter. Now she's happy her son's a louse.'

'And Adrianna?'

Vince shrugged. 'She married a biker. What can I say?'

'So the moral is all kids cause havoc and parents just have to pray.'

'And drink.' Vince grinned. 'Keeps me in business.'

Not an option at the moment. Maybe this was why instead of going home—before she had thought about where she was going or why—Natalie cycled to South Yarra, and looked up at Liam's apartment. It fronted onto Toorak Road with a balcony, blinds open.

She could see Liam through the window, sitting on the sofa with James, both focused on the television. After a few minutes Megan joined them, kissing Liam's cheek before snuggling up to him.

Natalie felt her eyes moisten. Angry at herself, she got back on her bike and rode home. She stopped off at the Ducati showroom window to pick out her next motorbike. It was probably just as well they were closed and she couldn't take it there and then.

Natalie arrived at Declan's for her weekly appointment fifteen minutes early. Time for a coffee? High Street was a happening place for foodies and there were plenty of options. She propped the bike against Declan's fence and bent over to put the lock on, catching movement in the room beyond out of the corner of her eye. Declan's office. A woman in a blue dress: blonde, not his wife with her red curls. Was he finishing with a patient?

She decided she didn't need more caffeine and withdrew down the street a couple of houses, to let his patient escape unseen. From her position, the landscape fell away to the flat inner-city suburbs of Collingwood and Fitzroy, and she had a great view of the skyline of Melbourne: cranes, half-built buildings, St Patrick's spire. The sound of the tram came rumbling down the nearby street and there was really no other city in the world she could have been in.

Instead of admiring it, she used the time to check Twitter and see if there was any way she could work out the identity of the know-it-all tweeters. Especially the ones mentioning her.

@KidsReallyMatter's avatar was a cartoon picture of two small children hugging. Their profile stated they were a coffee-loving atheist who swore a lot and—in case there was any doubt—cared about kids. They seemed to tweet mainly on social issues, relatively calmly. Articulate—as far as you could tell in 140 characters… but they knew something about her,

Natalie was sure. Possible identities? Any of the staff who had looked after her. Someone at the College? And Lauren. Would she? Payback for the affair—or for still being in Liam's life?

@ManUnderFire had an avatar picture of Stewie from *Family Guy*. The handle suggested he was a bit pathetic—or at least defensive. The profile read: *Straight white male. If you hate me already, don't waste your time. Plenty of others doing that.* Maybe a guy whose wife had run off and taken his kids… but that was more @MyBitchinRules, who had his own photo—apparently—and no profile. @ManUnderFire read to her as powerless, someone who had perhaps been bullied at school and now didn't have anything better to do with his time. He had plenty of opinions about what the government should do in a string of tweets about child abuse, largely siding with those who had been wrongly accused.

@lizar82's avatar looked like it was a cover of a Mills and Boon romance. If 82 was her birth year, she and Natalie were the same age. A romantic? Quirky profile—tea-drinking dreamer who wanted to live on an island and not wear clothes. Her timeline included many retweets of outrage about asylum seeker policies, but mostly it was conversations with people she seemed to know: *sorry to hear about your sister* or *see ya next week*; the occasional *you knobhead whoever you are* to someone who had said something she disagreed with.

The minutes ticked by and no one came out of Declan's house. She frowned. Declan was a stickler for time. A patient would have left at ten minutes to the hour. Perhaps a supervisee, then?

Natalie knocked and opened the door; Declan's office was open and he was sitting waiting. No sign of the blonde.

'I thought you had a patient.'

'No, I've had the afternoon off,' Declan said. 'Enjoyed a round of golf.'

'With the woman that was here?' It really wasn't like Declan. Nor was his response. Only an instant, but she knew that look: guilt. Bloody men. She felt a sense of enormous disappointment. Idealising her supervisor was stupid but perhaps inevitable. He'd helped her survive the year of rehab, and kept her on the straight and narrow since her first bipolar episode as an intern. But that didn't mean he wasn't human.

'Have you seen Mark La Brooy's column?' she asked, slamming down a copy on his desk. 'I renotified. You were right. Chelsea did give me something I could use in court… though not with a name attached.' She paused. 'What the fuck am I going to do?'

'About Chelsea? It's in the hands of the court.' He waved the paper. 'About La Brooy? Nothing.'

'What do you mean nothing?'

'I have spoken to Ken Rankin.'

No surprise there. Natalie had never met him but she had a feeling that was about to change.

'He and I agree that weighing into this debate will make things worse. We can't control the media.'

'So we just let them say what they like?'

Declan shrugged. 'These columnists have opinions. Educated readers can sort out the real issues.'

'So, the College is just going to let me be crucified?'

Declan looked at her sternly. 'One columnist has mentioned you once.'

'I'm all over fucking Twitter.'

Declan frowned. 'We need to sit and watch, Natalie. The College is across the situation.'

'And the Medical Board?'

'There is nothing to answer for, Natalie.'

Yet.

'You haven't done anything wrong,' Declan added.

'So they don't want me to come in?'

He hesitated. 'Not at this stage.' Meaning, one more thing and she was toast.

Time to forget about personal issues. And tweets. She thrust the picture she had brought into his hands.

'Chelsea's nightmare.'

Declan nodded. 'Did she talk about it?'

'A monster,' said Natalie. 'Jenna had been wording her up that the sessions were about nailing Malik. So I didn't want to come straight out and ask her if it was him.'

Declan waited for her to go on.

Natalie couldn't sit still: she started to walk around the office. 'She said in the earlier part of the session she was sad not to be staying at her father's and was angry at me. When I asked would the monster in her nightmares come in that bedroom, she said no.'

'It might be useful to ask her to draw her family,' said Declan as he looked at the picture. He spent a few moments deep in thought. The ticking of the clock in the hall seemed to echo down the corridor as Natalie waited, counting the ticks and feeling as confused as Chelsea.

'You have to understand that at eight, Chelsea may exist in two different realities. As children develop and form their sense of who they are, they evaluate themselves and their experiences against their important role models, the people they love. For a child, the crucial other is the parent, who is seen as all-knowing, powerful and omnipotent.'

Declan let this sink in before he continued. 'What happens if that parent is also scared, and no longer powerful? Let us suppose *Jenna's* reality is that Malik is the abuser. To exist in a relationship with her mother, Chelsea must incorporate this view even if it isn't happening—or if it is and Chelsea doesn't experience it as abuse.'

'What about when Chelsea is with her father?'

'Assuming he is the abuser, the abuse isn't necessarily scary but part of what makes their relationship special— because it has yet to be evaluated and processed in the light of maturing and later relationships. But once the abuse is in the real world—named and reacted against, then Chelsea will be confused and frightened. At the moment, she is perhaps somewhere in between.'

'So if Malik isn't abusing her—say the schoolteacher is…'

'Certainly possible. But this type of abuse over time... Family are more likely. Was Jenna abused herself?'

'She says not.' Natalie thought for a moment. 'She has an avoidant style, so minimises negatives in her childhood, tendency to idealise... It's not impossible.' Natalie remembered the parents' story of the unexplained stopping of Little Athletics. Because someone had abused her there?

'That would distort Jenna's views and distort Chelsea's world even more.'

Natalie tried to put herself in Chelsea's shoes. 'So if Malik wasn't guilty—let's say his brother is, if we're keeping it in the family—she can't tell her mother because Jenna has so strongly convinced herself Malik is responsible? And confused Chelsea with this?'

Natalie thought of all the adults she had worked with who had delayed for years telling their parents what had happened. Chelsea was only eight. She didn't understand what was being done to her—and couldn't talk about it because it would fracture the already unstable world she lived in. And Jenna, unintentionally, might be making it even more unstable if her belief that Malik was the abuser was not true.

If Malik *was* responsible... then, in time, Chelsea could be helped to adopt a view of him that was her own, but likely to be compatible with Jenna's.

But if not? Then it meant Chelsea's monster was still out there with access to her. And no one to help her.

Natalie sat in the waiting room wishing herself anywhere else on the planet but here. At least the only other patient sitting on one of the mismatched antique chairs didn't have a baby, but she looked a good deal further along than Natalie.

Natalie ignored her, not wanting to do pregnancy talk any more than she wanted to do baby talk. Something happened to women when they had babies that made Natalie want to run and hide. Would it happen to her without her noticing? Or would she flee at the first sight of this alien within her?

Her mother, for all their problems, had always been there. It wasn't like Natalie had a maternal role model of escape, and not like she had ever run away from anything before. Why was she feeling such a desperate need to escape now? Nerves. Lack of support. She could imagine Declan saying to her *you don't have to do this alone*. But alone she was. Her choice.

Liam had left text and voice messages—she hadn't answered any of them. When she had proof—when they both knew—who the baby's father was, then they could discuss options. The current uncertainty—more in his mind than hers—made their relationship too complicated. As if it wasn't complicated enough already.

All three of them had taken the test, and the magic of modern genetic analysis had been performed. Some of the bean's cells were in her blood. For two thousand dollars—extra because she wanted both men tested, so there would be no doubt in either man's mind—they had extracted the component that was alien to her, running around in her blood, and compared the genetic profile to the DNA in Liam's and Damian's blood sample.

She could ask if it was a girl or a boy; decided not to. Declan undoubtedly would say she was defending against the reality. The test couldn't tell her the other thing she wanted to know. *Will my baby have bipolar?* It didn't matter, not really. It was just that life was tough enough without an extra burden. She figured that she'd just have to work on best evidence: the bean would have a risk, but if she kept its early childhood 'good enough' then there was a chance that the genes, even if they were present, would not play out.

Now she was about to find out the result to the question that *could* be answered, without either Liam or Damian with her.

Would Liam want the child once she had confirmation that it was his? Would he fall in love with it at birth? Would he want to be there with her, or had he already moved on, decided it was too much trouble managing everyone's needs, her, his ex, their children—at the same time?

And if (however unlikely) it was Damian's? Living together for the kid wasn't her style; friends with benefits wasn't his. Natalie winced at the idea of weekend handovers, but figured they'd work it out without the need for the Family Court. Maybe he'd sleep on the couch and help out with the night feeds that Declan was so worried would tip her bipolar over the edge. They might well—night shifts had, back when she was an intern.

Alex Lascelles called her in. Today he was wearing a velvet jacket with gold brocade. Natalie had to resist the temptation to rub her hands over it as she walked past. He performed a quick check-up then handed her the paperwork from the lab. She thanked him and left.

Natalie was still taking in the results as she made her way out of the private clinic wing through the crowds in the main hospital foyer.

If she had noticed Liam's ex-wife earlier she would have taken a different route.

Lauren intercepted her outside the florist's. She was dressed, as always, in an impeccable suit, this one probably made for her in Italy, or in Paris en route to some WHO meeting or medical conference. Natalie looked up from the paperwork and, as she saw Lauren, had to step around a shop assistant to avoid her. Some ten centimetres shorter than Lauren, Natalie instinctively stepped another foot further away—into the floral display around some Spring Racing Carnival cut-outs—and squared her shoulders.

Lauren must have seen something aggressive in the stance. 'Oh, please,' she said. 'Just try. It would make my day.'

With hospital staff to witness? Natalie could just imagine trying to explain it Declan. After the day she'd been having, Natalie felt more like diving in front of a tram herself than pushing Lauren under one—even if she was tweeting as @KidsReallyMatter.

'I don't think we have anything to say to each other.' Natalie was jammed between the promotional cut-out and Lauren; she wondered if she could move the display so she could walk away.

'You think not?' Lauren's eyes glinted. 'You had the nerve to give advice to *my* son.'

Shit. What had James told her?

'Lauren, grow up. This is about you and Liam, not me or your children.'

Lauren's self-satisfied expression sent a shiver through her. Natalie could only hope it didn't show.

'Actually, it's about who *my* children spend time with.'

Meaning not some nutter? Natalie felt the old mix of rage and shame well inside her, the feelings that led her to deny she had bipolar, that made her fear her own evaluations of herself. When she was depressed it led her to think she wasn't as good as everyone else, that she'd be better off dead. Maybe Lauren just meant she was a home-wrecker; Natalie felt guilty about that too, but it didn't bite as deep—neither Lauren nor Liam were blameless in that matter.

Natalie wasn't unwell now. She didn't want to see Lauren on her butt—at least not if Natalie had to put her there. She wanted Lauren to see reason. To let Liam and her live their own life—and not to harm James and Megan in the process.

Nothing she said was likely to be heard. Didn't mean she wouldn't try.

'Your issue is with Liam. You chose him and then you chose to leave him. Decide which it is you are grieving and get on with it.'

Natalie was edging away when Lauren grabbed her arm. It took some self-control not to attempt a kick-boxing manoeuvre but as it happened, because she kept moving, the result was the same. Lauren hadn't seen the shop assistant kneeling on the floor mopping up a spill. When she sidestepped into the water she slipped and ended up crashing onto the table, buckets of water and flowers descending with her, followed by smiling pictures of race-goers in fascinators. The lavender roses that landed in her lap were a nice final touch.

Malik was pacing the waiting room when Natalie got to her office.

'He's been here an hour,' Beverley told her, covering the phone mouthpiece. 'And he was crying.' Hand removed. 'No, not fruitcake. We want the French wedding cake, the one...'

Natalie went to deal with Malik.

'I've only got ten minutes, Malik.'

'Please.' His eyes were indeed full of tears; his puppy-dog look would have melted women harder than Natalie. Or maybe it was her hormones.

'They won't let me see either of them,' said Malik. 'The workers say they will get an intervention order out if I go within a kilometre of the house—*my* house, Doctor King! My own house, my children. Jenna won't even let me speak to them on the phone; she is turning them against me, they will hate me.'

Natalie crossed her arms. 'Malik, this isn't about you.'

At her tone, Malik slumped into the chair. Maybe they didn't have to worry about Egyptian mothers—Ama probably pulled him into line in exactly this manner.

'Chelsea is being abused, do you understand?'

Malik nodded slowly. 'This is what they tell me. So I have come to ask. Are you sure, I mean, really sure? Could Jenna not have told her to say things? Bribed her?'

'No, Malik. I'm not saying she hasn't done that too, but this is stuff that can't be made up.'

210

Malik's head dropped into his hands. A minute passed before he spoke; Natalie had to strain to hear him as he hadn't moved.

'Do you know, when Chris was born I saw him only on Skype? Do you know how that is, to see someone so small, so in need of your protection but you cannot be there? Cannot touch your own flesh and blood?' Malik slowly raised his head and looked at Natalie. 'When I was allowed to return he had already grown, but he looked at me and I never wanted him to stop looking. I am his father.'

'You're still his father,' said Natalie. 'But both children must be protected until it is clear what the risk to them is.'

'How is Chelsea?' Malik's eye twitched. 'After Chris was born, I saw Chelsea differently. She was four, but it was as if I am looking and seeing her for the first time as well. Still a child, not so much bigger than Chris. Does having a child make you hear differently? She was always very... able to speak for herself. She got more demanding, but I didn't find it annoying, I saw that she was really asking for... reassurance. Now, Doctor King, who is there to give it to her? Not Jenna, who is about her new job, or Jenna's mother, who is about her next drink.'

Another minute passed.

'Do you know,' Malik said, voice now firmer, 'what it is like to look at the beds they are meant to be sleeping in? The edginess I couldn't explain when I had Chris and had to hand him back, it was because the emptiness that was about to follow would last another week. Now they say it will be forever. Always, I will be empty inside.'

Natalie watched him, trying not to react. This wasn't acting—this was real and raw. But it didn't mean he wasn't an abuser. It had all been about *him*.

'I read,' Malik continued, 'about abuse. This Royal Commission, how the lawyers are made ill hearing these stories, that they have nightmares. And do you know what I think?'

Natalie shook her head.

'I think, that if you are right, this is what my little Chelse will be living. A nightmare grown men and women cannot bear.' He leaned in closer to her.

Natalie looked at him hard. Was this the psychopath lying because he knew what she needed to hear to believe him? She saw pain in his eyes and could not convince herself that he didn't truly feel for Chelsea—which meant she couldn't convince herself he'd abuse her.

'And then I think,' said Malik, with absolute conviction, 'that when I find who has done this, I will kill him.'

Natalie arranged to meet Liam at *his* choice of cocktail bar, rather than her local. The Everleigh was upstairs, on the grungy-hip Gertrude Street in Fitzroy, through a discreet doorway and up a staircase that led into a New York-style bar. Liam was sitting in one of the booths with a martini — and a lime soda for her.

'How are James and Megan?'

'Getting by.' Liam was looking at her, trying to guess the answer.

'And Lauren?' She hoped he didn't pick the tightness in her voice. Wondered what Lauren had told him about the flower-shop fiasco.

'Still wishing she'd had two girls and that I hadn't been the father of either of them.'

'Well they're the only children you'll be having in the immediate future.'

Why was it that she could break things gently to patients but in her personal life she almost relished the impact of the unadorned truth? Declan would believe it was to protect herself against rejection. On this occasion, he'd have been right.

Liam took a breath, then a sip of his drink. 'So, what are your plans?' He didn't appear to be — anything. Not angry, not disappointed, not surprised. And, thank Christ, not concerned for her either. Or if he was, smart enough not to show it.

'I guess I'll start negotiating the first-week sleepover.

For the bean. Damian made it clear he would be pursuing parental rights.'

There was a long silence; they had both withdrawn so she had no hope of reading his thoughts, but he surprised her nevertheless.

'Seems like I was right. He knew something we didn't.'

Did he? A million to one… it happened, she supposed.

'Your relationship with McBride. Any chance you'd like to have one?'

Any chance? She thought guiltily of Damian squeezing her hand over ice-creams. He would never trust her; didn't get her like Liam did. And it wasn't what she wanted. Did that matter? Wouldn't it be better for the bean if she took the picket fence with Damian? It was probably the best option for her own mental health. Her mother had apparently come around to taking the safe option and was still happily married nearly thirty years later. It would be better for Liam and his children too. *This isn't just about you.*

'It's not where I see it heading at the moment.'

Liam nodded, drained his drink. 'Okay, then. So, no change.'

'What do you mean?' Natalie wondered if the stress was dulling her mind. 'You made it very clear your support was DNA-dependant. Yours didn't come up.'

Liam hesitated. 'No, Natalie. I never said that. I said I would fulfil my obligations to the child were it mine — by which I meant financial, and in the role of father. A role not without its challenges as you know from recent times, but' — he looked briefly a little sad, or at least reflective — 'the most important thing I ever took on.' He took a breath. 'My offer to support you, see where our relationship went, was separate from the pregnancy and the identity of the father.'

It took a full twenty seconds before Natalie could find the words to respond. 'You'd consider a relationship with someone who was pregnant to another man?'

'I've done the considering.' He looked directly at her. 'I wanted it to be very clear that no child is a bargaining chip —

not in my life. I didn't think that was what you were doing when you said you thought I was the father, but given it was only one time—well, I wasn't sure, okay? Seems I was right. Since we've been seeing each other, I believe you really did think the baby was mine. Just like I believe you wouldn't have told Lauren about our affair. So again: let me be very clear. I said I was prepared to see where our relationship went, and I still am.'

Natalie didn't trust herself to speak.

Liam brushed her hair off her cheek and kissed her forehead. 'Think about it, okay? I want you to do what's right for you. For your kid. God knows, being with me isn't going to be easy.'

'You got the result?'

Declan must have a sixth sense.

'Yes. It…' She didn't want to talk about it, yet knew she needed to. 'The bean's…. Damian's.'

'I gather that isn't what you were hoping for.'

'It doesn't matter. I'm not taking charity from either of them.'

'Either?'

Natalie rubbed her temple. 'I don't understand where he's coming from. Liam's said he's happy to have a relationship, even though he isn't the kid's father; Damian has said he wants a relationship, but only if he is attached by DNA. But as everyone keeps telling me, this isn't just about me. What's best for the bean? What am I meant to do?'

'*Meant* to do, Natalie? You know better than that.'

'I don't, that's the trouble.' The tremor in her voice frightened her. She took a breath, stared hard at Declan.

'You know enough about good relationships,' he said.

'Then neither,' Natalie said dully. 'Neither of them trusts me. Can't say I blame them.'

'Trust can be earnt.' Declan was using the fatherly tone he'd perfected; Natalie wondered what his kids thought of him as a dad. 'But you first have to trust yourself. The relationship can only be right for the other person if it's right for you as well.'

Jenna and Malik flashed through her mind. Chelsea and Chris's neediness. Her mother and Craig. Need versus want. How much it was possible to compromise between the two—and what happened to the child in the middle?

'I'm still angry at my mother for not telling me who my father is.'

Declan leaned in, so she could see his face clearly; kind eyes that revealed their concern about her. 'Natalie, when you are managing several things, you need to decide which is the least important, or the one that can be put on hold—and let it go. You think your father's identity is relevant now?'

'Yes. It… it's getting in the way. Me as a mother, me settling down… it's like I can't find myself until I know.'

Truth was, she felt paralysed in making decisions about Damian and Liam, and the feeling was eerily similar to that paralysis she felt when she woke from her nightmares.

Declan looked like he was wrestling with something. 'Have you tried to think about it from your mother's point of view? Why she made that decision?'

'No,' Natalie lied. She didn't feel like defending her mother, even if intellectually her mother taking the safe option—Craig—made sense. She added, trying to bring the reality into focus, 'It's not like it matters. My father wasn't around. He's probably dead anyway.'

Declan's eye twitched.

Natalie stopped short. 'You know.'

Declan didn't say anything. Had her mother told him something, all those years ago when Declan had first taken her into therapy at sixteen?

'Did he abuse me? Did he have bipolar?' Natalie added, thinking how much that mattered to her, despite never knowing him, despite everything. 'They had a lot to deal with. Craig came to the rescue, we all lived happily ever after. I get it.'

'As a child, being rescued by your real father was a fantasy, Natalie. Your mother had some practicalities to consider as well as what she—and you—wanted.'

Natalie shrugged, irritated that he was redirecting her. 'I know—and Craig did a good job.' Yet she had held on to the belief that men were unreliable all the same. Trust. Declan said trust in herself had to come before it could happen in a relationship. But she was running out of time. Liam wasn't going to wait forever. 'I know my mother won't tell me,' she said finally. 'I'm guessing he had bipolar genes, he was apparently vertically challenged if my height is anything to go by; I'm my father's daughter.'

'And your mother's. And your stepfather's.'

'And now I know who this one's father is,' said Natalie, looking down. She was still barely showing. 'I need to work out if he's the only one that's going to be around.' Damian would be around for his child. But did she want Liam around for her? And in the mix: was it fair to him and his children?

'You have a lot on your plate, Natalie. Everything need not be decided at once.'

Natalie couldn't sleep. Lying looking at the ceiling she knew she should take more quetiapine but she needed to think. And she was afraid the nightmare would come again. She had been three years old when Craig came on the scene. So any abuse... any memories of her father...must predate that. She closed her eyes, tried to let herself slip back into the past, feel and hear the sounds of her childhood.

Zilch, zero and nothing.

Triggers? Natalie ran through normal childhood objects hoping something would take her back. A teddy bear had popped up in her dreams. She didn't know if she'd ever even had one. *Round and round the garden, like a... teddy bear.* For a second he was there, the man she had thought of as her father. She could hear him, almost feel him. And it didn't feel... bad. Did it? She thought of Declan's explanation about how Chelsea would have, at the age of eight, compartmentalised the experiences. At three—more than thirty years ago—Natalie would have done more than that. The memories would be walled off. Maybe her mother was right, that it wouldn't be good for anyone if she found the sealed compartment and opened it. Particularly now, when she had so much on her plate and the bean needed her to be strong.

But Natalie had never, ever run from anything. She threw off the bedclothes and went downstairs. The baby book had been abandoned somewhere among the journal articles. Bob stirred on his stand and looked at her curiously before announcing, 'Let him go,' and turning his back on her. She'd always thought that this particular saying of Bob's was to do with Liam but maybe it was more aptly applied to her father. And she would let him go—when she knew what she was letting go of.

She flipped through the book. There were, she knew, no unidentified males in the photos. There were photos with her and her mother and Nan. One of her sitting by a cupboard covered in chocolate. She had found the Easter egg stash and was sharing the spoils with what might have been a soft toy; it was partially obscured. The cupboards were green. These, or maybe all that chocolate, made her feel a little nauseated.

She looked at the young version of herself, a child in a world she didn't remember. Much younger than Chelsea, younger even than Chris. Had this infant told her mother something? Had her mother known intuitively, or caught her father in the act—one moment, changing all of their lives forever? Her mother marrying Mr Predictable while Natalie wasted her childhood—and beyond—looking for the father she had idealised instead of realising he was a monster?

Natalie pulled the chocolate photo out of its place and put it under the light. Among the half-unwrapped Easter eggs was a small brown soft toy. She was staring at the teddy bear with its one eye as her own baby, eighteen weeks into its gestation, gave its first definite kick. All she could think of was how fearful she was for both it and herself. She had no idea if that was about emotions from the past invading her current thoughts, or the uncertain future she was facing.

There was no problem filling in time when she couldn't sleep. Twitter never died, nor the people on it, despite the encouragement of others. The Mark La Brooy fan club were tweeting about immigration (largely against) and hours earlier @KidsReallyMatter had been on an extended rant about her ex, thinly disguised as commentary on child support policy.

Kids Really Matter @KidsReallyMatter: *Easy to hide income if you know how.*

Liza R @lizar82: *@KidsReallyMatter Then they have kids for weekend and spend big. Heroes while we're struggling.*

My Bitchin Rules @MyBitchinRules: *@KidsReallyMatter @lizar82 You're hanging with the wrong guys, ladies.*

Liza R @lizar82: *@MyBitchinRules F*K OFF.*

Kids Really Matter @kidsreallymatter: *@lizar82 Blocked.*

In her head, Natalie wrote #GETALIFE. She was about to turn her phone off when another tweet popped up.

Kids Really Matter @KidsReallyMatter: *So over work.* Lauren, after finishing a report in the early hours? A nurse, home after a late shift?

Man Under Fire @ManUnderFire: *Tell me about it. No support, pay is shit.*

Someone else couldn't sleep.

Liza R @lizar82: *Don't talk to me about no support.*

Kids Really Matter @KidsReallyMatter: *@lizar82 #PsychBitch still giving you grief?*

What? Natalie felt her heart start pumping. Her fingers hovered over the icon with the feathered pen, itching to tap out a response. She hadn't yet. Her profile still said zero tweets. But she just couldn't let this go.

Liza R @lizar82: *@KidsReallyMatter not about to trust anyone to help.*

Kids Really Matter @KidsReallyMatter: *@lizar82 particularly if her brain's fried.*

Brain fried: surely that meant the electroconvulsive therapy that had brought her out of her deep depression eight months ago. Natalie was typing before she thought. The rage that went through her was so strong she thought that the phone might break under the pressure of her fingers.

U will b FUCKING DISBARRED U'LL NEVER WORK AGAIN U BITCH HOW CAN U WORK AS A HEALTH PROFESSIONAL U HAVE NO ETHICS?

Then she did break the phone—hurled across the room and heard the crack as it hit the wall.

Breathe, she heard Declan tell her. A quetiapine. A hot chocolate. Anything. She'd ring the clinic tomorrow. Make sure they found out who it was. And then she really would make sure they never worked again. And if it was Lauren? She'd have a one-to-one chat. No holds barred. There would be more than flowers cascading down on the other woman.

The receptionist at the clinic where she had been treated was reluctant to put her through to the general manager until Natalie pulled the doctor card—and the possibility of a reporting to the Health Complaints Commissioner. He called her back within minutes.

Natalie had met Gavin Boreman but remembered little of him other than a moustache that belonged in a seventies porno. Now he listened to her rant—which included her assurance that his clinic wasn't going to fucking get away with this just because they were private, as well as her promise to hold him accountable even if she had to chop off his balls and fry them for breakfast—without comment.

'Well?' she asked finally. 'What are you going to do about it?'

'Doctor King, I doubt very much there is anything I can do about anything on social media. I have to believe my staff would not divulge anything confidential. I'll send a memo around but I'm afraid that's all I can do.'

He was probably right, but it didn't make her feel any better. She hung up while he was still talking. Put her head in her hands.

The powerlessness meant the rage had nowhere to go. Just made her restless and tense and feel like she wanted to punch something. All she wanted was a normal life… for just a little while. For the bean. And… for herself. She had to know she was going to be okay. Her child, relationship, job. It was why she had been taking her pills like such a good girl. And would keep doing so.

She silently prayed to a god she didn't believe in: *Let it be enough*. And then went back to work.

'I can't get Chelsea out of the car.' Jenna was standing in the waiting room, wearing a T-shirt with a picture of Pink on it and the red corduroy trousers.

The previous appointment had been cancelled. 'No one to bring her,' a man, presumably Stephen Radford, had told Beverley. Natalie had had to chase Jenna to reschedule.

'What's the point?' Jenna had been irritable. 'I agree with my parents—you found out enough for the court now.'

And Jenna had got what she wanted.

'It's not just about having someone to blame, Jenna,' said Natalie. 'This is about helping Chelsea deal with it.'

This was what appeared to clinch it—Chelsea obviously wasn't coping.

'She's getting as impossible as Chris!' Jenna looked slightly embarrassed as she said it. Or maybe it was just the awkwardness, given the last time they had spoken, Jenna had hung up on Natalie.

Natalie already knew that Jenna struggled to take charge, that in the face of opposition from her children she preferred to take the easy option rather than risk their anger. She wondered fleetingly how Jenna had stood up to Malik... the thought that followed was lost before she could grasp it, though she sensed it was an important one. *Concentrate*. She focused on Chelsea not getting out of the car. It may have been as much about her trust issues with Natalie as it was about her relationship with her mother.

'How has she been?' Natalie asked.

Jenna hesitated. 'Okay.'

'Really okay?'

'No... but at least she's not having to see Malik.' Jenna paused. 'Thank you.'

'I'm sorry it took so long to get something concrete. There's a lot she's pretty confused about.'

'Chelsea knows her own mind, I assure you.' There was an edge of resentment. Natalie recognised it as Jenna's moment of regression to when her own feelings hadn't been acknowledged; having met Mickie, it made sense. But it was Jenna who had to take the initiative with Chelsea, and help her to recover and make sense of what had happened to her.

'How do you think she's feeling, Jenna?'

'Pissed off at me.'

'Because?'

'Well, she didn't want to come here for one thing.'

'So why did you bring her?'

'Because you...' she stopped herself. 'Because I want her to have any help she can get.'

'Help to what?'

'To manage... to not be scarred by all this.'

'Because you feel guilty?'

'I haven't done anything. I'm the one protecting her.'

'But you exposed... you didn't save her from it happening.' Natalie touched her lightly on the arm. 'Jenna, I'm not blaming you. You've done all you could. But guilt isn't about logic. It's

223

about the fact that you want the best for your child, want them never to hurt and never to have anything go wrong, and life isn't like that.'

'I do feel kind of bad.'

'And when Chelsea gets angry it makes you feel worse, right?'

Jenna nodded.

'But under the anger, what do you think she's feeling?'

Jenna paused. Finally she said, 'Scared.'

'And if you don't stick with her and give her the message that you can cope with her anger, how do you think that will make her feel?'

'Even more scared.'

Natalie nodded. 'Now with that in mind, let's go get her out of the car, shall we?'

Jenna looked ambivalent.

'Pretend,' said Natalie. 'Pretend you're... I don't know, Kim Kardashian. No one can say no to you. Firm... but kind.'

'Yeah?' The Kardashians probably didn't do 'kind'.

'Maybe not quite as much nude-selfie.'

Jenna didn't seem to find this amusing. Natalie let her go ahead, and she opened the car door. 'Come on, Chelsea. Doctor King's here.'

Chelsea looked at her mother, sulkily.

'Come on, Chelsea. Please.'

'No one can say no to you,' said Natalie softly.

Jenna took a breath. 'Delaying just means we'll get home later.'

Chelsea flashed her mother a look. More thirteen than eight.

Jenna straightened her shoulders, crossed her arms. Chelsea looked at Natalie and whether it was her mother's change of tone or being outnumbered, she wriggled out of the car and ran ahead. Natalie gave Jenna the thumbs-up, and went after her.

'Can we play in the sand?' Chelsea—the eight-year-old version—asked, sitting in front of the table and trying to work out how to take the lid off. There was a new air of bravado about her—as Natalie eased the cover from its protective position she hoped this didn't translate to her turning the room into Desert Storm like her brother had.

Chelsea went over to the shelves, looking at the Disney characters.

'Why don't you have a family play down at the beach?' suggested Natalie.

Chelsea wandered to another shelf. 'Have you seen *Finding Dory*?'

Natalie felt like punching her fist in the air. No, but at least she knew what it was. 'Nemo and his dad help find Dory's parents, right?'

'Yeah.' Chelsea put a fish which could have been Nemo on the sand. 'Nemo's dad already found him, even though he went down drains and ended at the dentist.'

The relevance of the topic was obvious. Dory had to find both parents though—Chelsea had her mother.

Chelsea found a mermaid and put it next to the fish, then added a starfish. Her, Chris and her mother?

'Anyone else in the family?' Natalie asked.

'They're having a holiday by themselves.'

'Are they going to go swimming?'

'No. They're going to sit in the sun.'

'And what's going to happen?'

'The mermaid is going to get sunburnt and have to go to hospital.'

Natalie wished she had Declan watching. What the hell did that mean? And was this beach in Egypt? 'Maybe...' Natalie got up and found what she was looking for. 'The mother found an umbrella just in time and put the children in the shade.' She put the umbrella down next to the mermaid and Chelsea moved the fish near it. She frowned. 'It's going to get hot so she's going to swim after all.' The mermaid was moved out of the sand onto the glass top. Chelsea looked up to the shelf and selected another figure and put it down nearby.

A shark.

'So, what's going to happen now?' Natalie asked, careful not to react.

Chelsea seemed frozen.

'Perhaps someone can save the mermaid?' said Natalie softly, mindful that a starfish, if that was meant to be Jenna, was a bit under-resourced for the task. Natalie selected a whale and put it between the shark and the mermaid. 'How about this?'

Chelsea shook her head, but then her expression cleared and she smiled. She went to the doll's house where Aladdin was still in residence. 'He's going to call a genie and save her.'

Natalie smiled. Then she looked back at the doll's house. *Of course.* She and Declan had misinterpreted the scene. Aladdin—Malik—was not trying to get into Princess Jasmine's bedroom. He was guarding it to stop *anyone else* getting in. Was that reality, or was Chelsea separating the good and bad versions of her father into two people?

It was the end of the day before Winona rang her back.

'You need to look for someone other than Malik,' said Natalie.

'What?'

'I think there's a real possibility she's being abused by someone other than Malik. Her behaviour's getting worse, for one thing.'

'So, what do you expect us to do? We've assessed her home environment as safe.'

'What about her teachers?'

'I'm not an investigator. Do you know how many cases I have on my books at the moment?'

It wasn't really the point. If her suspicions were right, Protective Services was failing Chelsea. As were her family —and so was Natalie.

'You really want to do these songs?' asked Shaun, surveying her list. He pushed his straw hat to the back of his head and looked up at her.

'Sure do.' Being pregnant was not going to get in her way. Well, it would eventually—Tom had suggested that she needed to think about Gil's partner Cassie taking over some time soon, at least until after the bean made an appearance.

Shaun caught a look from Tom and shrugged. 'You're the boss.'

Not really—Shaun carried at least as much weight as she did, but he was humouring her.

They were all her favourites for when she wasn't getting enough sex. Usually one or two on a given night was enough. But on this list, among 'Because the Night', 'Fucking Perfect' and 'When Doves Cry' there were some of their own, even more pointedly sexual, songs. Natalie wanted to enjoy herself and not worry about whether Damian was going to turn up. Worry about nappies, prams and the whole shebang—that would happen soon enough.

She threw herself into the songs, felt alive and electric and the audience went with her energy. The dance floor was crowded from the second song and continued when Shaun duetted with her on some hard rock tunes. She wasn't showing—not really. She hadn't been able to get into her leather trousers or skirt but the military style black and red jacket that covered her butt also covered the bump.

They'd done a couple of encores after the last bracket when Natalie decided what her final song would be.

'Time for a quiet one, do you think?'

Shaun looked surprised. The whole band were sweating under the lights and Tom had been muttering he was getting too old for this, but until this moment Natalie hadn't shown the slightest hint she was flagging. She told him what she wanted to sing and he looked even more stunned. 'You want me to do the duet?'

'Sure,' she said. It would make it easier.

Shaun shrugged. The place went quiet and she didn't think that there was a single sound in the entirety of the pub as she sang, accompanied only by Shaun, her own version of Christina Aguilera's 'Just a Fool'. She was already well into it when she wondered why it had popped into her head. Wasn't sure it had been a good choice in the circumstances—more applicable to Liam. This was not about her regret around her relationship with Damian. And the hurt, and what she was missing? All Liam.

She took her time about coming back to the bar, wanted to be sure she was in control; this was too important to fuck up. Benny was watching Damian as she joined him.

Damian raised his eyebrow, but didn't say anything.

Natalie poured herself more water.

'What was that about?' Damian finally asked.

Natalie leaned forward. 'Look, I don't want you to get the wrong idea.'

'What? That you care or something? Unlikely.'

Natalie felt the sting of his words, but didn't doubt that she deserved them. 'It's yours.'

There was a silence that seemed to extend across the room, but the rest of the room didn't matter anymore.

'The DNA test?'

'Yes.' She handed him the paperwork and he opened it slowly, staring in disbelief.

'You still want to be a dad?'

'Looks like I'm going to be.'

'Yeah, well being a father is a bit more than a sperm donation.'

'I want to be there.' Jesus, the man had tears in his eyes.

Natalie tried to imagine the discussions about schools, parenting practices, holiday arrangements. Maybe they could do it by email. She gritted her teeth. They were both intelligent adults; all they needed to do was put their child first. Maybe they would agree on a lot of things anyway. Damian was a grown-up—and she was working on it. Trying to not equate mature with boring.

'I haven't really thought about the details,' said Natalie.

'We could make it work.'

Natalie looked at him. *He's in love with you* Liam had said. *Children are better off if their parents stay together*, Damian had said. They both knew that wasn't always true. But he'd been making a point with Liam. He'd been waiting for the result.

'You're assuming it's over with Liam.'

Damian flinched. 'O'Shea. You've told him it's not his?'

'While you and I were together, Damian, I slept with Liam once. I didn't ask for it but I didn't stop him. My bad. And I didn't tell you then because… I don't know, we hadn't had the "we're exclusive" talk. And I didn't want to hurt you.' Or to lose his trust.

She took a breath. 'Would you have stuck around? If I *had* told you? Or stayed if the DNA test said it was his?'

Damian didn't need to say anything.

'Okay? So I was right.' She stood up, suddenly exhausted. 'The bean? We'll cope. And for its sake, I'll do everything I can to make sure you're the best dad the kid can have.'

Just a fool? That pretty much summed her up.

When she got home, James O'Shea was on her doorstep.

Natalie stared at him, wondering what on earth he was doing there. In the next instant, she thought that, regardless

229

of why, it must have taken a good deal of courage. Maybe he was coming to tell her to leave his dad alone. Whatever, she wasn't about to give him a hard time.

'James. You must be a shit-hot navigator. This isn't the easiest place to find.'

The tension in his shoulders eased a little, but the line of his mouth was still straight, lips pursed.

'Where's my dad?'

Natalie looked at him closely. He was in jeans and a T-shirt but she doubted if this was how he normally looked when he left home. The clothes were dirty and the T-shirt—it was black so it was hard to tell, but it looked like it had blood on it. More blood in his hair; in the dim light she couldn't make out where it had come from. That needed to be looked at—and if she told him Liam wasn't there, and not likely to be any time soon, he would take off.

'Come on up.' She opened the door, figuring he was still young enough to take notice of a firm adult directive, even one from a woman he had major issues with.

He paused, then pushed past her up the stairs. Natalie took a deep breath and smiled briefly. If her mother could see her now—about to get everything she had delivered as a teenager and probably a whole heap more. Mothers. Lauren. Natalie took a quick look along the laneway; no sign of her—yet—then followed the battered James upstairs.

James looked around as though he'd landed on Mars. Compared to his house in Hawthorn, her warehouse probably was like another planet. He stopped dead at the top of the stairs when he saw her housemate.

'Bob,' she said as the bird cocked his head, taking in the new comer with interest, 'meet James O'Shea.'

'You're a star,' Bob announced, and launched himself onto the boy's shoulder.

James seemed a little shaken, which gave her a moment to take a good look at him. It was worse than she'd thought. The blood had probably come from his nose, but that wasn't the major injury. Judging from the swelling, there was a good chance he had a depressed fracture of his cheekbone.

'Shoo him off,' Natalie said mildly, walking to her freezer and grabbing a tea towel en route. 'He's quoting—misquoting—"Hurricane". Doubt you've heard of it'—she came over to him, ice packed into the cloth—'but it's quite apt.'

James looked at her angrily. She shooed Bob back to his perch and handed the icepack to the boy. 'Song about Rubin Carter. He was almost the world middleweight champion. Boxing. The pack's for your cheek.'

It took James a moment to make sense of what Natalie had said. He gingerly applied the icepack.

'I presume you've tried your father's mobile.'

'Yeah.' The boy now looked like he was either going to cry or run. He didn't appear to have thought about what he'd do if he'd found himself trapped in the Other Woman's den without his dad.

'Take a seat and I'll find him,' Natalie said. This was what James wanted, not her questioning him about what happened. They might get to that. 'And don't worry, your mother will never hear from me that you're here.' She fancied there was a slight release of breath, but that could have been wishful thinking. And it might have been hers.

Her mobile, amazingly, still worked, even though the screen beneath the crack was barely readable. Liam's mobile was ringing out. She tried his office, and his flat in South Yarra. Hovered over another number she'd put in her phone directory, just in case, and hit it.

Tania's mobile answered on the third ring.

'Sorry to bother you,' said Natalie, glad the other woman couldn't tell how much her heart was racing, pleased her voice was cool, that it even had a hint of amusement in it. 'Natalie King here. Is Liam there by any chance?'

'Natalie.' There was a pause, and she imagined Tania's hand over the speaker, while performing a frantic mime.

'Natalie.' Liam's voice this time. Sounding guilty? No

231

way to tell. It wasn't her business, at least not with respect to this phone call or this moment. 'Is there a problem?'

'Yes. Your son needs you. Now.'

Liam arrived fifteen minutes later. By the time he got there Natalie had reminded James she was a doctor and confirmed her suspicions, or at least to the extent that was possible without an X-ray. Between grunts she'd also deduced that he'd been somewhere he shouldn't have been and that alcohol was involved, though he wasn't coming across as intoxicated. Natalie left James petting Bob with one hand—the bird had raised his crest and asked, 'How do you feel?'—and grasping the icepack with the other. She went down to open the door so she could bring Liam up to speed.

'And Liam?' she said quietly, grabbing his arm.

Liam looked ready for the worst.

'You have one brave kid there. Facing me on my turf because he desperately needed his dad—took a lot of guts. He's even had the good grace to be civil. Haul him over the coals later; this is not the time.'

'Other guy look as bad?' Liam asked, giving his son's shoulder a squeeze.

'She,' James stole a look a Natalie, 'thinks I might have broken it.'

'Mate, I doubt you did it on your own, but we'd better get it seen to or your mother will think I'm negligent.'

James looked panic stricken. 'If Mum finds out...'

If his mother found out where he was it'd be Natalie on her arse among the flowers next time.

'I have a great network of surgeons,' Natalie interjected.

She told Liam where to take James, then pulled out her phone.

With Liam and James gone, the warehouse seemed cold and empty. Maybe it was the rage, the ruminations about Twitter, the 'brain's fried' comment that accentuated her loneliness, the sense that she'd been abandoned.

I don't need anyone, she told herself, then texted Declan. His response was immediate: *Breakfast?*

The pot of coffee was ready again, along with a plate of croissants, newspapers put aside. Declan looked worried. Was it how she looked? Her hair had kind of gone wild. There had been more important things to worry about than the hairdresser. He listened as he drank his coffee and pulled the croissant into tiny pieces.

The tweets, the breach of confidentiality, the outrage she felt. The powerlessness. Gavin Boreman and his fucking bureaucratic bullshit.

'Do you know who these Twitter people are?'

'No.'

'Realistically, can you find out?'

'The police could.'

'Will they, on the basis of this?'

She could ask Damian. Didn't like her chances. 'No.'

'Then let it go, Natalie.' Declan's tone was firm. She thought of his advice, about choosing what was important and what was not.

'This is my reputation, Declan. Ken Rankin and the Medical Board…'

'No.' Declan shook his head. 'Even if this is a smear campaign, we'll deal with it.'

Natalie felt her stomach drop, thought of the tweet she had sent.

'But you need to understand… you can't afford to… look I don't profess to understand Twitter. But I understand its potential. And you don't need it, Natalie.'

'I know.' She did know. It was just hard not to respond. Hard to let the unfairness, the one-sided bile, go unchallenged.

'Natalie, you're doing well. But we need to think about... maybe you'd be better back on lithium.'

No, she wanted to scream.

But the bean had all its bits now—the heart risk no longer existed. The risks at delivery were... manageable. She swallowed. 'Not yet.' She saw Declan's expression. 'I will if I need to, okay? But I'll... stop looking at Twitter.' And get her priorities straight.

Liam turned up again the following evening. Natalie didn't have the energy to tell him to piss off. 'Is James okay?' Natalie pulled the long white wrap her mother had given her tightly around herself.

'Out of surgery and doing fine.' Liam looked as if it had been him that was attacked. 'Thanks for the help. Your friend was brilliant with him.'

Natalie waited, resisting the urge to stroke his cheek, grab his hand and pull him into bed with her.

'About Tania. We were working. I'd left my phone in the car.'

Natalie shrugged. 'Whatever.'

She wondered what his sadness was about. James and his current circumstances? Lauren and his fucked marriage? Her and their fucked relationship? Tania and whatever the fuck she'd interrupted? She didn't trust her judgment on many of these options, but his kids? There, she was one hundred per cent sure. He loved them. And flawed as Liam was, he did his best as a father.

'James is a really good kid,' said Liam. 'I don't mean he isn't messing up at the moment, but I think this might really have scared him. He and some mates were in a park drinking and a couple of older guys got stuck into them.'

There was a long silence before she spoke. She didn't want it to sound like she was being a bitch, but from James's point of view it was the big question.

'Why didn't he go to Lauren?'

Liam rubbed his temples. 'Lauren's angry. At me. At men. In general. Right now James seems to be included.'

'I suggest you both need to pretend I was never the go-between here.'

'No,' said Liam, sounding firmer than he had for some time. She closed her eyes. 'This is about what's best for the kids,' he said. 'Lauren and I need to try to act like adults and keep our stuff out of it. Though I can't say I know how to manage her side of that interaction, only my own.'

'When she wants child care, surely she'll want you onboard?' asked Natalie.

'Lauren is brilliant at outsourcing the practical needs. She has her mother if all else fails, but she'll probably resort to a mix of latchkey parenting and sending me bills for nannies. At one stage when the kids were young, she had two nannies doing alternating shifts.'

'Because you didn't pull your weight?' She didn't look at him.

'No, because I did my share hoping she'd meet me halfway. It was pretty hard for her to do that when she was at overseas conferences and meetings. I only ever missed one play Megan was in; she was a tree and I had a murder trial. Lauren missed plays, speech nights, virtually every sports match.'

If Lauren had accepted Liam outsourcing the sex the way she had of her mothering duties, they'd still have been together. They'd been attracted as intellectual equals but led parallel lives. It wasn't the sort of relationship Natalie wanted. Would she and Liam be capable of something more? At least they had an interest in each other's work. As well as the sex.

She heard him stand up as he spoke and closed her eyes again, didn't want to look at him, figured he'd read her stillness for what it was, how she had learnt as a child, to protect herself from her father abandoning her, her mother being emotionally unavailable while dealing with all the shit life generated. No Irish accent was going to overcome a basic survival skill.

He didn't touch her. Just stood so close she could feel his breath, so close she could smell the smell that she would always know as his, earthy and male, sexy and thick with just the right pheromones because all it made her want to do was drag him to bed.

Liam waited for her to open her eyes and look at him. Then he spoke. Not with the heavy Irish accent he used when he wanted to seduce her and get over her defences—just the natural light tones that only hinted at his origins.

'Three things. One, up front. Yes, I slept with Tania. Once. After Lauren and I broke up and before you and I started seeing each other again. Not last night. And incidentally, she was the only woman I saw in that time. It was a mistake. Though unfortunately Tania didn't entirely agree.

'Two. You weren't responsible for breaking up my marriage. I was. And so was Lauren. I knew the risk, and honestly? I think she was glad I took it. Gave her an excuse for me to be the bad guy. She'd wanted out for a long time—hasn't wanted anything from me except keeping up appearances and looking after the children since they started school.

'And three? I… I'm not happy with what I see in the mirror when I look. I feel torn and can't ever feel I am being who I want to be because I'm pulled in opposing directions.' He ran his hand through his hair. 'Natalie, I am sorry if I am saying this wrong. This emotional chitchat isn't my thing. But I'm forty-three years old and crazy about someone who, quite frankly, everyone has told me is totally wrong for me. I don't know how to juggle that, your thing with McBride and my kids, but I'm trying. I want to be there for you, I want there to be an "us"… but I don't want to get in the way if you want something else.'

He looked at her and in his gaze she saw all the longing that had been there since the first time she'd slept with him.

Knew her own longing was just as strong. Doubted the wisdom in it for them both.

If she loved him, really loved him… shouldn't she put him first? He was trying to do that for her… give her an out, an option of a simpler life with Damian. This wasn't his child—and by asking Liam to stay with her, he risked losing his kids: their mother was much more likely to poison them against him if Natalie was on the scene. She should know more than anyone how much children needed their father. Then there was the issue of managing life with the bean, dealing with his kids, living arrangements, feeling… pinned down.

'I don't know, Liam. I'm not sure what's best or what I want.'

'Take your time.'

She turned away, didn't want him to see the lie, and the tears in her eyes. Her hand went to the bean, who just then gave a kick. As if to remind Natalie that, whether Liam and she acknowledged it or not, she didn't *have* that much time.

Beverley showed Natalie four wedding invitations. 'Which do you like best?'

It was easier to go with the flow than to tell her the truth, which was that she didn't like any of them.

'This one.' It had lots of roses on it and Natalie thought it was unlikely anyone under the age of eighty would go for it.

Beverley frowned. 'I don't know. A bit too, well, flowery…'

The phone pulled Beverley back to what she was being paid for. 'It's for you.'

It was Gaylene Ambrose, Chelsea's class teacher.

'Is something wrong?'

'I'm not sure. I was after some advice. About how to handle an episode… Well, how to handle Chelsea really.'

The child who had always been good. Had her oppositional behaviour escalated?

'I could drop by after school.'

'Could you? I'll be in the classroom.'

Natalie was at the school shortly after 4 p.m. Gaylene looked up when she heard the door and smiled.

'Thanks for coming by. I've had one of those days where you want to have a bottle of wine or two after.'

'Involving Chelsea?'

'Among others. Do you have time to go the café?'

It was not the café Ted Beahre had taken her to; this one

was more glass-fronted displays and bakery goods. They had shut down the coffee-maker but they could do wine—a chardonnay for Gaylene. And a mineral water for Natalie.

'Look,' said Gaylene when they'd settled into the back corner with their drinks. 'I may be overreacting. And I guess after your visit I was more... well, watching out for Chelsea.'

Natalie nodded, taking a sip of her drink. She doubted it was an overreaction; Gaylene struck her as being very solid. But she might have been more observant than normal—all the better to help her understand and assist Chelsea.

'It was just so out of character,' Gaylene continued. 'But she actually attacked Matilda. Who can be annoying, but Chelsea has always been very tolerant, at least when Amy isn't around. And Amy wasn't around.'

'Can you start at the beginning?'

'They were in the playground and I was on duty. I didn't see the start. One of the boys told me Chelsea slapped Matilda. When I got there, Matilda was crying. But I heard Chelsea say she was fat and no boy would ever look at her.'

'Were those her words?'

'No.' Gaylene looked uncomfortable. 'She said no boy would ever have sex with her.'

Natalie winced. 'Did you speak to either of them afterwards and find out anything more?'

'I was pretty shocked, to be honest. I mean I'm used to kids swearing but this was... kind of clinical.' Gaylene twirled her wine glass on the tabletop. 'I took both girls to the classroom and spoke to them. Matilda didn't say anything very much then, though later when I forced Chelsea to say sorry, Matilda said she didn't want a boyfriend anyway because they were stupid.'

'And Chelsea's explanation?'

'That Matilda keeps annoying her, and that she is fat and needs to lose weight. I pointed out that that was being very unkind and normally... normally I'm sure Chelsea would have at least listened to me. But it seemed to go over the top of her head, like nothing I said mattered.'

Because at the end of the day, grown-ups were letting her down. The result was either depression—which was how Chelsea had initially looked—or getting angry and acting out. That's where they were now.

'Can I ask something off the record?' asked Natalie.

Gaylene looked at her without replying.

'Protective Services have stopped Chelsea's father's access,' said Natalie. 'But I'm not convinced she's still safe. Is there anyone you know of... anyone else that might...'

Gaylene shook her head. 'It's always Jenna or her mother who picks Chelsea up. I've never seen anyone else, apart from Malik.'

'I know you wouldn't want to implicate anyone without proof, but...' Natalie took a breath. 'Any rumours, anything about any of the male staff? Gardeners? Maintenance men?'

'You think it might be happening at school?'

'I just want to look at every possibility.'

Gaylene shook her head. 'The male teachers are never one-on-one with the kids—we aren't even allowed to touch them when they're hurt, we've all gone so PC. Chelsea occasionally goes to aftercare so I suppose there are gardeners and maintenance guys around then, but... It just couldn't happen. You have to be signed in and out.'

'You're sure?'

The hesitation was so brief it would have been easy to ignore, but Natalie was watching for it. 'I won't say where I heard it.'

Gaylene sighed. 'I really don't want to get him into trouble and I don't think there was an ounce of truth in it.'

'What?'

'Last year. Matilda's mother accused one of the teachers of facilitating her ex being able to see Matilda. And I mean even if he did, it was his wife he was reported to be violent towards, not the children.' But in her eyes Natalie saw the doubt.

'And the teacher?'

'He was investigated and found not to have done anything wrong.'

Natalie thought of the sports teacher's defensiveness.

'Ted Beahre, right?'

Gaylene nodded.

Liam rang just as Natalie reached Declan's, an hour early. The school was on the way and there hadn't been time to go home first, so—another café stop. She hovered over the call, wondered if ignoring him would give him the message she couldn't bring herself to verbalise. In the end, she weakened.

'Fucking bitch. She's refusing to let me see Megan. Says my drinking has caused James to go off the rails and she doesn't want me and my *relationships* to traumatise her too.' Liam was the one sounding traumatised.

'She's just playing games. And Megan… give her time.'

'Yeah, well Lauren's timing is impeccable. I was pulled out of the Royal Commission to deal with it. The Commissioner went ballistic and wouldn't let me back in.'

Natalie thought of Declan's advice. 'Sometimes when you have too many balls in the air you need to pick the least important and let it drop.'

'Yeah, well that isn't my daughter.'

'What does she want, Liam? Lauren I mean? She surely doesn't want you back. This is about making you suffer because she is.'

'Fine. But it shouldn't be Megan who suffers.'

No one wanted their kids to suffer—yet it was hard to avoid, whether in unhappy marriages that stayed together or unhappy ones that separated.

Right now, James needed them both if his teenage years weren't going to become a litany of truancy, drugs and police involvement. If anyone knew that, it was Natalie.

Talking to Declan would help. Just being in his office would help the stress roll off her. She pictured molecules of adrenaline and cortisol racing around her body and skipping gleefully over the placenta. Evil molecules—she put beards on the cortisol and lycra on the adrenaline and became absorbed in the fantasy, wondering which of the LGBTTQQIAAPPH2O they fitted.

When she saw the car pull out from the street opposite she recognised it. It was her mother's.

As she walked towards Declan's, she wondered if she was mistaken. Her fantasy of stress molecules was only just below the delusion level. Maybe she was going manic; her meds would be diluted with weight gain; when you factored in the sleep deprivation, she was at risk of relapse, even with the extra medication Declan had suggested she take. But it didn't feel like mania. Irritation maybe—worry about Chelsea, lack of sleep, nightmares. Surely within the bounds of normal? She hit the fence in anger, hurting her hand. She hated this, hated having to constantly challenge and question herself. Couldn't she just be... What? Not normal. Just a *bit* more stable?

Natalie stood outside Declan's house and office. She could see him faintly through the heavy lace. He was watching her. Her mother's phone number had been on his pad. The blonde woman on the golf morning. Her mother—a blonde—leaving via the road that went to his back lane just now. It was her mother who had arranged for Declan to see her back then, when she was sixteen, and she'd obviously given him background on the family then. And he'd treated Natalie in psychotherapy. Which made him an unusual supervisor—he knew a lot about her. And about Jan. Her mother refused to tell her who her father was; could it have been because she was protecting Declan rather than Natalie? Because he was married? She stared at the window, then turned, unfastened her bike, and rode home.

There was a large bunch of flowers on the doorstep.

The card said *We can make this work—for our baby's sake. Damian.*

Declan had left a message on her voicemail: *Natalie, ring me.*

Quite aside from the missed appointment, Natalie knew why Declan had called. There was a letter from the College in her mailbox. She considered not reading it. Surely Lauren wouldn't have complained?

She hadn't. But Gavin Boreman had. And they had scheduled a hearing.

Natalie took an extra quetiapine and went to sleep.

'I was wondering if you could do some drawings for me,' said Natalie.

Chelsea was back to being subdued. She'd slouched into the office without even saying hello, after another missed appointment. Jenna had claimed it wasn't her fault: she had to work and so did her father. Mickie had been unwell.

'Draw your school and your friends, maybe? And your teachers if you want.'

'I already drew me and Amy.'

'How about Matilda? Or your teachers?'

'I had a fight with Matilda.'

'What about?' Natalie sat down on the floor with her back to the window. The light caught Chelsea's curled locks and made them seem very blonde. Still a pretty child, but for a moment her expression made her look older—and pure mean girl. As quickly as it had come it disappeared. Natalie wondered if the veneer would end up dominating. Natalie had gone down the biker-girl route, maybe for much the same reason: to protect herself. Anything was better than vulnerability.

'She was horrible.'

'Matilda was?'

'Yes.'

'What did she say that was horrible?'

Chelsea shrugged. 'It doesn't matter. Mummy says her father hit her mother.'

Maybe poor Matilda, in seeking solidarity against fathers, had stirred Chelsea's desire for her father to rescue her. Exploring her relationship with Ted Beahre would have to wait.

'Families can be very confusing can't they?' said Natalie. 'Sometimes doing a drawing of them can help make some sense of the confusion.'

Chelsea seemed more enthusiastic about this. She chose an A3 size sheet and looked at it then Natalie. 'Can I draw it like I want them to be?'

'Sure.'

Chelsea drew her father first, starting with his head and then body and limbs, finishing with a full head of hair. She then drew herself next to him, holding his hand. Neither of them had a smile. Next she identified Jenna, holding her other hand, in jeans and a beret.

'Mummy got the beret in France,' Chelsea said, adding a little colour. After a moment, she added Chris on the other side of her mother. 'He's playing in the mud and got into trouble,' she said, explaining the brown colouring on his face.

'Is there anyone else in your family?'

'Nanna and Grandpa and Teta and Uncle Youssef.'

'Do you want to draw them too?'

'They won't fit. I said this is how I want the family to be.'

'Good point,' said Natalie, nodding. But did this mean there was a reason for not wanting Youssef in the picture? 'So how about your family now? Can you draw them?'

Chelsea started humming as she drew, but with little life to the sound. Was it a depressed version of 'Teddy Bears' Picnic'?

'Do you know the words to that song?' Natalie asked, remembering this was the child that didn't like the football as much as the club songs.

'Sure.' Chelsea kept drawing without looking up.

Natalie started singing the words. After a moment Chelsea joined in. Their memories of the words differed in one spot — was it a little girl or a teddy bear that had to be good to get a treat?

Later Natalie wondered if it was distracting Chelsea through the singing that caused the child to lose concentration and draw what she wasn't meant to.

Chelsea drew Jenna first, herself on one side, and then on the other what Natalie initially thought was going to be Chris. Except she did him as a stick figure. And then added Chris at her mother's feet. One figure that didn't belong, and drawn in a regressed manner.

'Who's that?'

'Luke.' Chelsea looked up at Natalie, eyes wide. In them Natalie saw the girl's recognition of her mistake. She grabbed the picture and screwed it up, threw it, and went to sit in the chair at the opposite side of the room.

Natalie felt her heart pounding. Chelsea had given away a secret and didn't want Natalie to betray her.

'Is Luke your mother's boyfriend?'

Chelsea looked miserable. 'I hate him,' she whispered.

'And you miss your daddy.'

Chelsea nodded, tears rolling down her cheeks.

This cleared something up for Natalie. She'd wondered how Jenna had managed to put her children above the man in her life, Malik. But she hadn't. There was another man in her life, who had helped her escape one problem only to create another. Natalie had accused Jenna and Malik of letting their own issues get in the way of seeing their children's needs — but she'd been doing the same thing. Wary of trusting men, Natalie had been blind to this fundamental difference between her and Jenna: Jenna had a deep-seated need for male approval that dominated her choices. The missed appointments made sense now, too — Jenna had been afraid this might come out.

'Chelsea.' Natalie knelt in front of her, put a hand on her hand. 'This is going to be really tough, and it isn't your fault. Can you trust me to try and sort it out? Maybe I can help you get some time with your daddy, but it might not be straight away.'

The little girl leaned forward and fell into Natalie's arms,

Natalie could feel the child's whole body shake and it felt like she was shattering into millions of pieces that would never, could never, be put back together.

What the hell did she do now? Natalie wished that Declan was there instead of her. The weight of the responsibility was greater than she had ever felt with her adult patients, and all the worse because she knew that barely beneath the surface was her own unprocessed trauma. She didn't want to stuff this child up—and was afraid her own wounds were so dangerously close to the surface she wasn't able to see clearly.

She looked at the clock. Declan would be seeing patients. She was going to have to handle this herself.

'Can I call Mummy in to see what we need to do?' she asked when the sobs had turned into sniffs. Chelsea held onto her so tightly that Natalie wondered if she'd squash the bean.

She thought of Gaylene not being allowed to touch children in the schoolyard. She probably wasn't meant to either, but no way in hell was she going to reject this child who was so desperate—and had chosen finally to trust her.

It took another ten minutes to convince Chelsea to let her go to the phone, to tell Beverley to send Jenna in. Natalie was sitting next to Chelsea on the chair when she arrived. Chelsea was looking down into her hands.

'Jenna, Chelsea's been pretty upset,' said Natalie. She took a breath. Steadied her anger, not sure how much was her own at her mother from long ago redirected to Jenna. Or just plain fury that this woman had let her boyfriend abuse her daughter. 'And I'm going to have to ask you to promise me something.'

Jenna looked at her daughter. 'Chelsea, are you okay?'

'She'll be fine, but she needs to be safe.'

Jenna stiffened.

'Is there anyone we don't know about that might make Chelsea feel unsafe, Jenna?'

Jenna's look clouded over. Not guilt, not anger. Natalie

tried to grasp it but it was gone too quickly. 'No. She's safe at home with me.'

'And your boyfriend, Jenna?'

'I don't…' Jenna looked at Chelsea and stopped.

'Promise me you won't have him in your house, Jenna, when Chelsea is there. That's all I ask.'

'I don't know what you're talking about.'

'Promise me.'

'Whatever.' Jenna glared at Natalie. 'You don't know anything. Chelsea, come on. We're going home.'

Natalie couldn't stop them leaving. But in Chelsea's look as she left was something worse than anger or accusation of failure—it was a loss of hope.

Winona was not answering. Natalie left a message and another with the on-call team to contact her urgently. Then she cycled to Declan's.

If Declan had been seeing her mother and knew more than she did about her past, she needed to get over it, infuriating as it was. And if it was more than that? She'd deal with it. For Chelsea's sake as much as her own and the bean's. And she couldn't afford not to have him on side at a disciplinary hearing.

She didn't think she could have done much different with Chelsea and Jenna but she felt guilty all the same. On the bike ride her thoughts were jumbled but there was a recurring theme. Anger. Anger she felt towards Jenna. Then guilt. Guilt at failing Chelsea. But somehow that guilt was also tied up with her dream, and with anger at her mother and guilt she seemed to be carrying for something she had done as a child. Something she could no more have been responsible for than Chelsea was for being abused.

She sat outside Declan's house for half an hour before deciding to knock. Looked across at Melbourne basking in the sunshine, the roof of a new complex glistening as the rays reflected off it. This wasn't just about being a good therapist. She also had to try to be a good mother, and she needed Declan's help for both tasks. Pregnancy made it hard not to focus internally. Every kick was like, *hey Mum, think of me*. Her. A mother. There was something not so bad about the thought.

Who was she then not to give her mother the same chance to make mistakes? Who was Natalie to say now, thirty-odd years later, that Jan hadn't wanted it to be different? Natalie's issue wasn't with the absent father—it was in trusting her mother.

Declan was alone, or at least not with a patient: no sound of his wife cooking or watching television in the background. He didn't look surprised to see her, and in his concern she could see an element of relief. They sat in their usual chairs, no offer of tea or wine, and he waited for her to begin.

'I'm sorry I missed the last appointment,' Natalie began.

Declan was seated in his usual chair, regarding her with a grave air.

'My mother has been here at least a couple of times, right?' Natalie didn't wait for an answer. 'I will ask her again for the truth, and perhaps I'll get it. But right now...' Emotion threatened to choke her up. She stopped, wouldn't meet his eye. She poured out what had happened with Chelsea and Jenna.

'I really didn't want to let her leave,' Natalie finally said. 'But I had to, didn't I? Was there something else I should have done?'

Declan leaned forward. His hand covered hers. 'The only thing you need to do now is take a breath. I know you care. But you're the therapist, not mother or auntie or foster carer. You need to keep a distance to be able to see clearly.'

'I should have seen Jenna needed a relationship to survive. Both the dependency and the histrionic aspects of her personality were clear markers and I missed them. I wanted to think she'd grown up.' Like Natalie wanted herself to. 'But I can't believe she let the bastard—'

'Slow down, Natalie.'

Natalie took several breaths.

'You don't *know* anything,' said Declan. 'Jenna didn't

251

want to see what she couldn't handle, simple as that. It doesn't mean she wilfully allowed anyone to abuse her child. Just lacked the capacity to judge.'

Natalie saw the passing look again on Jenna's face. Dissociation? Something was still wrong about it, but it slipped past her again.

'You know Gavin Boreman rang the College. He was… unimpressed.' Declan was taking the report seriously, but it was hard to tell how he felt about it.

Had she really been that out of line? Or was he stigmatising her too, using his knowledge of her having been ill to cover himself?

'He'd be more unimpressed with @KidsReallyMatter if it happened to be one of his nurses,' she said.

Declan smiled. Well, almost. 'As it happens, exactly what I said.'

'Thank you, Declan.' Natalie relaxed her fingers—her nails had almost broken the skin of her palm.

'But this is potentially serious, Natalie. We'll get through this meeting at the College, but you should have a lawyer present. To be safe.'

He'd said 'we'. It was the only good thing about this. Chelsea, Liam… and her own past that seemed intent on nagging relentlessly at her: there was too much in her head at the moment for her to process or even worry about dealing with it at the moment. Better to let Declan take it on.

'I think you need to consider offering to cut your workload. You'll have to soon anyway.'

'It's not fair. I'm fine.' Natalie sunk back in the chair.

Declan patted her hand and sat back, waiting.

'I realised something,' said Natalie slowly. 'As I was cycling here. About myself.' She looked up at the ceiling. 'I've been angry at my mother for not telling me about my father, all these years. But something happened when I saw Jenna and Chelsea together, locked in their pain and guilt. I'm actually angry at myself. I don't know quite what for, but something way back. I think I'm to blame and rather than deal with it, I blamed my mother.'

'You were little more than an infant, Natalie.'

Natalie looked at Declan, for a moment, wondering about just how well he knew Jan, how much she had confided in him. 'You know how important you've been in my life. Part therapist, part… father. You were there for me when no one else was, in a way no one else could have been. I know my mother wanted to be, but I was too angry, too… hurt, and I needed someone to blame. When I was diagnosed with bipolar, it was like I was being punished.'

'I think your mother may have felt the same, Natalie. If she could have taken the burden from you, she would have.'

Natalie bit her lip, took a moment to get her emotions in check. 'I went into medicine for me, Declan. But psychiatry — that was because of you, and I've never regretted it. You've helped me accept my illness, maybe even accept that it limits me, although saying that makes me want to scream.' She paused and wiped the tear that threatened to weaken her. Declan looked like he wanted to hug her, but they both knew it would undo her.

'Please Declan… I may be about to be prevented from practising yet all I can worry about is my past. I don't even begin to understand why, but my subconscious is leaking. Badly. Do you know what happened when I was a child? Who my father is? I know she's rung you. Visited you.'

Declan sighed. 'I knew your mother before I met you,' he said. 'I regret not telling you that but if you recall, when you met me at sixteen, with your leg and hip in traction, you weren't very fond of your mother and my link to her might have prevented you letting me in. She called me to see you — trusted me because she knew me.'

Natalie crossed her arms, never taking her eyes off him. She would not let him get away with a lie. *How* had her mother known him?

Declan smiled. 'Truth was, when I saw you in that ICU

bed with tubes and pins and metal frames, you were just any other patient; you know I care about all my patients and you weren't going to be any different.'

'And then?'

Declan leaned forward; his smile had a sad edge. 'The moment you looked at me and heard I was a psychiatrist—you yelled, "Bloody shrink," in case you've forgotten—you had me engaged.'

Natalie frowned. Why hadn't he answered her question?

'That look of bugger off was clear,' said Declan, 'and maybe that was all your biological father. But I also saw all the stubbornness, determination and resilience that is your mother. I knew I was going to keep turning up until you finally gave in.' Which she had. But not until after at least five visits spent mostly in silence.

'Natalie,' said Declan quietly, 'your mother has seen me recently for advice. She has been desperate to help you, and terrified of sending your relationship back into the past anger and silence.'

And as she left, though Declan still hadn't answered her question, her thank you and the hug she gave him were entirely genuine. If it was fatherly on his part, she couldn't say.

Liam had left her a message to say he'd parked the Lotus in her cul de sac while he had a mediation session regarding child access around the corner, and to suggest dinner. She left him a message now so he wouldn't think the car had been stolen, took the spare keys that were still in her warehouse and drove to Warrandyte.

For the first time Natalie could ever recall, she felt she needed her own mother. Who had continued to be there, despite all the tension that her absent father had created between them.

'Jan, love,' Craig called from the balcony as he watched Natalie slam the door. 'That racket was Natalie in the race car.' The spray of stones had hit the garage door and sent Hercules hobbling for cover.

'Natalie, what a…' Jan stopped herself. 'Natalie. What's wrong?'

'Did I have a teddy bear as a kid?'

Jan looked at her blankly.

'I mean, like, a special one?'

Jan had had time to process the question. 'Yes. You wouldn't sleep without it.'

'What happened to it?'

'No idea.' Jan frowned. 'If I kept it, I would have put it in the box of stuff I dropped off when you moved.'

'Not there.' Natalie had looked. Twice.

'Might have got caught up in Maddison's stuff,' Craig suggested. 'She was a big doll kid; wouldn't part with anything.'

Maddison's stuff, as it turned out, was still in the house. Natalie disappeared into Maddison's old room without answering their questions.

'We'll get a new one for your baby,' Craig yelled after her.

'Do you want a tea or coffee?' Jan added.

Maddison's room was unchanged from the day she'd left to marry Miles. Pale pink walls — Natalie's room had been red and black and had since been repainted — with Laura Ashley floral curtains and a white bedspread on a single four-poster bed. The cupboards were full. Everything from Barbie and her caravan to a collection of antique dolls Nan had added to each birthday. Natalie looked at their dead eyes and they still gave her the creeps.

On the top shelf were the Beanie Babies. Natalie struggled to see them decorating her warehouse; but one beanie babe, to her amusement, was a cockatoo. She didn't think Maddison would miss it.

Among the pile there were three teddy bears. A large pink one with a valentine heart — must have been from some boyfriend prior to Miles. An antique one, probably from Nan. And a third faded yellow one. Natalie picked the last one up — why was it familiar? It wasn't the one from her dreams. For one thing, this had both eyes.

'That's it,' said Jan from the door.

Natalie turned around. 'No, it's not the one I meant.'

'Actually you're right. You never really did take to it. The one you had before this teddy fell apart. Had wires sticking out that were dangerous so we sent it off to the doll hospital and this one came back.'

Natalie stepped down from the stool, still holding the yellow bear. Took the cockatoo as well and went back to the kitchen. She slumped on a chair as Jan poured tea for them all and Craig found some fruit cake only he would eat.

'I want to say...' Shit. Why was this so hard? Natalie steeled herself. 'I want to say sorry. To you both.'

Craig sat down after slapping her shoulder. 'Nothing to say sorry for.'

Natalie half-laughed. 'Craig, you deserve a medal for surviving all I did to you. But this... Mum this is about you and me.'

Jan flashed an anxious look at Craig.

'Your mum did the best—'

'I know.' Natalie put her hand on her stepfather's arm. 'I'm not here to blame anyone about anything.'

'I won't go back to all that Natalie, I just won't.'

Natalie looked long and hard at her mother, as if she was seeing her for the first time. Every previous occasion they had had this conversation it had been: 'I won't tell you' pitched against 'You owe me and I want to know'.

Now when Natalie looked at her mother she saw someone she had never seen before. Not the angry matriarch holding the power, but a mother who was scared, and who loved her daughter and thought she was doing the right thing.

'It's okay,' said Natalie. 'That's what I wanted you to know. I mean, really okay. I'd like to know, sure. But I was three years old and you did what you thought was best. I won't ask again. But I love you both for doing your best and sticking around even after I made it pretty impossible. You did good, Mum.'

Winona rang back as Natalie was approaching home.

She sounded grumpy. 'The on-call team rang me at home. I work long enough hours without being chased. They said you were insistent.'

'The Essa case? There's a boyfriend on the scene.'

There was a long silence. Winona's job had already given her the air of someone older than she probably was. This case wasn't going to help.

'We're going to have to do an after-hours unscheduled visit to spring him then,' Winona finally said. 'She's denied having a boyfriend to us.'

That didn't make Natalie feel much better—she should have known to look harder for reasons to explain Jenna's flight into health. Instead she'd bought the fairy tale Jenna had constructed for herself as well as everyone else.

'What'll happen to Chelsea and Chris?'

'If we can't trust her to keep this guy out, then we'll take them to her parents' I guess. Until the court decides tomorrow.'

'You'll do it tonight?' Natalie felt her stomach sink as she remembered Chelsea's look. She'd asked the girl to trust her.

'Yep.'

'Can I come?'

'What? Why?'

'I'm working with Chelsea. I'm worried she'll blame herself. And she doesn't know any of you guys. She's already been traumatised enough, so if I can go with her to her grandparents'…'

'Makes sense. And if I have to do after-hours, I guess you can too. Meet you outside Jenna's house in an hour.'

The house that had once been both Jenna's and Malik's was a small stand-alone weatherboard along a narrow street where inner-city hip met the burbs. Some of the houses had been renovated, with landscaped gardens and windows craning for city views. Others, like Jenna's, had peeling paint and eighties-style balconies.

They spent three minutes banging on the front door, to no response. Natalie was pretty sure there had been music on when they'd arrived. It was nine o'clock so the children would have been in bed—but Jenna must have seen them coming from the window of the front room.

'Jenna,' Winona finally yelled, 'we know you're there. If you don't open up we'll call the police.'

There was a sound from the other side of the door and it flew open. Jenna stood in the doorway. 'What do you want?' She saw Natalie and for a moment looked shocked.

'We need to confirm that the children are safe,' said Winona, looking into the darkness beyond Jenna.

'Well they are.' Jenna started to close the door but Winona put her foot in it.

'We'll just come back with the cops, Jenna.'

'You do that.' Jenna flashed Natalie a look of unalloyed fury. She kept pushing the door until Winona removed her foot.

'What now?' said Natalie.

'We get the police,' said Winona, stepping gingerly on the door-stop foot.

'By which time Luke will have done a runner.'

'And we'll be sitting in the car watching. I have tinted windows for a reason.' Her car was also a good deal less obvious than the yellow Lotus.

It took half an hour for a police car to cruise down the street. But by that stage they had seen a skinny tall man in his late twenties or early thirties leaving, tucking his shirt into his trousers and looking around furtively. Natalie had her phone out and took what she hoped was a photo; the screen was barely visible since she'd thrown it across her warehouse.

'Probably won't need it,' said Winona. 'My guess is it'll take the cops less than half an hour to work who he is and where he lives.'

Jenna opened the door sullenly to one bald cop and one red-haired one.

'We saw him leave, Jenna,' said Winona. 'So you can either tell us his name or not, your choice. But we're taking the children to your parents'.'

Jenna looked like she was going to faint. 'You can't. I made him go. No way would he ever touch my kids.'

'I asked you to promise to not have him here, Jenna,' said Natalie. Jenna really seemed to believe he wasn't responsible. And her children would suffer for her poor judgment.

'You don't frickin' know anything.' Jenna's scream made them all jump—which, fortunately for Natalie, put the bald copper in between her and Jenna so his chest got the brunt of the slap that had been aimed at her. The constable held Jenna's arms firmly.

'It's *not* Luke. Why the frickin' hell do you think I had to hide him? Because I knew what you lot'—she looked angrily at Winona—'would think. But I *know* it isn't. Now they'll give her back to Malik.'

'You need to calm down Jenna,' said Winona. It was clear that she had done this too many times; she looked weary but showed none of the emotions Natalie was wrestling with.

'For Chelsea and Chris's sake,' Natalie added. This got a result. Jenna started sobbing and slumped; constable baldy lowered her into a chair.

'Will you ring your parents, Jenna, or will I?' Winona

was sticking to protocol. The order helped Jenna regroup. The phone call was short and after she hung up she went to get Chris and Chelsea, who appeared ten minutes later in dressing gowns and slippers. Chris looked like he had been woken; Chelsea looked scared but managed a small smile for Natalie.

This time it was Jenna's haunted look that lodged in Natalie's mind as Winona ushered the kids out the door. The resonance with Chelsea's was startling, and again Natalie's mind took her back to earlier in the day: the look of dissociation, if that's what it was, when Natalie had confronted her about the boyfriend.

'The children will have to go with me,' said Winona, looking at the Lotus. Not a standard issue government car—besides it only took one passenger.

'I'll come back and get it later.' Natalie wanted to stay with Chelsea. She had a promise to keep.

She gave the girl a hug and sat in the back seat with her and her brother.

'Your mum loves you,' said Natalie softly. 'She'll get help, okay? You don't need to worry about her.'

Chelsea nodded silently. Later during the drive she snuck her hand into Natalie's and it stayed there until they drew up in front of a large double-storey house in Balwyn. Established middle class. Chelsea's hand tightened. 'I want my mummy.'

'I know, Chelsea,' said Natalie. 'This is only temporary, okay? And I'm sure your mum will come and stay here too until it gets sorted.'

'And Daddy?'

'Maybe you'll get to see Daddy now, too.'

There was a small brief smile; but tears were still running down Chelsea's cheeks as Mickie engulfed her. Stephen stood on the porch, looking drawn.

'Bloody hell,' Winona muttered.

'What?' But then Natalie got it too. Mickie smelled like a brewery.

Chelsea wriggled away. She looked to her grandfather and then Natalie, her anxiety palpable.

Why was nothing ever easy?

'Come Chelsea, Chris.' Stephen Radford moved to help his wife stand upright. He looked vaguely apologetic. The children didn't move, turning as Jenna's car drew up. Chelsea ran to her mother but Chris stepped closer to his grandfather, looking dazed.

'I'll look after them all,' Stephen said to Winona and Natalie. 'I always have.' His gaze, resting on Natalie, seemed to suggest he would do a better job than she had.

Winona left the children in Jenna's and her father's care, then dropped Natalie back at her car. It was midnight. Natalie had half a dozen messages and missed calls from Liam. To make matters worse, someone had dragged a key along the entire length of the Lotus. Natalie fancied Jenna or Luke as the perpetrator and wondered how many days' —or weeks'— work it would take to pay for the paint job. She left the car at Liam's apartment with a note under the windscreen wiper and caught a cab home without talking to him.

At 6 a.m. Natalie lay looking at the ceiling, wondering what had woken her.

Guilt. The feeling was there again, wrapped around a sense of longing and fear. The bean turned over.

'Great, kid,' said Natalie, wondering if its early-morning gymnastics had roused her, rather than her memories telling her she was the cause of her father leaving. No amount of *I was only a child* seemed to settle it. Perhaps because she no longer felt affinity with the child she had been then. But this feeling was not just the usual emptiness that came with the image of a one-eyed teddy bear. Its replacement, the yellow teddy, was sitting next to her bed watching her. 'No, it's not about you,' Natalie muttered and turned it face down.

Jenna. Or Chelsea. Something about them was gnawing at her. She couldn't pinpoint what. Surely nailing down what Jenna was hiding had solved the mystery? Her mind oscillated between the two; mother and daughter. Repeating patterns. Like her with the bean's father, mirroring her own mother and her father. Except Damian was going to be around. She hadn't completely repeated the pattern. He had sent a text saying *Hi, how's it going?* She hadn't responded, hadn't acknowledged the flowers. Didn't know what to say, or what she felt. She knew he'd be a good dad, though. As Liam was.

As Jenna had thought Malik would be. And then had thought Luke was. Her own needs had clouded her judgment. Natalie was certain hers wouldn't. Almost certain. Unlike

Jenna she didn't need a man for her sense of self-worth. She had lived alone a long time, could continue to do so. Wanting Liam wasn't the same as needing him. Anyway, she was pushing him away so hard he'd give up eventually.

Natalie pulled herself out of bed in frustration. She had almost reached the place where her mind would reveal the message it was holding for her, but mundane realities had intervened again. Maybe she just needed to deal with that and let the court deal with Jenna and Chelsea.

But after she'd showered and sat down with the paper, the worry at the back of her mind was gnawing at her again—a nagging, irrational sense that Jenna was right. Was she overanalysing or was there a seed of something germinating?

Luke. Just because Jenna had hidden his existence didn't mean he was abusing Chelsea. Natalie reflected back on her sessions with Chelsea. The monster had been nonspecific. Chelsea hated Luke—but it might only be because he had replaced her father.

Natalie might have been blinkered by her obsession with good fathers. What if it wasn't a father at all—or at least not Chelsea's? What about Ted Beahre? Or Youssef? Or Matilda's father?

Natalie was about to head into Yarra Bend but she rang and said she'd be in late morning. Instead, she went to the Children's Court.

Winona was standing outside Courtroom 2, talking to Harvey Alcock. Probably not enough notice for the Dictator. Or else this hearing was straightforward. Maybe Katlego Okeke had them worried about wasting taxpayers' money. Winona looked surprised to see Natalie.

'We don't need to call you,' said Alcock, tucking his shirt into his trousers.

'It could be the schoolteacher.'

Alcock raised an eyebrow. Winona frowned. 'What makes you think that?'

'No one wanted to point the finger at him,' said Natalie. 'But Chelsea was trying to miss sport. And there had been another issue with him about supporting a dad seeing his kid. The point is, Chelsea doesn't like Luke but she didn't actually say he was the abuser.'

'It's always the de facto,' said Winona. 'It was the reason I liked Malik for it—he didn't change Chelsea's nappies, just came along later. Same thing with Luke. Takes on the mother but with the eye on the daughter; seen it happen over and over, and the women can't see what's going on in front of their eyes.'

Because they don't want to and... Natalie lost the thought as Winona continued.

'Same with the straight physical abuse—I've had two tragedies in the last year because the mother's left the kid with a de facto who had a short fuse. Subdural haemorrhage, both of them. One died in hospital, other's brain damaged.'

Natalie thought of how hard it must be for a male primary school teacher: much less opportunity than a partner to abuse the child, and a lot more scrutiny. Winona was probably right. Probably.

Because of the short notice, neither Jenna nor Malik nor their lawyers were present and the duty magistrate was not Louise Perkins.

Magistrate Kincaid seemed to do a perfunctory read, then looked at Alcock. 'So what are you proposing?'

'That the mother reside with her parents.'

'So the maternal grandparents will have custody?'

'Yes, your Honour, technically.'

Kincaid frowned. 'Technically. What does that mean?'

Alcock briefly conferred with Winona. 'The maternal grandmother is still being assessed.'

Meaning they weren't sure if Mickie could keep off the booze.

'And the father? Mr... Essa?'

'We can leave that until the hearing with her Honour, Louise Perkins.'

Kincaid frowned. 'But you are saying there is now no suggestion that the father has been abusing the child? And there are concerns about the maternal grandmother?'

'Malik's not Chelsea's father.' Jenna had burst through the doors, looking flustered, and yelling. Li Yang was at her side.

Kincaid frowned.

'Li Yang, your Honour,' she said crisply. 'Technically Mr Essa adopted my client's older child, but we maintain that he is abusing her and my client opposes any access.'

Kincaid looked irritated. 'This is the case, is it not, that has attracted the attention of the media?' He glared at Alcock. 'Where's your QC?'

'Your Honour, this is an emergency hearing. We discovered only last night that Ms Radford had been exposing her children to an abusive de facto.'

'Your Honour, there is no evidence of that at all,' said Li Yang. Of abuse or the exposure? Natalie felt increasingly that this hearing was going to be one-sided.

'Sit down Ms Yang.' Kincaid was going a gentle shade of puce. 'Mr Alcock, where are the children now?'

'With my parents,' Jenna interjected. 'But I want them with me.' Her agitation was evident—she looked like she hadn't slept.

'Ms Yang, have your client remain quiet or I'll evict her.' Kincaid sounded as if his preference would have been to evict everyone. He turned to Alcock. 'Are they safe or not with the Radfords?'

'Well your Honour...'

Natalie couldn't contain herself any longer. 'They could go to the paternal grandmother.'

'No! Malik will get them then.' Jenna's outburst had her lawyer yanking hard on her arm.

Kincaid looked back and forth between Jenna and Natalie, and settled on Natalie. 'Who are you?'

'Chelsea's psychiatrist.'

Kincaid rubbed his temples. 'Let's swear you in then and see what sense you make of this.'

As Natalie recited the oath, Li Yang and Jenna began a hurried exchange while Alcock and Winona did likewise.

'So, Doctor King,' said the magistrate. 'Are you able to shed any light on where the Essa children could be placed?'

'Chelsea is showing definite signs of being abused,' said Natalie. 'But it still isn't clear by whom, and… the man we… I and Protective Services…. saw leaving Jenna's house last night, has yet to be investigated. I *believe*.'

Harvey cleared his throat. 'May I ask the witness some questions?'

'Yes, yes; and then you also, Ms Yang. But—' The magistrate indicated his watch.

'And what do you know about this man, Doctor King?' said Alcock.

'Jenna had denied she was seeing anyone; he may work with her.' Natalie saw Jenna look down. 'And Chelsea doesn't like him.'

'What are your concerns about the Radfords?'

'Mrs Radford apparently drinks. Jenna has mentioned this and she was intoxicated when we dropped the children there last night.'

Kincaid rolled his eyes.

'And is Ms Radford capable of caring for her children at her parents' house?'

Was she? There was something nagging at Natalie, but was it Jenna or her own dreams? She thought of her assessments: *impartial*. 'From what I've seen, yes.'

Alcock had the answer he wanted. Li Yang was on her feet.

'Are you a hundred per cent positive that Mr Essa is not abusing Chelsea?'

One hundred per cent? Was it ever possible to be that certain of anything? 'I am as confident as I can be in dealing with a confused eight-year-old. She clearly loves him and he her.'

'The abuse started after he started having access, Doctor King.' Li Yang turned to Kincaid. 'We have had a professor of psychiatry stating he is a psychopath and bad parent.'

Natalie felt sick. She was sure she was right… she had to be. She thought of Wadhwa talking about his nose twitching; the bulls in the pen together. Li Yang was looking at her as if she was the Antichrist.

'Associate Professor Wadhwa did not see Mr Essa with Chelsea, nor did he see Chelsea herself. I have. Individual sessions as well as the ones with her parents.' Natalie knew she sounded defensive and wished she could be more detached. For court, at least.

'Are you *really* so sure, Doctor King, that you'd risk exposing an innocent eight-year-old to more abuse?'

I'm not the one who hid the boyfriend, Natalie wanted to scream. Her head started to ache and her vision was going fuzzy. When she closed her eyes the one-eyed teddy bear was staring accusingly at her.

'Are you so confident that Mrs Essa will not leave her son alone with the children?' Li Yang continued.

Natalie paused. Thought about Youssef. About Malik saying he'd kill the abuser if he found him and wondered if that would extend to family. 'I… Mrs Essa has organised rooms for the two children at her house.' There, they would be safe, surely. 'But… no, I can't guarantee she won't leave her sons with them.' Or hightail it to the Middle East with them in shipping containers. She thought of Okeke, took a deep breath. 'I do not know if there is any foundation to the concern, but Malik's brother is going to Egypt and Jenna has raised concerns they might try to take the children.'

'Do the children have passports?'

'No, your Honour,' Li Yang said. Reluctantly.

Kincaid drummed his fingers on the table. 'This needs to be dealt with by her Honour, Louise Perkins. This court only needs to deal with a short-term solution to keep the child safe, not ensure parental rights or establish who is abusing the child.' His eyes narrowed. 'You, Ms Radford, lied. Therefore, I cannot possibly trust your judgment and am frankly sick of parents thinking they can wave the abuse card willy-nilly without evidence. And we *do* have evidence you and your mother are unsuitable—' He glared at Alcock. 'I see your case comes up in three weeks and that paternal access with his mother supervising was only ceased after the abuse became apparent, of which Doctor King has cleared him. I note he hasn't been given a chance to be here today, but assuming he and his mother are still able to have the children, Protective Services is to deliver them to Mrs Essa's this afternoon.'

Jenna was still screaming when the security guards came in, and Natalie stood up, only to find the dizziness escalating to send stars into her vision until she fainted.

Natalie had a bruise on her forehead, but otherwise she felt fine. Just a combination of skipping breakfast, dehydration and pregnancy. The court clerk found her a glass of water and stayed with her after everyone else had left, until she eventually convinced him to let her make her own way home.

Winona was still outside. She'd just ended a call. 'Malik was ecstatic,' she said. She glared at Natalie. 'You'd better be right. I still think he's a sleaze.'

Natalie's head was already throbbing—this didn't help. She looked around. 'What happened to Jenna?'

'She took off home. I've sent the police to stop her doing a runner with the kids. She was yelling that it wasn't fair she had to pick between her kids and Luke. I could see them all taking off together.'

'Are the police going to investigate?' asked Natalie. 'I mean as to who abused Chelsea?'

'Luke? Yes. After that?' Winona shrugged.

On the walk home, Natalie left phone messages for both Malik and Jenna. To Jenna she reiterated that she was sure Malik was safe… and Malik she told not to leave the children with anyone, not even male friends… or family. She hoped he would understand her concern, even if he didn't share it. And she reminded him of Chelsea's next appointment.

As soon as she put the phone down it rang—her rooms.

'Natalie?'

'Yes Bev?'

'I know you aren't looking at Twitter, but…'

Natalie's stomach dropped.

'Check out @lizar82.'

She still hadn't replaced her phone. It was hard to even see the Twitter icon let alone the messages on the cracked screen. But she could see enough.

Man Under Fire @ManUnderFire: *#PsychBitch tar us all with same brush*

Liza R @lizar82: *F*cking #PsychBitch just took my kids*

Natalie rang Beverley back. 'Can you look up Jenna Radford's file for me? Give me her full name?'

Bingo. 'Jenna *Eliza* Radford.' Plus a birth year of '82· plus that prim little asterisk—like the way Jenna always said 'fricking'.

Did it matter? No; Declan was right. She was going to let it go. @KidsReallyMatter could be Lauren, could be a nurse. Could be Mr Boreman's receptionist. If that was how they dealt with their anger it was probably better to pity them than be sucked in.

She checked Twitter one last time before deleting her account. It still read zero tweets. She had never hit the tweet button.

Liam turned up late after a no-show from his children. He looked like he'd lost weight, and there were grey bags under his eyes. Natalie didn't have the heart to tell him to bugger off.

'You need to see someone,' said Natalie, giving him a whiskey, which he downed in one gulp. 'Someone neutral who can help you… let you talk about this.'

'I'm fine.'

Sure he was.

'Just need a good night's sleep. And my car needs a new paint job.'

Natalie winced. 'Send me the bill.'

'Bound to happen with the company I keep. I'm amazed it

didn't happen earlier, parking it here.' He paused 'I wish this wasn't so hard on you. But as if the kids and Lauren aren't stressful enough…'

Natalie turned around, looked at him. 'What?'

Liam poured himself another whiskey. 'Remember Michael?'

'Your star witness, right? Going to nab your paedophile teacher.'

Liam nodded as he sat down and put his feet up on the table covered with papers. 'Ex-star witness.'

'Oh, Liam, I'm sorry. He won't present at the commission?'

'He started to yesterday. Gruelling. I can't tell you… Well, I just don't know how you deal with it. He kept breaking down in tears.' Liam's voice choked. He took a breath. 'Didn't turn up today. I just heard they found him. Hanged himself.'

'Shit.' Natalie felt dizzy again and sat down. The one-eyed teddy bear was back in her thoughts.

'They gave me a copy of the note.' Liam shook his head. 'I just don't get it.'

'Why he killed himself?' Natalie thought of her own moments of intense darkness when there appeared no end in sight, only the welcome idea of the absence of pain. Of anything other than the place you were in.

'No, that I get.' He threw a piece of paper on the table and Natalie picked it up. It was a photocopy of Michael's last thoughts. Rambling, mostly incoherent. A set of regrets. But one line jumped out.

I can't live with myself. I did it too. Tell the kid I'm real sorry.

'Your abuse victim became an abuser,' said Natalie softly.

Natalie thought of the borderline patients, treated as annoyances in the emergency department after yet another overdose, of the chaos of their childhood being acted out in drug use and criminal acts — and sometimes committing abuse themselves. When your emotions were a mess of impulses and drives you could neither understand or control, it could be reassuring to identify with the abuser rather than take the victim role.

'We're good at sympathising about their abuse; can try to imagine how horrific, how terrifying, how soul destroying it was. But when kids are abused it affects them at the core... and we aren't so good at sympathising with those long-term effects.'

Liam nodded. He looked at her. 'I've prosecuted these bastards. Willingly, gladly, thrown the fucking book at them. Lowest of the low. But this man... I knew him. Felt sorry for him. He did those things too... but Christ, he was a *victim*.'

Neither Malik nor Jenna returned her calls. Winona had answered her phone and given a curt report of the scene that had unfolded at the Balwyn home. Jenna had turned on her mother and blamed her, and had to be physically restrained. Ama and Malik had been there to collect the children, who had apparently been exposed to their mother's hysterical rants and accusations.

And Katlego Okeke was on the attack in the *Guardian*. Headline: 'Bad parenting comes in all colours'.

> *A month ago, Mark La Brooy published an 'I was right' article. Without any apparent review of the legal proceedings, and certainly without troubling himself to go to the Children's Court to see the reality of the case for himself, he decided that a girl's father was a child abuser and should be denied even supervised access. Not exactly La Brooy's usual position, but the man was Muslim. Or apparently so—I guess all Egyptians are Muslims in his world. A few weeks later, the court agreed with him, based largely on an assessment of the child by a psychiatrist. No matter that La Brooy has demeaned this psychiatrist as 'junior' and 'unstable' and 'female'. He's happy to accept her judgment when it agrees with his own expert opinion.*
>
> *I know about this article not because I follow*

272

*La Brooy's column, but because it incited a Twitter
storm of abuse towards me. It's not the first time my
opinions have provoked this sort of reaction, but it's
always depressing to be confronted by people who
see the world, literally, in black and white.*

*Life is more complicated than that and this case
was no exception. It seems the psychiatrist was right
about the abuse but wrong about the source. The
mother had lied about another man in her life—one
of the 'de factos' that La Brooy so often cites as the
prime abusers.*

*So, Mark. Everything fits. Seems that it was the
de facto. You'd have got it right if you hadn't let
racism get in the way.*

Not for the first time, Natalie wished these columnists would
look at the complexities rather than take one fact and run with
it. The court—and psychiatrists—took time with evidence
that was limited to start with—and very rarely, in fact, black
and white. Okeke was right about that. But the imperfect
system was all they had. Natalie felt exhausted just thinking
about how La Brooy would respond. Let alone Twitter.

She wondered how Chelsea was holding up; hoped the
strengths she had seen in the girl would offer some protection.

It helped that Malik brought the child in, on time, and that
she was full of excitement about her new bedroom.

'Thank you, Doctor King,' said Malik.

'Thank me by keeping her safe,' said Natalie softly, out
of earshot of Chelsea. 'We don't know for sure that Jenna's
boyfriend did anything.'

'*I* am sure.' Malik's voice was steely. 'Chelsea tells me
she hates this man. Before Jenna met me there were several
boyfriends. Drug users. Dealers, I think. It was these I worried
about when she went to work. I know now I must have the
children. She is not fit.'

'She's still their mother, Malik.'

'My mother can care for them.' Malik's dismissiveness was chilling. 'See, Chelsea is doing well. I will care for her and Chris.'

Chelsea herself had no wish to talk about her mother, and throughout the session redirected the conversation to her toys. Staying on message—or, more precisely, off message. But it was her overbrightness that left Natalie worried; it was masking her true feelings. The ones that would cause her problems years later—as they had with Liam's witness, Michael.

When she got home, Damian was sitting in his Camry waiting for her outside her warehouse. *It's best for the children to have their parents together*. That's what she'd wished her whole childhood.

'Dinner,' he said firmly. 'No excuses.'

'I'm still seeing O'Shea.' Well, sort of. Being with her wasn't working for Liam or his kids.

Damian didn't look at her. 'We need to talk.'

The new restaurant on Smith Street served bread and a shared platter; they both stuck to water.

'I have some information for you,' said Damian. Natalie felt a wave of relief—he meant *work*.

'This is totally, and I mean *totally* off the record, you understand?'

'Yes.' Damian did things by the book. If he was breaking a rule it had to be something big. Something important.

'That teacher you asked about?'

Ted Beahre. Shit. 'Yes.'

'Nothing on him.'

Natalie let her breath out. Brilliant.

'But…' There was a silence while Natalie wondered what the 'but' meant. 'He was briefly working at the same school as one of the guys named by the Royal Commission.' Damian cleared his throat. 'And the business where he was reported?'

'Yes.'

'It involved a parent with whom he was or is friends. At his current school. Chelsea's school.'

274

Matilda's father. 'And?'

'That parent is facing charges of possession of pornography. Underage girls. His daughter may well have been abused.'

'Poor Matilda.'

Damian frowned. 'Her name... off the record... is not Matilda. It's Amy.'

Natalie suddenly didn't feel hungry. Just very tired. Chelsea spent lots of nights at Amy's. She pulled out some money to cover half the tab.

'I'll pay,' he said. 'Consider it child support.'

Whatever. Natalie stood to leave, then paused. 'Damian, tell me something. Why did you think this kid was yours? You did, didn't you, right from the start?'

Damian leaned back in his chair. 'From the start? No. What I told you was what the specialist told me.'

Natalie sensed there was more. Waited.

Damian sighed, shifted in his seat. 'I went back, to talk to him.'

'And?'

'I hadn't quite understood first time round. The one in a million? That was the chances of Caitlin and me having a baby together.'

Natalie stared at him, her mind racing over long-ago lessons from her medical course.

'Apparently there was a problem with my sperm and her eggs, or the uterine environment or something. Different woman... different circumstances, different figures.' He looked at her. 'I'm sorry, Natalie.'

You don't need contraception, I'm infertile. And she'd believed him. But then, so had he.

Damian stood up, put his hands on her shoulders. 'When you finally realise O'Shea won't stick around, I'm here for you.'

He'd look after his mistake. But that didn't mean they were right for each other. Or that Liam didn't want her, baby or no baby.

Mark La Brooy's column was headed: 'What about the Real Victims?'

The social justice warriors are out in force, he began, implying their influence was behind the court's *reckless indifference* to child welfare.

> *The court couldn't move fast enough to return access to the de facto—an Egyptian man and recent immigrant. I will say it again: my problem is not with the man's religion (and certainly not his colour—Islam is not a race). It is with the court affording him privileged treatment because of it. More importantly, that privileged treatment is given priority over the children's welfare.*
>
> *Go back and read my articles on this case. You will see at the heart of them a concern for the welfare of children. Now go to the internet and trawl through the articles of identity politicians and the feminist left. You will see little or no concern for the children—just an obsession with racial and religious sensitivities.*

Then a few paras of self-justification culminating in the usual pompous formula:

*I make no apology for using the 'wrong' language or
sharing an unpalatable fact. Better that than aiding
and abetting those who would abuse our children.*

Absolute refusal to take a step back and a lot of water-muddying. No interest in finding a cooperative way forward; bonus virtue signalling. Natalie decided she'd have to give up reading these columns too. They made her want to punch a wall. Or Mark La Brooy.

'Twitter,' Bev told her, 'has released a shit storm.' She showed Natalie the screen search for @*SayItStraight68*—La Brooy's handle—but it was blank. 'He's been suspended,' Bev explained. 'For abuse. Some of his posts have been deleted but the one I saw had been retweeted thousands of times—he was very crude and personal about Okeke; called her a ho and used the word "ape"—didn't actually call her that, but anyone could see... Wouldn't be surprised if he gets the sack.'

Natalie doubted that anything in his article would cost him his job. But maybe, like her, he took to Twitter in the late evening—perhaps fuelled by a drink or two. It sounded like his tweets were less measured than his columns.

After her meeting with Ken Rankin, she and La Brooy might be lining up together for unemployment benefits.

Tonight was Natalie's last gig; Gil's partner Cassie was going to take over until the bean was born. Maybe for a lot longer. Natalie gave Tom a hug. She felt uncharacteristically nostalgic.

Tom put his sticks down and hugged her back. 'You okay?'

Was she? Natalie tipped her head down, tied her hair into a knot and pulled on the blonde spiked wig that she used for the stage.

'Can't see you pushing a pram.' Shaun was shaking his head. He wasn't alone. Nappies. Mothers' groups. Car seats and strollers. Jesus.

Singing made it easy to forget—she picked the hardest,

sexiest and most edgy of their repertoire and lost herself in the music and words.

'You're on fire tonight,' Liam was sitting waiting for her at the bar. Vince brought her a water.

'Hope he's going to make an honest woman of you.' Vince glared at Liam.

Natalie laughed. 'Vince, no one says that anymore.'

'I do. I'm old school.' Vince left to tend to other patrons as Liam took a call. His tension went up a notch; it only took a moment for Natalie to work out it was his ex-wife.

'I know it is, Lauren,' he said. 'I tell you, he didn't want me there… no…'

'She's playing you,' said Natalie loud enough for him— and possibly Lauren—to hear.

Liam frowned, shook his head and left the pub, still talking on the phone.

Natalie watched him go. She would never ask him to choose between herself and his kids—but at some stage he was going to have to decide whether his loyalties lay with her or Lauren.

Tonight, Lauren won. As Liam was driving he sent a text: *Family crisis, sorry.*

She tried not to think about him. About the pending disciplinary hearing. About the future. Tried also to forget about Blake's phone message. *Don't know if this is what you were after Nat, but looks like Youssef's Mum's going as well. To Egypt or wherever.* There wasn't anything she could do about it. Ama was entitled to go wherever she wanted—and she'd probably cancel now she had the children with her.

Unless she'd booked her trip when she got the children? Natalie felt her skin prickle. Damian wasn't likely to stake out the airport to check for kids on false passports. She left a message on Li Yang's phone. Maybe she would.

Natalie was not the only one to pick that La Brooy was on the back foot. Okeke's column didn't need to mention his name.

White supremacy has never gone away. It sits just below the surface, waiting to break through as soon as someone outside the club gets uppity.

Of course, it's all about fear. And no one is more pathetic than those whose fear turns to bluster as they try to shut down conversation and dissent. White men have never had to grow up being called a black slag, being told their only worth was as a sexual object. This is not Islamic culture; it's rife in western countries driven by white men. What they fear about change is that they just might not continue to get away with this frat boy behaviour and instead actually have to be responsible for themselves.

This didn't make Natalie feel any better than La Brooy's column. Anger in whatever form, justified or not, was draining. As she downed the dregs of her coffee and headed to work, she thought about the morning meditation she'd used when she was living on the coast. Vowed to replace the morning paper with it.

When Natalie arrived on her bike at her rooms, Jenna, who was waiting in the car park, jumped out of her car to chase her. Natalie waited outside the back entrance, ready to slam the door shut.

Jenna looked more upset than angry.

'Can we talk?'

This case seemed to be full of unpaid overtime with interviews crammed into spaces that didn't exist. 'Come in. I don't have long.'

Natalie sent her in to her room and stuck her head into the office. 'Your favourite patient is here,' she said to Beverley. 'Any chance of two coffees?'

Beverley didn't just smile. She beamed. 'Not a problem. Mark La Brooy's been sacked, by the way. The paper has apologised too, for what it's worth.' Beverley handed her a sheet of paper. 'Here's the list of songs we want at the wedding.' Natalie glanced at it—the first two were 'Ave Maria' and 'Amazing Grace'.

'Beverley, no way.'

'You'll be great,' said Beverley, ignoring her as she went off to the kitchen. Natalie shook her head.

Jenna was sitting in the chair, bolt upright. She started when Natalie came in.

'I want to start by saying I'm sorry.' Jenna sounded more stressed than sorry, as if she'd rehearsed her lines. Probably had. With Li Yang coaching.

'Sorry for what, Jenna?'

'Not telling you about Luke.'

Natalie sat down; she wondered if she looked any better than Jenna, who appeared to have aged several years. Her red trousers were almost hanging off her. The eating disorder may well have flared up.

'He's an okay guy. Really.'

'I'm not the one you need to tell this to, Jenna.'

'Yes, you are.' Jenna's words came fast, and too intense. 'I want you to understand.' She took a breath. 'I met him at work.' Jenna saw Natalie's look. 'I only started dating him *after* I broke off with Malik.'

Maybe.

'He's got way more in common with me than Malik. We both did science degrees, he likes the same television shows, bushwalking. He doesn't... he doesn't drink, do drugs. And he doesn't...' Jenna fought to find the words. 'He doesn't make me feel like I'm less than him, you know? Malik always needed to feel... superior. A little comment, a snide remark. It wore me down, and I never really saw it until I was out of it.'

'Jenna, no one is here to judge your choice of men. If you want to go into therapy to make sense of those choices, fine, but not now and not with me. This is about keeping your daughter safe. About providing her and Chris with a stable environment.'

'You think I don't know that?' Jenna's — *lizar82's* — anger fired up, and she instantly looked less tired. 'I didn't want Malik to know about Luke. I told you about him checking up on me, right?'

Natalie nodded.

'Well I really didn't know how he'd react. He *is* unpredictable. And very... old world. Male honour, that kind of thing. I was worried. I'm still worried. Someone threw paint over Luke's car — we couldn't prove it was Malik, but it had to have been.'

I'll kill him, he'd said.

'When I had the feeling that something was really wrong with Chelsea I wasn't stupid, okay?' said Jenna. 'But Luke has *never* been with the kids without me there. Usually they are with my mum, or before, with Ama. When I said I knew it couldn't be him, I really did know. He's good with Chris too, helps me be firm like you showed me that time.'

It was hard not to believe her; she certainly seemed to believe what she was saying.

Natalie thought back to Chelsea not liking the man who usurped her father. To the monster with the large phallic symbol.

'Could Chelsea have seen you two… together?'

Jenna frowned. 'You mean… like having sex?'

Natalie nodded.

'No.' The answer was too quick, not thought through. Jenna's expression was all teenage sulk. 'You aren't listening to me. I've seen… I've seen how Malik looks at her, right? I know this isn't going to stand up in court but I *know* he doesn't think about her as a kid. Or at least, he has this, this… sense of ownership. It's creepy.'

Maybe this was what Wadhwa had picked up. Had she missed it? She thought about how dismissive Malik had been of Chelsea needing her mother, his usual reflective capacity obliterated by his own anger and needs. But the same was happening with Jenna.

'She was missing him, Jenna.'

'She's frickin' *eight*. What the hell would she know?' Jenna banged the table. 'I tell you this started before Luke ever met her. It isn't him. And I don't trust Malik not to get on a frickin' plane with them. His business, his uncle? They're fricking criminals, okay? If anyone can get false passports, they could. My father thinks we should do it first—disappear, I mean. He's always been against me seeing you but I was stupid enough to trust you.'

'Chelsea's being abused, Jenna. Putting your head in the sand won't make it go away.' Could it be someone other than Luke? Jenna was convincing. 'Have you considered… Youssef? Teachers at school? Has she been over to stay at friends' places?'

Jenna's response was again too quick. 'It has to be Malik, okay?' There was an almost pleading edge to her tone; like she was desperate for Natalie to believe her. But why?

'The police took her. Forcibly. Do you know how it makes me feel knowing she's there, that I let them take her?' Jenna looked at Natalie. 'You got kids? Would you let a paedophile even live next door to your fricking kids?'

Jenna shook her head and got up to go. 'If Malik thinks

this is the end, he's mistaken. I'll never give up.' She turned back at the door. Her green eyes stared coolly back. 'I'll kill him rather than let him have my daughter. I'm not taking a chance she ends up in the Middle East. I'd rather spend the rest of my life in prison knowing I saved her than leave her with that bastard.'

When Natalie got home, after leaving several messages at Malik's, at his mother's and on his mobile, Liam was waiting for her. He'd been leaving messages too, explaining why he'd taken off from the pub and not gone home with her. Something about James refusing to do a school debate unless he turned up. Really, it hadn't mattered what the reason was — just something that helped her make up her mind.

'Can we talk?' he said.

'I've got a meeting at the College in an hour.' Natalie left the door open behind her as she and Bob went upstairs. Liam closed it softly behind him and followed.

'You know I'm sorry, right?'

'Yes, Liam, I know that.' Natalie wished she didn't feel so tired, physically and mentally. The pregnancy? Her bipolar? She was probably just tired of her life being out of control. And she so didn't need this just before meeting with Rankin. 'And I know you have to put your children first. I wouldn't expect or want anything different.'

'I sense a "but".'

He looked tired, and sad. She saw the corner of his eye twitching under the unruly black curl, as it did when he got stressed; the tightness in his shoulders. He'd pulled his tie off, left his suit jacket in the car. She couldn't think about his mouth and how it tasted and how he made her feel, because it would weaken her. Involuntarily her hand went to the bean — and Liam took the movement and all its significance in. She was sure he had reached the same decision as her if he was honest with himself—it was just hard.

'I was wrong,' said Liam softly. 'I let Lauren manipulate me; she knows my buttons and pushed them.'

'Did James do his debate?'

'It was over before I got there, which she well knew.' He stepped closer, put his hands on her shoulders. 'I'm meeting for mediation, in an hour, just around the corner from here. I won't let it happen again.'

But he wouldn't risk losing his kids. 'What does Lauren want?'

'Revenge. To see me suffer. You too, I dare say.'

'Let's go a little deeper, shall we? What does she want for your kids?' Natalie looked at him, steeled herself.

Liam shrugged. 'To be high achievers. We argued on this. I want them to follow their dreams, she wants them to go to university. Doctors, lawyers, CEOs... Not what she said, but I know she'd feel like she'd failed if they weren't.'

'And how about from you, when you were together, what did she want?'

'A trophy. A smart ambitious man who would look good on her arm. But then she also needed a house-husband who would put her needs first.'

'Love? Adoration? Respect?'

'Respect.' Liam answered automatically. 'To prove to her father she's better than her brother.'

Natalie nodded. Now she had all the pieces to make sense of Lauren's narcissistic traits; under stress anything that wasn't perfect would be cut off and denigrated.

She looked at him. This was the moment she had to step in and take the reins. This wasn't just about her. Being torn between her and his children was ripping Liam in two, and aggravating Lauren. He looked haggard and lost, and she felt like she had done it to him. And she knew how much not having a father could mess you up.

So she wasn't going to do that to her child—or Liam's.

For James, Megan and the bean—for the adolescent she once was, the person she wanted to be—the mother she wanted to be, she would do this, no matter how much pain it caused her.

'You're meeting with her, right?'

Liam nodded.

'Nothing will work if revenge is all she's after, but here's a suggestion.' They had to, surely, be better at putting their children first than Jenna and Malik? 'Rule One: don't be cocky. That will remind her of the revenge motive. Think dignified.'

Liam frowned, but he was taking onboard what she was saying. He knew the importance of the performance. In court, he was the master. But he was too close to this matter to brief himself.

'You basically want to show yourself as the perfect father and perfect ex-husband, the intellectual equal who will be accommodating'—she saw him starting to shake his head and raised her hand—'insofar as it involves the children.'

Liam looked sceptical.

'Rule Two, go out of your way to show respect for her job. I know grovelling isn't your thing'—Natalie grinned at his expression—'but this is the time. You know, those serious respectful looks you flash at the jury after you've delivered a statement that expects them to disregard everything the defence has told them?'

Liam had the grace to smile.

'And Rule Three?' Natalie paused. She couldn't look at him, was afraid she might tear up. 'Find a way of telling her she's right.'

'Right about what?'

'Whatever you like. She knows you pride yourself on being totally ethical; doesn't mean you don't get it wrong sometimes. You need to be sincere—I mean she really, really needs to believe you, but on this, she will want to. Narcissists hate to be criticised and seen to be wrong—they get defensive quickly and then you've lost the argument. Smart people get around them by getting them onside.'

Liam stared at her. If it was for her insight into Lauren, or her take on him, she wasn't sure.

'I suggest you say it about me,' Natalie said, her voice hard. 'Tell her she was right about me. That I've fucked your life up.'

Liam frowned.

'This isn't going to work Liam, you and me. I can't do this. You said you couldn't look at yourself in the mirror if you weren't true to yourself? Well as it happens —' Her voice started to crack. She stopped and hardened her expression against the vulnerability she saw in Liam's, the flash of pain as he saw what she intended. 'Neither can I. This is too hard. I thought we could get through it but we can't. Go back to your children, Liam.'

'Fuck that, Natalie. That isn't your choice to make. Lauren and I aren't ever getting back together. They're my children, my decision. You know I love you. And I know you love me. Stop thinking you can be fucking noble or something.'

Maybe he hadn't decided it was over, but he'd see the sense in it.

'I'm not being noble,' she said. She certainly didn't feel it, she just felt wretched and empty, the loneliness that would engulf her the moment he walked out the door punching her in the stomach. 'I want my child to have a father. The biological one I never got to have. A simple life like the one my mother chose. A life that won't stress me and will keep me well.'

Liam looked like she'd slapped him. 'McBride? He... you... you're saying you don't love me?'

Natalie closed her eyes. Thought of his children. Thought of the bean. Thought of how much she did love him, how much he was the only man she could ever see herself with. Thought about Jenna and Chelsea and Malik. And couldn't lie. Or at least not about that. 'You chose your children, Liam. I'm choosing mine.'

Liam stared at her. Without saying a word, he walked out. Bob helpfully added, 'Let him go!'

Natalie's mobile went as soon as the door slammed. A private number.

'Is this Doctor King?' A man's voice she didn't recognise. A slight accent.

'Yes.'

'This is Youssef Essa. You left a message.'

'For your brother—Malik. I'm trying to get in touch with him. Have you seen him?' And by the way, are you planning on doing a runner with your niece and nephew?

'He was at my mother's,' said Youssef.

'I rang there and no one answered.'

'That is because they were at the school.' Youssef sounded agitated.

'Did something happen?'

'Yes,' said Youssef. 'My brother wanted me to tell you thank you and that he will take care of Chelsea.'

Natalie's stomach dropped. 'What happened, Youssef?'

'I do not know what happened. But my mother called Malik and he went to the school. He was upset.'

Natalie had her bike halfway out the door when she saw Liam had left his Lotus parked there. He must have been planning to see her after his mediation session. She pushed the bike back and found the spare keys. She could get to the school and still make it in time to the College. Four-thirty. Would anyone still be there?

As it happened, yes. Ama, Gaylene, Ted Beahre and a man in his fifties that Natalie didn't know—along with two police officers. Chris was a little distance off in the playground, watching them all. Natalie recognised the gaunt Senior Constable Hudson from when he had chased after her stalker a year or so earlier, and the red-haired PC from the encounter with Luke.

'What happened?'

Gaylene looked to the man Natalie didn't know. Ted Beahre just glared and mumbled something about not being responsible. Natalie looked at him sharply.

Tony Hudson frowned at Natalie. 'What's your interest in this?' His South African accent made him sound like he had a cold.

'I'm Chelsea's psychiatrist,' said Natalie, turning her attention away from Ted Beahre. 'How is she? Where is she?'

'This we do not know,' said Ama. She looked unsure whether to be angry or frightened. 'I came to get her and they say she has gone.'

'Aftercare signed her out,' the unidentified man said. 'We hadn't been advised that her mother was no longer authorised.'

Jenna. At least that meant Chelsea wasn't going to be smuggled away to the Middle East. But she would be with Luke.

'I always said Mr Essa was fine,' said Ted with an *I told you so* look. Mainly to Natalie, whom he had edged closer to. 'A wrongly accused father, plus a protective mother and with due respect, experts who don't have the full picture. A pretty lethal cocktail.'

Lethal cocktail? Natalie remembered the tweet that used the very same words. Now she had no doubt—Ted Beahre was @ManUnderFire.

'This isn't about you,' Natalie said, shaking her head. 'And you should see someone professional rather than bleat your animosity all over Twitter.'

Ted Beahre looked like he had been struck. And then as if he might cry.

'Have you tried her house?' Natalie asked no one in particular. She looked at her watch. Shit, could she make it to the College in fifteen minutes?

SC Hudson looked irritated. 'We have a constable there now—no sign of anyone. It's Doctor King, isn't it?'

Natalie nodded.

'I don't suppose you know the full name of Ms Radford's boyfriend?'

'No,' said Natalie pulling out her phone. 'First name Luke. This is a photo of him.' It wasn't great quality, but Hudson had her send it to him anyway.

'I suggest you take the little fella home,' Hudson said to Ama. 'We have your details. We'll call as soon as we know something.'

Ama nodded and called to Chris, who joined her as she headed towards the gate. Natalie ran after her. 'Where's Malik?' she asked.

'Where do you think?' Ama stopped abruptly and turned to Natalie. 'The system here, it is a joke. In my country, children are protected by the law, by their families.'

Natalie didn't bother arguing that Jenna was family. 'So what is Malik doing?'

Ama's eyes narrowed. 'He is being a man. A father.'

Ama took Chris's hand and left Natalie watching—and wondering. Could Malik know where Luke lived? She thought about how he had followed Jenna, watched her at work. Had he done more than that? Vandalised Luke's car?

Natalie looked at her watch. She could easily work out Luke's name—and maybe where he lived. 4.59 p.m. What chance Beverley was still at work? Natalie rang her mobile.

'Are you still in the rooms?'

'Just left,' said Beverley.

'Can I get you to do me a favour?' In peak hour it would take Natalie an hour to get to the office. 'Look in Jenna

Radford's file for her workplace—it's a pathology lab, I just need to know the name.'

There was a long pause. 'Both songs?'

'Both songs.'

'Diagnostic Laboratory Services in Richmond,' Beverley told her cheerfully two minutes later.

'Bev, another favour. Can you ring the College and my medical indemnity insurers and tell them…' Tell them what? That she was on a mission to stop children being abused, whisked off to Egypt, and generally save the world? Yeah, that'd go down well. 'Tell them I'm dealing with a psychiatric emergency.' And that she had to put her patient first. Even if it meant they told her she wasn't ever going to be able to see patients again. Even if she had to go through a full psychiatric examination and court hearing to be reinstated. She had to help Chelsea. And, just maybe, Jenna and Malik too. She had always known that this case was going to be about choices. She just didn't know that in the end it might cause her to lose everything except her integrity.

Natalie voice-dialled the laboratory: 'I was talking to one of your lab techies a while ago. I need to ask him something. Luke. Is he there?'

'Sorry, Luke is on sick leave today.'

Bad sign.

'Damn. I'll try Monday then. Can you tell me who to ask for? Luke what?'

'Luke Karlsson.'

'K and two S's?'

'I guess.'

It took several interactions with an automated voice at directory assistance before she got an operator.

'Do you know the suburb?'

'No,' said Natalie. 'I think inner city though.'

'I have an L Karlsson in Northcote and one in North Melbourne.'

Natalie went for the Northcote one, noticing that she'd missed a call from Declan, no doubt waiting at the College and wondering where she was.

The Margaret Karlsson who answered was married to Lars and didn't know a Luke. She tried the North Melbourne number. No answer. Natalie tried directory assistance again.

'Williamstown?'

Maybe… but it would be a bit of a commute across the Westgate Bridge to his work in Richmond.

'More eastern or northern, probably?'

'How about Thornbury?'

A woman answered. Jenna's voice. Natalie hung up. She already had the address from directory assistance. She programmed it into the GPS. Fifteen minutes' drive. She pushed the pedal a little. Maybe less. At least she was on the right side of town; if Malik was coming from his place, or from work, he'd have a longer drive.

She thought of SC Hudson. But she didn't have his number. She rang Damian.

'Can you find SC Hudson's phone number?'

'Natalie, I'm not your personal assistant. Or anything else in your life, something you seem to want to make a point of. You want Hudson, call the station he's with.' Damian sounded irritable. 'I'm Homicide.' He hung up.

She tried her local police station and was put in a queue. Great.

Her mind went back to Jenna and Malik. *It has to be Malik*. It was like Jenna needed to be right about Malik. Natalie replayed the scene… the pleading tone had been almost childlike. The occasional flashes of dissociation were also a regression. *He's always been against me seeing you*. Buckling now to her father, as she had to Malik, and now Luke, or… Natalie's hand clenched on the steering wheel as the pieces fell into place.

Luke Karlsson's house was a weatherboard set back from the road with a neat front garden and a carport to one side.

There was a blue Honda parked in it. Someone was home. Natalie pulled the Lotus up outside. There were no nearby parks so she propped it half across the driveway; if it stopped them escaping, all the better. She was still on hold at the police station; she hung up.

The house looked quiet. No obvious sign of an emergency. No way was Jenna or Malik going to deliberately hurt Chelsea. Perhaps she could talk some common sense into Jenna before Malik arrived, then take Chelsea back to Ama's.

It was a plan, at least.

Just not a very good one.

It wasn't Luke who answered the door, but Jenna. Her expression transformed from nervous expectation to anger. 'Why don't you just frickin' leave me alone?'

'If I go, it'll be the police next. Or Malik.'

'Go away, you'll ruin everything. *Again*.' Jenna looked nervously past her. There was no sign of anyone. 'He applied for passports,' she said. 'They took photos of Chelsea. At the pharmacy.'

Shit. 'Tell your lawyer. The court case is in three weeks, Jenna. Let it be decided properly. This will go against you.'

'And it hasn't already?' Jenna glared at her. 'I thought you would be on my side. I frickin' asked to see you so my psych history wouldn't be held against me but what good did that do me?'

'This isn't about your psych history, Jenna.'

'It doesn't matter anymore. No one believes me because they think I'm nuts, or a woman or 'cause of some crappy legal technicality. But I *know*. I told you I wouldn't sit by and see my daughter abused. Or taken overseas. Fuck off. *Now*.'

The door slammed.

So much for that plan.

Natalie rang the police station again and this time got through. SC Hudson wasn't there.

'It's urgent,' said Natalie. 'Tell him I've found the child he's looking for.' The PC took down the address but didn't sound overly interested. It probably had 'custody dispute' against the job description, and they'd be about as popular as DV callouts.

Natalie sat in the car. Jenna's retort replayed in her mind. What was Jenna afraid she would ruin? *Again*. Natalie had stood up for Malik—was that all it was about?

Jenna. Histrionic. Liked the drama, to be the centre of attention. Manipulated the men in her life.

What had she hoped to achieve by taking Chelsea? She can't have planned to do a runner, because she didn't have Chris.

A truck turned into the driveway, running up and over the pavement in order to avoid the Lotus. It still managed to clip the bumper bar; the car shuddered and Natalie groaned. *Easy Tiger Imports*. Malik.

Malik didn't appear to notice Natalie, or if he did, he wasn't wasting time acknowledging her. He was out of the car and running to the front door.

Shit. No sign of any police.

He is being a man. A father.

Malik had ended up in hospital at twelve defending his dead father's honour. Because he was being taunted that his father was a coward for not standing up to gunmen.

Be a man. Unlike your father. Was this what Ama had taught her sons?

No rules… I will kill him.

Natalie leapt out of the car without thinking.

'No Malik, don't do it,' she screamed. 'Your children need you caring for them, not in jail.'

Malik's stare stopped her dead. 'Keep away, go now. This is not your fight,' he said.

'Let the police handle it, Malik. You go in there and something goes wrong, it will go against you.' Like if you kill Luke. 'Right now, the police are on your side. They'll be here soon.' Hopefully.

Which Jenna must know. Natalie's mind was racing.

Jenna wasn't stupid. She can't have thought she would get away with kidnapping Chelsea.

No—Jenna had known this would happen. Knew if she took Chelsea, Malik would come after her. And maybe Malik knew where Luke lived. He'd thrown paint over Luke's car.

Jenna hadn't run; she knew that the police would take Chelsea back and the court would not look positively at her behaviour. Why take Chelsea then, except to get Malik here—and why do that unless…

'It's a trap, Malik.'

Malik hadn't taken his eyes off her. 'Leave now.'

'She wants you to go in, Malik.' Natalie went up to him. 'I don't know what she's got planned, but if anything happens… it's hers and Luke's word against yours.' Providing Natalie left—and didn't ruin everything. She grabbed Malik's arm. 'Come back to the car, Malik. The police will get Chelsea, and after this you'll probably get custody of them both. Long term.'

There was a flash behind Malik's eyes that Natalie caught a glimpse of, that she couldn't make sense of. Regret?

'It is too late,' he said.

Too late. What had he done?

'The door will be unlocked, Malik. Jenna wants you to walk in—it won't end well.'

Malik didn't appear to be listening. 'Just leave!'

'Malik, it's you who needs to leave.'

Malik stepped forward and grabbed her arm.

'What the fuck?' said Natalie.

In his other hand was a gun.

As Natalie had predicted, Jenna had left the front door unlocked. Her expression when Natalie entered, ahead of Malik, was of fury. Until she saw the gun. Probably a good thing Jenna didn't also have one—and that there was no sign of Luke.

'Where is Chelsea?' Malik's voice had an edge that betrayed his nervousness. He pushed Natalie ahead of him. 'Both of you, sit.' He waved them over to a large couch covered with a throw and cushions.

Natalie took a quick look at Jenna; there was no sense of fear in her expression. Natalie grabbed her arm and pulled her down to sit beside her. She didn't want anyone aggravating Malik. The gun didn't sit comfortably in his hand—he would be no marksman. Which might have been reassuring if she was fleeing from him in bushland. Here it was more frightening—he was just as likely to kill one of them by mistake.

'Where is Chelsea?'

'Do you really think I'd have her here waiting for you?' Not frightened at all.

'Where have you put her, you bitch?' Malik took a step towards them, but at least wasn't pointing the gun with any specific intent.

'Stop this now,' said Natalie. 'Listen to me, Malik. This is not how you show you are a man, nor a good father. Is this what you want Chris and Chelsea to grow up knowing? That you are in jail? That you killed their mother?'

'They will know I protected them from her boyfriend, a man who abuses an eight-year-old girl. He and Jenna are the criminals, not me.' He looked around warily. 'Where is he? Have you let him take her?'

'You will never have her, Malik. Never.' Jenna's voice was chilling; this *was* a set-up—and she intended to do whatever was necessary to ensure Malik was either in jail or dead. But what was her plan? Was Luke going to jump out of a cupboard?

Natalie felt she was running out of time. 'You're sinking to their level, Malik,' she said in a rush. 'You told me your father was an honourable man—are you sure this is his version of honour? Holding unarmed women hostage?'

'She has no honour!' said Malik. 'And is no mother to either of her children. She lets this man touch her daughter.'

'No, Malik. She didn't.'

This time her voice was firm. The idea that had been brewing in the car after she left the school had developed clarity. 'You have both been trying to be good parents. But neither of you knew what was going on. Who was abusing Chelsea.'

They looked at her.

'I want to talk to you both,' said Natalie. 'About Chelsea. But you need to sit down, Malik.'

Malik hesitated. 'Chelsea?' he yelled. There was silence; Natalie could feel the house was empty. Jenna's smirk, too, suggested her daughter wasn't about to come out of hiding and run to Malik.

'She isn't here,' said Natalie. 'And you need to hear what I have to say. Sit.'

Malik narrowed his eyes. Moved backwards, keeping Natalie and Jenna in his sight as he checked that the kitchen was empty.

'You have five minutes,' he said. 'Then Jenna must tell me where Chelsea is, or I swear I will shoot her.'

The gun might keep Jenna in her seat. Natalie wondered which story to tell; one that would deflect the blame, or the one she thought was the truth—the one she had been blind to, even in the face of her own nightmares telling her the answer.

'I didn't think either of you was lying.' At least not about the abuse. 'Jenna, I know you love your kids. Sometimes you struggle, but your intentions were always to do the right thing by your daughter. Even now, you think you're doing what you have to. You too, Malik. You wanted to keep Chelsea safe. You were both trying to protect Chelsea and thought it was too risky to leave it to the legal profession or us psychiatrists. You both thought we might get it wrong, and your children would suffer.'

Malik's grim expression suggested she had this right. Jenna's was harder to read. And it was Jenna that she had to judge carefully. Natalie took a quick look at the gun in Malik's hand.

'Somebody has been hurting Chelsea, though. For a while, I thought it might have been her sports teacher, Ted Beahre.'

Malik frowned, looked to Jenna. Natalie might convince him. Deep down, Jenna knew the real answer. Was this the time for the truth? Was the time ever going to be right if it had been buried this deep, for this long?

'I even had him checked out,' Natalie continued. 'But Chelsea's monster was not at her school. Malik, she saw you as her saviour.' Putting Aladdin *outside* the bedroom door.

To stop the monster coming in.

'Which had me thinking, like you, Malik, that it had to be Luke.'

'It fricking wasn't Luke.' Jenna sat forward.

'I know Jenna. Stay with me, okay? This is going to be tough but you want what's best for Chelsea, and unless you hear what I have to say, then she will *never* be safe, no matter what you do to Malik. Like I said, she's been hurt. You have to face the truth to be able to help her recover.'

Jenna's look was hostile. Natalie thought about her advice

to Liam. There was enough similarity between narcissists and histrionics on this point to use the same advice herself. 'I was wrong not to trust you Jenna. I know you love your children and would do anything for them.'

The hostility eased a fraction.

'But we were both wrong about something else, and to explain that I have to tell you a story. It won't take long.' Natalie didn't have long; Malik was getting restless. *It's too late.*

'There once was a little girl, who really, really, wanted her parents to love her. But her mother wasn't very well, and her younger siblings needed a lot of attention. So to get noticed she helped around the house and got a lot of praise, and this made her feel pretty good. But her mother wasn't getting any better and noticed her less and less, and so she had to become like a grown-up and do far too much work at home. And her daddy kept telling her what a good girl she was, and how much he loved and appreciated her. It made her feel she was important, and she learned how to make her daddy love her more and more.

'But he made her keep a secret. The secret came with a price, but she didn't understand that because she was only a child, and the bigger and scarier it was, the more angry and overwhelmed she was by it. Until one day it got so hard, she decided she wanted to… disappear?' Natalie looked to Jenna for clues in the tightness of her lips, the eyes that seemed to be looking nowhere. 'Maybe she thought if she didn't eat, her mother would notice her then, and help. But your mother didn't notice, did she Jenna? There's never been anyone who could really make you feel better.'

Malik frowned. 'What is this you are talking about?'

'Imagine, Malik, that your father was a hero, that he'd saved his friend and didn't die. How would that have changed your life? You loved him… but you also hated him for letting you down, for dying. You've never felt quite good enough, that you had something to prove. Jenna loved and hated her parents too, and she's never resolved it because the only way to manage the conflicts and the secrets was to un-know them. What kept her together was the certainty she was loved—but she's never allowed herself to scrutinise that. Her trauma was far worse than yours, Malik.'

Denial—a powerful mechanism that had protected Jenna all these years. And it was about to crumble. Jenna's psyche scar had never quite kept the lid on—symptoms bubbling up at critical times; eating disorders, drugs, alcohol; the need for drama to recreate that specialness again and again. But until now the core of Jenna, the vulnerable child, had been kept safe from what she hadn't been able to deal with then. The child who wanted love, still, as an adult, needed to believe she was special, even when it put her daughter in harm's way.

Could Jenna face it now? For Chelsea?

Natalie started to sing softly. About teddy bears getting together for a surprise picnic, about having to wear a disguise, about having a wonderful time.

The colour was draining out of Jenna's cheeks. Her eyes were glassy.

Natalie remembered what Chelsea had sung, the words she had got wrong... except she hadn't. She had sung the words she had been taught by her grandfather. 'If my girl's been good today...'

'No...' the voice that came from Jenna was childlike but with pain woven into the sound as if it was woven into the very fabric of her being. 'You can't know that song, it's our song.' Her eyes suddenly focused. 'Ours.'

'No, Jenna. He sang it to Chelsea too.'

Jenna seemed to shrink, as if the couch was swallowing her up. She started to curl up, shaking her head. 'No, no,' she whispered. 'He wouldn't. It was just me, only me...'

Malik stood up. 'What is this about?

'It was Chelsea's grandfather, Malik. He first abused Jenna as a child—and more recently, Chelsea.'

Malik was shaking his head. 'This is... monstrous.' He

looked at Natalie as if he couldn't quite make sense of what she had said. 'This changes nothing. It still shows she is not fit to look after our children. Where is she, Jenna?'

'She isn't here and you need to go.' Natalie spoke with as much authority as she could manage. And for a moment it looked like she'd succeed. Malik turned to leave.

'No. Wait.' Jenna's voice was so soft they almost didn't hear her. 'Malik? Where is Chris?'

Malik stopped and turned around. Looked at his ex-wife. 'Right now? Where you will never, ever get him, you bitch. On a plane home.'

Jenna looked frozen, as if she couldn't quite comprehend what she was hearing. That if she refused to hear it, maybe it wouldn't be true.

Malik waved the gun at her. Natalie stood up and faced Malik.

'You aren't going to shoot either of us Malik,' Natalie said as she took out her phone and started to hit triple zero.

She was right about the gun—it was one of the replicas from Blake's shipment. But that didn't stop Malik launching himself at Natalie, barrelling into her, and sending her sprawling, her abdomen taking the full force of his weight as she twisted and fell onto the arm of the couch.

The sensation was immediate—the bean felt like it had done a complete somersault.

Bile filled Natalie's mouth as lights started to flicker at the edge of her peripheral vision. She groaned and rolled over; fell to the floor, with Malik half on the couch and half on the floor beside her.

Even if she'd had something to hit him with she wouldn't have been able to manage it—just breathing was hard enough. Nor would she have been able to focus on looking for the phone or speaking on it if she had found it. *It's too early* was all she could think, as waves of regret seemed to pass through her whole body.

What had Malik intended? Natalie didn't know, though

she was pretty sure Chris wasn't on any plane yet. If so, there would have been no need for Malik to take Chelsea before the police arrived. More than likely Ama, Youssef and Chris were at the airport waiting for Malik and Chelsea. Whether Malik wanted to harm Jenna and Natalie, or just immobilise them, only he would ever know.

Natalie saw him try to stand, wondered if he would kick her, and curled up to protect the bean. Its level of activity suggested distress, and it might be in its last moments of life. What happened next was a blur. She remembered saying sorry to the bean, feeling an overwhelming sense that she was never going to get a chance to be a mother. The shattering regret that came with the realisation.

There was a blood-curdling scream, and she couldn't make sense of where it had come from. Malik's expression was more bewilderment than anything else; it seemed out of keeping with the sound. He fell onto one knee, face white, toppling over. Natalie managed to shift sideways so that he didn't fall directly on top of her—instead she found her legs pinned underneath his prostrate body.

She half-raised herself. Looked to Jenna, who had now picked up the gun and was watching her ex-husband. She turned and their eyes locked. 'I had to,' she said calmly. 'He was going to kill us both.'

Malik hadn't moved. Natalie slowly turned towards him. Tried to make sense of the blood that was spreading across the back of his shirt, away from the knife handle that was protruding from between his ribs. Not arterial, she thought, too dark, too slow. Too far off centre to get the aorta or vena cava, the big blood vessels. But internally? Right side; it might have got his liver. Might well kill him.

Kill him. Blood. A lot of it. Her memories would come when the time was right, Declan had said. And as Natalie battled to stay conscious, it seemed like the time had come.

For a moment, she was in another room, in another time, thirty years earlier. And there was blood there too.

Childhood memories, walled up in their own little capsule
—but now the walls were crumbling.

Two uniformed policemen came through the door from
the kitchen, guns drawn. Several things happened at once.

Jenna swung around, Malik's fake gun in her hand, and as
they yelled, 'Drop it,' Natalie screamed, 'It isn't real,' and a
gunshot was fired.

Or at least she thought that was what happened. But maybe
she was seeing things too, because she was sure it was Liam
who was holding her before she passed out. She thought she
said to him, 'Tell Damian I'm sorry about the bean.'

Natalie woke in hospital. She wanted to yell *I don't belong here, it's too early*; instead she focused on looking at a white ceiling as she was wheeled from the emergency department to ultrasound, back to the ED, then to the ward.

The room had mildew, and there was a vase of orchids in one corner. The low swish of a ceiling fan drowned out the voices of the nurses handing over at the end of the shift. It took her back to the ICU, to rehab. After the motorbike accident, hospital had been her home for nearly a year. Back then, she couldn't move. Now she didn't want to.

She was going to lose the bean. Of course she was. What sort of mother would she have been anyway? She pictured Damian picking up his daughter—dressed in a mini-goth outfit—and them fighting over what was appropriate. They'd told her it was a girl, heart still beating when she'd arrived, but the placenta...

She looked at the fan and counted rotations. Tried not to picture the daughter Damian might never get to dance with.

Liam was there when she got to the hospital. He *had* been at Luke's house: he'd arrived at the same time as the police, but hadn't been allowed in the ambulance.

'My car has a tracker,' he told her. 'I was thinking up how many charges I could bring against you and McBride.'

'Damian? What did he have to do with anything?'

'I figured that's whose house it was. Thought the cops

there were his mates. You can imagine my surprise when I walked into…' He shook his head. 'Just get better, okay? Do what you're told for a change?'

He paused. 'No matter what happens, remember all parents have regrets at times. Be kind to yourself. If you lose the… bean… it was an accident.'

Natalie stared after him as Liam was ushered out to allow another medical examination. Hadn't she told him to piss off? She closed her eyes and concentrated on not crying. Listened as she was told she'd be confined to bed to give the bean any chance at all.

She did the police interview in the hospital room the next morning. Damian watched as she gave her statement. She told SC Hudson that they needed to talk to Stephen Radford about the abuse rather than Luke, but he appeared to have already heard this and wanted to focus on the assault.

'Malik Essa attacked you when you went to call the emergency line?'

'Yes.'

'And what happened then?'

'Until then,' said Natalie, 'Malik had us both at gunpoint. He'd made it clear that he wanted Chelsea and that he was then going with—or following—the rest of his family and his other child to Egypt. Jenna took the only chance she had to stop him.'

She had always known this case might force her to choose between the truth and loyalty to her patient. *The law is my domain*, Liam had told her. *Let the judge decide*.

And Declan: *You're not Solomon*.

'You thought he was going to kill you?'

Natalie hesitated. 'By the time I tried to call the police, I was pretty sure the gun wasn't real.'

'How could you tell?'

'I knew he imports replica guns.' Natalie anticipated the next question. 'Sorry: patient confidentiality. But…' She looked directly at SC Hudson. 'He attacked me. He may have killed my unborn child.'

SC Hudson paused, frowned. 'So, you were both in the living room, right?'

'Yes.'

'Can you tell me how Jenna came to have the knife?'

'I don't know when she got it.'

'You were going in and out of consciousness?' SC Hudson asked.

'Yes.'

'So while Malik was attacking you, she could have gone to the kitchen?'

Natalie paused. 'Is that what she said?'

'Can you answer the question, please?'

'Yes, it's possible.' And it was. Without her having to play Solomon.

After SC Hudson left, Damian didn't mince words.

'You're dangerous, you know that, right?'

Natalie shrugged. 'Chelsea and Jenna are okay?'

'Yes. Chelsea was with Luke—they were waiting for a phone call from Jenna. She'd told Luke that she wanted to discuss things without the children there—told him she could do better with Malik one on one.' Damian's expression suggested he didn't believe a word of it.

'And Malik?'

'Stable in ICU. Lost a lot of blood from the liver nick, but they think he'll make it.'

'Did they find Chris?'

'The plane hadn't taken off. They all had Egyptian passports. Might be fake, but they were good enough to get them through.'

'Hadn't Jenna's lawyer put an alert on to stop them being allowed to go?'

'No idea.' Maybe her lawyer had contacted the passport office, rather than Border Force.

'Will they be charged?' asked Natalie.

'Jesus, I'd like to throw the book at the lot of you. Stephen Radford will be brought in for some serious questioning. Seems Jenna's keen to press charges, both in her own right and for her daughter. Other charges? Ama for trying to take the child illegally? Yes. Malik? A string. Jenna?' His eyes narrowed.

If it were up to him, Natalie thought: yes. But SC Hudson's questions hadn't been designed to elicit anything other than the simplest answer.

In the end, at least Jenna was trying. Better for Chelsea to have her than essentially lose both parents and both sets of grandparents in one day.

Natalie nodded, stared at the ceiling. 'You're feeling guilty you flipped me off. Don't be, Damian. Wasn't your fault. I'm… I'm sorry about the bean, if… you know.'

Damian was still fuming. 'You aren't a fucking police-woman, Natalie. And if you were, you'd know better. You're pregnant. What the hell were you thinking?'

He got up to leave. 'Did Liam speak with you?' she asked suddenly, thinking of what Liam had told her.

Damian stopped in the doorway. 'He seemed to be under the impression we were an item.' He paused. 'I told him that was my fantasy, not yours. You obviously love the jerk, Natalie. Seems he feels the same.' The brief puzzled expression confirmed for Natalie what she had always known. Damian was a decent bloke, but it wasn't in him to do what Liam was prepared to do—raise another man's child. Not with her, anyway.

Her hospital room seemed to have a revolving door. No sooner had Damian left than her mother was there.

'Declan would probably tell me not to yell at you for worrying me half to death. Again.'

'And he'd be right.'

'You gave us all a scare. Even Blake. He nearly passed out when he heard the police almost shot you because of a replica gun.'

Natalie gave her mother a wry smile.

'And Maddison...' says you can even have first name option. Her choice is Lauren if it's a girl.'

Natalie managed to stop herself laughing. Just. 'Tell her it's fine—that one's all hers.'

Jan looked at her awkwardly, fiddled with the flowers. 'Declan said you know that I've been asking him for advice.'

Natalie nodded.

'It... he hasn't told you it's more than that. I've known him... for a long time.'

Natalie stared at her mother. *Declan's my father.* If Jan knew what she was thinking, she didn't rush to confirm or deny. She looked the way she always did, right before Natalie launched into an attack and they would both end up angry, not speaking for days.

This time Natalie stopped the words that had already formed. The *You lied*, the *You had no right*. In her mother's awkwardness, even now at fifty-five, she saw the woman Jan had once been. The lioness, fiercely protective if misguided.

More than that, she saw herself. The uncertainty in her own eyes every time she looked in the mirror and asked herself, *Should I try and make it work with Damian, for the bean* versus *The bean will be happy if I am... and Liam is more right for me despite everything.*

This time, Natalie took a breath. Said to her mother, 'Declan is a good listener and... you found a wise counsel for me.'

Her mother must have sensed the unspoken question. 'I saw him when you were two years old, Natalie.'

Ah. His patient, not his girlfriend. Thank God. It might have taken her another thirty-four years to forgive Declan for not telling her.

'Actually,' Jan said, sitting on the chair by the bed, 'you saw him.'

'*I* saw him?'

Jan nodded. 'You were nearly three. Very verbal—full sentences. You could do a good argument even then.'

They both smiled, cautious smiles that identified a vulner-ability for them both, though Natalie only half-knew where her mother was going. She closed her eyes, remembered the blood seeping across Malik's shirt. How it had taken her back to another bloody scene from long ago. 'Teddy Bears' Picnic' and another teddy bear song, 'Round and Round the Garden'. She felt a wave of guilt and shame—pain that made no sense, yet was there in her gut as if it had been yesterday.

'Then…' Jan waited for Natalie to open her eyes, locked with them, a silent plea to be forgiven. Before, Natalie had seen only her own pain and reacted defensively with anger. Now she sat with it. Allowed the inner turmoil of a three-year-old to bubble inside, despite the panic that threatened to push her to the edge.

'You stopped talking. Wouldn't say a word. To anyone.'

'Declan helped me speak again.' Which was why she had trusted him in the midst of her adolescent anger. Part of her had recognised him, years later.

Jan nodded.

Natalie looked at the tears rolling down her mother's face. 'Why, Mum? Why did I stop talking?'

Her mother broke away from Natalie's gaze, and for a moment Natalie thought she would leave. But she got up and walked over to the window, gazing out over the busy street below.

'Declan tells me I have to tell you. That you're ready.' Jan took a breath. 'I hope he's right because I'm not sure I am. And I'm breaking a promise to do it.'

'A promise to my father?'

Jan nodded. 'In the end… you are more important than he ever was. I only ever kept it because I thought it was best for you. Declan says it's not—last time I saw him he was pretty blunt—and he's right. Lately I've kept my mouth shut because it's easier for me.'

There was a long pause while Jan gathered her thoughts. Her courage.

'Your father was part of my brief rebellion,' Jan said. 'Nan didn't like him and made the mistake—' Jan shook her head. 'One I didn't learn from. Remember I told you Eoin was no good for you?'

Eoin who died in the bike smash that put sixteen-yearold Natalie in hospital for a year. 'Yes. It made him so much more attractive.'

'Which was exactly what happened with your father,' Jan said. 'It wasn't that he was that bad a guy, but he was from a very different kind of family and pretty wild.'

What sort of wild?

'We went out for a few months. I... we'd already broken up when I found out I was pregnant.'

Repeating patterns. Natalie shook her head at the stupidity of life. How on earth had she managed that?

'We tried to make it work for a while. He and his family wanted us to get married. Nan thought we should too—old school. But...' Jan shrugged. 'I already knew Craig. I've loved him since I was fifteen. He was my best friend's brother; he had another girlfriend when I was going out with your father.'

She'd always loved *Craig*? Natalie stared at her mother. Her life-long fantasy was that her father had been the love of Jan's life; that she'd settled for Craig... Of course her mother loved Craig. It was why they were so damn happy. Craig. The stepfather who she had given hell—because she had played out on her mother's feelings of guilt. And who, despite everything, had been a great father to her.

'He waited for me,' said Jan quietly. 'Didn't put on pressure, just waited for me to sort it out. And was there to catch us both.'

Like Liam.

'What happened, Mum?'

'Oh, your father adored you. Made it harder not to keep trying.' Jan had the grace to give Natalie an apologetic look. 'Not that he was any use, of course. Never changed a single nappy, never stopped long enough to do anything practical that a baby needed. He was good at getting you out of bed; didn't seem to realise babies need to sleep as well. But God, you loved him. Your eyes lit up every time he came into the room. *Dad* was your first word and you'd call for him when you were upset. It was me that had to manage the fallout, though.'

Natalie caught the remnant edge in her mother's voice. Being fair wasn't part of the deal kids gave you. The parents had to be the adults.

'You never said Dad again, after. Ever. You started talking again, but it was like you'd wiped everything.'

Which she had; dissociation and denial was how the brain coped with trauma, and the trauma had been enough to keep the memory buried. Right up until the last few months, when working with Chelsea had touched the memories and the bloodshed in Luke's house had ripped the last of the scab away.

I am standing at the door, and in my hand is my favourite teddy bear that goes with me everywhere. I must have come into the room ahead of my mother, because this memory does not have her in it, only me, calling Daddy and expecting him to pick me up in his arms and throw me into the air, to sing songs and whirl me around in that breathless moment where I am loved; where I am the centre of the universe.

But something is wrong. His eyes are glazed and he isn't looking at me. Then there is water. Water everywhere and it's not the way the bath normally is. It's red; and I hear screams and my one-eyed teddy is lying in a puddle staring at me, blaming me, and then my Daddy disappears. And I am left with the certainty that I killed him.

'We'd had a fight the night before,' her mother was saying, over thirty years later. 'And you and I had gone to stay at Nan's. He had been very… erratic. I didn't understand then, but…'

'He had bipolar.'

Jan nodded. 'Undiagnosed. I'd tried to get him to see someone but he wouldn't. He… he'd slashed his wrists to the bone and there he was in the bath. It was…' She shuddered. 'Terrifying. And you saw him first.'

'Oh, Mum.' Natalie held her arm out and her mother took her hand, giving it a clumsy squeeze. 'It's not your fault.'

'It felt like it was. I blamed myself for arguing, for leaving him alone. I blamed myself for getting pregnant… Not for having you, but… Well, when you were an idea rather than a person it would have been easier… But then I felt guilty for thinking that, for subjecting you to… For mucking up Craig's life. In the end, I just had to get on with it. And part of that was leaving Nick and his family behind.'

Nick. Her father had a name.

'Did his family… want to be involved?'

Jan nodded. 'I didn't have any beef with them, but in the end, they respected my wishes, more or less.'

It took Natalie a few seconds to process this. 'What do you mean: more or less?'

Jan looked abashed. 'You know your uncle.'

Natalie stared. Suddenly it became obvious. 'Vince.'

Jan nodded.

Natalie's head started to spin. Vince, who had offered to give the band their first gig, who had kept them on as regulars from the start. Who had found the warehouse for her and who gave her unasked-for fatherly—or rather avuncular—advice.

It wasn't just Vince. She knew her cousins. Benny with his pink mohawk and Adrianna and her biker husband and…

Natalie stared at her mother. 'He's not dead.'

Jan sighed. 'No, he's not dead.'

Nick. Vince's brother who led the back-up singers at

Adrianna's wedding. Who had a not-bad singing voice; who had danced with her. She started to shake, tears rolling down her cheeks. Pulled her mother into her.

Then she caught sight of someone else in the doorway. 'Hello Craig,' she said between sobs. And then something she had never been able to say before. 'Hello Dad.'

Liam had texted to say he was coming. She thought about asking her mother to get her a sexy black nightie and then thought better of it. If Liam and she were going to make it, then it would have to be warts and all. She flicked the television on to try and distract herself as she waited. The weekly media wrap-up was on—and this week's guests were Mark La Brooy and Katlego Okeke.

'Can you explain why you defended Mark, why you asked the *Herald Sun* to reinstate him?'

Defended? What the…?

'Of course.' Okeke looked magnificent in warrior red. 'I was defending the integrity of the vilification law, not him.' She flashed a look at La Brooy, pasty, overweight, leaning back with shirt half-hanging out and pencil end in his mouth where a cigarette might otherwise have propped. 'For it to be an offence, I have to be offended. I wasn't. For that I'd have to respect his opinion. Takes more than what he's got to get under my *black* skin.'

La Brooy's anger looked entirely counterfeit.

Natalie hit the off button. Okeke might not have been offended. But Natalie was, by both of them. They were revelling in the drama, the confrontation. She doubted either of them had ever given a shit about Malik, Jenna, Chelsea or Chris. Not really.

At least she was off the hook with the College. Declan had phoned to say that in the light of the news coverage of the case—largely with a positive spin on her involvement— and her medical crisis, Rankin had put the complaint aside. Subject to continued monitoring by Declan.

'It didn't hurt,' added Declan, 'that, reading between the lines, Boreman thinks one of his nurses might be your @*KidsReallyMatter*. He told Rankin he might have over-reacted.'

Then Liam was there.

He stood in the doorway and they just looked at each other. He still seemed tired but there was something different, Natalie thought. A calm that hadn't been there before. And he was still the sexiest man she had ever met.

'You'd be wanting a visitor, would you?' he finally said.

'Depends.' On whether…whether it was the right thing.

Pushing him away, she'd been acting out her childhood guilt and inability to trust herself. And it was herself she needed to trust. Through everything, she had never wavered in how she had felt about him.

'Depends on you being quiet and listening,' said Liam. He pulled the chair closer to her bed. 'While you were gallivanting around in my Lotus…'

Natalie winced. 'About that—'

Liam's look stopped her. 'I was in a mediation session with Lauren.'

She had forgotten that—she'd had a few other things on her mind. She turned to the monitor, watched the line that said the bean was holding steady, for now.

'I did what you told me,' he went on. 'Said she was right.' Liam watched Natalie's expression and leaned in. 'I told her she was right that our children mattered more than anything. I told her I trusted her to know that us both being happy, with or without partners, was going to make them happier in the long run too.'

Natalie opened her mouth to speak, but he pushed on. 'I saw someone last week. They offered us counselling through the Royal Commission and after Michael killed himself, I needed to get some stuff off my chest. Your advice, I recall. I haven't had a drink in a week. I want it to stop being a problem before it's a bigger one.' He took a breath. 'They repeated something you'd told me. I was being driven by guilt.'

As her mother had been. As Natalie had been—guilt buried in her childhood that had shaped her, just as it had shaped Jenna.

'I don't want you to have to choose between them and me, Liam.'

'And I would never want you to choose between the bean'—they both paused awkwardly, looking at the line on the monitor—'and any children we might have together.' He saw her expression. 'If you, we, want them, okay? We should both choose to do what's right for our kids—but not because of guilt.'

'It won't be easy.'

'No, it won't. But working less will help.'

Like Declan had said—letting go of the least important things.

'You can't leave the Royal Commission, Liam.'

'No, I can't.' He smiled. 'But I can leave the Office of Public Prosecutions.'

'No.'

'Too late. I put my resignation in.'

'But… what will you do?'

Liam shrugged. 'Take time out, sell the Lotus, live off the proceeds. Grow olives. Maybe even do defence law. I can try and live among all your…ah… collections of stuff… if that's where you want to be. Just…we do it together. All the way.'

She thought of her father, her mother and Craig. Another pattern repeating. But maybe with improvements gained through insight. She was a psychiatrist after all—it had to count for something.

EPILOGUE

'Do you have a moment?'

Natalie turned around, recognising the voice. Jenna. Standing in her waiting room without an appointment.

She didn't, but she'd find one.

'I've come to say thank you.'

'For what, Jenna?' Natalie watched her patient wrestle with all she was dealing with, deciding how best to answer. Thanks for lying—or at least not telling the whole truth? Or thank you for making me face my inner demon at last, and maybe save my daughter? Natalie had referred Jenna to a therapist, and there was enough material there to keep her in work for a few years to come.

'I came to you because I didn't want my children taken off me.' She shrugged. 'I have them, and Malik won't get them.'

Natalie sighed.

'He may not have been abusing Chelsea, but he still thought he owned them,' said Jenna. 'I'd have always wondered, every access, whether I would ever see them again.'

'Were you planning on killing him?'

Jenna looked at Natalie hard. 'If I had to, yes.'

'You were going to hope they'd accept self-defence?'

Jenna gave a fleeting smile. 'As it was, I had to save you.'

'You could have gone to jail.'

'Yes, but better that than leaving my child…' She stopped, blinked away a tear. 'I'm still coming to terms with… I've had dreams for years, but now… Now I remember. Perhaps I always did, but was too scared to face it.' Tears rolled down her cheeks. 'I will never forgive myself... how could I have not... have faced it? For my daughter?'

'Be kind to yourself Jenna. You're facing it now. It will take time, and your children need you.'

'He left, you know. My father,' said Jenna quietly. 'Thailand, the police think. He had an escape plan... went to the airport as soon as the police called him in for questioning. My mother moved in to help me. It's too late to heal all the scars, but we're trying.' She looked at Natalie. 'I want this to stop here, this generation. Thank you... for finding the therapist. She's been great with us all. Even helping me deal with Chris.'

When she left, Natalie watched her go to the car where Mickie and Chelsea were waiting. Three generations of traumatised women... finding strength together.

She never had to sing 'Ave Maria' at Beverley's wedding, which was just as well. She probably couldn't have done it with a straight face. Liam had told her he'd record it and play it every time they had an argument. They weren't having many, though. She'd even cleaned up the living area. More or less.

She was in the last verse of 'Amazing Grace', which had been hard enough — Beverley and Jack with their arms around each other, looking slightly nauseating but, dare she admit, strangely sweet and very happy — when her waters broke.

Still too early. But despite the partial tear, her placenta had managed to get the bean through to thirty-six weeks, and that would be enough. The paediatrician could manage it from there.

When Sienna — dark brown tuft on her head like her dad's — opened her eyes and looked directly at her mother, for the first time in Natalie's life, she felt free of her past.

And in the same moment, she knew what it was like to love someone so much, so overwhelmingly, that she would do anything, *anything*, without limits, to protect her.

ACKNOWLEDGMENTS

This story draws on a lot of the difficult work done by Protective Services, the Children's Court Clinic and Children's Court, with whom I work. Though they are often not loved by the clients who find themselves there, they try to do, as far as is possible, what is best for the child, as do the clinicians who do the ongoing work with these families.

While it isn't possible always to get the outcomes we would like, every little bit of insight and support that can be given to a parent may help their child.

The idea for this book had its first incarnation in a manuscript called *Kate and Cathie*, written twenty-five years ago when my children were young, one page a day for a year until I had something I could edit. It got some encouraging feedback (it is still my mother's favourite, at least prior to *Two Steps Forward*) and some interest from publishers but never got over the line. I have used the concept here in a grittier, more real way than I did then. Back then I spent time with my friend Janine's daughter Annabelle to flesh the child character out—but Chelsea has benefited from experience with my own daughter Dominique, and niece Samantha (who gave me the modern-day answer to what an eight-year-old would like if she had three wishes).

My early readers need to be thanked—heaps and heaps. Erina Reddan and Tania Chandler, both wonderful writers themselves, gave me invaluable feedback. Some got Version One with a very different 'father' conclusion, some readers got this version, and I apologise if I've omitted any of you: Sue Hughes, Janifer Willis and his Honour Graham McDonald. My children Daniel and Dominique both gave their thoughts—Daniel's particularly useful because he was doing a placement at the Children's Court Clinic at the time.

Thanks also to Michael Heyward and the great team at Text who had to help me juggle the publication of two books in six months: Mandy (editor extraordinaire), W. H. Chong and Jess Horrocks for the cover designs, Jane Finemore, Kate Sloggett and Lucy Ballantyne.

Finally, as always, my thanks to Graeme, who is along on the journey of each book with me; on plot ('Noooo... not the Mafia...'), character ('Noooo... she's meant to be a psychiatrist not an action hero...' and 'No, Liam would not let Damian into the delivery room...'), when I'm stuck ('What happened to the plan?') and then first reader, last reader and chief cheerleader. The whole process is so much richer and more enjoyable (and has a better outcome, of course) having you there.